Love[illegible]
Love[illegible] Dance

MARY HIGGINS CLARK

First published in Arrow 1992
29 30 28

First published in the United Kingdom by Century 1991
Arrow Books
The Random House Group Limited
20 Vauxhall Bridge Road, London SW1V 2SA
www.randomhouse.co.uk
Addresses for companies within The Random House Group Limited can be found at:
www.randomhouse.co.uk/offices.htm
The Random House Group Limited Reg. No. 954009
A CIP catalogue record for this book is available from the British Library.

Pour les notes en marge du texte
© Larousse, 2015
21, rue du Montparnasse
75283 Paris Cedex 06

HARRAP's® est une marque de Larousse SAS
www.harrap.com

ISBN 978 2 81 870325 0

About the author

MARY HIGGINS CLARK is the author of many suspense novels; three collections of short stories[1]; a historical novel, *Mount Vernon Love Story*; a memoir, *Kitchen Privileges*[2]; and a children's[3] book, *Ghost Ship*, illustrated by Wendell Minor.
She is also the coauthor with Carol Higgins Clark of several holiday[4] suspense novels: *Deck the Halls*[5], *He Sees You When You're Sleeping*[6], *The Christmas Thief*[7], *Santa Cruise*[8] and *Dashing Through the Snow*[9]. More than ninety million copies[10] of her books are in print in the United States alone, and her books are worldwide[11] bestsellers.

1. nouvelles
2. [Entre hier et demain]
3. pour enfants
4. dont l'histoire se passe au moment de Noël
5. [Trois Jours avant Noël]
6. [Ce soir je veillerai sur toi]
7. [Le Visiteur de Noël]
8. [La Croisière de Noël]
9. [Le Mystère de Noël]
10. exemplaires
11. dans le monde entier

DIRECTION DE LA PUBLICATION : Carine Girac-Marinier

DIRECTION ÉDITORIALE : Claude Nimmo

NOTES EN MARGE : Natalie Pomier

RÉVISION DES NOTES : Marianne Mouchot

RELECTURE : Joëlle Narjollet

INFORMATIQUE ÉDITORIALE : Philippe Cazabet, Marie-Noëlle Tilliette

CONCEPTION GRAPHIQUE : Uli Meindl

MISE EN PAGES : Cynthia Savage

FABRICATION : Rebecca Dubois

Remerciements à Josephine Lyon

Mot de l'Éditeur

Vous aimeriez lire en langue originale, mais le vocabulaire, les expressions figurées ou la syntaxe vous arrêtent parfois ?

Cette collection est faite pour vous !

Vous trouverez en effet, en note dans la marge, une traduction de certains mots et expressions qui vous permettra d'avancer facilement dans votre lecture.

Nous n'avons pas cherché à vous donner une traduction littéraire de l'ouvrage et nous nous sommes parfois écartés du sens littéral pour vous fournir le sens qui convient le mieux à l'histoire. Aussi les mots sont-ils traduits dans le contexte du texte original.

Les expressions figées anglaises sont, bien entendu, rendues par une expression équivalente en français.

Les allusions à des réalités culturelles du monde anglo-saxon sont expliquées également dans la marge, pour vous aider à mieux comprendre la trame de l'histoire.

Vous aurez ainsi, en regard du texte original, tout le savoir-faire d'un dictionnaire rien que pour vous et adapté à ce livre !

Notre objectif est de vous mener jusqu'au mot FIN en vous donnant les clés nécessaires à la compréhension du récit.

Laissez-vous gagner par l'angoisse, l'humour et le suspense qui règnent chez les maîtres de la littérature anglo-saxonne.

Lire en VO ? You can indeed!

For my brother Johnny's boys,
Luke and Chris Higgins,
and for his granddaughter, Laura.

With love.

What is a friend?
A single soul[1] dwelling[2] in two bodies.
— Aristotle[3]

1. seule âme
2. logée
3. Aristote

Acknowledgments

ENDLESS THANKS[1] to all who gave so much input and encouragement[2] in the writing of this book—my editor, Michael V. Korda; his associate, senior editor Chuck Adams; my agent, Eugene H. Winick; Robert Ressler, Associate Director of Forensic[3] Behavioral Services. Kudos[4] to my daughter, Carol Higgins Clark, for her research, comments and suggestions and for burning the midnight oil[5] with me as we raced to deadline[6]. And of course, special thanks to the rest of my family and friends, who endured my usual self-doubting about whether or not I could tell this story; their saintly patience will have the cathedrals fighting for their bones[7].

1. Mille mercis
2. ont fortement contribué et m'ont tant encouragée
3. médico-légal
4. Bravo
5. avoir travaillé toute la nuit
6. à l'approche de la date limite
7. vu leur patience de saints, on s'arrachera leurs reliques

Coup de pouce pour vous aider à bien comprendre le début de l'histoire...

C'est Charley qui lui avait dit de tuer Nan il y a quinze ans... Et il semblait s'être fait oublier. Mais Charley a repris la main, il lui a enjoint de passer des petites annonces... et il a tué sept autres filles.

Charley se fait de plus en plus pressant. Encore deux et on arrête !

I
MONDAY
February 18

THE ROOM was dark. He sat in the chair, his arms hugging his legs[1]. It was happening again. Charley wouldn't stay locked[2] in the secret place. Charley insisted on thinking about Erin. *Only two more*, Charley whispered[3]. *Then I'll stop.*

He knew there was no use protesting[4]. But it was becoming more and more dangerous. Charley was becoming reckless[5]. Charley wanted to show off[6]. *Go away, Charley, leave me alone*, he begged[7]. Charley's mocking laugh[8] roared through the room[9].

If only Nan had liked him, he thought. If only she'd invited him to her birthday party fifteen years ago ... He'd loved her so much! He'd followed her to Darien with the present he'd bought her at a discount house[10], a pair of dancing slippers[11]. The cardboard shoebox[12] had been plain and cheap[13], and he'd taken such trouble[14] to decorate it, drawing a sketch of the slippers[15] on the lid[16].

Her birthday was on March twelfth, during spring break[17]. He'd driven down to Darien to surprise her with the present. He'd arrived to find her house ablaze with lights[18]. Cars were being parked by valets.[19] He'd driven slowly past, shocked and stunned[20] to recognize students from Brown there.

It still embarrassed him to remember[21] that he'd cried like a baby as he turned around to drive

1. serrant les jambes de ses bras
2. refusait de se laisser enfermer
3. murmura
4. que ça ne servait à rien de protester
5. incontrôlable
6. se faire remarquer
7. supplia
8. Le rire moqueur
9. résonna dans toute la pièce
10. chez un soldeur
11. chaussures de danse
12. boîte en carton
13. très quelconque
14. s'était donné tant de mal
15. en dessinant les chaussures
16. couvercle
17. les vacances de Pâques
18. tout illuminée
19. Des voituriers garaient les voitures.
20. ébahi
21. Il était encore tout gêné en se souvenant

back. Then the thought of the birthday gift made him change his mind. Nan had told him that every morning at seven o'clock, rain or shine[1], she jogged in the wooded area near her home. The next morning he was there, waiting for her.

He remembered, still vividly today[2], her *surprise* at seeing him. *Surprise*, not pleasure. She'd stopped, her breath coming in gasps[3], a stocking cap[4] hiding her silky blond hair, a school sweater[5] over her running suit[6], her feet in Nikes.

He'd wished her a happy birthday, watched her open the box, listened to her insincere[7] thanks. He'd put his arms around her. "Nan, I love you so much. Let me see how pretty your feet look in the slippers. I'll fasten them[8] for you. We can dance together right here[9]."

"Get lost![10]" She pushed him away, threw the box at him, started to jog past him.

It was Charley who had run after her, grabbed her[11], thrown her to the ground[12]. Charley's hands squeezed her throat[13] until her arms stopped flailing[14]. Charley fastened the slippers on her feet and danced with Nan, her head lolling[15] on his shoulder. Charley lay her[16] on the ground, one of the dancing slippers on her right foot, replacing the Nike on her left.

A long time had passed. Charley had become a blurred memory[17], a shadowy figure[18] lurking somewhere in the recesses of his mind[19], until two years ago. Then Charley had started reminding him about Nan, about her slender, high-arched feet[20], her narrow ankles, her beauty and grace when she danced with him …

Eeney-meeney-miney-mo. Catch a dancer by the toe.[21] Ten piggy toes[22]. The game his mother used

1. quel que soit le temps
2. comme si c'était hier
3. essoufflée
4. un bonnet
5. un pull de l'université
6. par-dessus le jogging
7. du bout des lèvres
8. Je vais attacher la bride
9. ici même
10. Fiche-moi la paix !
11. l'avait attrapée
12. jetée par terre
13. l'avait prise à la gorge, serrant
14. de s'agiter dans tous les sens
15. sa tête ballant
16. l'avait allongée
17. vague souvenir
18. une silhouette floue
19. tapie dans un coin de sa tête
20. la cambrure de ses pieds fins
21. [comptine type Am stram gram, pour désigner ici une danseuse]
22. orteils

to play when he was small. *This little piggy went to market.*[1] *This little piggy stayed home.*

"Play it ten times," he used to beg when she stopped. "One for each piggy toe."

His mother had loved him so much! Then she changed. He could still hear her voice. *"What are these magazines doing in your room? Why did you* take those *pumps*[2] *from my closet*[3]*? After all we've done for you! You're such a disappointment to us."*

When he reappeared two years ago, Charley ordered him to place ads[4] in the personal columns[5]. So many ads. Charley dictated[6] what he had to say in the special one[7].

Now seven girls were buried on the property[8], each with a dancing slipper on the right foot, her shoe or sneaker[9] or boot on the left …

He'd begged[10] Charley to let him stop for a while. He didn't want to do it anymore. He'd told Charley that the ground was still frozen—he couldn't bury them, and it was dangerous to keep their bodies in the freezer[11] …

But Charley shouted, "I want these last two to be found. I want them found just the way I let Nan be found."

Charley had chosen these last two the same way he had chosen the others after Nan. They were named Erin Kelley and Darcy Scott. They had each answered two different personal ads he'd placed. More important, they had each answered his *special* ad.

In all the replies[12] he'd received, it was *their* letters and pictures that had jumped out at Charley[13]. The letters were amusing, the cadence of the language attractive[14], almost like hearing Nan's voice, that self-deprecating wit[15], that dry,

1. [autre comptine, qui joue sur le nom enfantin de l'orteil, « doigt de cochonnet »]
2. escarpins
3. dans mon placard
4. de faire paraître des annonces
5. dans la rubrique des rencontres
6. lui avait dicté
7. sa petite annonce spéciale
8. enterrées dans le jardin
9. sa basket
10. supplié
11. congélateur
12. Parmi toutes les réponses
13. qui, pour Charley, sortaient du lot
14. leur style était rythmé et alléchant
15. son autodérision pleine d'esprit

intelligent humor[1]. And there were the pictures. Both were inviting[2] in different ways ...

Erin Kelley had sent a snapshot[3] of herself perched on the corner of a desk[4]. She'd been leaning forward a bit as though speaking, her eyes shining, her long, slim[5] body poised[6] as though she were waiting to be asked to dance[7].

Darcy Scott's picture showed her standing by a cushioned windowseat[8], her hand on the drapery[9]. She was half-turned toward the camera[10]. Clearly, she'd been surprised when her picture was taken. There were swatches of material[11] over her arm, an absorbed, but amused, expression on her face. She had high cheekbones[12], a slender frame[13], and long legs accentuated by narrow ankles, her slim feet encased in[14] Gucci loafers[15].

How much more attractive they would be in dancing slippers! he told himself.

He got up and stretched[16]. The dark shadows falling across the room no longer disturbed him. Charley's presence was complete and welcome. No more nagging voice begged him[17] to resist.

As Charley willingly receded[18] into the dark cave from which he had emerged, he reread Erin's letter and ran his fingertips over her picture[19].

He laughed aloud[20] as he thought of the beguiling[21] ad that had summoned Erin to him[22].

It began: *"Loves Music, Loves to Dance."*

1. son sens de l'humour caustique et intelligent
2. l'attiraient
3. photo
4. assise sur le bord d'un bureau
5. mince
6. figé
7. qu'on l'invite à danser
8. debout à côté du siège rembourré d'un rebord de fenêtre
9. une main sur le rideau
10. l'appareil photo
11. des échantillons de tissu
12. des pommettes saillantes
13. une silhouette svelte
14. chaussant
15. des mocassins
16. s'étira
17. Il n'était plus harcelé par une voix le suppliant
18. retournait de son plein gré
19. passa les doigts sur la photo
20. tout haut
21. très alléchante
22. conduit Erin droit vers lui

II
TUESDAY
February 19

COLD. SLUSHY. Raw[1]. Terrible traffic[2]. It didn't matter. It was good to be back in New York.

Darcy happily tossed off her coat[3], ran her fingers through her hair[4], and surveyed[5] the neatly separated mail[6] on her desk. Bev Rothhouse, skinny, intense, bright[7], a night student at[8] Parsons School of Design and her treasured secretary[9], identified the stacks[10] by order of importance.

"Bills[11]," she said, pointing to the extreme right. "Deposit slips[12] next. Quite a few of them."

"Substantial, I hope," Darcy suggested.

"Pretty good," Bev confirmed. "Messages over there. You've got requests to furnish two more rental apartments[13]. I swear, you certainly knew what you were doing when you opened a secondhand business[14]."

Darcy laughed. "Sanford and Son. That's me."

Darcy's Corner, Budget[15] *Interior Design* was what the placard on the office door read[16]. The office was in the Flatiron Building[17] on Twenty-third Street.

"How was California?" Bev asked.

Amused, Darcy heard the note of awe[18] in the other young woman's voice. What Bev really meant was, "How are your mother and father? What's it like to be with them? Are they really as gorgeous[19] as they look in films?"

1. Un froid sale et pénétrant
2. Une circulation
3. fut soulagée d'enlever son manteau
4. se passa la main dans les cheveux
5. regarda
6. le courrier soigneusement trié
7. une jeune femme maigre, sérieuse et intelligente
8. qui suivait des cours du soir à
9. était une secrétaire très précieuse
10. les différentes piles
11. Les factures
12. Les récépissés
13. pour meubler 2 autres appartements en location
14. cette brocante
15. pour petits budgets
16. voilà ce qu'il y avait sur sa plaque à l'entrée
17. [célèbre gratte-ciel triangulaire]
18. le soupçon d'admiration
19. sensationnels

The answer, Darcy thought, is, Yes, they're gorgeous. Yes, they're wonderful. Yes, I love them and I'm proud of them. It's just that I've never felt comfortable[1] in their world.

"When are they leaving for Australia?" Bev was trying to sound offhanded[2].

"They left. I caught the red-eye back[3] to New York after seeing them off[4]."

Darcy had combined a visit home with a business trip to Lake Tahoe, where she'd been hired[5] to decorate a model ski house[6] for budget-priced[7] buyers. Her mother and father were embarking on an international tour[8] with their play[9]. She wouldn't see them for at least six months.

Now she opened the container[10] of coffee she'd picked up[11] at a nearby lunch counter[12] and settled down[13] at her desk.

"You look great," Bev observed. "I love that outfit[14]."

The square-neck[15] red wool dress and matching coat[16] were part of the Rodeo Drive shopping tour her mother had insisted upon. "For such a pretty girl, you never pay enough attention to your clothes, darling," her mother had fussed[17]. "You should emphasize[18] that wonderful ethereal quality." As her father frequently observed, Darcy could have posed for the portrait of the maternal ancestor for whom she had been named[19]. The original Darcy had left Ireland after the Revolutionary War to join her French fiancé, an officer with Lafayette's forces. They had the same wide-set[20] eyes, more green than hazel[21], the same soft brown hair streaked with gold[22], the same straight nose.

"We've grown a bit since then," Darcy enjoyed pointing out[23]. "I'm five eight[24]. Darcy the First was a shrimp[25]. That helps when you're trying to look

1. je ne me suis jamais sentie à l'aise
2. parler d'un air dégagé
3. le vol de nuit pour rentrer
4. après leur départ
5. eu un contrat
6. un chalet modèle
7. à petit budget
8. tournée
9. pièce de théâtre
10. gobelet [fermé]
11. qu'elle avait acheté en passant
12. snack-bar
13. s'installa
14. ta tenue
15. à encolure carrée
16. le manteau assorti
17. dit, chagrinée
18. accentuer
19. dont elle portait le nom
20. très écartés
21. noisette
22. rehaussés de mèches dorées
23. aimait à souligner
24. Je fais plus de 1,70 m
25. crevette

ethereal." She had never forgotten when she was six and overheard[1] a director[2] comment, "How ever did two such stunning[3] people manage to produce that mousy-looking[4] child?"

She still remembered standing perfectly still[5], absorbing the shock. A few minutes later when her mother tried to introduce her to someone on the set[6], "And this is my little girl, Darcy," she had shouted "No!" and run away. Later she apologized for being rude[7].

This morning when she got off the plane[8] at Kennedy, she'd dropped her bags[9] at the apartment, then come directly to the office, not taking time to change into her usual working garb[10], jeans and a sweater[11]. Bev waited for her to start sipping the[12] coffee, then picked up the messages[13]. "Do you want me to start getting[14] these people for you?"

"Let me give Erin a quick call first."

Erin picked up[15] on the first ring[16]. Her somewhat preoccupied greeting told[17] Darcy that she was already at her worktable. They'd been college roommates together[18] at Mount Holyoke. Then Erin had studied jewelry design[19]. Recently she'd won the prestigious N. W. Ayer award[20] for young designers.

Darcy had also found her professional niche[21]. After four years of working her way up[22] in an advertising[23] agency, she had switched careers[24] from account executive[25] to budget interior decorating. Both women were now twenty-eight, and they were as close[26] as they'd been when living together in school.

Darcy could picture Erin at her worktable, dressed in jeans and a baggy[27] sweater, her red hair held back by a clip[28] or in a ponytail[29], absorbed by her work, unaware of outside distraction[30].

1. avait entendu
2. un réalisateur
3. d'une beauté aussi frappante
4. aussi terne
5. être restée figée
6. plateau
7. malpolie
8. après avoir débarqué
9. était passée déposer ses valises
10. d'enfiler sa tenue de travail habituelle
11. pull
12. à boire son
13. prit la pile de messages
14. à rappeler
15. décrocha
16. sonnerie
17. Son « allô » distrait était signe pour
18. partagé une chambre d'étudiantes
19. la création de bijoux
20. prix
21. créneau
22. passés à gravir les échelons
23. de pub
24. était passée de
25. directrice comptable
26. proches
27. trop grand
28. barrette
29. queue de cheval
30. ne laissant rien la distraire

The preoccupied "hello" gave way to a whoop of joy[1] when Erin heard Darcy's voice.

"You're busy," Darcy said. "I won't keep you.[2] Just wanted to report that I've arrived, and, of course, I wanted to see how Billy is."

Billy was Erin's father. An invalid, he'd been in a nursing home[3] in Massachusetts for the past three years.

"Pretty much the same," Erin told her.

"How's the necklace[4] going? When I phoned Friday you sounded worried[5]." Just after Darcy had left last month, Erin had landed a commission from[6] Bertolini Jewelers to design a necklace using the client's family gems[7]. Bertolini was on a par with[8] Cartier's and Tiffany's.

"That's because I was still terrified the design might be off base[9]. It really was pretty intricate[10]. But all is well. I deliver it tomorrow morning and if I say so myself,[11] it's sensational. How was Bel-Air?"

"Glamorous." They laughed together, then Darcy said, "Update me on[12] Project Personal."

Nona Roberts, a producer at Hudson Cable Network, had become friendly with Darcy and Erin at their health[13] club. Nona was preparing a documentary on personal columns—about the kind of people who placed and answered the ads; their experiences, good or bad. Nona had asked Darcy and Erin to assist[14] in the research by answering some of the ads. "You don't have to see anybody more than once," she'd urged[15]. "Half the singles[16] at the network[17] are doing it and having a lot of laughs[18]. And who knows, you might meet someone terrific. Anyhow[19], think about it."

Erin, typically the more daring[20], had been unusually reluctant[21]. Darcy had persuaded her it could be fun. "We won't place our own ads," she

1. fit place à un cri de joie
2. Je ne vais pas te prendre longtemps.
3. en maison de retraite [médicalisée]
4. collier
5. avais l'air inquiète
6. décroché une commande de
7. les joyaux
8. aussi réputé que
9. que le concept ne fonctionne pas bien
10. assez chargé
11. je ne devrais pas m'envoyer des fleurs mais
12. Raconte-moi les derniers épisodes du
13. de gym
14. de l'aider
15. insisté
16. La moitié des célibataires
17. qui travaillent pour la chaîne
18. s'amusent bien
19. En tout cas
20. d'habitude la plus fonceuse des deux
21. étonnamment réticente

argued[1]. "We'll just answer some that look interesting. We won't give our addresses, just a phone number. We'll meet them in public places. What's to lose?[2]"

They had started six weeks ago. Darcy had had time for only one date[3] before she left on the trip to Lake Tahoe and Bel-Air. That man had written he was six one[4]. As she told Erin afterward, he must have been standing on a ladder when he measured himself[5]. Also he'd claimed he was[6] an advertising executive. But when Darcy threw out a few names of[7] agencies and clients, he was totally at sea[8]. A liar and a jerk[9], she reported to Erin and Nona. Now, smiling in anticipation[10], Darcy asked Erin to fill her in on her most recent encounters[11].

"I'll save it all for tomorrow night[12] when we get together with Nona," Erin said. "I'm writing every detail down in that notebook you gave me for Christmas. Suffice it to say[13], I've been out twice more since we talked. That brings the total to eight dates in the last three weeks. Most of them were nerds[14] with absolutely no redeeming social value[15]. One it turned out I'd met before.[16] One of the new ones was really attractive and needless to say[17] hasn't called back. I'm meeting somebody tonight. He sounds okay, but let's wait and see."

Darcy grinned[18]. "Obviously, I haven't missed much. How many ads have you answered for me?"

"About a dozen. I thought it would be fun to send both our letters to some of the same ads. We can really compare notes[19] if those dudes[20] call."

"I love it. Where are you meeting tonight's prize[21]?"

"In a pub off[22] Washington Square."

"What does he do?"

"Corporate law.[23] He's from Philadelphia. Just relocating here[24]. You can make[25] tomorrow night, can't you?"

1. avait fait valoir
2. Qu'avons-nous à perdre ?
3. rendez-vous
4. faisait 1,85 m
5. ça devait être une fois monté sur une échelle
6. avait prétendu être
7. avait glissé dans la conversation quelques noms d'
8. avait été complètement paumé
9. Menteur et con
10. d'avance
11. de lui raconter ses dernières rencontres
12. soir
13. Disons déjà que
14. des crétins
15. qui n'ont rien pour compenser
16. Il y en a un que j'avais déjà croisé.
17. bien entendu
18. sourit
19. partager nos impressions
20. ces types
21. le gros lot de ce soir
22. qui donne sur
23. Droit des affaires.
24. Il vient s'installer ici.
25. être là

with him. The producers had managed to find a young actress who bore a startling resemblance to[1] Nan. The docudrama showed her jogging; the figure[2] watching her from the protection of the trees; the confrontation; the attempt to escape, the killer tackling her[3], choking her[4], pulling the Nike from her right foot and replacing it with a high-heeled slipper[5].

The commentary was delivered by an announcer whose sonorous voice sounded gratuitously horrified[6]. "Was it a stranger who accosted beautiful, gifted[7] Nan Sheridan? She and her twin celebrated their nineteenth birthday the night before at the family mansion[8]. Did someone Nan knew, someone who perhaps toasted her[9] on her birthday, become her killer? In fifteen years no one has come forward with[10] a shred of information[11] that might solve this hideous crime. Was Nan Sheridan the random[12] victim of a deranged monster, or was her death an act of personal vengeance?"

A montage of closing shots followed.[13] The house and grounds from a different angle. The phone number to call "if you have any information." The last closeup[14] was the police photo of Nan's body as it had been found, neatly placed on the ground, her hands folded together on her waist, her left foot still wearing the Nike, her right foot in the sequined[15] slipper.

The final line: "Where are the mates to this sneaker, to this graceful evening shoe[16]? Does the killer still have them?"

Greta Sheridan had watched the program dry-eyed[17]. When it was finished, she'd said, "Chris, I've gone over it in my mind[18] so often. That's why I wanted to see this. I couldn't function after Nan died, couldn't think. But Nan used to talk to me so

1. ressemblait terriblement à
2. silhouette
3. qui la plaquait au sol
4. l'étranglait
5. une chaussure de danse à talon haut
6. était inutilement théâtrale
7. la talentueuse
8. grande maison
9. qui avait peut-être levé son verre à sa santé
10. personne n'avait fourni
11. la moindre information
12. prise au hasard
13. La séquence avait fini par une série de prises de vue.
14. gros plan
15. à sequins
16. la 2e basket et le 2e escarpin
17. sans verser une larme
18. J'ai repensé à tout ça

much about everyone at school. I … I just thought that seeing that program might make me recall[1] something that could be important. Remember the day of the funeral[2]? That huge crowd.[3] All those young people from college. Remember Chief Harriman said that he was convinced her killer was sitting there among the mourners[4]? Remember how they had cameras set up[5] to take pictures of everyone in the funeral home[6] and at church?"

Then, as though a giant hand had smashed[7] her face, Greta Sheridan had broken into heart-rending sobs[8]. "That girl looked so much like Nan, didn't she? Oh Chris, I've missed her so much all these years. Dad would still be alive[9] if she were here. That heart attack[10] was his way of grieving[11]."

I wish I'd taken an ax to every television in the house[12] before I let Mother watch that damn program, Chris thought as he ran down the corridor to his office. The fingers of his left hand drummed[13] on the desk as he grabbed[14] the phone. "Mother, what's wrong?"

Greta Sheridan's voice was tense and unsteady[15]. "Chris, I'm sorry to bother you during the auction, but the strangest letter just came[16]."

Another fallout from that stinking program[17], Chris fumed[18]. All those crank letters[19]. They ranged[20] from psychics[21] offering to conduct seances to people begging for money in exchange for their prayers. "I wish you wouldn't read that garbage[22]," he said. "Those letters tear you apart[23]."

"Chris, this one is different. It says that in memory of Nan, a dancing girl from Manhattan is going to die on the evening of February nineteenth in exactly the way Nan died." Greta Sheridan's voice rose. "Chris, suppose this isn't a crank letter? Is there anything we can do? Is there anyone we can warn[24]?"

1. m'aiderait peut-être à me souvenir de
2. l'enterrement
3. Cette foule.
4. l'assistance en deuil
5. qu'ils avaient installé des caméras
6. au funérarium
7. venait de s'écraser sur
8. éclaté en sanglots déchirants
9. serait encore en vie
10. crise cardiaque
11. sa façon de faire son deuil
12. Si seulement j'avais cassé toutes les télés de la maison à coups de hache
13. Il tapotait de la main gauche
14. en prenant
15. tendue et tremblante
16. je viens de recevoir une lettre très bizarre
17. Encore une retombée de cette stupide émission
18. ragea
19. lettres d'illuminés
20. avaient un éventail, allant
21. médiums
22. ces âneries
23. te chamboulent
24. prévenir

DOUG FOX pulled on his tie, carefully twisted it into a precise knot[1], and studied himself in the mirror. He'd had a facial[2] yesterday and his skin glowed[3]. The body wave had made his thinning hair seem abundant[4] and the sandy rinse[5] completely covered the touch of gray that was emerging at his temples[6].

A good-looking guy, he assured himself[7], admiring the way his crisp white[8] shirt followed the lines of his muscular chest[9] and slim waist. He reached for[10] his suit jacket, quietly appreciating the fine feel[11] of the Scottish wool. Dark blue with faint pinstripes[12], accented by the small red print[13] on his Hermès tie. He looked every inch the part[14] of the investment banker, upstanding citizen[15] of Scarsdale, devoted husband of Susan Frawley Fox, father of four lively, handsome youngsters[16].

No one, Doug thought with amused satisfaction, would suspect him of his other life: that of the single[17] freelance illustrator with an apartment in the blessed anonymity[18] of London Terrace on West Twenty-third Street, plus a hideaway[19] in Pawling and a new Volvo station wagon[20].

Doug took a final look in the long mirror, adjusted his pocket handkerchief, and with a glance to make sure[21] he hadn't forgotten anything, walked to the door. The bedroom always irritated him. Antique French provincial furniture, damn place done by an upscale[22] interior designer, and Susan still managed to make it look like the inside of Fibber McGee's closet[23]. Clothes piled on the chaise, silver toilet art-

1. la noua soigneusement
2. Il s'était fait faire un soin du visage
3. brillait
4. La Mini-vague redonnait un volume factice à ses cheveux clairsemés
5. le rinçage blond cendré
6. sur ses tempes
7. se dit-il d'un air convaincu
8. bien blanche
9. torse musclé
10. attrapa
11. douceur
12. avec de fines rayures
13. motif
14. avait vraiment l'air
15. citoyen intègre
16. beaux enfants pleins de vie
17. célibataire
18. dans le merveilleux anonymat
19. pied-à-terre discret
20. break
21. s'étant assuré d'un coup d'œil
22. chic
23. lui donner un air de pagaille sans nom [allusion à un feuilleton radio américain]

icles haphazardly strewn[1] over the top of the dresser[2]. Kindergarten[3] drawings taped on the wall[4]. Let me out, Doug thought.

The kitchen was the scene of the usual mayhem.[5] Thirteen-year-old Donny and twelve-year-old Beth jamming[6] food in their mouths. Susan warning that the school bus was down the block[7]. The baby waddling around[8] with a wet diaper[9] and grubby[10] hands. Trish saying she didn't want to go to kindergarten[11] this afternoon, she wanted to stay home and watch "All My Children" with Mommy.

Susan was wearing an old flannel robe[12] over her nightgown[13]. She had been a very pretty girl when they were married. A pretty girl who'd let herself go[14]. She smiled at Doug and poured him[15] coffee. "Won't you have pancakes or something?"

"No." Would she ever stop asking him to stuff his face[16] every morning? Doug jumped back[17] as the baby tried to embrace[18] his leg. "Damn it, Susan, if you can't keep him clean, at least don't let him near me. I can't go to the office looking grubby."

"Bus!" Beth yelled[19]. "Bye, Mom. Bye, Dad."

Donny grabbed his books. "Can you come to my basketball game tonight, Dad?"

"Won't be home till late, son. An important meeting. Next time for sure, I promise."

"Sure." Donny slammed the door as he left[20].

Three minutes later, Doug was in the Mercedes heading for the train station, Susan's reproachful[21] "Try not to be too late" ringing in his ears[22]. Doug felt himself begin to unwind[23]. Thirty-six years old and stuck[24] with a fat wife, four noisy kids, a house in the suburbs. The American Dream. At twenty-two he'd thought he was making a smart move[25] when he married Susan.

1. en vrac
2. sur la commode
3. d'enfant
4. punaisés au mur
5. Dans la cuisine, c'était le bazar habituel.
6. qui enfournaient
7. en vue
8. trottinant
9. une couche mouillée
10. sales
11. à la maternelle
12. robe de chambre
13. chemise de nuit
14. qui s'était laissée aller
15. lui servit
16. de se gaver
17. fit un bond en arrière
18. mettre ses bras autour de
19. hurla
20. sortit en claquant la porte
21. réprobateur
22. qui résonnait encore dans ses oreilles
23. à se détendre
24. coincé
25. il s'était cru malin

Unfortunately, marrying the daughter of a wealthy man[1] wasn't the same as marrying wealth. Susan's father was a tightwad[2]. Lend[3], never give. That motto[4] had to be tattooed on his brain.

It wasn't that he didn't love the kids or that he wasn't fond enough of Susan. It was just that he should have waited to get into this paterfamilias routine[5]. He'd thrown his youth away.[6] As Douglas Fox, investment banker, upstanding citizen of Scarsdale, his life was an exercise in boredom[7].

He parked and ran for the train, consoling himself with the thought that as Doug Fields, bachelor[8] artist, prince of the personals[9], his life was swift and secretive[10], and when the dark needs came[11] there was a way to satisfy them.

1. richard
2. un radin
3. Prêter
4. devise
5. avant de se lancer dans cette routine de père de famille
6. Il avait gâché sa jeunesse.
7. positivement ennuyeuse
8. célibataire
9. petites annonces
10. speed et secrète
11. ses envies malsaines lui venaient

III
WEDNESDAY
February 20

On Wednesday evening, Darcy arrived at Nona Roberts's office promptly at six-thirty[1]. She'd had a meeting with a client on Riverside Drive and phoned Nona to suggest they cab over[2] to the restaurant together.

Nona's office was a cluttered[3] box in a row[4] of cluttered boxes on the tenth floor of the Hudson Cable Network. It held a somewhat battered oak desk[5] piled with[6] papers, several filing cabinets, the drawers of which did not fully close[7], shelves of[8] reference books and tapes, a distinctly uninviting-looking love seat[9], and an executive swivel chair[10] which Darcy knew no longer swiveled. A plant which Nona consistently forgot to water[11] drooped wearily[12] on the narrow windowsill[13].

Nona loved that office. Darcy privately[14] wondered why it didn't destroy itself by spontaneous combustion. When she arrived, Nona was on the phone, so she went out seeking[15] water for the plant. "It's begging for mercy[16]," she said when she returned.

Nona had just completed the call[17]. She jumped up[18] to embrace Darcy. "A green thumb I have not.[19]" She was wearing a khaki wool jumpsuit[20] that faithfully followed the lines of her small frame. A narrow leather belt with a white-gold clasp[21] sculpted in the form of linked[22] hands cinched her waist[23]. Her

1. à six heures et demie pile
2. qu'elles prennent un taxi pour aller
3. tout en désordre
4. rangée
5. un bureau en chêne hors d'âge
6. encombré de
7. caissons dont les tiroirs ne fermaient pas
8. des étagères couvertes de
9. un petit canapé vraiment peu accueillant
10. fauteuil pivotant
11. oubliait systématiquement d'arroser
12. pendouillait
13. rebord de la fenêtre
14. intérieurement
15. chercher
16. Elle demande grâce
17. venait de finir sa conversation
18. se leva d'un bond
19. Je n'ai pas la main verte.
20. combinaison
21. une boucle en or blanc
22. entrelacées
23. lui ceignait la taille

medium-blond hair, streaked with touches of gray, was blunt-cut and barely reached her chin[1]. Her animated face was interesting rather than pretty.

Darcy was glad to see that the pain in Nona's dark brown eyes had been almost completely replaced by an expression of wry humor[2]. Nona's recent divorce had hit her hard. As she put it, "It's traumatic enough turning forty[3] without your husband bumping you[4] for a twenty-one-year-old nymphet[5]."

"I'm running late[6]," Nona apologized. "We're meeting Erin at seven?"

"Between seven and seven-fifteen," Darcy said, her fingers itching[7] to skim the dead leaves[8] from the plant.

"Fifteen minutes to get over there, provided I throw myself in front of an empty cab[9]. Terrific. There's one thing I'd like to do before we go. Why don't you come with me and witness the compassionate side of television[10]."

"I wasn't aware[11] it had one." Darcy reached for her shoulder bag[12].

All the offices rimmed[13] a large central area which was crowded with[14] secretaries and writers at their desks. Computers hummed and fax machines clattered.[15] At the end of the room, an announcer was on camera giving a news update[16]. Nona waved a general greeting[17] as she passed. "There isn't a single unattached person[18] in that maze[19] who isn't answering the personal ads for me. As a matter of fact[20], I suspect there are some supposedly attached[21] guys who are also quietly getting together with an intriguing box number."

She led Darcy into a screening room[22] and introduced her to Joan Nye, a pretty blonde who didn't look more than twenty-two. "Joan does the obits[23],"

1. coupés en un carré très court
2. ironique
3. d'atteindre la quarantaine
4. ne vous plaque
5. lolita
6. à la bourre
7. très tentée
8. d'enlever les feuilles mortes
9. si j'arrive à prendre un taxi au vol
10. voir le côté compatissant de la télévision
11. Je ne savais pas
12. son sac à main [à bandoulière]
13. bordaient
14. où étaient entassés
15. On entendait le bourdonnement des ordinateurs et le cliquetis des fax.
16. bulletin d'informations
17. fit bonjour de la main à tout le monde
18. un ou une seul(e) célibataire
19. dédale
20. En fait
21. a priori en couple
22. une salle de visionnement
23. s'occupe des nécros

she explained. "She just finished updating an important one and asked me to take a look at it[1]." She turned to Nye. "I know it will be fine," she added reassuringly.

Joan sighed[2]. "I hope so," she said, and pushed the button to start the film rolling.

The face of film great[3] Ann Bouchard filled the screen. The mellifluous[4] voice of Gary Finch, the Hudson Cable anchorman[5], was properly subdued[6] as he began to speak.

> "Ann Bouchard won her first Oscar at the age of nineteen, when she replaced ailing[7] Lillian Marker in the 1928 classic *Perilous Path* ..."

Film clips of Ann Bouchard in her most memorable roles were followed by highlights of her personal life[8]: her seven husbands, her homes, her well-publicized battles with studio executives[9], excerpts[10] of interviews throughout her long career[11], her emotional response to receiving[12] a lifetime achievement award[13]: "I have been blessed[14]. I have been loved. And I love you all."

It was over. "I didn't know Ann Bouchard died," Darcy exclaimed. "My God, she was on the phone with my mother last week. When did that happen?"

"It didn't," Nona said. "We prepare the celebrity obits in advance just the way the newspapers do[15]. And we regularly update them[16]. The farewell[17] to George Burns has been revised twenty-two times. When the inevitable occurs, we just have to drop in the lead[18]. The rather irreverent name[19] for the project is the Toodle-oo Club."

"Toodle-oo Club?"

"Uh-huh. We do the final portion and say toodle-oo[20] to the deceased[21]." She turned to Nye. "That was terrific. I'm positively blinking back tears.[22] Incidentally[23], have you answered any new personals?"

1. d'y jeter un coup d'œil
2. soupira
3. la star de ciné
4. mélodieuse
5. présentateur
6. avait la sobriété de rigueur
7. alors souffrante
8. les moments importants de sa vie privée
9. ses célèbres conflits avec les producteurs
10. des extraits
11. tout au long de sa carrière
12. son émotion quand elle reçut
13. un prix couronnant sa carrière
14. J'ai eu une chance extraordinaire
15. comme ça se fait dans la presse écrite
16. nous les mettons à jour régulièrement
17. Les adieux
18. ajouter la séquence d'ouverture
19. Le surnom irrévérencieux
20. tchao
21. au défunt
22. J'en ai les larmes aux yeux.
23. À propos

Nye grinned. "It may cost you, Nona. The other night I made a date to meet some jerk. Naturally got caught in traffic. Double-parked my car[1] to rush in and let him know I'd be right back[2]. Rushed out[3] to find a cop ticketing me[4]. Finally found a garage six blocks away and when I came back—"

"He was gone," Nona suggested.

Nye's eyes widened[5]. "How did you know?"

"Because I've heard this from some other people. Don't take it personally. Now we'd better run[6]." At the door Nona called over her shoulder, "Give me the ticket[7]. I'll take care of it.[8]"

In the cab on the way to meet Erin, Darcy found herself wondering what it was that made someone pull a trick like that[9]. Nye was genuinely attractive[10]. Was she too young for the man she had met? When she answered the ad she must have given her age. Did he have some image in mind that Nye didn't fit[11]?

It was a disquieting thought[12]. As the cab bumped and lurched through[13] Seventy-second Street traffic, she commented, "Nona, when we started answering these ads, I thought of it as a joke[14]. Now I'm not so sure. It's like having a blind date[15] without the security of being introduced to the guy because he's the best friend of somebody's brother. Can you imagine any man you know doing that? Even if for some reason Nye's date hated the way she dressed or wore her hair or whatever, all he had to do was have a quick drink and say he was rushing for a plane. He still gets away fast and doesn't leave her feeling like a fool[16]."

"Darcy, let's face it[17]," Nona said. "From all the reports I'm hearing[18], most of the people who place or answer these ads are pretty insecure[19]. What's a

1. Je me suis garée en double file
2. que je revenais tout de suite
3. Je suis ressortie en courant
4. et je suis tombée sur un flic en train de me mettre un P-V
5. la regarda, ébahie
6. on ferait mieux de filer
7. le P-V
8. Je m'en occuperai.
9. ce qui poussait les gens à faire un truc pareil
10. vraiment jolie
11. à laquelle Nye ne correspondait pas
12. une pensée troublante
13. se frayait difficilement un chemin dans
14. j'ai pris ça à la rigolade
15. une rencontre arrangée mais
16. une andouille
17. regardons les choses en face
18. D'après tout ce qu'on me raconte
19. ne sont pas très équilibrés

lot more scary[1] is that just today I got a letter from an FBI agent who'd heard about the program and said he wants to talk to me. He'd like us to include a warning[2] that these ads are a natural for sexual psychopaths[3]."

"What a lovely thought!"

As usual, Bella Vita offered encompassing warmth.[4] The wonderful, familiar garlicky[5] aroma was in the air. There was a faint hum of talk and laughter[6]. Adam, the owner[7], greeted them[8]. "Ah, the beautiful ladies. I have your table." He indicated one by the window.

"Erin should be along any minute[9]," Darcy told him as they were seated[10]. "I'm surprised she isn't waiting. She's always so prompt[11], it actually gives me a complex."

"She's probably stuck in traffic," Nona said. "Let's order wine. We know she'll have chablis."

Half an hour later, Darcy pushed her chair back. "I'm going to phone Erin. The only thing I can imagine is that when she delivered the necklace she designed for Bertolini's, there might have been some adjustment needed. She loses track of time[12] when she's working."

The answering machine[13] was on[14] in Erin's studio apartment. Darcy returned to the table and realized Nona's anxious expression mirrored her own feelings[15]. "I left a message that we're waiting for her and to call here if she can't make it[16]."

They ordered dinner. Darcy loved this restaurant, but tonight she was hardly aware of[17] what she was eating. Every few minutes she glanced at[18] the door hoping that Erin would come flying in[19] with a perfectly reasonable explanation of why she had been delayed[20].

1. inquiétant
2. que nous ajoutions une mise en garde indiquant
3. un outil idéal pour les prédateurs sexuels
4. Bella Vita offrait un accueil toujours aussi chaleureux.
5. de la cuisine à l'ail
6. On entendait les rires et les conversations en fond sonore
7. propriétaire
8. vint les accueillir
9. devrait arriver d'une minute à l'autre
10. prenaient place
11. ponctuelle
12. perd la notion du temps
13. répondeur
14. branché
15. reflétait ce qu'elle-même ressentait
16. venir
17. ne savait plus trop
18. jetait un coup d'œil vers
19. arriverait en courant
20. pour son retard

She did not come.

Darcy lived on the top floor of a brownstone[1] on East Forty-ninth Street, Nona in a co-op on Central Park West. When they left the restaurant they took separate cabs, promising that whoever heard from Erin first[2] would contact the other.

The minute she got home, Darcy tried Erin's number again. She tried an hour later, just before she went to bed. This time she left an emphatic[3] message. "Erin, I'm worried about you. It's Wednesday, 11:15. I don't care how late you get in[4], call me."

Eventually, Darcy fell into an uneasy sleep.[5]

When she awakened[6] at 6 a.m., her immediate thought was that Erin had not called.

JAY STRATTON stared out the corner window[7] of his thirtieth-floor apartment in Waterside Plaza on Twenty-fifth Street and the East River Drive. The view was spectacular: the East River arced by[8] the Brooklyn and Williamsburg Bridges, the twin towers to the right, the Hudson behind them, the streams of traffic[9], agonizingly slow in the evening rush hour[10], flowing well enough now[11]. It was seven-thirty.

Jay frowned[12], a gesture that caused his narrow eyes to become almost invisible. A head of dark brown hair, expensively cut and attractively threaded with gray[13], helped to foster his cultivated look of casual elegance[14]. He was aware[15] of the tendency of his waistline to thicken[16], and exercised vigorously. He knew he looked a bit older than his age, which was thirty-seven, but that had proved to

1. immeuble en grès rouge
2. la première à avoir des nouvelles d'Erin
3. plus insistant
4. Quelle que soit l'heure à laquelle tu rentres
5. Darcy finit par sombrer dans un sommeil agité.
6. se réveilla
7. regardait par la fenêtre d'angle
8. passant sous les voûtes
9. le flot de la circulation
10. à l'heure de pointe
11. commençait à se fluidifier
12. fronça les sourcils
13. parsemés d'un beau gris
14. renforçaient son élégance faussement décontractée
15. conscient
16. qu'il commençait à prendre du ventre

be an advantage. He'd always been considered unusually handsome by most people.

Certainly the newspaper magnate's widow[1] whom he'd escorted to the Taj Mahal casino in Atlantic City last week had found him attractive, though when he had mentioned that he'd like to have some jewelry created for her, her face turned to stone[2]. "No sales pitch[3], please," she snapped[4]. "Let's understand that.[5]"

He hadn't bothered with her again[6]. Jay did not believe in wasting time[7]. Today he'd lunched at the Jockey Club and while he waited for a table he'd started chatting with an older couple. The Ashtons were in New York on holiday celebrating their fortieth anniversary[8]. Obviously well-heeled[9], they were somewhat at loose ends[10] outside their familiar North Carolina surroundings[11] and responded eagerly to his conversational overtures[12].

The husband had looked pleased at Jay's query as to whether he'd[13] chosen a suitable piece of jewelry for his wife to commemorate[14] their forty years together. "I keep telling Frances that she ought to let me buy her some real nice jewelry but she says to save the money for Frances Junior."

Jay had suggested that at some time in the distant future[15], Frances Junior might enjoy wearing a lovely necklace or bracelet and telling her own daughter or granddaughter that this was a very special gift from Grampa to Nana[16]. "It's what royal families have been doing for centuries," he explained as he handed them his card[17].

The phone rang. Jay hurried to answer it. Maybe it was the Ashtons, he thought.

It was Aldo Marco, the manager at Bertolini's. "Aldo," Jay said heartily[18]. "I was planning to call you. All's well, I trust[19]?"

1. veuve
2. elle avait pris un air très froid
3. Gardez vos boniments
4. avait dit sèchement
5. Soyons clairs là-dessus.
6. pris la peine de la revoir
7. n'était pas le genre à perdre son temps
8. anniversaire de mariage
9. aisés
10. un peu désorientés
11. leur Caroline du Nord
12. semblèrent ravis quand il entama la conversation
13. quand Jay lui demanda s'il avait
14. le bijou adéquat pour fêter dignement
15. dans plusieurs années
16. de Papy à Mamie
17. en leur tendant sa carte de visite
18. d'un ton enjoué
19. je suppose

"All is certainly not well.[1]" Marco's tone was icy[2]. "When you introduced me to Erin Kelley I was most impressed with her and her portfolio. The design she submitted was superb and as you know, we gave her our client's family gems to reset[3]. The necklace was supposed to have been delivered this morning. Miss Kelley failed to keep the appointment[4] and has not answered our repeated messages. Mr. Stratton, I want either that necklace or my client's gems back immediately."

Jay ran his tongue over his lips[5]. He realized the hand holding the phone was damp[6]. He had forgotten about the necklace. He chose his answer carefully[7]. "I saw Miss Kelley a week ago. She showed me the necklace. It was exquisite[8]. There must be some misunderstanding[9]."

"The misunderstanding is that she has failed to deliver the necklace, which is needed for an engagement party[10] Friday night. I repeat, I want it or my client's gems back tomorrow. I hold you responsible to execute one or the other alternative. Is that clear?"

The sharp click of the phone sounded[11] in Stratton's ears.

1. Non, ça ne va pas bien du tout.
2. glacial
3. à remonter
4. ne s'est pas présentée à son rendez-vous
5. se passa la langue sur les lèvres
6. moite
7. soigneusement ses mots
8. extrêmement raffiné
9. un malentendu
10. soirée de fiançailles
11. Le claquement sec du téléphone résonna

MICHAEL NASH saw his last patient, Gerald Renquist, at five o'clock on Wednesday afternoon. Renquist was the retired[12] CEO[13] of an international pharmaceutical company. Retirement had thrown[14] a man whose personal identity was linked to the intrigue and politics of the boardroom[15] to the status of unwilling sideliner[16].

12. à la retraite
13. P-DG
14. Sa mise à la retraite avait réduit
15. conseil d'administration
16. à l'état de spectateur malgré lui

"I know I should consider myself lucky," Renquist was saying, "but I feel so damn useless[1]. Even my wife pulled that old saw on me[2]—'I married you for better or worse, but not for lunch.' "

"You must have had a game plan for retirement[3]," Nash suggested mildly[4].

Renquist laughed. "I did. Avoid it at all cost.[5]"

Depression, Nash thought. The common cold of mental illness.[6] He realized he was tired and not giving Renquist his full attention. Not fair[7], he told himself. He's paying for me to listen. Still[8], it was a distinct relief[9] when at ten of six[10] he was able to wrap up the session[11].

After Renquist left, Nash began to lock up[12]. His office was on Seventy-first and Park, his apartment on the twentieth floor of the same building. He went out through the door that led to the lobby[13].

The new tenant[14] in 20B, a blonde in her early thirties, was waiting for the elevator. He fought down irritation[15] at the prospect of riding up with her[16]. The undisguised interest in her eyes was a nuisance[17], as were her almost inevitable invitations to drop in for a drink[18].

Michael Nash had the same problem with a number of his women patients. He could read their minds. Nice-looking guy, divorced, no children, mid-to-late thirties, available[19]. A diffident reserve had become second nature to him.[20]

At least tonight the new neighbor[21] did not repeat the invitation. Maybe she was learning. When they stepped from[22] the elevator, he murmured, "Good night."

His apartment reflected the precise care he took with[23] everything in his life. Ivory flax upholstery on[24] the twin[25] sofas in the living room was repeated on the dining room chairs surrounding the

1. tellement inutile
2. m'a sorti ce vieil adage
3. des projets pour la retraite
4. doucement
5. L'éviter à tout prix.
6. L'équivalent du rhume pour la santé mentale.
7. Ce n'est pas juste
8. Cela dit
9. il fut franchement soulagé
10. 17h50
11. mettre un terme à la séance
12. ferma son bureau
13. menait dans le hall
14. locataire
15. réprima son agacement
16. à l'idée de se retrouver dans le même ascenseur qu'elle
17. pénible
18. passer boire un verre
19. libre
20. C'était devenu une seconde nature de se tenir sur ses gardes.
21. voisine
22. sortirent de
23. l'attention méticuleuse qu'il prêtait à
24. Le lin ivoire qui recouvrait
25. deux

round oak table. That table had been a find at an antique auction[1] in Bucks County. The area carpets had muted[2] geometric patterns[3] on an ivory background. A wall of bookcases, plants on the windowsills, a Colonial[4] dry sink[5] which served as a bar, bric-a-brac he'd gathered[6] on trips abroad[7], good paintings. A comfortable, handsome room.

The kitchen and study[8] were to the left of the living room, the bedroom suite and bath to the right. A pleasant apartment and an attractive complement to the big place in Bridgewater that had been his parents' pride and joy[9]. Nash was often tempted to sell it, but knew he'd miss riding[10] on weekends.

He took off[11] his jacket and debated between watching the tail end[12] of the six o'clock news or listening to his new compact disc, a Mozart symphony. Mozart won. As the familiar opening bars softly filled the room, the doorbell rang[13].

Nash knew exactly who it would be. Resigned, he answered it[14]. The new neighbor stood holding an ice bucket[15]—the oldest trick in the book[16]. Thank God he hadn't started to mix his drink. He gave her the ice, explained that no, he couldn't join her[17], he was on his way out[18], and steered her to[19] the door. When she was gone, still twittering about[20] "Maybe next time," he made straight for[21] the bar, mixed a dry martini, and ruefully[22] shook his head.

Settling on the sofa near the window, he sipped the cocktail, appreciating its smooth, soothing[23] taste, and wondered about the young woman he was meeting for dinner at eight o'clock. Her response to his ad had been downright[24] amusing.

His publisher[25] was ecstatic about[26] the first half of the book he was writing, the book analyzing the

1. venait d'une vente aux enchères d'antiquités
2. discrets
3. motifs
4. de style XVIIIe s.
5. comptoir
6. qu'il avait rapportés
7. de ses voyages à l'étranger
8. le bureau
9. fait la fierté de ses parents
10. que ça lui manquerait de ne plus monter à cheval
11. retira
12. la toute fin
13. on sonna à la porte
14. alla ouvrir
15. seau à glace
16. une très vieille ficelle
17. se joindre à elle
18. sur le point de sortir
19. la reconduisit vers
20. jacassant encore un
21. alla droit sur
22. tristement
23. réconfortant
24. carrément
25. éditeur
26. ravi de

people who placed or answered personal ads, their psychological needs, their flights into fantasy in the way they described themselves[1].

His working[2] title was *The Personal Ads: Quest for Companionship or Departure from Reality?*[3]

1. les descriptions fantaisistes qu'ils font d'eux-mêmes
2. provisoire
3. Faire des rencontres ou chercher à fuir la réalité ?

IV
THURSDAY
February 21

DARCY SAT at the dinette[1] table, sipping coffee and staring unseeingly[2] out the window at the gardens below. Barren now, scattered with unmelted snow[3], in the summer they were exquisitely planted[4] and manicured to perfection[5]. The prestigious owners of the private brownstones they backed[6] included the Aga Khan and Katharine Hepburn.

Erin loved to come over when the gardens were in bloom[7]. "From the street you'd never guess they exist[8]," she'd sigh. "I swear, Darce, you sure lucked out[9] when you found this place."

Erin. Where was she? The minute she woke up and realized that Erin had not phoned, Darcy had called the nursing home in Massachusetts. Mr. Kelley's condition[10] was unchanged. The semi-comatose state could go on indefinitely, although he was certainly getting weaker[11]. No, there had been no emergency[12] call to his daughter. The day nurse[13] really couldn't say if Erin had made her usual phone call last evening.

"What should I do?" Darcy wondered aloud. Report her missing?[14] Call the police and inquire about accidents[15]?

A sudden thought made her shiver[16]. Suppose Erin had had an accident in the apartment. She had a habit[17] of tilting back in her chair[18] when she was

1. du coin repas
2. le regard vide
3. Avec seulement quelques taches de neige résiduelle pour toute couleur
4. regorgeaient de plantes magnifiques
5. parfaitement entretenus
6. sur lesquels ils donnaient
7. en fleurs
8. on ne soupçonne même pas leur existence
9. as eu une sacrée veine
10. L'état de santé
11. il ne faisait aucun doute qu'il s'affaiblissait
12. en urgence
13. infirmière de jour
14. Signaler sa disparition ?
15. pour savoir s'il y avait eu des accidents
16. la fit frémir
17. le tic
18. se balancer en arrière sur sa chaise

concentrating. Suppose she'd been lying there[1] unconscious all this time!

It took her three minutes to throw on[2] a sweater and slacks[3], grab a coat and gloves. She waited agonizing[4] minutes on Second Avenue before getting a cab.

"One-oh-one[5] Christopher Street, and please hurry."

"Everybody says 'hurry.' I say take it easy[6], you'll live longer." The cabbie[7] winked[8] into the rearview mirror[9].

Darcy turned her head. She was in no mood[10] to banter[11] with the driver. Why hadn't she thought of the possibility of an accident? Last month, just before she went to California, Erin had dropped by for dinner[12]. They'd watched the news. One of the commercials[13] showed a frail old woman falling and getting help by touching the emergency signal on a chain around her neck. "That'll be us in fifty years," Erin had said. She'd imitated the commercial, moaning[14], "Hel-l-l-p, hel-l-l-p! I've fallen, and I can't get up!"

Gus Boxer, the superintendent[15] of 101 Christopher Street, had an eye for[16] pretty women. That was why when he hurried to the lobby to answer the persistent ring of the doorbell, his annoyed scowl[17] was quickly replaced by an ingratiating twist of his mouth[18].

He liked what he saw. The visitor's light brown hair was tossed by the wind[19]. It fell forward on her face[20], reminding him of the Veronica Lake movies he stayed up to watch[21]. Her hip-length[22] leather jacket was old but had that classy[23] look that Gus had come to recognize since taking this job in Greenwich Village.

1. Et si elle gisait
2. pour enfiler
3. un pantalon
4. qui lui parurent interminables
5. 101
6. calmez-vous
7. chauffeur de taxi
8. lui fit un clin d'œil
9. rétroviseur
10. n'était pas d'humeur
11. à plaisanter
12. était passée dîner
13. publicités
14. en geignant
15. gardien
16. repérait
17. son air contrarié
18. une sorte de rictus mielleux
19. balayés par le vent
20. Ils lui retombaient sur la figure
21. qu'il regardait tard dans la nuit
22. qui lui descendait jusqu'aux hanches
23. chic

His appraising eyes[1] lingered[2] on her long, slim legs. Then he realized why she looked familiar. He'd seen her a couple of times with 3B, Erin Kelley. He opened the vestibule door and stepped aside[3]. "At your service," he said in what he considered to be a winning manner[4].

Darcy walked past him, trying not to show her distaste. From time to time, Erin complained about the sixty-year-old Casanova in dirty flannel. "Boxer gives me the creeps[5]," she'd said. "I hate the idea he has a master key to my place[6]. Once I walked in and found him there and he gave me some cock-and-bull story[7] about a leak[8] in the wall."

"Was anything ever missing?" Darcy had asked.

"No. I keep any jewelry I'm working on in the safe[9]. There's nothing else worth pocketing[10]. It's more that he has a nasty, flirtatious way about him that makes my skin crawl[11]. Oh well. I've got a safety bolt[12] when I'm inside and the place is cheap. He's probably harmless[13]."

Darcy came straight to the point[14]. "I'm concerned[15] about Erin Kelley," she told the superintendent. "She was supposed to meet me last night and didn't show up[16]. She doesn't answer her phone. I want to check her apartment. Something may have happened to her."

Boxer squinted[17]. "She was okay yesterday."

"Yesterday?"

Thick lids drooped over faded eyes.[18] Parted[19] lips were moistened[20] with his tongue. His forehead collapsed into erratic lines.[21] "No, I'm wrong. I seen her[22] Tuesday. Late afternoon. She come in with some groceries[23]." His tone became virtuous. "I offered to carry 'em up for her."

"That was Tuesday afternoon. Did you see her go out or return Tuesday evening?"

1. Son regard qui la jaugeait
2. s'attarda
3. s'écarta
4. d'un ton qu'il pensait charmeur
5. me fait flipper
6. un passe pour entrer chez moi
7. m'a sorti un prétexte foireux
8. fuite
9. coffre-fort
10. de tentant
11. me donne des boutons
12. cran de sûreté
13. inoffensif
14. alla droit au but
15. inquiète
16. n'est pas venue
17. plissa les yeux
18. De lourdes paupières voilèrent ses yeux délavés.
19. entrouvertes
20. humidifiées
21. Son front se plissa dans tous les sens.
22. J'l'ai vue
23. des sacs de courses

"Nope. Can't say I did.[1] But listen, I'm not a doorman[2]. Tenants have their own keys. Delivery guys[3] gotta use the intercom[4] to get let in[5]."

Darcy nodded[6]. Knowing it was useless, she had rung Erin's apartment before she buzzed for the[7] superintendent. "Please. I'm afraid there may be something wrong. I've got to get into her place. Do you have your passkey?"

The twisted smile returned. "You gotta understand, I don't normally let people into an apartment just because they wanna go in. But I seen you with Kelley. I know you're friends. You're like her. Classy. Good-lookin'."

Ignoring the compliment, Darcy started up the stairs.

The stairs and landings[8] were clean but dreary[9]. The patched walls[10] were battleship gray[11], the tiles on the steps uneven[12]. Walking into Erin's apartment had the effect of going from a cave into daylight[13]. When Erin moved[14] here three years ago, Darcy had helped her paint and paper[15]. They'd hired a U-Haul[16] and made forays[17] into Connecticut and New Jersey for garage-sale furnishings.

They'd painted the walls a stark[18] white. Colorful Indian rugs were scattered[19] over the scratched[20] but polished parquet floor. Framed[21] museum posters[22] were arranged over a studio couch[23] that was covered in bright red velour and piled with vividly assorted throw pillows[24].

The windows faced the street. Even though the sky was overcast[25], the light was excellent. Under the windows a long worktable held Erin's supplies[26] neatly placed side by side: torch, hand drill[27], files[28] and pliers[29], ring clamps[30] and spring tweezers[31], soldering block[32], gauges[33], drills[34]. Darcy had al-

1. Nan, j'crois pas.
2. portier
3. Les livreurs
4. l'Interphone
5. pour qu'on les laisse rentrer
6. acquiesça de la tête
7. avant d'appuyer sur le bouton du
8. les paliers
9. tristes
10. Les murs colmatés
11. gris acier
12. le carrelage des marches était irrégulier
13. de se retrouver au grand jour en sortant d'une grotte
14. avait emmenagé
15. à tapisser
16. loué un camion
17. fait des expéditions
18. austère
19. un peu partout
20. rayé
21. encadrées
22. Des affiches
23. canapé convertible
24. couvert de coussins de couleurs vives
25. couvert
26. le matériel
27. perceuse
28. limes
29. pinces
30. étaux
31. pinces coupantes [à ressort]
32. bloc de soudage
33. gabarits
34. forets

ways been fascinated to watch Erin at work, her slender fingers skillfully[1] handling[2] delicate gems.

Next to the table was Erin's one[3] extravagance, a tall chest[4] with several dozen narrow drawers. A nineteenth-century pharmaceutical cabinet[5], the bottom drawers were a facade concealing a safe[6]. One easy chair[7], a television, and a good stereo system completed the pleasant room.

Darcy's immediate impression was a surge of relief[8]. There was nothing out of order[9] here. Gus Boxer at her heels, she walked swiftly[10] into the tiny kitchen, a small windowless cubicle[11] that they'd painted a bright yellow and decorated with framed tea towels[12].

The narrow hallway led to the bedroom. The pewter and brass[13] bed and a two-on-three dresser[14] were the only furniture in the closet-sized room. The bed was made. There was nothing out of place.

Clean, dry towels were on the rack in the bathroom. Darcy opened the medicine chest[15]. With a practiced eye[16], she noted that Erin's toothbrush, cosmetics and creams were all there.

Boxer was becoming impatient. "Looks okay to me. You satisfied?"

"No." Darcy went back into the living room and walked over to the worktable. The message machine showed twelve calls had come in[17]. She pressed playback[18].

"Hey, I don't know—"

She cut off[19] Boxer's protest. "Erin is missing. Have you got that straight?[20] She's *missing*. I'm going to listen to these messages and see if they might somehow give me an idea of where she might be. Then I'm going to call the police and inquire about accidents. For all I know,[21] she's unconscious

1. avec dextérité
2. maniant
3. unique
4. grande commode
5. meuble d'apothicaire
6. dont les tiroirs du bas, en trompe-l'œil, cachaient un coffre-fort
7. fauteuil
8. un immense soulagement
9. Rien n'était en désordre
10. vite
11. cagibi
12. des torchons
13. en étain et en cuivre
14. une commode à 5 tiroirs
15. l'armoire à pharmacie
16. En connaisseur
17. indiquait douze appels
18. appuya sur lecture
19. interrompit
20. Vous avez pigé ?
21. Si ça se trouve,

in a hospital somewhere. You can stay here with me or if you're busy, you can go. Which is it?[1]"

Boxer shrugged[2]. "I guess it's okay to leave you here."

Darcy turned her back on him[3], reached into her purse[4], and took out her notebook[5] and pen. She did not hear Boxer leave as the messages began. The first one had come on Tuesday evening at six forty-five. Someone named Tom Swartz. Thanks for answering his ad. Just discovered a great little inexpensive[6] restaurant. Could they meet for dinner? He'd phone again.

Erin was supposed to meet[7] Charles North on Tuesday evening at seven o'clock at a pub near Washington Square. By quarter of seven[8] she had undoubtedly already left[9], Darcy thought.

The next call came in at seven twenty-five. Michael Nash. "Erin, I certainly enjoyed meeting you and hope you might be free for dinner sometime this week. If you have a chance[10], call me back this evening." Nash left both his home and office numbers.

Wednesday morning the calls began at nine o'clock. The first few were run-of-the-mill business-related[11]. The one that made Darcy's throat close[12] was from an Aldo Marco of Bertolini's. "Miss Kelley, I am disappointed you did not keep[13] our ten o'clock appointment. It is essential that I see the necklace and be sure there is no last-minute adjustment necessary. Please get back to me immediately.[14]"

That call had come in at eleven[15]. There were three more follow-ups[16] from the same man, increasing in irritation and urgency[17]. Besides Darcy's own messages, there was another one concerning the Bertolini assignment[18].

1. Qu'est-ce que vous préférez ?
2. haussa les épaules
3. lui tourna le dos
4. fouilla dans son sac à main
5. carnet de notes
6. bon marché
7. censée retrouver
8. À 18h45,
9. elle était forcément déjà partie
10. Si vous avez une minute
11. concernaient le travail normal
12. qui serra la gorge de Darcy
13. que vous ne soyez pas venue à
14. Merci de me rappeler au plus vite.
15. datait de 11h
16. trois autres appels
17. chacun plus pressant et plus véhément
18. commande

"Erin, this is Jay Stratton. What's going on? Marco's bugging me for[1] the necklace and holding me responsible for bringing you to him[2]."

Darcy knew that Stratton was the jeweler who had given Erin's portfolio to Bertolini's. His message came in around seven Wednesday evening. Darcy started to push the rewind[3] button, then paused. Maybe it would be better not to erase these[4]. She looked in the phone book[5] for the number of the nearest precinct[6]. "I want to report someone missing[7]," she said when the call was answered. She was told that she would have to come in personally[8], that this kind of information about a competent adult[9] could not be accepted over the phone.

I'll stop there on my way home, Darcy thought. She went into the kitchen and made coffee, noting that the only milk container[10] was unopened. Erin started her day with coffee and always drank it light[11]. Boxer had seen her with groceries Tuesday afternoon. Darcy looked into the garbage pail[12] under the sink[13]. There were a few odds and ends[14], but no empty milk container. She wasn't here yesterday morning, Darcy thought. She never got back Tuesday night.

She brought the coffee back to the worktable. A daily reminder was[15] in the top drawer[16]. She flipped through it[17], starting with today. There were no appointments listed[18]. Yesterday, Wednesday, there were two: Bertolini's, 10 A.M.; Bella Vita, 7 P.M. (Darcy and Nona).

In the preceding weeks, there were notations of dates[19] with names of men unfamiliar to Darcy[20]. They were usually scheduled[21] between five and seven o'clock. Most of them had the meeting place listed[22]: O'Neal's, Mickey Mantle's, P. J. Clarke's, the

1. n'arrête pas de me réclamer
2. me tient pour responsable puisque c'est moi qui vous ai présentés
3. rembobiner
4. de ne pas les effacer
5. l'annuaire
6. du commissariat le plus proche
7. signaler une disparition
8. venir en personne
9. un adulte en pleine possession de ses facultés
10. l'unique brique de lait
11. le prenait toujours avec beaucoup de lait
12. la poubelle
13. l'évier
14. quelques bricoles
15. Il y avait un agenda
16. tiroir du haut
17. le feuilleta
18. aucun rendez-vous
19. un certain nombre de rendez-vous (galants)
20. que Darcy ne reconnaissait pas
21. la plupart du temps prévus
22. donnaient le lieu du rendez-vous

Plaza, the Sheraton ... all hotel cocktail lounges[1] and popular pubs.

The phone rang. Let it be[2] Erin, Darcy prayed as she grabbed it. "Hello."

"Erin?" A man's voice.

"No. This is Darcy Scott. Erin's friend."

"Do you know where I can reach[3] Erin?"

Disappointment, intense and overwhelming, swept over Darcy.[4] "Who is this?"

"Jay Stratton."

Jay Stratton had left the message about the Bertolini jewelry. What was he saying?

"... if you have any idea where Erin is, please tell her that if they don't get that necklace, they'll file a criminal complaint[5]."

Darcy's eyes flickered to[6] the pharmaceutical cabinet. She knew that Erin kept the combination[7] in her address book under the name of the safe company. Stratton was still talking.

"I know Erin kept that necklace in a safe in her studio[8]. Is there any possibility you can check to see if it's there?" he urged[9].

"Hold on a minute[10]." Darcy put her hand over the speaker[11], then thought, What a dumb thing to do[12]. There's no one here I can ask. But in a way[13] she was asking Erin. If the necklace wasn't in the safe, it might mean that Erin had been the victim of a robbery[14] when she attempted to deliver it[15]. If it was there, it was almost certain proof[16] that something had happened to her. Nothing would have kept[17] Erin from delivering the necklace on time.

She opened Erin's address book and turned to D. Next to Dalton Safe was the series of numbers. "I have the combination," she told Stratton. "I'll wait for you to come here. I don't want to open Erin's

1. des bars
2. Pourvu que ce soit
3. joindre
4. Une amère déception submergea Darcy.
5. vont porter plainte
6. lança un regard à
7. avait noté la combinaison
8. son atelier
9. insista
10. Ne quittez pas
11. mit une main sur le combiné
12. Quel geste stupide
13. d'une certaine façon
14. se l'était fait voler
15. en allant le déposer
16. la preuve quasi irréfutable
17. Rien n'aurait pu empêcher

safe without a witness[1]. And in case the necklace is here, I'll want a receipt for it from you[2]."

He said he'd be right over[3]. After she replaced the receiver[4], Darcy decided that she'd ask the superintendent to be present as well. She didn't know anything about Jay Stratton except that Erin told her he was a jeweler and the one who got her the Bertolini commission.

While she waited, Darcy went through[5] Erin's files[6]. Under "Project Personal," she found sheets of personal columns torn from magazines and newspapers. On each page a number of the ads were circled[7]. Were these the ones Erin had answered, or had thought about answering? Dismayed[8], Darcy realized that there were at least two dozen of them[9]. Which, if any of them, had been placed by Charles North, the man Erin was to meet on Tuesday evening?

When she and Erin agreed to answer the personal ads, they'd gone about it systematically[10]. They'd had inexpensive letterheads made[11] with only their names at the top. They'd each chosen a favorite snapshot to send when requested[12]. They'd spent a hilarious evening composing letters they had no intentions of sending[13]. "I love to clean clean clean," Erin had suggested, "my favorite hobby is doing the wash by hand. I inherited[14] my grandmother's scrub board[15]. My cousin wanted it too. It caused a big family fight. I get a little nasty during my period[16], but I'm a very good person. Please call soon."

They had finally come up with[17] what they decided were reasonably alluring responses[18]. When Darcy was leaving for California, Erin had said, "Darce, I'll send yours out about two weeks before you're due back[19]. I'll just change a sentence here or there to fit the ad[20]."

1. sans témoin
2. je vous demanderai d'établir un reçu
3. qu'il allait venir tout de suite
4. avoir reposé le combiné
5. parcourut
6. les dossiers
7. entourées
8. Consternée
9. plus d'une vingtaine
10. elles s'y étaient prises avec méthode
11. s'étaient fait faire un papier à en-tête tout simple
12. sur demande
13. qu'elles n'avaient aucune intention d'envoyer
14. J'ai hérité de
15. la planche à laver
16. deviens un peu agressive quand j'ai mes règles
17. fini par rédiger
18. des réponses raisonnablement allèchantes
19. ton retour
20. pour que ça corresponde à l'annonce

Erin didn't own a computer[1]. Darcy knew she typed out[2] the responses on her electric typewriter[3] but did not Xerox them[4]. She kept all the input[5] in the notebook she carried in her purse: the box numbers of the ads she answered, the names of the people she called, her impressions of the ones she dated[6].

Jay Stratton leaned back in the cab[7], his eyes half-closed. The speaker[8] behind his right ear was blaring[9] rock music. "Will you turn that down?[10]" he snapped.

"Man, you trying to deprive me of my music?" The cabbie was in his early twenties. Wispy, snarled hair[11] hung around his neck[12]. He glanced over his shoulder[13], caught the look[14] on Stratton's face, and, muttering under his breath[15], lowered the volume[16].

Stratton felt sweat forming in his armpits[17]. He had to pull this off.[18] He tapped his pocket. The receipts Erin had given him for the Bertolini gems and for the diamonds he'd given her last week were in his wallet[19]. Darcy Scott sounded smart[20]. He mustn't arouse the slightest suspicion[21].

The nosy[22] superintendent must have been watching for him. He was in the foyer when Stratton arrived. Obviously, he recognized him. "I'll bring you up," he said. "I'm supposed to stay while she opens the safe."

Stratton swore to himself[23] as he followed the squat figure[24] up the stairs. He didn't need two witnesses.

When Darcy opened the door for them, Stratton's face was set in a pleasant, somewhat-concerned expression. He had planned to sound reassuring, but

1. n'avait pas d'ordinateur
2. tapait
3. machine à écrire
4. ne les photocopiait pas
5. toutes les infos
6. à qui elle fixait des rendez-vous
7. s'installa sur la banquette du taxi
8. haut-parleur
9. beuglait
10. Vous voulez bien baisser cette musique ?!
11. Des cheveux filasse tout emmêlés
12. lui pendouillaient dans le cou
13. jeta un œil par-dessus son épaule
14. vit l'expression
15. marmonnant dans sa barbe
16. baissa le son
17. sentait la sueur perler sous ses bras
18. Il fallait qu'il réussisse ce coup.
19. portefeuille
20. intelligente
21. éveiller le moindre soupçon
22. trop curieux
23. jura en silence
24. la silhouette trapue

1. lui indiqua qu'il valait mieux éviter les banalités
2. bloc
3. faire la liste de tout ce que nous allons trouver
4. tourna ostensiblement le dos
5. tournait le cadran
6. s'accroupit
7. des pochettes
8. recouvraient les étagères
9. Je vais vous passer tout ce qu'il y a dedans
10. Et vous le notez.
11. effleurait le sien
12. allumait
13. à la recherche d'un cendrier
14. fit exprès de renverser
15. les pierres étincelantes s'éparpiller
16. se précipita pour les ramasser
17. maudissant sa maladresse
18. soigneusement
19. on peut faire de beaux bijoux fantaisie avec
20. des pierres de lune

the worry in Scott's eyes warned him against banalities[1]. Instead, he agreed with her that something must be dreadfully wrong.

Smart girl, he thought. Darcy had obviously memorized the combination of the safe. She was not about to let anyone know where Erin kept it. She had a pad[2] and pen ready. "I want to itemize everything we find[3] in there."

Stratton deliberately turned his back[4] while she twisted the dial[5], then crouched[6] beside her as she pulled the door open. The safe was fairly deep. Boxes and pouches[7] lined the shelves[8].

"Let me hand everything out to you[9]," he suggested. "I'll describe what we find. You write it down.[10]"

Darcy hesitated, then realized it was a sensible suggestion. He was the jeweler. His arm was brushing against hers[11]. Instinctively, she moved aside.

Stratton looked over his shoulder. An irritated-looking Boxer was lighting[12] a cigarette and glancing around the room, probably searching for an ashtray[13]. It was Stratton's only chance. "I think that velvet case is the one Erin kept the necklace in." Reaching for it, he deliberately knocked[14] a small box onto the floor.

Darcy jumped as she saw the glitter of stones scattering[15] around her and scrambled to collect them[16]. An instant later Stratton was beside her, cursing his carelessness[17]. They searched the area thoroughly[18]. "I'm sure we got them all," he said. "These are semiprecious, suitable for good costume jewelry[19]. But more important ..." He opened the velvet case. "Here's the Bertolini."

Darcy stared down at the exquisite necklace. Emeralds, diamonds, sapphires, moonstones[20], opals, and rubies were set in an elaborate design that reminded her of the medieval jewelry she'd seen in portraits at the Metropolitan Museum of Art.

"Lovely, isn't it?" Stratton asked. "You can understand why the manager at Bertolini's was so upset[1] at the prospect of something happening to it[2]. Erin is remarkably gifted[3]. She not only managed to create a setting[4] that made those stones look ten times their own considerable value[5], but she did it in the Byzantine style. The family who commissioned[6] the necklace was originally from Russia. These gems were the only valuable possessions[7] they were able to take when they fled in 1917."

Darcy could visualize Erin sitting at this worktable, her ankles around the rungs of the chair[8], the way she used to sit when she was studying in college. The sense of impending[9] disaster was overwhelming[10]. Where would Erin willingly[11] go without delivering this necklace on time?

Nowhere *willingly*, she decided.

Biting her lip[12] to keep it from quivering[13], she picked up[14] the pen. "Will you describe this for me and I think we should identify every precious stone in it so there's no question that any are missing[15]."

As Stratton removed other pouches, velvet cases, and boxes from the safe, she noticed that he was becoming increasingly more agitated. Finally he said, "I'm going to open the rest all at once, then we'll list them." He looked directly at her. "The Bertolini necklace is here, but a pouch[16] I gave Erin with a quarter of a million dollars worth[17] of diamonds is gone."

Darcy left the apartment with Stratton. "I'm going to the police station to file a missing-person report[18]," she told him.

1. si contrarié
2. à l'idée qu'il ait pu disparaître
3. a un don
4. sertir les pierres
5. d'une façon qui les faisait paraître dix fois plus précieuses
6. avait commandé
7. objets de valeur
8. les chevilles enroulées autour des pieds de la chaise
9. imminent
10. terrible
11. de son plein gré
12. Se mordant la lèvre
13. pour l'empêcher de trembler
14. reprit
15. pour établir avec certitude qu'il n'en manque aucune
16. pochette
17. d'une valeur de 250 000 $
18. signaler la disparition

"You're absolutely right," he said. "I'll take care of getting the necklace to Bertolini's immediately and if we haven't heard from Erin[1] in a week, I'll contact the insurance company[2] about the diamonds."

It was exactly noon when Darcy entered the Sixth Precinct on Charles Street. At her insistence that something was terribly wrong[3], a detective[4] came out to see her. A tall black man in his mid-forties with military bearing[5], he introduced himself as Dean Thompson and listened sympathetically[6] as he tried to allay her fears[7].

"We really can't file a missing-person report for an adult woman[8] simply because no one has heard from her for a day or two," he explained. "It violates[9] freedom of movement. What I will do if you give me her description is check it against accident reports[10]."

Anxiously, Darcy gave the information. Five feet seven[11], one hundred and twenty pounds[12], auburn hair, blue eyes, twenty-eight years old. "Wait, I have her picture in my wallet."

Thompson studied it[13], then handed it back[14]. "A very attractive woman." He gave her his card and asked for hers. "We'll keep in touch.[15]"

Susan Frawley Fox hugged[16] five-year-old Trish and guided her reluctant feet[17] to the waiting school bus that would take her to the afternoon session of kindergarten. Trish's woebegone face[18] was on the verge of crumbling into tears[19]. The baby, firmly held under Susan's other arm, reached down[20] and pulled Trish's hair. It gave the needed excuse.[21] Trish began to wail[22].

1. si nous n'avons pas de nouvelles d'Erin
2. la compagnie d'assurance
3. Comme elle insistait qu'il y avait vraiment quelque chose d'anormal
4. policier
5. d'allure martiale
6. compatissant,
7. tout en essayant de dissiper ses craintes
8. ouvrir une enquête pour la disparition d'une femme majeure
9. C'est contraire au principe de
10. c'est que je vais la comparer avec la liste des accidentés
11. 1m70
12. 54 kilos
13. l'observa attentivement
14. la lui rendit
15. Je vous tiendrai au courant.
16. fit un gros câlin à
17. la conduisit un peu de force
18. l'air abattu,
19. sur le point de fondre en larmes
20. se pencha
21. Ce fut le prétexte.
22. pleurer

Susan bit her lip, torn between annoyance[1] and sympathy. "He didn't hurt you and you're not staying home."

The bus driver, a matronly woman[2] with a warm smile, said coaxingly[3], "Come on, Trish. You sit right up here near me."

Susan waved vigorously and sighed with relief as the bus pulled away[4]. Shifting the baby's weight[5], she hurried from the corner back to their rambling[6] brick and stucco home. Patches of snow still covered isolated sections of the lawn[7]. The trees seemed stark and bloodless against[8] the gray sky. In a few months the property would be lush with flowering hedges[9] and the willows[10] would be heavily laden with[11] cascades of leaves. Even as a small child[12] Susan had studied the willows for the first hint of spring[13].

She shoved the side door open[14], heated a bottle[15] for the baby, brought him to his room, changed him, and put him down for a nap[16]. Her quiet time had begun: the hour and a half before he woke up. She knew she should get busy. The beds weren't made. The kitchen was a mess[17]. This morning Trish had wanted to make cupcakes, and spilled batter was still lumped[18] on the table.

Susan glanced at the baking pan on the countertop[19] and half-smiled. The cupcakes looked delicious. If only Trish wouldn't carry on so about[20] kindergarten. It's almost March, Susan worried. What's it going to be like when she's in the first grade[21] and has to be gone all day?

Doug blamed Susan for Trish's reluctance to go[22] to school. "If you'd go out more yourself, have lunch at the club, volunteer for some committees, Trish would be used to being minded by other people[23]."

1. la contrariété
2. une matrone
3. d'un air enjôleur
4. repartit
5. Replaçant le bébé sur sa hanche
6. biscornue
7. la pelouse
8. se détachaient, sans vie, sur
9. regorgerait de buissons en fleurs
10. saules
11. chargés de
12. Toute petite déjà,
13. à l'affût des premiers signes du printemps
14. ouvrit la porte de derrière
15. biberon
16. le mit au lit pour la sieste
17. sens dessus dessous
18. il restait des petits tas de pâte à gâteau
19. plan de travail
20. ne faisait pas une telle allergie
21. sera au CP
22. disait que c'était la faute de Susan si Trish n'aimait pas aller
23. aurait l'habitude d'être gardée par quelqu'un d'autre

Susan put the kettle on[1], sponged[2] the table, and fixed[3] a grilled cheese and bacon sandwich. There is a God, she though gratefully as she reveled in the blessed silence[4].

Over a second cup of tea, she permitted herself to face the anger that was burning inside her. Doug hadn't come home again last night. When he stayed in for late meetings he used the company suite at the Gateway Hotel near his office in the World Trade Center. He got furious when she called him there. "Damn it, Susan, unless there's an earth-shattering emergency[5], give me a break[6]. I can't be called out of meetings[7] and by the time they're over it's usually[8] well past midnight."

Taking the tea with her, Susan got up and walked down the long hail[9] to the master[10] bedroom. The antique full-length standing mirror[11] was in the right-hand corner opposite the wall of closets[12]. Deliberately, she stood in front of it and appraised herself[13].

Thanks to the baby's exploring fingers, her short, curly brown hair was disheveled[14]. She seldom bothered with makeup[15] during the day but really didn't need it. Her skin was clear and unlined[16], her complexion[17] fresh. At five feet four[18] she could certainly afford to lose fifteen pounds[19]. She'd been one hundred and five when she and Doug were married fourteen years ago. Sweats[20] and sneakers had become her daily wardrobe[21], especially since Trish and Conner were born.

I am thirty-five years old, Susan told herself. I could lose some weight[22], but contrary to what my husband thinks, I am not fat. I'm not a great housekeeper[23], but I know I'm a good mother. A good cook[24], too. I don't want to spend my time outside the house when I have young children who need

1. mit de l'eau à bouillir
2. passa une éponge sur
3. se prépara
4. en savourant le calme
5. une urgence absolue
6. fiche-moi la paix
7. ne peux pas être dérangé en pleine réunion
8. elles finissent en général
9. le grand couloir
10. principale
11. La psyché d'époque
12. en face de la penderie encastrée
13. se jaugea
14. ébouriffés
15. ne prenait presque jamais le temps de se maquiller
16. sans rides
17. teint
18. Avec son 1,62 m
19. une demi-douzaine de kilos
20. Les survêtements
21. ses vêtements de tous les jours
22. du poids
23. bonne ménagère
24. cuisinière

me. Especially since their father won't give them the time of day[1].

She swallowed[2] the rest of the tea, her anger building[3]. Tuesday night when Donny came home from the basketball game, he had been in the never-never land between ecstasy and misery[4]. He had sunk the winning shot[5]. "Everybody stood up and cheered for me[6], Mom!" Then he added, "Dad was practically the only father who wasn't there."

Susan's heart had wrenched[7] at the pain in her son's eyes[8]. The babysitter had canceled[9] at the last minute, which was why she hadn't been able to be at the game either. "This is an earth-shattering event[10]," she'd said firmly. "Let's see if we can reach Dad and tell him all about it."

Douglas Fox was not registered at[11] the hotel. There was no conference room in use. The suite kept for personnel of Keldon Equities was not being occupied.

"Probably some dumb new operator[12]," Susan had told Donny, trying to keep her tone even[13].

"Sure, that's it, Mom." But Donny wasn't fooled[14]. At dawn[15], Susan had awakened[16] to the sound of muffled sobs[17]. She'd stood outside Donny's door, knowing that he wouldn't want her to see him crying.

My husband doesn't love me or his children, Susan told her reflected image. He lies to us[18]. He stays in New York a couple of nights a week. He's bullied me into[19] almost never calling him. He's made me feel like a fat, frowsy[20], dull[21], useless clod[22]. And I'm sick of it[23].

She turned from the mirror and analyzed the cluttered bedroom. I could be a lot more organized, she acknowledged[24]. I used to be. When did

1. ne leur accorde jamais une minute
2. avala
3. sentant la colère monter
4. ne savait s'il devait être fou de joie ou déprimé
5. avait marqué le panier gagnant
6. m'a applaudi
7. avait eu un pincement au cœur
8. devant la douleur dans les yeux de son fils
9. s'était décommandé(e)
10. un grand jour
11. ne figurait pas sur le registre de
12. une réceptionniste pas très dégourdie
13. de garder un ton neutre
14. n'était pas dupe
15. À l'aube
16. avait été réveillée
17. par des sanglots étouffés
18. nous ment
19. Il me force à
20. débraillée
21. ennuyeuse
22. crétine finie
23. j'en ai ma claque
24. s'avoua-t-elle

I give up[1]? When did I become so damn discouraged that it wasn't worth trying[2] to please him?

Not hard to answer. Nearly two years ago, when she was pregnant with the baby[3]. They'd had a Swedish au pair, and Susan was sure that Doug had had an affair[4] with her.

Why didn't I face it then? she wondered as she began to make the bed. Because I was still in love with him? Because I hated to admit my father was right about him?

She and Doug had been married a week after she was graduated from[5] Bryn Mawr. Her father offered her a trip around the world if she'd change her mind. "Under that schoolboy charm, there's a foul-tempered sneak[6]," he had warned her.

I went into it with my eyes open, Susan acknowledged, as she returned to the kitchen. If Dad had known the half of it[7], he'd have had a stroke[8], she thought.

There was a pile of magazines on the wall desk in the kitchen. She riffled through them[9] until she found the one she was looking for. An issue[10] of *People* with an article about a female private investigator[11] in Manhattan. Professional women hired her[12] to check out[13] the men they were considering marrying[14]. She also handled[15] divorce cases.

Susan got the phone number from information[16] and dialed it[17]. When she reached the investigator, she was able to make an appointment for the following Monday, February 25th. "I believe my husband is seeing other women," she explained quietly. "I am thinking of divorce, and I want to know all about his activities."

When she hung up she resisted the temptation to simply sit and continue to think things through[18]. Instead, she attacked the kitchen vigorously. Time

1. ai-je laissé tomber
2. me suis-je persuadée que ça ne valait plus la peine
3. attendait le bébé
4. liaison
5. la fin de ses études à
6. un faux jeton avec un caractère de cochon
7. avait su la vérité
8. fait une attaque
9. les feuilleta
10. Un numéro
11. une femme détective privé
12. l'engageaient
13. pour enquêter sur
14. qu'elles envisageaient d'épouser
15. s'occupait aussi des
16. en appelant les renseignements
17. le composa
18. à ruminer

to shape up this place.[1] By summer, with any luck[2], it would be on the market.

It wouldn't be easy raising[3] four children alone. Susan knew that Doug would pay little if any attention to the kids[4] after the divorce. He was a splashy spender[5] but cheap in hundreds of little ways[6]. He'd balk at[7] adequate child support[8]. But it would be a lot easier to live on a tight budget[9] than to go on with this farce[10].

The telephone rang. It was Doug, complaining again about the damn late meetings these last two nights. He was exhausted today and they still hadn't settled everything[11]. He'd be home tonight, but late. Real late.

"Don't worry, dear," Susan said soothingly[12]. "I understand perfectly."

The country road was narrow, winding[13], and dark. Charley didn't pass a single other car. His driveway was almost hidden by brush[14] at the point where it intersected the road. A secret and quiet place, removed from curious eyes[15]. He'd bought it six years ago. An estate sale.[16] Estate giveaway was more like it.[17] The place had been owned by an eccentric bachelor who as a hobby renovated it himself.

Built in 1902, the exterior was unpretentious. Inside, the renovation had consisted of turning the entire first floor[18] into one open room[19], complete with a kitchen area and fireplace[20]. Wide plank oak flooring[21] shone with a satiny finish[22]. The furniture was Pennsylvania Dutch, austere, handsome.

1. Il est temps de mettre un peu d'ordre.
2. un peu de chance
3. d'élever
4. s'occuperait peu, voire pas du tout, des enfants
5. très dépensier
6. radin sur bien des détails
7. rechignerait à payer
8. une pension alimentaire correcte
9. sur un budget serré
10. de laisser perdurer cette situation grotesque
11. n'avaient toujours pas réglé tous les détails
12. d'un ton apaisant
13. sinueuse
14. par les broussailles
15. à l'abri des curieux
16. À une vente aux enchères.
17. Une vente pour trois fois rien, plutôt.
18. à transformer le rez-de-chaussée
19. en une seule pièce
20. avec coin cuisine et cheminée
21. Le parquet de larges lattes de chêne
22. avait une brillance satinée

Charley had added a long upholstered couch covered in maroon[1] tapestry, a matching chair, an area rug[2] between the couch and fireplace.

The second floor[3] was exactly as he'd found it. Two small rooms made into one decent-sized bedroom. Shaker[4] furniture, a carved headboard[5] bed and tall chest. Both made of pine. The original tub[6], freestanding on claw feet[7], had been left in the modernized bath[8].

Only the basement[9] was different. The eight-foot freezer[10] that no longer held an ounce of food[11], the freezer where, when necessary, he left the bodies of the girls. Here, ice maidens[12], they'd waited for their graves[13] to be dug[14] under the warming rays of the spring sun. There was a worktable in the basement as well, the worktable with a stack of ten cardboard shoe boxes[15]. There was only one left[16] to decorate.

A charming house nestled[17] in the woods. He'd never brought anyone here until two years ago when he'd begun to dream about Nan. Before that, owning the house had been enough. When he wanted to escape, this was his retreat[18]. The aloneness.[19] The ability to pretend that he[20] was dancing with beautiful girls. He'd play old movies on the VCR[21], movies in which he became Fred Astaire and danced with Ginger Rogers and Rita Hayworth and Leslie Caron. He'd follow Astaire's graceful movements until he could step with his every step[22], mimic[23] the way Astaire would turn his body. Always he sensed Ginger and Rita and Leslie and Fred's other partners in his arms, their eyes worshipful[24], loving the music, loving the dance.

Then one day, two years ago, it was over[25]. In the middle of the dance, Ginger drifted away[26] and Nan was in Charley's arms again. Just like the moments after he killed her, waltzing on the jogging path[27],

1. bordeaux
2. un petit tapis
3. premier étage
4. [style américain dépouillé]
5. à tête de lit sculptée
6. La baignoire d'origine
7. avec ses pieds griffus
8. salle de bains
9. sous-sol
10. Le congélateur de 2,50 m de long
11. ne contenait plus la moindre nourriture
12. devenues princesses de glace
13. tombes
14. soient creusées
15. où étaient empilées dix boîtes à chaussures
16. Il n'en restait qu'une
17. nichée
18. refuge
19. Se sentir seul.
20. Pouvoir faire comme s'il
21. magnétoscope
22. jusqu'à ce qu'il arrive à reproduire chacun de ses pas
23. à imiter
24. d'adoration
25. terminé
26. s'était évaporée
27. quand ils valsaient tous deux sur le chemin de terre

her light, svelte body so easy to hold, her head lolling on his shoulder.

When that memory came back, he'd run to the basement and taken the mates of the sequined dancing slipper and the Nike that he'd left on her feet from the shoe box[1] and cradled them in his arms[2] while he swayed to[3] the music on the stereo[4]. It was like being with Nan again, and he'd known what he had to do.

First he'd set up[5] a hidden video camera so he could relive every single moment of what was to happen[6]. Then he'd begun to bring the girls here one by one. Erin was the eighth to die here. But Erin would not join the others in the wooded fields that surrounded[7] the house. Tonight he would move Erin's body. He had decided exactly where he would leave her.

The station wagon moved silently down the driveway, around to the back of the house. He stopped at the metal doors that led to the basement.

Charley's breath[8] began to come in short, excited gasps[9]. He reached for the handle[10] to open the back door of the wagon, then stood irresolutely[11]. Every instinct warned him not to delay. He must lift Erin's body from the freezer, carry it to the car, drive back to the city, leave it on the abandoned Fifty-sixth Street dock bordering[12] the West Side Highway. But the thought of watching the video of Erin, of dancing with her just one more time, was irresistible.

Charley hurried around the house to the front door, let himself in[13], snapped on the light[14], and without bothering to remove his overcoat[15] ran across the room to the VCR. Erin's tape[16] was on top of the others on the cabinet. He popped it in[17] and sat back on the couch, smiling in anticipation[18].

1. pris dans la boîte la chaussure de danse et la Nike faisant la paire avec celles qu'il lui avait laissées aux pieds

2. les avaient serrées dans ses bras

3. en se balançant au rythme de

4. chaîne HI-FI

5. installé

6. de ce qui allait se produire

7. le terrain boisé autour de

8. La respiration de Charley

9. s'accéléra et devint haletante

10. poignée

11. s'arrêta, indécis

12. qui longe

13. entra

14. alluma vite la lumière

15. sans même enlever son manteau,

16. La cassette

17. la glissa dans l'appareil

18. d'avance

The tape began to play.

Erin, so pretty, smiling, coming in the door, exclaiming with delight over the house[1]. "I envy you this haven[2]." He fixing a drink for them. She sitting curled on the couch[3]. He sitting across from her[4] in the easy chair, getting up and setting a match to the kindling[5] in the fireplace.

"Don't bother to light a fire," she'd told him. "I really must get back.[6]"

"Even for half an hour it's worth it[7]," he'd assured her. Then he'd turned on the stereo, muted[8], soft, and pleasant, the songs of the forties. "Our next date is going to be at the Rainbow Room," he said. "You enjoy dancing as much as I do[9]."

Erin had laughed. The lamp beside her accentuated the glints of red[10] in her auburn hair. "As I wrote when I answered your ad, I love to dance."

He'd stood up, held out his arms[11]. "How about now?" Then, as though struck by a thought, said, "Wait a minute. Let's do this right.[12] What shoe size are you?[13] Seven?[14] Seven and a half? Eight?"

"Seven and a half narrow.[15]"

"Perfect. Believe it or not, I have a pair of evening slippers that should fit you[16]. My sister asked me to pick up a pair she had ordered[17] in that size. Like the good big brother I did as I was told. Then she phoned and told me to take them back[18]. She'd found a pair she liked better."

Erin had laughed with him. "Just like a kid sister.[19]"

"I'm not going to be bothered running around returning them." The camera stayed on her, catching her smiling, content expression as she looked around the room.

He'd gone up to the bedroom, opened the closet where boxes of new evening shoes were lined up[20] on the shelf. He'd bought the ones he'd chosen for her

1. faisant des compliments sur la maison
2. havre de paix
3. assise lovée sur le canapé
4. assis en face d'elle
5. petit bois
6. Il faut vraiment que je rentre.
7. ça vaut la peine
8. en sourdine
9. autant que moi
10. reflets roux
11. lui avait tendu les bras
12. Faisons les choses comme il faut.
13. Vous chaussez du combien ?
14. Du 38
15. Un petit 38,5.
16. qui devrait vous aller
17. commandée
18. de les rendre
19. C'est typique des petites sœurs.
20. alignées

in a variety of sizes. Pink and silver. Open toes[1] *and backs*[2]*. Heels as narrow as stilettos*[3]*. A gossamer ankle strap*[4]*. He reached for the pair that were seven and a half narrow and carried them down, still wrapped in tissue*[5]*.*

"Try these on[6]*, Erin."*

Even then, she wasn't suspicious[7]*. "They're lovely."*

He'd knelt and slipped off[8] *her ankle-top leather boots*[9]*, his hands impersonal. She'd said, "Oh, really, I don't think ..." Ignoring her protest, he'd fastened the*[10] *slippers on her feet.*

"Will you promise to wear these next Saturday when we go to the Rainbow Room?"

She had lifted her right foot a few inches off the carpet[11] *and smiled at the sheer beauty of the shoes*[12]*. "I can't accept these as a gift*[13] *..."*

"Please." He had smiled up at her[14]*.*

"Well, let me buy them from you. The funny thing is, they'd go perfectly with a new dress I've only worn once."

It had been on the tip of his tongue to say[15]*, "I saw you in that dress." Instead, he'd murmured, "We'll talk about payment later." Then he'd put his hand on her ankle, letting it linger just enough to begin to alert her*[16]*. He'd stood up, gone over to the stereo. The cassette he had specially prepared was already in place. "Till There Was You" was the first song. The Tommy Dorsey orchestra began to play and the unforgettable*[17] *voice of the young Frank Sinatra filled the room.*

He walked back to the couch and reached for Erin's hands. "Let's practice."

The look he'd been waiting for came into Erin's eyes. That tiny first flicker of awareness[18] *that something wasn't quite right*[19]*. She recognized the subtle change in his tone and manner*[20]*.*

1. Ouvertes au bout
2. sur le talon
3. des talons aiguilles
4. Une bride en voile léger sur la cheville.
5. emballées dans leur papier de soie
6. Essayez-les
7. ne s'était toujours pas méfiée
8. lui avait retiré
9. bottines
10. attaché la bride des
11. quelques centimètres au-dessus du tapis
12. tellement elle était séduite par la beauté de ces chaussures
13. en cadeau
14. levé la tête vers elle en souriant
15. Il avait été à deux doigts de lui dire
16. prolongeant le contact juste assez pour l'inquiéter
17. inoubliable
18. La toute première réalisation
19. tout à fait normal
20. son attitude

Erin was like the others. They all reacted the same way. Speaking too quickly, nervously. "I think I really had better start back[1]*. I have an early appointment tomorrow morning."*

"Just one dance."

"All right." Her tone had been reluctant.[2]

When they began to dance, she seemed to relax. All the girls had been good dancers, but Erin was perfection. He'd felt disloyal thinking she might even be better than Nan. She was weightless[3] *in his arms. She was grace. But when the last notes of "Till There Was You" faded away*[4]*, she stepped back*[5]*. "Time to go."*

Then when he said, "You're not going anywhere," Erin began to run. Like the others, she slipped and slid[6] *on the floor he had polished so lovingly*[7]*. The dancing slippers became her enemy as she scurried to escape him*[8]*, raced toward the door to find it bolted*[9]*, pushed the panic button on the alarm system to learn it was a farce*[10]*. It emitted a hollow maniacal laugh*[11] *when touched, a little extra bit of irony that set most of them sobbing*[12] *as he reached for their throats*[13]*.*

Erin had been particularly satisfying. At the end she seemed to know it was useless to plead[14] *and in an animal burst of strength*[15] *she fought him, clawing at*[16] *the hands that gripped her slender neck. It was only when he twisted*[17] *that heavy gold necklace around her throat and she began to lose consciousness that she had whispered, "Oh God, please help me, oh Daddy. ..."*

When she was dead, he danced with her again. No resistance now in that lovely body. She was his Ginger, his Rita, his Leslie, his Nan, and all the others. When the music stopped, he took off her left slipper and replaced it with her boot.

1. crois vraiment que je ferais mieux de partir
2. Elle acceptait à contrecœur, ça s'entendait.
3. si légère
4. se turent
5. s'était écartée
6. avait glissé
7. avec tant de soin
8. essayait d'accélérer pour lui échapper
9. et s'aperçut qu'elle était verrouillée
10. et se rendit compte que c'était un leurre
11. le rire forcé d'un fou
12. qui déclenchait presque à chaque fois leurs larmes
13. les saisissait à la gorge
14. qu'il était inutile de le supplier
15. sursaut de force presque animal
16. enfonçant ses ongles dans
17. avait tordu

The video ended as he carried her body down to the basement, where he laid her[1] in the freezer and placed the other slipper and boot in the waiting shoe box.

Charley got up from the sofa and sighed. He rewound[2] the videotape, removed it, and turned off the VCR. The cassette tape he had prepared for Erin was still in the stereo. He pressed "Play."

As the music filled the room, Charley hurried downstairs and opened the freezer. Lovely, lovely, he sighed as he saw the still face[3], the bluish veins that showed in the ice-blue skin. Tenderly, he reached for her.

It was the first time he'd danced with one of the girls whose body he had frozen. It was a different but thrilling[4] experience. Erin's limbs[5] weren't pliant now[6]. Her back would not bend in a dip[7]. Her cheek pressed against his neck, his chin rested on the auburn hair. That hair once so soft, now beaded with frost[8]. Minutes passed. Finally, as the third song was ending, he twirled her around[9] one last time, then, satisfied, glided to a halt[10] and bowed[11].

It had all begun with Nan fifteen years ago on March thirteenth, he thought. He kissed Erin's lips just the way he had kissed Nan's. March thirteenth was three weeks away[12]. By then[13] he would have brought Darcy here and it would be over[14].

He realized that Erin's blouse[15] was beginning to feel damp[16]. He must get her to the city. Holding her in one arm, he half-dragged her[17] to the stereo.

As he turned off the dials, Charley did not notice that an onyx ring with a gold *E* slipped from Erin's frozen finger. Neither did he hear the faint ping[18] as it landed on the floor[19] and lay almost hidden in the fringe on the rug[20].

1. l'allongea
2. rembobina
3. le visage figé
4. palpitante
5. Les membres
6. ne pliaient plus
7. ne se cambrait plus
8. étaient maintenant perlés de givre
9. la fit virevolter
10. s'arrêta dans une glissade
11. salua
12. dans trois semaines
13. D'ici là
14. tout serait fini
15. le chemisier
16. être humide
17. la traîna
18. le tintement
19. de la bague tombant par terre
20. restant à demi cachée parmi les franges du tapis

V
FRIDAY
February 22

DARCY STARED unseeingly at the blueprint[1] of the apartment she was decorating. The owner was spending a year in Europe and was specific about her needs. "I want to rent the place furnished[2], but I'm putting my own things in storage[3]. I don't want some klutz[4] burning a hole[5] in my carpets or upholstery[6]. Fix the place up tastefully[7] but cheaply. I hear[8] you're a genius at that."

Yesterday after she'd left the police station, Darcy had forced herself to follow up[9] a "Moving/Everything Must Go[10]" sale in Old Tappan, New Jersey. She'd hit a bonanza of[11] good furniture that was practically a giveaway[12]. Some of it would exactly suit this apartment; the rest she'd store for future jobs.

She picked up her pen and sketching pad[13]. The sectional[14] should be on the long wall, arcing to face the windows. The ... She laid down the pen[15] and put her face in her hands. I have got to get this job finished. I've got to concentrate, she thought desperately.

A memory came unbidden.[16] The week of finals[17] of their sophomore year[18]. She and Erin holing up[19] in their room, cracking the books[20]. The music of Bruce Springsteen coming from the stereo in the next room, echoing through the walls, tempting

1. les plans
2. le louer meublé
3. je vais mettre mes affaires au garde-meubles
4. qu'un gros plouc
5. fasse des trous de cigarette
6. sur mes fauteuils
7. Décorez-le avec goût
8. Il paraît que
9. à aller assister
10. Cause déménagement : Tout doit disparaître
11. était tombée sur un filon de
12. étaient pratiquement donnés
13. son carnet à dessins
14. canapé modulable
15. posa son stylo
16. Un souvenir lui revint.
17. des derniers partiels
18. 2e année de fac
19. calfeutrées
20. le nez dans leurs bouquins

them to join the celebrants whose exams were over. Erin lamenting[1], "Darce, when Bruce is playing, I can't concentrate."

"You've got to. Maybe I can buy us earplugs[2]."

Erin, a mischievous look on her face[3]: "I've got a better idea." After dinner they'd gone to the library. When it was closing, they hid in stalls in the bathroom[4] until the security guards left[5]. They'd settled themselves on the seventh floor at the desks by the elevator, where fluorescent lights burned[6] all night, and studied in perfect peace[7], letting themselves out through[8] a window at dawn[9].

Darcy bit her lip, realizing she was on the verge of tears again[10]. Impatiently, she dabbed at her eyes[11], reached for the phone, and called Nona. "I tried you[12] last night, but you were out[13]." She told her about going to Erin's apartment, about Jay Stratton, about finding the Bertolini necklace, about the missing diamonds.

"Stratton's going to wait a few days to see if Erin shows up[14] before he makes a report to the insurance company. The police can't accept a missing-person report because it interferes with[15] Erin's right to freedom of movement."

"That's nonsense[16]," Nona said flatly[17].

"Of course it's nonsense. Nona, Erin was meeting someone Tuesday night. She'd answered his ad. That's what worries me. Do you think you should call that FBI agent who wrote to you and talk to him?"

A few minutes later, Bev poked her head[18] in Darcy's office. "I wouldn't bother you[19], but it's Nona." There was sympathetic understanding in her face.[20] Darcy had told her about Erin's disappearance.

Nona was brief. "I left a message for the FBI guy to call. I'll get back to you when he does."

1. qui se plaignait
2. des boules Quies
3. la mine espiègle
4. les toilettes
5. les vigiles soient partis
6. où des néons restaient allumés
7. avaient étudié en paix
8. avant de sortir par
9. au petit matin
10. à nouveau sur le point de pleurer
11. se tamponna les yeux
12. t'ai appelée
13. était sortie
14. réapparaît
15. enfreindrait
16. absurde
17. sans ambages
18. passa la tête
19. Désolée de vous déranger
20. Elle avait un air compatissant.

"If he wants to meet you. I'd like to be there." When Darcy hung up[1], she looked across the room at the coffee brewer on a side table[2] near the window. She made a new pot, deliberately heaping a generous amount[3] of ground coffee[4] into the filter.

Erin had brought along a thermos of strong, black coffee that night they had hidden in the library. "This makes the gray cells stand at attention[5]," she had announced after the second cup.

Now, after the second cup, Darcy was finally able to fully concentrate on the apartment plan. You're always right, Erin-go-bragh, she thought as she reached for her sketchpad.

1. raccrocha
2. regarda la cafetière à l'autre bout du bureau, sur une petite table
3. prenant soin de mettre une bonne dose
4. café moulu
5. maintient les cellules grises en alerte

VINCE D'AMBROSIO returned to his twenty-eighth-floor office from the conference room in the FBI headquarters[6] on Federal Plaza. He was tall and trim, and no one observing him would doubt that after twenty-five years he still held the record for the mile run at his high school alma mater[7], St. Joe's, in Montvale, New Jersey.

His reddish-brown hair was cut short. His warm brown eyes were wide-set. His thin face broke easily into a smile[8]. People instinctively liked and trusted Vince D'Ambrosio.[9]

Vince had served as a criminal investigative officer in Vietnam, completed his master's degree[10] in psychology on his return, then entered the Bureau[11]. Ten years ago, at the FBI training academy[12] on the Quantico Marine Base near Washington, D.C., he'd helped set up[13] the Violent Criminal Apprehension Program[14]. VICAP, as it was called, was

6. quartier général
7. lycée
8. souriait facilement
9. Vince D'Ambrosio plaisait aux gens et leur inspirait confiance.
10. avait fini sa maîtrise
11. intégré le FBI
12. centre de formation
13. à mettre sur pied
14. Programme d'arrestation des auteurs de crimes violents

a computerized national master file[1] with a particular emphasis on[2] serial killers.

Vince had just conducted[3] an update session on[4] VICAP for detectives from the New York area who had taken the VICAP course[5] at Quantico. The purpose[6] of today's meeting had been to alert them that the computer which tracked seemingly unrelated crimes[7] had sent out a warning signal[8]. There was a possible serial killer loose[9] in Manhattan.

It was the third time in as many weeks[10] Vince had delivered[11] the same sobering news[12]: "As you all are aware[13], VICAP is able to establish patterns in[14] what heretofore[15] have been considered isolated cases. The VICAP analysts and investigators have recently alerted us to a possible connection[16] between six young women who have vanished[17] in the past two years.

"All of them had apartments in New York. No one is sure whether they were actually *in* New York when they disappeared. They're all still officially listed as missing persons. We now believe that is a mistake[18]. Foul play is a probability.[19]

"The similarities between these women are striking[20]. They are all slender and very attractive. They range in age[21] from twenty-two to thirty-four. All are upscale in background and education.[22] Outgoing. Extroverted.[23] Finally, every one of them had begun to regularly answer personal ads. I am convinced we have another personal-ad serial killer out there, and a damn clever one[24].

"If we are right, the profile of the subject is the following: well-educated; sophisticated; late twenties to early forties; physically attractive. These women wouldn't have been interested in a diamond-in-the-rough[25]. He may never have been arrested for a violent crime but could have a juvenile history of being

1. fichier national informatisé
2. centré surtout sur
3. venait de présenter
4. une mise à jour de
5. formation sur VICAP
6. L'objectif
7. qui recensait des crimes apparemment isolés
8. venait d'émettre un avertissement
9. en train de sévir
10. en 3 semaines
11. annoncé
12. la même nouvelle glaçante
13. le savez tous
14. faire des rapprochements entre
15. jusqu'ici
16. lien
17. disparu
18. une erreur
19. Il est probable qu'elles ont été victimes d'un meurtre.
20. frappantes
21. Elles sont d'un âge compris entre
22. Elles viennent toutes d'un milieu aisé et cultivé.
23. Très extraverties.
24. c'est un type très futé
25. un type en or sous des dehors frustes

a Peeping Tom[1], maybe stealing[2] women's personal items[3] at school. His hobby could be photography."

The detectives had left, all promising to be on the lookout for[4] any reports of missing young women who fit[5] that category. Dean Thompson, the detective from the Sixth Precinct, lingered behind the others[6]. Vince and he had met in Vietnam and had remained friends over the years.

"Vince, a young woman came in yesterday, wanting to file a missing-person report on a friend of hers, Erin Kelley, who hasn't been seen since Tuesday night. She's a young woman who fits the profile you've described. *And* she was answering a personal ad. I'll stay on top of it.[7]"

"Keep me posted.[8]"

Now, as Vince flipped through[9] the messages on his desk, he nodded with satisfaction[10] when he saw that Nona Roberts had called him. He dialed her[11], gave his name to her secretary, and was immediately put through[12].

He frowned as Nona Roberts's troubled voice explained, "Erin Kelley, a young woman I talked into[13] answering personal ads for my documentary, has been missing since Tuesday night. There is no way[14] Erin would have dropped out of sight[15] unless she'd been in an accident, or worse. I'd stake my life on that.[16]"

Vince looked at his list of appointments. He had meetings in the building the rest of the morning. He was due at the Mayor's office[17] at one-thirty. Nothing he could skip[18]. "Would three o'clock work out for you?[19]" he asked Roberts. After he replaced the receiver, he said aloud, "Another one."

1. un passé de voyeur
2. a peut-être volé
3. des effets personnels féminins
4. de rester à l'affût de
5. rentrant dans
6. resta en arrière
7. Je vais surveiller ça de près.
8. Tiens-moi au courant.
9. en faisant défiler
10. hocha la tête, satisfait
11. l'appela
12. elle la lui passa immédiatement
13. que j'avais convaincu de
14. Il est totalement impossible
15. qu'Erin ait disparu sans explications
16. J'en mettrais ma main au feu.
17. était censé être dans le bureau du maire
18. qu'il ne pouvait annuler
19. Est-ce que 15 h vous irait ?

A MOMENT AFTER she telephoned Darcy about the three o'clock appointment with Vincent D'Ambrosio, Nona received an unexpected[1] visit from Austin Hamilton, CEO and sole[2] owner of Hudson Cable Network.

Hamilton had an icy, sarcastic manner which his staff[3] regarded with intense apprehension[4]. Nona had managed to talk Hamilton into the personal-ads documentary despite the fact that his initial reaction had been: "Who cares about a bunch of losers[5] meeting other losers?"

She had secured[6] his reluctant go-ahead[7] by showing him the pages upon pages of personal ads in magazines and newspapers. "It's the social phenomenon of our society," she'd argued[8]. "These ads aren't cheap to place. It's the old story. Boy wants to meet girl. Aging executive[9] wants to meet wealthy[10] divorcée. The point is[11], does Prince Charming find Sleeping Beauty[12]? Or are these ads a colossal and even humiliating waste of time[13]?"

Hamilton had grudgingly agreed[14] that there might be a story there[15]. "In my day," he'd pointed out[16], "you met people socially[17] at prep school[18] and college[19] and at coming-out parties[20]. You acquired a select group of friends and through them met other social equals[21]."

Hamilton was a sixty-year-old professional preppie[22], and the consummate snob[23]. He had, however, singlehandedly built[24] Hudson Cable and his innovative programming was a serious challenge to[25] the three big networks.

1. inattendue
2. unique
3. son personnel
4. redoutait
5. une bande de minables
6. décroché
7. son accord réticent
8. fait valoir
9. Cadre vieillissant
10. riche
11. La question est
12. sa Belle au bois dormant
13. perte de temps
14. admis à contrecœur
15. quelque chose à en tirer
16. fait remarquer
17. on faisait des rencontres
18. lycée
19. à la fac
20. aux soirées de fin d'études
21. d'autres personnes du même milieu
22. BCBG
23. un snob absolu
24. développé tout seul
25. menaçait sérieusement

When he stopped in Nona's office his mood was frosty[1]. Even though he was as always impeccably dressed, Nona decided that he still managed to remain remarkably unattractive[2]. His Savile Row[3] suit[4] did not quite conceal[5] his narrow shoulders and thickening waist. His sparse hair[6] was tinted a silvery blond shade that did not succeed in looking natural. His narrow lips, which were capable of selectively breaking into a warm smile[7], were set in an almost invisible line. His pale blue eyes were chilly[8].

He got right to the point[9]. "Nona, I'm damn sick[10] of this project of yours. I don't think there's an unattached person in this building who isn't placing or answering personal ads and wasting time comparing results ad nauseam[11]. Either wrap this project up fast[12] or forget it."

There was a time to placate[13] Hamilton; a time to intrigue him. Nona chose the second option. "I had no idea how explosive this personal-ads business[14] might be." She fished on her desk for[15] the letter from Vincent D'Ambrosio and handed it to Hamilton. His eyebrows went up[16] as he read it.

"He's coming here at three o'clock." Nona swallowed. "As you can see, he points out that there's a dark side to these ads. A good friend of mine, Erin Kelley, answered one on Tuesday night. She's missing."

Hamilton's instinct for news overcame his petulance[17]. "Do you think there's a connection?"

Nona turned her head, abstractly noted[18] that the plant Darcy had watered[19] two days ago was beginning to droop again. "I hope not. I don't know."

"Talk to me after you meet with this guy."

Disgusted, Nona realized Hamilton was salivating over the potential media value[20] of Erin's disappear-

1. il était d'humeur glaciale
2. très peu séduisant
3. [rue de Londres célèbre pour ses couturiers et ses tailleurs chics]
4. costume
5. n'arrivait pas à cacher
6. Ses cheveux clairsemés
7. capables à l'occasion de sourire chaleureusement
8. froids
9. n'y alla pas par quatre chemins
10. j'en ai ma claque
11. à n'en plus finir
12. vous bouclez le projet
13. Il y avait des moments où il fallait apaiser
14. histoire
15. farfouilla sur son bureau pour retrouver
16. Il leva un sourcil
17. calma son irritation
18. vit vaguement
19. arrosé
20. à l'idée du potentiel médiatique

ance. With a visible effort to sound sympathetic, he said, "Your friend's probably fine. Don't worry."

When he was gone, Nona's secretary, Connie Frender, poked her head in the door. "Are you still alive?"

"Barely.[1]" Nona tried to smile. Had she ever been twenty-one? she wondered. Connie was the black counterpart[2] of Joan Nye, the Toodle-oo Club president. Young, pretty, bright, smart[3]. Matt's new wife was now twenty-two. And I'll be forty-one, Nona thought. With neither chick nor child[4]. Lovely thought.[5]

"This single black female[6] wishes to meet anyone who breathes[7]," Connie laughed. "I've got a whole new batch[8] of responses from some of the box numbers[9] you wrote to. Ready to look at them?"

"Sure."

"Want some more coffee? After Awesome Austin[10], you probably need it."

This time Nona knew her smile was almost maternal. Connie did not seem to know that offering the boss a cup of coffee was frowned upon[11] by some feminists. "I'd love one.[12]"

She returned with it five minutes later. "Nona, Matt's on the phone. I told him you were in conference and he said it was vital that he talk to you."

"I'm sure it is." Nona waited for the door to close and took a swig of coffee[13] before she reached for the phone. Matthew, she thought. Meaning of the name? Gift of God.[14] For sure.[15] "Hi, Matt. How are you and the prom queen[16]?"

"Nona, is it possible for you to stop being nasty[17]?" Had he always sounded this querulous[18]?

"No, it really isn't." Damn, Nona thought. After nearly two years, it still hurts to talk with him.

1. À peine.
2. l'homologue noire
3. intelligente
4. Sans nana et sans gosse.
5. Super.
6. dame noire célibataire
7. n'importe qui de vivant
8. un lot complet
9. boîtes poste restante
10. un entretien avec Hamilton la Terreur
11. mal vu
12. Avec plaisir.
13. but une gorgée de café
14. Don de Dieu.
15. Ben voyons !
16. ta midinette
17. désagréable
18. eu ce ton plaintif

"Nona, I was wondering. Why don't you buy me out of the house[1]? Jeanie doesn't like the Hamptons. The market's still lousy[2] so I'll give you a real break on the price[3]. You know you can always borrow[4] from your folks[5]."

Matty the moocher[6], Nona thought. Marriage to the child-bride[7] had reduced Matt to this. "I don't want the house," she said quietly. "I'm going to buy my own place when we unload this one[8]."

"Nona, you love that place. You're just doing this to punish me."

"See you." Nona broke the connection[9]. You're wrong, Matt, she thought. I loved the house because we bought it together and cooked lobsters[10] to celebrate our first night in it and every year we did something else to make it even greater. Now I want to start absolutely fresh[11]. No memories.

She began to go through the new batch of letters. She'd sent out over a hundred[12] to people who had placed recent ads requesting them to share their experiences. She'd also persuaded the cable anchorman, Gary Finch, to invite people to write in about[13] the results of personal ads they'd either placed or answered and the reason they no longer would do it.

The result of the on-air announcement[14] was proving to be a bonanza. A relatively small number wrote ecstatically about meeting "the most wonderful person in the world and now we're engaged[15]" … "living together" … "married."

Many others expressed disappointment. "He said he was an entrepreneur. Meaning[16] he's broke[17]. Tried to borrow money the first time I met him." From Bashful[18] Single White Male: "She criticized me all through dinner. Said I had a nerve[19] putting[20] in the ad that I was attractive. Boy, did she make

1. tu ne me rachèterais pas ma part de la maison
2. Le marché est encore mou
3. je te ferai un bon prix
4. emprunter
5. à tes parents
6. le profiteur
7. femme-enfant
8. on se sera débarrassés de celle-ci
9. mit fin à la conversation
10. des homards
11. repartir à zéro
12. Elle en avait envoyé plus d'une centaine
13. d'inciter les spectateurs à raconter
14. l'annonce télévisée
15. fiancés
16. Ce qui veut dire
17. qu'il est fauché
18. timide
19. que j'étais gonflé
20. de mettre

me feel lousy[1]." "I started getting obscene phone calls in the middle of the night." "When I got back home from work I found him sitting on my doorstep[2] sniffing coke[3]."

Several letters were unsigned[4]. "I don't want you to know who I am, but I'm sure one of the men I met through a personal column is the man who burglarized[5] my house." "I brought a very attractive fortyish executive[6] home and found him trying to kiss my seventeen-year-old daughter."

Nona felt heartsick at[7] the final letter in the pile. It was from a woman in Lancaster, Pennsylvania. "My twenty-two-year-old daughter, an actress, disappeared almost two years ago. When she did not return our calls, we went to her New York apartment. It was obvious that she had not been there in days. She was answering personal ads. We are frantic[8]. There has been absolutely no trace of her."

Oh God, Nona thought, oh God. Please let Erin be all right.[9] Her hands trembling, she began to sort through[10] the letters, adding the most interesting to one of three files: *Happy About Ads. Disappointed. Serious Problem.* The last letter she held out[11] to show Agent D'Ambrosio.

At one o'clock Connie brought her in[12] a ham and cheese sandwich. "Nothing like a little[13] cholesterol," Nona commented.

"There's no point in ordering tuna for you[14] when[15] you never eat it," Connie commented.

By two, Nona had dictated letters to potential guests[16]. She made a note to herself to invite a psychiatrist or psychologist to be on the program[17]. I ought to have someone who can do a wrap-up analysis[18] of the whole personal-ads scene[19], she decided.

1. elle m'a vraiment sapé le moral
2. sur le seuil devant chez moi
3. de la cocaïne
4. anonymes
5. a cambriolé
6. cadre d'une quarantaine d'années
7. fut bouleversée par
8. fous d'inquiétude
9. Faites qu'Erin soit saine et sauve.
10. trier
11. Elle mit la dernière lettre de côté
12. lui apporta
13. Rien de tel qu'un peu de
14. te prendre du thon,
15. puisque
16. pour inviter d'éventuels participants
17. participer à l'émission
18. une synthèse
19. du monde des petites annonces de rencontre

Vincent D'Ambrosio arrived at quarter of three. "He knows he's early," Connie told Nona, "and doesn't mind waiting[1]."

"No, that's fine. Ask him to come in."

In less than one minute, Vince D'Ambrosio forgot the remarkable discomfort of the green love seat in Nona Roberts's office. He considered himself a good judge of people and liked Nona immediately. Her manner was straightforward[2], pleasant. He liked her looks[3]. Not pretty but attractive, especially those large reflective[4] brown eyes. She wore little if any makeup[5]. He also liked the touches of gray in her dark blond hair. Alice, his ex-wife, was also blond but her sunny tresses[6] were the result of regular appointments at Vidal Sassoon. Well, at least now she was married to a guy who could afford them[7].

It was obvious that Roberts was desperately worried. "Your letter coincides with the most recent responses I've been receiving," she told him. "People writing about meeting thieves[8], moochers, addicts[9], lechers[10], perverts. And now ..." She bit her lip. "And now, someone who never would have dreamed of answering a personal ad and did it as a favor to me[11] is missing."

"Tell me about her."

Nona was fleetingly grateful that Vince[12] D'Ambrosio did not waste time with empty reassurances[13]. "Erin is twenty-seven or -eight. We met six months ago in our health club. She, Darcy Scott, and I were in the same dance classes and became friendly. Darcy will be here in a few minutes." She picked up the letter from the woman in Lancaster and handed it to Vince. "This just arrived."

1. ça ne le gêne pas d'attendre
2. Elle était directe
3. la trouvait agréable à regarder
4. songeurs
5. paraissait à peine maquillée
6. mèches blondes
7. en avait les moyens
8. des voleurs
9. des drogués
10. des obsédés sexuels
11. ne l'a fait que pour me rendre service,
12. brièvement reconnaissante à Vince
13. de ne pas perdre de temps à la rassurer par des banalités

Vince read it quickly and whistled silently[1]. "Somebody didn't file a report with us. This girl isn't on our list. She brings the count up to[2] seven missing."

In the cab on the way to Nona's office, Darcy thought of the time[3] she and Erin had gone skiing at Stowe their senior year of college[4]. The slopes[5] had been icy, and most people had headed for the lodge[6] early. At her urging[7], she and Erin went for one last run[8]. Erin hit a patch of ice[9] and fell, her leg snapping under her[10].

When the patrol[11] came with the meat wagon[12] for Erin, Darcy skied beside her, then accompanied her in the ambulance. She remembered Erin's ashen[13] face, Erin trying to joke[14]. "Hope this doesn't affect my dancing. I plan to be queen[15] of the stardust ballroom[16]."

"You will be."

At the hospital, when the X-rays were developed[17], the surgeon[18] raised his eyebrows. "You really did a job on yourself[19], but we'll fix you up[20]." He'd smiled at Darcy. "Don't look so worried. She'll be fine."

"I'm not just worried. I feel so damn guilty[21]," she'd told the doctor. "Erin didn't want to make the last run."

Now as she entered Nona's office and was introduced to Agent D'Ambrosio, Darcy realized she was experiencing exactly the same reaction. The same relief[22] that somebody was in charge[23], the same guilt that she had urged Erin to answer the ads with her.

"Nona only asked if we wanted to *try* them. I was the one who pushed[24] Erin to do it," she told D'Ambrosio. He took notes as she talked about the phone call on Tuesday, about Erin's saying she was

1. mima un sifflement
2. Avec elle, on en est à
3. repensa à la fois où
4. pendant leur dernière année de fac
5. pistes
6. étaient retournés au chalet
7. Comme Darcy avait insisté
8. avaient fait une dernière descente
9. avait glissé sur une plaque de glace
10. se fracturant la jambe
11. les secours
12. l'ambulance
13. blême
14. plaisanter
15. J'ai l'intention de devenir la reine
16. des thés dansants
17. une fois les radios développées
18. chirurgien
19. ne vous êtes pas ratée
20. on va vous remettre sur pied
21. si coupable
22. soulagement de savoir
23. prenait les choses en main
24. C'est moi qui ai poussé

meeting someone named Charles North in a pub near Washington Square. She noticed the change in D'Ambrosio's manner when she spoke about opening the safe, about giving the Bertolini necklace to Jay Stratton, about Stratton's claim that there were diamonds missing.

He asked her about Erin's family.

Darcy stared at her hands[1].

Remember arriving at Mount Holyoke first day of freshman year[2]? Erin already there, her suitcases[3] piled neatly in the corner. They'd sized each other up[4], both liked what they saw. Erin's eyes widening as she recognized[5] Mother and Dad but not losing her composure[6].

"When Darcy wrote to me this summer introducing herself, I didn't realize that her parents were Barbara Thorne and Robert Scott," she'd said. "I don't think I ever missed one of your films." Then she added, "Darcy, I didn't want to settle in[7] until you were here. I thought you might have a preference about which closet or bed you wanted."

Remember the look Mother and Dad exchanged. They were thinking, what a nice girl Erin is. They asked her to join us for dinner.

Erin had come to college alone. Her father was an invalid, she explained. We wondered why she never even mentioned her mother. Later she told me that when she was six, her father developed multiple sclerosis[8] and needed a wheelchair[9]. Her mother took off[10] when she was seven. "I didn't bargain for this[11]," she'd said. "Erin, you can come with me if you want."

"I can't leave Daddy all alone. He needs me."

Over the years, Erin completely lost touch with[12] her mother. "The last I heard[13] she was living with some guy who owned a charter sailboat[14] in the

1. fixa ses mains
2. la première année de fac
3. valises
4. Elles s'étaient observées
5. surprise de reconnaître
6. gardant son calme
7. installer mes affaires
8. avait commencé à souffrir de sclérose en plaques
9. fauteuil roulant
10. avait quitté la maison
11. Je ne m'attendais pas à ça
12. avait perdu de vue
13. Aux dernières nouvelles,
14. propriétaire d'un voilier de location

Caribbean." She was at Mount Holyoke on a scholarship[1]*. "As Daddy says, being immobilized gives you plenty of time to help your kid with her homework*[2]*. If you can't pay for college, at least*[3] *you can help her get a free ride*[4]*." Oh Erin, where are you? What's happened to you?*

Darcy realized that D'Ambrosio was waiting for her to answer his question. "Her father's been in a nursing home in Massachusetts for the last few years," she said. "He's not aware of much anymore.[5] I guess I'm the closest thing Erin has to a relative besides him.[6]"

Vince saw the pain in Darcy's eyes. "In my business I've observed that having one good friend can beat[7] having a passel of relatives[8]."

Darcy managed a smile. "Erin's favorite quote is from Aristotle. 'What is a friend? A single soul[9] dwelling in two bodies[10].' "

Nona got up, stood beside Darcy's chair, and put her hands reassuringly on her shoulders. She looked squarely at D'Ambrosio[11]. "What can we do to help find Erin?"

A LONG TIME ago, Petey Potters had been a construction worker. *"Big jobs,"* as he liked to boast[12] to anyone whose ear he could get[13]. "World Trade Center. I usta be out[14] on one of them girders[15]. Tell ye[16], the wind wuz whippin' so[17] ye wondered if ye were gonna stay up there." He'd laugh, a wheezy chortle[18]. "Some view[19], lemme tell ye[20], some view."

But at night the thought of going back up on the girder began to get to[21] Petey. A coupla shots of

1. boursière à Mount Holyoke
2. devoirs à la maison
3. au moins
4. on peut l'aider à ne pas devoir payer ses études [par une bourse au mérite]
5. Il n'est plus conscient de grand-chose.
6. Après lui, c'est pour ainsi dire moi le plus proche parent d'Erin.
7. peut être mieux
8. une grande famille
9. Une seule âme
10. dans deux corps
11. regarda D'Ambrosio droit dans les yeux
12. s'en vanter
13. quiconque voulait bien l'écouter
14. J'travaillais
15. une de ces poutres en acier
16. J'vous dis pas
17. le vent soufflait si fort
18. d'un rire rauque
19. Une vue fantastique
20. mon vieux
21. tracasser

1. Un ou deux verres de whisky
2. ensuite, une ou deux bières
3. lui iradiait l'estomac
4. Un poivrot bon à rien.
5. pestait contre son père
6. un sacré numéro
7. cuvait son vin
8. asile de nuit
9. un refuge de l'Armée du salut
10. [littéralement : je plonge]
11. Ça rate jamais.
12. la Bible
13. de s'avancer
14. de rendre grâce au Créateur
15. ce souvenir amusait encore
16. le vieux clochard
17. d'aluminium
18. de vieux chiffons
19. avec lesquels il avait fabriqué une sorte de tente
20. adossée au vieux terminus désaffecté
21. Des clopes.
22. Les poubelles
23. qu'on pouvait rapporter pour récupérer la consigne
24. une raclette
25. toutes sales à cause de lui
26. de lui faire signe que non
27. une vieille chouette

rye[1], a coupla beer chasers[2], and the warmth would flow into the pit of his stomach[3] and spread through his body.

"You're just like your father," his wife began to scream at him. "A no-good drunk.[4]"

Petey never got insulted. He understood. He'd start to laugh when his wife ranted about Pop[5]. Pop had been some card[6]. He'd disappear for weeks at a time, dry out[7] in a flophouse[8] on the Bowery, and then come back home. "When I'm hungry, it's no problem," he'd confided to eight-year-old Petey. I go to the Salvation Army shelter[9], take a dive[10], get a meal, a bath, a bed. Never fails.[11]"

"What's 'take a dive' mean?" Petey had asked.

"When you go to the shelter, they tell you about God and forgiveness and we're all brothers and we want to be saved. Then they ask anyone who believes in the good book[12] to come forward[13] and acknowledge his Maker[14]. So you get religion. You run up, fall on your knees, and shout something about being saved. That's taking a dive."

Nearly forty years later the memory still tickled[15] the homeless derelict[16] Petey Potters. He'd created his own shelter, a combination of wood and tin[17] and old rags[18] that he'd piled together into a tentlike structure[19] against the sagging, shuttered terminal[20] on the abandoned West Fifty-sixth Street pier.

Petey's needs were simple. Wine. Butts.[21] A little food. Litter baskets[22] were a constant supply of cans and bottles that could be redeemed for the deposits[23]. When he was ambitious, Petey took a squeegee[24] and a bottle of water and stood at the Fifty-sixth Street exit of the West Side Highway. No drivers wanted their car windows smeared by his efforts[25], but most people were afraid to wave him away[26]. Only last week he'd heard an old bat[27] explode to the driver of a Mercedes, "Jane, why do you allow yourself to be held up like this[1]?"

Petey had loved the answer. "Because, Mother, I don't want to have the side of this car scratched[2] if I refuse."

Petey didn't scratch anything when he was rejected. He just went on to the next car, armed with his squirt bottle[3], a coaxing[4] smile on his face.

Yesterday had been one of the good days. Just enough snow so that the highway became messy and windshields[5] got sprayed with dirty slush[6] from the tires[7] of cars ahead of them. Few people had refused Petey's ministrations[8] at the exit ramp[9]. He'd made eighteen bucks[10], enough for a hero sandwich[11], butts, and three bottles of dago red[12].

Last night he'd settled inside his tent, wrapped[13] in the old army blanket the Armenian church on Second Avenue had given him, a ski cap[14] keeping his head warm, a tattered greatcoat[15], its moth-eaten fur collar cozy around his neck[16]. He'd finished the hero[17] with the first bottle of wine, then settled down to puffing and sipping[18], content and warm in an inebriated haze[19]. Pop taking a dive. Mom coming back to the apartment on Tremont Avenue, worn out from scrubbing[20] other people's houses. Birdie, his wife. *Harpie*, not Birdie. That's what they shoulda called her.

Petey shook with mirth[21] at the play on words[22]. Wonder where she was now. How about the kid? Nice kid.

Petey wasn't sure when he heard the car pull up[23]. He tried to force himself to wakefulness[24], instinctively wanting to protect his territory. It better not be cops trying to knock over his place. Nah. Cops didn't bother with this kind of shack[25] in the middle of the night.

1. tu te laisses toujours faire
2. qu'on me raye l'aile de ma voiture
3. son pulvérisateur
4. enjôleur
5. pour que les pare-brise
6. soient éclaboussés de boue et de neige fondue
7. pneus
8. les bons offices
9. bretelle de sortie
10. s'était fait 18 $
11. sandwich club
12. gros rouge
13. emmitouflé
14. bonnet de laine
15. un pardessus élimé
16. dont le col en fourrure mité lui réchauffait le cou
17. son sandwich
18. s'était installé pour savourer clope et pinard
19. les vapeurs de l'alcool
20. épuisée d'avoir briqué
21. rit de bon cœur
22. de son jeu de mots
23. s'arrêter
24. sortir de sa torpeur
25. ce type d'abri

Maybe it was a druggie[1]. Petey gripped the neck[2] of an empty wine bottle. Better not try to come in here. But nobody came. After a few minutes he heard the car start up again[3]; he peered out cautiously[4]. Taillights were disappearing[5] onto the deserted West Side Highway. Maybe somebody had to take a leak[6], Petey decided as he reached for the last bottle.

It was late afternoon when Petey opened his eyes again. His head had that empty, throbbing feeling[7]. His gut burned.[8] His mouth felt like the bottom of a birdcage[9]. He pulled himself up. The three empty bottles offered no consolation. He found twenty cents in the pockets of the greatcoat. I'm hungry, he whined[10] silently. Poking his head from behind[11] the piece of tin sheeting[12] that served as door[13] for his shelter, he decided that it must be late afternoon. There were long shadows on the dock. His eyes moved to focus on something that was clearly not a shadow. Petey squinted, muttered a profanity under his breath[14], and dragged himself to his feet[15].

His legs were stiff[16] and his gait clumsy[17] as he made his unsteady way to whatever[18] was lying on the pier[19].

It was a slim woman. Young. Red hair curling around her face. Petey was sure she was dead. A necklace was twisted into her throat. She was wearing a blouse and slacks. Her shoes didn't match.[20]

The necklace sparkled[21] in the fading light. Gold. Real gold. Petey licked his lips nervously[22]. Bracing himself for the[23] shock of touching the dead girl he reached around the back of her neck for the clasp[24] of the elaborate necklace. His fingers

1. un drogué
2. empoigna le goulot
3. redémarrer
4. pointa son nez avec précaution
5. Il vit des feux arrière disparaître
6. avait eu envie de pisser
7. le lançait
8. Il avait le bide en feu.
9. était pâteuse et puait
10. gémit
11. Sortant la tête de derrière
12. la feuille d'alu
13. qui faisait office de porte
14. jura tout bas
15. se releva péniblement
16. ankylosées
17. sa démarche mal assurée
18. se dirigeait d'un pas chancelant vers la forme qui
19. la jetée
20. Ses chaussures étaient dépareillées.
21. scintillait
22. se passa nerveusement la langue sur les lèvres
23. Se préparant au
24. le fermoir

fumbled.[1] Thick and unsteady, they could not get the clasp to release[2]. Christ, she felt cold.

He didn't want to break anything. Was the necklace long enough to pull over her head? Trying to ignore the bruised, blue-veined throat, he tugged at[3] the heavy chain.

Grimy fingerprints[4] streaked[5] Erin's face as Petey freed[6] the necklace and slipped it[7] in his pocket. The earrings[8]. They were good, too.

From a distance[9], Petey heard the whine of a police siren. Like a startled[10] rabbit he jumped up, forgetting the earrings. This was no place for him. He'd have to take his stuff[11], get himself a new shelter. When the body was found, just his being around here[12] would be enough for the cops.

An awareness of his potential danger sobered[13] Petey. On stumbling feet[14] he rushed back to the shelter. Everything he owned could be tied[15] in the army blanket. His pillow. A couple pairs of socks, some underwear[16]. A flannel shirt. A dish and spoon and cup. Matches. Butts. Old newspapers for cold nights.

Fifteen minutes later, Petey had vanished into the world of the homeless. Panhandling[17] on Seventh Avenue netted[18] four dollars and thirty-two cents. He used it to buy wine and a pretzel. There was a young fellow[19] on Fifty-seventh Street who sold hot jewelry[20]. He gave Petey twenty-five dollars for the necklace. "This is good, man. Try to get more like this."

At ten o'clock Petey was asleep on a subway grating[21] that radiated warm, dank air[22]. At eleven, he was being shaken awake[23]. A not-unkind[24] voice said, "Come on, pal[25]. It's going to be real cold tonight. We're going to take you to a place where you can have a decent bed and a good meal."

1. Il tâtonna des doigts.
2. n'arrivaient pas à ouvrir le fermoir
3. tira sur
4. Des traces de doigts sales
5. balayèrent
6. dégagea
7. le fourra
8. boucles d'oreilles
9. Au loin
10. effarouché
11. Il fallait qu'il prenne ses affaires
12. sa simple présence
13. dessoûla
14. D'un pas chancelant,
15. emporté
16. sous-vêtements
17. Faire la manche
18. lui rapporta
19. un jeune type
20. des bijoux volés
21. grille de métro
22. d'où émanait une vapeur chaude
23. quelqu'un le secoua pour le réveiller
24. plutôt aimable
25. mon vieux

AT QUARTER OF SIX on Friday evening, Wanda Libbey, snugly secure[1] in her new BMW, was inching her way along[2] the West Side Highway. Complacent in[3] the excellent shopping she'd done on Fifth Avenue, Wanda was still annoyed at herself[4] that she'd gotten such a late start back[5] to Tarrytown. The Friday night rush hour[6] was the worst of the week, a time when many quit New York for their country homes. She'd never want to live in New York again. Too dirty. Too dangerous.

Wanda glanced at the Valentino purse[7] on the passenger seat. When she'd parked in the Kinney lot[8] this morning, she'd tucked it firmly[9] under her arm and kept it there all day. She wasn't fool enough[10] to have it dangling from her arm[11] where someone might grab it[12].

Another damn traffic light.[13] Oh well, in a few blocks[14] she'd be on the ramp[15] and past[16] this miserable section of so-called highway.

A tap on the window made Wanda look swiftly[17] to the right. A bearded[18] face grinned in at her[19]. A rag[20] began to make swishing movements on[21] the windshield[22].

Wanda's lips snapped into a rigid line[23]. Damn. She shook her head vigorously. No. No.

The man ignored her.

I am not going to be held up by these people, Wanda fumed[24], jamming her finger on[25] the button that opened the passenger window. "I don't want—" She began to shriek[26]. The rag was thrown against the windshield. The bottle of fluid pinged off the

1. bien à l'abri
2. avançait au ralenti sur
3. Satisfaite de
4. s'en voulait encore
5. d'être partie si tard pour rentrer
6. heure de pointe
7. sac à main
8. parking
9. l'avait gardé bien serré
10. assez stupide
11. pour le laisser pendre à son bras
12. s'en saisir
13. Encore un feu rouge !
14. dans quelques centaines de mètres,
15. sur la bretelle de sortie
16. aurait dépassé
17. Un toc toc à la vitre lui fit regarder
18. barbu
19. lui faisait un large sourire
20. chiffon
21. balayer
22. pare-brise
23. serra les lèvres
24. rouspéta
25. le doigt pressant
26. crier

hood[1]. A hand reached into the car. She watched her purse disappear.

A squad car[2] was heading west on Fifty-fifth Street. The driver suddenly straightened up[3]. "What's that?" On the approach to the highway he could see traffic stopped, people getting out of cars. "Let's go." Siren blaring[4], lights flashing, the squad car lurched forward[5], skillfully weaving through the maze of moving traffic[6] and double-parked vehicles[7].

Still screaming with rage and frustration, Wanda pointed to the pier a block away. "My purse. He ran there."

"Let's go." The squad car turned left, then made a sharp right[8] as they roared onto the pier[9]. The cop in the passenger seat turned on the spotlight[10], revealing the shack Petey had abandoned. "I'll check inside." Then he snapped[11], "Hey, over there. Past the terminal. What's that?"

The body of Erin Kelley, glistening with sleet[12], the silvery slipper flashing[13] under the powerful beam[14] from the spotlight, had been discovered again.

DARCY LEFT Nona's office with Vince D'Ambrosio. They took a cab to her apartment and she gave him Erin's daily reminder[15] and her personal-columns file. Vince studied them carefully. "Not much here," he commented. "We'll find out who placed the ads she circled. With any luck[16], Charles North is one of them."

"Erin isn't the greatest record keeper[17]," Darcy said. "I could go back to her apartment and look

1. rebondit sur le capot
2. voiture de police
3. se redressa net
4. La sirène à fond
5. fonça
6. se faufilant habilement dans le dédale de la circulation
7. des véhicules en double file
8. vira à droite
9. en arrivant en trombe sur la jetée
10. alluma le projecteur
11. interpella sèchement
12. couvert de neige fondue scintillante
13. qui brillait
14. le faisceau puissant
15. l'agenda
16. un peu de chance
17. très bonne pour noter les choses

through her desk again[1]. It's possible I missed something[2]."

"That could help. But don't worry. If North's a corporate lawyer from Philadelphia, it'll be easy to trace him[3]." Vince stood up[4]. "I'll get on this right away.[5]"

"And I'm going back to her apartment now. I'll leave with you." Darcy hesitated. The light on the answering machine was blinking[6]. "Can you wait just a minute till I check the messages?" Attempting a smile she said, "There's always the chance Erin left one[7]."

There were two messages. Both were about personal ads. One was genial[8]. "Hi, Darcy. Trying you again. Enjoyed your note. Hope we can get together sometime. I'm Box 4358. David Weld, 555-4890."

The other was sharply different[9]. "Hey, Darcy, why do you waste *your* time answering ads and *my* time trying to reach you. This is the fourth time I've called. I don't like to leave messages, but here's this one. Drop dead.[10]"

Vince shook his head. "That guy has a short leash[11]."

"I didn't leave the answering machine on while I was away," Darcy said. "I suppose if anyone tried to reach me in response to the few letters I sent myself, they probably gave up[12]. Erin started answering ads in my name about two weeks ago. Those are the first calls I've gotten."

Gus Boxer was surprised and not especially pleased to respond to the buzzer and find the same young woman who had wasted so much of his time[13] yesterday. He was prepared to absolutely refuse[14] to allow her to enter[15] Erin Kelley's apartment again but did not get the chance[16]. "We've reported Erin's dis-

1. refouiller son bureau
2. que quelque chose m'ait échappé
3. de retrouver sa trace
4. se leva
5. Je m'y mets de ce pas.
6. clignotait
7. la possibilité qu'Erin en ait laissé un
8. très cordial
9. l'opposé
10. Va te faire voir !
11. se met en rogne facilement
12. ont sans doute fini par laisser tomber
13. lui avait fait perdre autant de temps
14. refuser catégoriquement
15. de la laisser entrer dans
16. n'en eut pas le temps

appearance to the FBI," Darcy told him. "The agent in charge[1] has asked me to go through her desk."

The FBI. Gus felt a nervous tremor go through his body[2]. But that was so long ago. He had nothing to worry about. A couple of people had left their names recently just in case a vacancy came up[3]. One good-looking gal[4] said it would be worth a thousand bucks under the table[5] if he put her at the top of the list. So if Kelley's friend was able to find out something happened to her, it would mean a nice piece of change in his pocket[6].

"I'm just as worried about that girl as you are," he whined[7], the unfamiliar sympathetic tone catching in his vocal cords[8]. "Come on up[9]."

In the apartment, Darcy immediately turned on all the lights against the impending dusk[10]. Yesterday, the place had seemed cheerful enough[11]. Today, Erin's continued absence[12] was leaving its mark[13]. A faint edging of soot was visible[14] on the windowsill. The long worktable needed dusting[15]. The framed posters that always gave brightness and color to the room[16] seemed to mock her[17].

The Picasso from Geneva. Erin had bought it on her one school trip abroad[18]. "I love this even though[19] it isn't my favorite theme," she'd commented. It depicted[20] a mother and child.

There were no further[21] messages on Erin's machine. A search of the desk revealed nothing significant[22]. There was a new cassette for the answering machine in the drawer. Possibly Agent D'Ambrosio would want the old tape, the one that contained messages. Darcy switched the two[23].

The nursing home. This was around the time Erin usually called it. Darcy looked up the number and dialed. The head nurse[24] on Billy Kelley's floor came to the phone. "I spoke to Erin as usual on Tuesday night

1. responsable de l'enquête
2. fut traversé d'un frisson nerveux
3. juste au cas où un appartement se libérerait
4. jeune femme
5. qu'il toucherait un bakchich de 1 000 $
6. il empocherait un joli pactole
7. gémit
8. d'un ton compatissant qui sonnait faux
9. Montez donc !
10. car la nuit tombait
11. encore l'air accueillant
12. l'absence prolongée
13. commençait à se faire sentir
14. On distinguait une fine couche de suie
15. avait besoin d'être épousseté
16. avaient toujours égayé
17. se moquer d'elle
18. pendant son seul voyage scolaire à l'étranger
19. même si
20. représentait
21. pas de nouveaux
22. n'apporta rien de nouveau
23. les intervertit
24. infirmière en chef

around five. I told her I think her father is quite near the end. She said she would spend the weekend in Wellesley." Then she added, "I understand she's missing. We're all praying that she's all right.[1]"

There's nothing more I can do here, Darcy thought, and suddenly felt an overwhelming desire[2] to go home.

1. Nous prions tous pour qu'il ne lui soit rien arrivé.
2. fut prise d'une irrésistible envie

It was quarter of six when she got back to her own place[3]. A hot shower was called for[4], she decided, and a hot toddy[5].

At ten past six, wrapped in her favorite flannel robe[6], steam rising from the toddy[7], she settled on the couch and pushed the remote control for[8] the television.

A story was breaking.[9] John Miller, the investigative crime reporter for Channel 4, was standing at the entrance to a West Side pier. Behind him in a roped-off area[10] a dozen policemen were silhouetted[11] against[12] the cold waters of the Hudson. Darcy turned up the volume.

"... body of an unidentified young woman was just discovered on this abandoned Fifty-sixth Street pier. She appears to have been the victim of strangulation[13]. The woman is slim, in her mid-twenties with auburn hair. She is wearing slacks and a multicolored blouse. A bizarre twist[14] is that she is wearing mismatched shoes[15], a brown leather ankle boot on her left foot, an evening slipper on her right."

Darcy stared at the television. Auburn hair. Midtwenties. Multicolored blouse. She'd given Erin a multicolored blouse for Christmas. Erin had been delighted[16]. "It has all the colors of Joseph's coat," she'd said. "I love it."

Auburn. Slim. Joseph's coat.

3. chez elle
4. s'imposait
5. un grog
6. peignoir
7. un grog fumant à la main
8. appuya sur la télécommande de
9. Il y avait un flash spécial.
10. derrière un cordon de sécurité
11. on distinguait une douzaine de policiers
12. devant
13. étranglée
14. Le point curieux
15. des chaussures dépareillées
16. ravie

The biblical Joseph's coat had been stained in blood[1] when his treacherous[2] brothers showed it to their father as proof of his death[3].

Somehow[4], Darcy managed to find in her purse the card Agent D'Ambrosio had given her.

Vince was just about to leave his office. He was meeting his fifteen-year-old son Hank at Madison Square Garden. They were going to have a quick dinner, then take in a Rangers game[5]. As he listened to Darcy he realized that he had been expecting this call[6]; he just hadn't thought it would come quite this soon[7].

"It doesn't sound good[8]," he told her. "I'll phone the precinct[9] where the body was found. Sit tight.[10] I'll get back to you.[11]"

When he hung up, he called Hudson Cable. Nona was still in her office. "I'll get right over to be with Darcy[12]," she said.

"She'll be asked if she can identify the body," Vince warned.

He called the Midtown North precinct and was put through to the head of the homicide squad[13]. The body had not yet been removed from the crime scene. When it reached the morgue, they'd send a squad car for Miss Scott. Vince explained his interest in the case[14]. "We'd be grateful for your assistance[15]," he was told. "Unless this turns out to be an open-and-shut case[16], we'd like to have it run through[17] VICAP."

Vince called Darcy back, told her about the squad car and that Nona was on the way[18]. She thanked him, her tone flat and unemotional[19].

1. barbouillé de sang
2. perfides
3. pour prouver qu'il était mort
4. Sans trop savoir comment
5. aller à un match des Rangers
6. il s'attendait à cet appel
7. que cela se produirait si tôt
8. Ça ne promet rien de bon.
9. commissariat du quartier
10. Ne bougez pas.
11. Je vous rappelle.
12. Je file chez Darcy pour qu'elle ne soit pas seule
13. le chef de la brigade criminelle
14. pourquoi il s'intéressait à cette affaire
15. Votre aide serait la bienvenue
16. Sauf s'il s'avérait qu'il s'agit d'une affaire toute simple
17. on aimerait entrer les détails dans le programme
18. n'allait pas tarder
19. d'un ton morne et détaché

1. à grands pas
2. parcourut
3. se réjouissait d'avance du luxe d'avoir
4. Pas le moindre projet.
5. était en face de
6. Juste en face du zoo
7. d'un tissu à motif héraldique
8. tapisserie moyenâgeuse
9. des paysages
10. Des scènes de chasse
11. tenture murale
12. complétaient
13. avait admirée avec espoir
14. à manches longues
15. pantalon de coton
16. Son verre à la main
17. mit le journal de 18 h
18. reportage
19. la douleur

CHRIS SHERIDAN left the gallery at ten past five and with long strides[1] walked[2] the fourteen blocks from Seventy-eighth and Madison to Sixty-fifth and Fifth. It had been a busy and highly successful week and he savored the luxurious freedom of knowing that he had[3] the whole weekend to himself. Not a single plan.[4] His tenth-floor apartment faced[5] Central Park. "Directly across from the zoo[6]," as he told his friends. Eclectic in taste, he'd mixed antique tables, lamps, and carpets with long, comfortable upholstered couches that he'd covered in a heraldic pattern[7], copied from a medieval tapestry[8]. The paintings were English landscapes[9]. Nineteenth-century hunting prints[10] and a silk-on-silk Tree of Life wall hanging[11] complemented[12] the Chippendale table and side chairs in the dining area.

It was a comfortable, inviting room, a room which in the past eight years many young women had eyed with hope[13].

Chris went into the bedroom, changed into a long-sleeved[14] sport shirt and chinos[15]. A very dry martini, he decided. Maybe later he'd go out for a plate of pasta. Drink in hand[16], he switched on the six o'clock news[17] and saw the same broadcast[18] Darcy was watching.

His compassion for the dead girl and identification with the grief[19] her family would experience was instantly replaced by horror. Strangled! A dancing shoe on one foot! "Oh, God," Chris said aloud. Could whoever murdered that girl have been the one who sent the letter to his mother? The letter that said a dancing girl who lived in Manhattan would die on Tuesday night exactly the way Nan died.

Tuesday afternoon, after his mother called, he'd contacted Glenn Moore, the police chief of Darien. Moore had gone to see Greta, had taken the letter, reassuring her it was probably from a crank[1]. He'd then called Chris back. "Chris, even if it's on the level[2], how do you begin to[3] protect all the young women in New York?"

Now Chris dialed the Darien police station again and was put through to the chief. Moore had not yet heard about the death in New York. "I'll call the FBI," he said. "If that letter is from the killer[4], it's physical evidence[5]. I have to warn you[6], the FBI will probably want to talk to you and your mother about Nan's death. I'm sorry, Chris. I know what that does to her."

AT THE ENTRANCE to Beefsteak Charlie's restaurant in Madison Square Garden, Vince threw an arm around[7] his son's shoulders. "I swear[8] you've grown[9] since last week." He and Hank were now eye to eye[10]. "One of these days, you'll be eating your blue plate off my head[11]."

"What the heck is[12] a blue plate?" Hank's lean[13] face with a sprinkling of freckles[14] across the nose[15] was the one Vince remembered seeing in the mirror nearly thirty years ago. Only the color of his gray-blue eyes had come from his mother's genes.[16]

The waiter beckoned to them[17]. When they were seated, Vince explained, "A blue plate used to be the special of the evening[18] at a cheap restaurant. Seventy-nine cents bought you[19] a hunk of meat[20],

1. lui assurant que ça venait sans doute d'un déséquilibré
2. même si c'était sérieux
3. comment espérer
4. a été envoyée par l'assassin
5. une preuve matérielle
6. vous prévenir
7. passa le bras autour des
8. Je suis sûr
9. que tu as grandi
10. maintenant de la même taille
11. en me dépassant d'une tête
12. Bon sang, c'est quoi
13. maigre
14. ses quelques taches de rousseur
15. sur le nez
16. Le gris bleu de ses yeux était la seule chose qu'il tînt de sa mère.
17. leur fit signe de s'installer
18. le plat du jour
19. Avec 79 cents, on pouvait acheter
20. un bon morceau de viande

a couple of vegetables, a potato. The plate was sectioned[1] to keep the juices from running together. Your grandfather loved that kind of bargain[2]."

They decided on hamburgers with everything piled on, french fries[3], salads. Vince had a beer, Hank a cola. Vince forced himself not to think about Darcy Scott and Nona Roberts going to the morgue to view the body of the murder victim. Rough as hell[4] for both of them.

Hank filled him in[5] about his track team[6]. "We're running at Randall's Island next Saturday. Think you can make it[7]?"

"Absolutely, unless ..."

"Oh, sure." Unlike his mother, Hank understood the demands of Vince's job. "You working on anything new?"

Vince told him about the concern[8] that a serial killer was on the loose[9], about the meeting in Nona Roberts's office, about the belief that Erin Kelley might be the dead woman found on the pier.

Hank listened intently[10]. "You think you ought to be in on this[11], Dad?"

"Not necessarily. This may be a local homicide solely for[12] the NYPD[13], but they have requested assistance from[14] the Behavioral Science Unit at Quantico and I'll help them as much as I can." He signaled for[15] the check[16]. "We'd better get started."

"Dad, I'm coming in again Sunday. Why don't I go to the game alone? You know your gut is telling you[17] to follow up on this case[18]."

"I don't want to pull that on you[19]."

"Look, the game[20] is sold out[21]. I'll make a deal with you.[22] No scalping[23], but if I sell your ticket[24] for exactly what you paid for it, I get to keep[25] the money. I've got a date[26] tomorrow night. I'm broke[27], and I can't stand to[28] ask Mom for a loan[29].

1. compartimentée
2. ce genre de bonne affaire
3. des frites
4. Ça allait être super dur
5. lui donna les dernières nouvelles
6. équipe d'athlétisme
7. que tu pourras venir
8. la peur
9. soit en train de sévir
10. attentivement
11. que tu devrais participer à l'enquête
12. ne concernant que
13. police new-yorkaise
14. demandé l'aide de
15. fit signe qu'on lui apporte
16. l'addition
17. ton instinct te dit
18. que tu devrais suivre l'enquête de près
19. te faire ce coup-là
20. le match
21. se joue à guichets fermés
22. Je te propose un marché.
23. Je ferai pas de bénef'
24. je revends ton billet
25. je garde l'argent
26. J'invite une fille
27. fauché
28. je déteste
29. un prêt

She sends me to that hunk of blubber[1] she married. So anxious for us to be buddies.[2]"

Vince smiled. "I swear you've got the makings of a con man.[3] See you Sunday, pal."

1. ce tas de graisse
2. Elle veut à tout prix qu'on soit potes.
3. Tu as l'étoffe d'un escroc !

ON THE WAY to the morgue, Darcy and Nona clasped hands[4] in the squad car. When they arrived, they were taken to a room off the lobby. "They'll come for you[5] when they're ready," the cop who had driven them explained. "They're probably taking photographs."

Photographs. *Erin, don't worry. Send your picture if they request it*[6]. *In for a penny, in for a pound.*[7] Darcy stared straight ahead[8], barely conscious of the room, of Nona's arm around her. Charles North. Erin had met him at seven o'clock on Tuesday night. A little more than a few short days ago. Tuesday morning she and Erin had joked about that date.

Darcy said aloud, "And now I'm sitting in the New York City morgue waiting to look at a dead woman who I'm sure is going to be Erin." Vaguely she felt Nona's arm tighten around her[9].

The cop returned. "An FBI agent's on the way. Wants you to wait for him before you go downstairs."

Vince walked between Darcy and Nona, his hands firmly under their elbows[10]. They stopped at the glass window that separated them from the still form[11] on the stretcher[12]. At Vince's nod[13], the attendant[14] pulled the sheet back from the victim's face.

But Darcy already knew. A strand of that auburn hair had escaped concealment[15]. Then she was

4. se tenaient la main
5. vous chercher
6. s'ils en demandent une
7. Quand le vin est tiré, il faut le boire.
8. regardait droit devant elle
9. la serrait un peu plus fort
10. les soutenant chacune fermement par le coude
11. la forme immobile
12. sur la civière
13. Quand Vince lui fit signe de la tête
14. l'employé
15. dépassait déjà du drap

seeing the familiar profile, the wide blue eyes now closed, the lashes dark shadows[1], the always smiling lips so still, so quiet.

Erin. Erin. Erin-go-bragh, she thought, and felt herself begin to sink into merciful darkness[2].

Vince and Nona grabbed her[3]. "No. No. I'm all right." She fought back the waves of dizziness[4] and made herself straighten up[5]. She pushed away the supporting arms[6] and stared at Erin, deliberately studying the chalky whiteness[7] of her skin, the bruises[8] on her throat. "Erin," she said fiercely[9], "I swear to you I will find Charles North. I give you my word[10] he is going to pay for what he did to you."

The sound of racking sobs echoed[11] in the stark[12] corridor. Darcy realized they were coming from her.

FRIDAY had been an extremely successful day for Jay Stratton. In the morning, he'd stopped at the Bertolini office. Yesterday, when he brought in the necklace, Aldo Marco, the manager, had still been furious at the delay[13]. Today, Marco was singing a different tune[14]. His client was ecstatic. Miss Kelley had certainly executed the concept[15] they had in mind[16] when they'd decided to have the gems reset. They looked forward to continuing[17] to work with her. At Jay's request, the twenty-thousand-dollar check was made out to[18] Jay as Erin Kelley's manager.

From there, Stratton went to the police station to file a complaint[19] about the missing diamonds. The copy of the official report in his hand, he'd headed for[20] the midtown[21] office of his insurance company. The distressed agent[22] told him that Lloyd's of

1. les cils ombrant la joue
2. se sentit partir dans les vapes avec délices
3. la rattrapèrent
4. lutta contre le vertige
5. s'obligea à se redresser
6. repoussa les bras qui la soutenaient
7. le blanc blafard
8. les bleus
9. avec rage
10. te donne ma parole
11. Des sanglots déchirants résonnèrent
12. nu
13. du retard
14. avait changé d'attitude
15. avait réussi à matérialiser le concept
16. qu'ils avaient imaginé
17. avaient hâte de continuer
18. établi à l'ordre de
19. porter plainte
20. s'était rendu
21. du sud de Manhattan
22. L'employée angoissée

London had reinsured[1] this packet of gems. "They'll undoubtedly post a reward[2]," she said nervously. "Lloyd's is getting terribly upset about the theft[3] of jewelry in New York."

At four o'clock, Jay had been in the Stanhope having drinks with Enid Armstrong, a widow who'd answered one of his personal ads. He'd listened attentively as she told him about her overwhelming loneliness[4]. "It's been a year," she'd said, her eyes glistening. "You know, people are sympathetic and they take you out occasionally[5], but it's a fact of life that the world goes two-by-two and an extra[6] woman is a nuisance[7]. I went on a Caribbean cruise[8] alone last month. It was absolutely miserable[9]."

Jay made the appropriate clucking sounds of understanding[10] and reached for her hand. Armstrong was mildly pretty, in her late fifties, good clothes but no style. He'd run into the type often enough.[11] Married young. Stayed home. Raised the kids and joined the country club. Husband who became successful but mowed his own lawn[12]. The kind of guy who made sure his wife was well provided for[13] after he keeled over[14].

Jay studied Armstrong's wedding and engagement rings[15]. All the diamonds were top quality. The solitaire was a beauty. "Your husband was very generous," he commented.

"I got these for our twenty-fifth anniversary[16]. You should have seen the pinpoint[17] he gave me when we got engaged[18]. We were such kids[19]." More glistening eyes.[20]

Jay signaled for another glass of champagne. By the time he left Enid Armstrong, she was excited about his suggestion that they get together next week. She'd even agreed to consider having him redesign her rings. "I'd like to see you with one im-

1. réassuré
2. Ils proposeront sûrement une récompense
3. le vol
4. à quel point elle se sentait seule
5. vous proposent des sorties de temps en temps
6. non accompagnée
7. c'est empoisonnant
8. croisière aux Caraïbes
9. déprimant
10. répondit par les onomatopées compatissantes de circonstance
11. Il avait souvent rencontré ce type de femmes.
12. qui est resté simple
13. serait à l'abri financièrement
14. après sa mort
15. l'alliance et la bague de fiançailles
16. anniversaire de mariage
17. le minuscule solitaire
18. nous nous sommes fiancés
19. si jeunes
20. De nouveau la larme à l'œil.

portant ring that incorporates all these stones. The solitaire and baguettes[1] in the center, banded on either side[2] by alternating diamonds and emeralds. We'll use the diamonds in your wedding ring and I can get some fine quality emeralds for you at a very reasonable price."

Over a quiet dinner at the Water Club, he pondered the pleasure of substituting a cubic zirconia for[3] the solitaire in Armstrong's ring. Some of them were so good even a jeweler's naked eye could be fooled[4]. But of course he'd have the new ring appraised[5] for her with the solitaire still in place. Amazing how single women fell for that[6]. "How thoughtful of you[7] to take care of the appraisal[8] for me. I'll take it right to my insurance company."

He lingered[9] at the bar of the Water Club after dinner. Good to relax. The business of being attentive and charming[10] with these old girls was exhausting even though the results were lucrative.

It was nine-thirty when he walked the few blocks from the restaurant back to his apartment. At ten he was wearing pajamas and a robe[11] newly purchased at Armani's. He settled on the couch with a bourbon on the rocks and turned on the news.

The glass shook in Stratton's trembling hands and liquor spilled unheeded on[12] his robe as he stared at the screen[13] and learned of the discovery of the body of Erin Kelley.

Michael Nash wondered ruefully[14] if he should offer free analysis to Anne Thayer, the blonde who so unfortunately[15] had bought the apartment next to his. When he left the office at ten of six on

1. des pierres taillées en rectangle
2. bordés de part et d'autre
3. savoura la perspective de substituer par un zircon
4. qu'à l'œil nu, même un bijoutier n'y voyait que du feu
5. il ferait évaluer la nouvelle bague
6. tombaient dans le piège
7. Comme c'est gentil de votre part
8. de vous occuper de l'évaluation
9. s'attarda
10. Passer son temps à se montrer attentionné et charmant
11. peignoir
12. il ne prêta aucune attention au cognac qui éclaboussa
13. l'écran
14. tristement
15. à son grand regret,

Friday afternoon, she was at the desk in the lobby, speaking to the concierge. As soon as she saw him, she dashed to[1] stand beside him and wait for the elevator. On the way up, she chatted[2] nonstop, as though she was on a countdown[3] to ensnare him[4] before they reached the twentieth floor.

"I went over to Zabar's today and got the most marvelous salmon. Fixed a platter of hors d'œuvres. My girlfriend was supposed to come over but can't make it[5]. Can't bear to see them go to waste.[6] I was wondering ..."

Nash cut her off[7]. "Zabar's salmon is great. Put it away.[8] It'll keep[9] for a few days." He was aware of the commiserating glance[10] of the elevator operator[11]. "Ramon, I'll see you in a few minutes. I'm on my way out.[12]"

He said a firm good night to the crestfallen[13] Miss Thayer and disappeared into his own apartment. He *was* going out, but not for an hour or so. And if he bumped into her then[14], maybe she'd start to get the message to leave him alone. "Dependent personality, probably neurotic, could get vicious[15] when crossed[16]," he said aloud, then laughed. Hey, I'm off work[17]. Forget it.

He was spending the weekend in Bridgewater. There was a dinner party at the Balderstons' tomorrow night. They always had interesting guests[18]. More important, he intended to use the better part of the next two days[19] working on his book. Nash acknowledged to himself[20] that he'd become so interested in the project that he was becoming impatient with distractions[21].

Just before he left, he tried Erin Kelley's number. He half-smiled as he heard the message in her lilting[22] voice: "This is Erin. Sorry to miss your call. Please leave a message."

1. se précipita pour
2. jacassa
3. faisait un contre-la-montre
4. pour le séduire
5. ne pourra pas venir
6. Je ne supporte l'idée d'un tel gâchis.
7. l'interrompit
8. Mettez-le au frigo.
9. Il se gardera
10. sentait bien le regard compatissant
11. du liftier
12. Je suis sur le point de ressortir.
13. toute déçue
14. tombait à nouveau sur elle à ce moment-là
15. devenir agressive
16. en cas de contrariété
17. je ne suis plus au travail
18. des invités
19. consacrer la majeure partie du week-end à
20. s'avoua
21. qu'il supportait de moins en moins ce qui l'en détournait
22. mélodieuse

"This is Michael Nash. I'm sorry to miss you, too, Erin. Tried you the other day. Guess you're away. Hope there isn't a problem with your father." He left his office and home number again.

The drive to Bridgewater on Friday night was as usual a traffic-clogged nuisance[1]. It was only when he passed Paterson on Route 80 that it began to let up[2]. Then with each mile the terrain became more countrylike[3]. Nash felt himself begin to relax. By the time he had driven through the gate of Scotshays, he had a total sense of well-being[4].

His father had bought the estate[5] when Michael was eleven. Four hundred acres[6] of gardens, woods, and fields. Swimming pool, tennis courts, stable[7]. The house copied from a manor in Brittany[8]. Stone walls, red-tiled roof[9], green shutters[10], white portico[11]. Twenty-two rooms in all. Half of them Michael hadn't bothered with in years[12]. Irma and John Hughes, the housekeeping couple[13], ran the place[14] for him.

Irma had dinner waiting[15]. She served it in the study. Michael settled in his favorite old leather[16] armchair to study the notes he would use tomorrow when he wrote the next chapter of his book. That chapter would concentrate on the psychological problems of people who, when they answered personal ads, sent in pictures of themselves that had been taken twenty-five years ago. He would concentrate on what factors made them try that ploy[17] and how they explained themselves when the date showed up[18].

That sort of thing had happened to a number of the girls he had interviewed. A couple of them had been indignant[19]. Some had been downright funny describing the encounter[20].

1. comme d'habitude un trajet embouteillé pénible
2. que la circulation devint plus fluide
3. rural
4. se sentait parfaitement détendu
5. la propriété
6. 160 hectares
7. une écurie
8. Bretagne
9. un toit de tuiles rouges
10. des volets
11. un porche
12. depuis des lustres
13. un couple de gens de maison
14. tenaient la maison
15. préparé le dîner
16. en vieux cuir
17. ce stratagème
18. l'autre arrivait au rendez-vous
19. outrées
20. avaient raconté la rencontre de façon hilarante

At quarter of ten, Michael turned the television on in anticipation of the news, then went back to his notes. The name Erin Kelley made him look up[1], startled[2]. He grabbed the remote control and pressed the volume frantically[3], causing the announcer's voice to shout through the room.

When the segment was finished, Michael flipped off the set[4] and stared at the dark screen.

"Erin," he said aloud, "who could do that to you?"

1. lui fit lever les yeux
2. stupéfait
3. avec frénésie
4. éteignit la télé

Doug Fox stopped for a drink at Harry's Bar on Friday evening before heading home to Scarsdale. It was a watering hole[5] for the Wall Street crowd[6]. As usual the bar was four deep[7] and the news on the television set was ignored. Doug did not see the bulletin[8] about the body that had been found on the pier.

If she was sure he was coming home, Susan usually fed the kids first[9], then waited to eat with him, but tonight, when he arrived at eight, Susan was in the den reading[10]. She barely raised her eyes when he came into the room and turned away from the kiss he tried to press on her forehead[11].

Donny and Beth had gone to the movies[12] with the Goodwyns, she explained. Trish and the baby were asleep. She did not offer to prepare anything for him. Her eyes went back to her book.

For a moment Doug stood uncertainly over her[13], then turned and went into the kitchen. She had to pull this attitude act[14] the one night I'm hungry, he thought bitterly[15]. She's just sore[16] because I didn't get home for a couple of nights and was so late last night. He opened the door of the refrigerator. The

5. un bar
6. traders
7. le bar était pris d'assaut
8. flash spécial
9. faisait dîner les enfants d'abord
10. dans le petit salon en train de lire
11. détourna la tête quand il voulut l'embrasser sur le front
12. au cinéma
13. resta debout à côté d'elle, un peu décontenancé
14. Elle avait choisi de faire la tête
15. avec amertume
16. Elle m'en veut juste

one thing Susan could do was cook.[1] With mounting anger[2] he decided that when he was able to make it home[3], the least she could do was to have[4] something ready for him.

He yanked out[5] packets of ham and cheese and went to the bread box. The weekly community newspaper[6] was on the kitchen table. Doug made a sandwich, poured[7] a beer, and began to skim the paper[8] as he ate. The sports page caught his eye[9]. Scarsdale had unexpectedly defeated[10] Dobbs Ferry in the midschool tournament[11]. The sudden-death winning basket[12] had been sunk[13] by second-stringer[14] Donald Fox.

Donny! Why didn't anyone tell him?

Doug felt his palms begin to sweat[15]. Had Susan tried to phone him Tuesday night? Donny had been disappointed and sullen[16] when Doug told him he couldn't make the[17] game. It would be just like[18] Susan to suggest they call with the news[19].

Tuesday night. Wednesday night.

The new telephone operator at the hotel. She wasn't like the young kids who willingly accepted the hundred bucks[20] he slipped them from time to time[21]. "Remember, any calls come in for me[22] when I'm not here, I'm in a meeting. If it's real late, I left a do-not-disturb."

The new operator looked like she posed for a moral majority ad[23]. He'd been still trying to figure out[24] how to snow her into lying[25] for him. He hadn't worried too much, however. He'd trained Susan not to phone him when he stayed in "for meetings."

But she *had* tried him Tuesday night. He was sure of it. Otherwise, she'd have had Donny phone him at the office Wednesday afternoon. And that dumb operator[26] had probably told her there was no meeting and no one was staying in the company suite.

1. La seule chose qu'elle fasse bien, c'était la cuisine.
2. De plus en plus énervé,
3. arrivait à rentrer tôt
4. la moindre des choses serait qu'elle ait
5. sortit rageusement
6. l'hebdo local
7. se versa
8. lire le journal en diagonale
9. attira son attention
10. à la surprise de tous, gagné le match contre
11. tournoi
12. panier gagnant [départageant 2 équipes]
13. marqué
14. le remplaçant
15. ses mains devenir moites
16. pris un air renfrogné
17. assister au
18. Ce serait bien le genre de
19. pour lui annoncer la nouvelle
20. prenaient volontiers les 100 $
21. qu'il leur glissait à l'occasion
22. si on m'appelle
23. avait l'air de sortir d'une affiche bien-pensante
24. de réfléchir à
25. la convaincre de mentir
26. gourde de standardiste

Doug looked around the kitchen. It was surprisingly neat[1]. They'd had the whole house renovated when they bought it eight years ago. The kitchen was a chef's dream. Center island[2] with sink and chopping board[3]. Plenty of counter space. Latest appliances.[4] Skylight.[5]

Susan's old man[6] had lent them the money for the renovation. He'd also lent them most of the down payment[7]. *Lent.* Not given.

If Susan got really sore[8] …

Doug tossed[9] the rest of the sandwich in the compactor[10] and brought his beer into the den.

Susan watched him enter the room. My handsome husband, she thought. She'd deliberately left[11] the newspaper on the table, knowing Doug would probably read it. Now he's sweating bullets[12]. He figured I probably called the hotel to let Donny give him the news. Funny, when you finally faced reality, it was amazing how clearly you could see things.

Doug sat on the couch opposite her. He's afraid to give me an opening[13], she decided. Tucking her book[14] under her arm, she got up. "The kids will be back about half past ten," she told him. "I'm going to read in bed."

"I'll wait for them, honey[15]."

Honey! He must be worried.

Susan settled in bed with the book. Then, knowing she was not able to focus on the print,[16] she laid it down and turned on the television.

Doug came into the bedroom just as the ten o'clock news began. "It's too lonesome out there.[17]" He sat on the bed and reached for her hand. "How's my girl?"

"Good question," Susan said. "How is she?"

1. bien rangé
2. Un îlot central
3. une planche à découper
4. Des appareils ménagers dernier cri.
5. Velux.
6. Le père
7. l'apport personnel
8. prenait les choses très mal
9. lança
10. la poubelle [avec compacteur de déchets]
11. avait fait exprès de laisser
12. il a les jetons
13. l'opportunité de lui dire ce que je pense
14. Son livre
15. chérie
16. se concentrer sur le texte
17. Je m'ennuie tout seul là-bas.

He attempted to pass it off as a joke[1]. Tilting her chin[2], he said, "She looks pretty good to me."

They both turned to watch the screen as the anchorman gave the headline news. "Erin Kelley, a prize-winning[3] young jewelry designer, was found strangled on the West Fifty-sixth Street pier. More after this."

A commercial.[4]

Susan glanced at Doug. He was staring at the screen, his pallor a ghastly white[5]. "Doug, what is it?"

He did not seem to have heard her.

"… Police are searching for Petey Potters, a drifter[6] who was known to have been living in this shack and may have observed the body when it was abandoned on this cold, debris-strewn[7] pier."

When the segment was completed[8], Doug turned to Susan. As though he had just heard her question, he snapped, "Nothing's the matter. Nothing." Beads of perspiration[9] were forming on his forehead.

At three in the morning, Susan was awakened from her own uneasy sleep[10] by Doug thrashing[11] beside her. He was mumbling[12] something. A name? "… no, can't …" The name again. Susan propped herself up[13] on one arm and listened intently.

Erin. That was it. The name of the young woman who'd been found murdered.

She was about to shake Doug awake when he suddenly quieted[14]. With growing horror[15], Susan realized why the newscast had so upset him[16]. Undoubtedly, he'd linked it to[17] that terrible time in college when he was one of the students questioned[18] about the girl who had been strangled.

1. de le prendre comme une blague
2. Lui relevant le menton
3. déjà primée
4. Une pub.
5. livide
6. un vagabond
7. couverte de débris
8. Une fois le reportage terminé
9. Des perles de sueur
10. tirée de son sommeil agité
11. qui se débattait
12. marmonnait
13. se souleva
14. mais il se tut d'un coup
15. De plus en plus horrifiée
16. l'avait ému à ce point
17. fait le rapprochement avec
18. interrogé par la police

VI
SATURDAY
February 23

On Saturday morning, Charley read the *New York Post* with intense fascination. COPYCAT MURDER[1] was the banner-sized headline[2].

The similarity of Erin Kelley's death to the *True Crimes* program about Nan Sheridan was the focus of the story[3] on the inside pages[4].

Someone had tipped an investigative reporter[5] from the *Post* about the letter to Nan Sheridan's mother warning that a young woman from New York would be murdered on Tuesday night. The reporter, quoting an unidentified source[6], wrote that the FBI was on the trail[7] of a possible serial killer. In the past two years, seven young women from Manhattan had disappeared after answering personal ads. Erin Kelley had been answering personal ads.

The circumstances of Nan Sheridan's death were rehashed in full[8].

Erin Kelley's background[9]; interviews with colleagues in the jewelry business. Their responses identical. Erin was a warm, lovely person, immensely talented. The picture the *Post* used was the one Erin had sent Charley. That delighted him.[10]

The network was going to repeat[11] the *True Crimes* episode about Nan's death Wednesday night. That would be so interesting to watch. Of

1. Meurtre à l'identique
2. disait la une du journal
3. était au centre de l'article
4. à l'intérieur
5. informé un journaliste d'investigation
6. qui citait une source anonyme
7. sur les traces
8. à nouveau exposées dans leur intégralité
9. Les origines et l'enfance
10. Il en fut ravi.
11. repasser

course he'd taped it[1] last month, but even so[2], to see it again, knowing that hundreds of thousands of people[3] would be playing amateur detective. *Who did it? Who was smart enough to get away with it[4]?*

Charley frowned. *Copycat.*

Copycat meant they thought someone else was imitating him. Anger rushed through him, stark, raging anger[5]. They had no right[6] not to credit him[7]. Just as Nan had had no right not to invite him to her party fifteen years ago.

He'd go back to the secret place in the next few days. He needed to be there. He'd turn on the video and dance in step with[8] Astaire. It wouldn't be Ginger, or Leslie, or Ann Miller in his arms.

His heart began beating faster.[9] This time it wouldn't even be Nan. It would be Darcy.

He picked up Darcy's picture. The soft brown hair, the slender body, the wide, inquiring eyes[10]. How much lovelier would that body be when he held it, rigid and cold in his arms?

Copycat.

Again he frowned. The anger was pounding at his temples[11], causing one of the terrible headaches to begin[12]. It is I, Charley, alone[13] who has the power of life and death over[14] these women. I, Charley, broke through the prison of the other soul[15] and now dominate him at will[16].

He would take Darcy and crush the life from her[17] as he had crushed it from the others. And he would confound the authorities with his genius[18], confuse[19] and bewilder their tiresome minds[20].

Copycat.

The people who wrote that should see the shoe boxes in the basement. Then they'd know. Those boxes that contained one shoe and one dancing

1. il l'avait enregistré
2. quand même
3. des centaines de milliers de gens
4. avait été assez habile pour ne pas se faire prendre
5. une colère noire
6. Ils n'avaient aucun droit
7. de ne pas lui attribuer ce meurtre
8. en rythme avec
9. Les battements de son cœur s'accélérèrent.
10. ses grands yeux curieux
11. faisait battre ses tempes
12. déclenchant un de ces terribles maux de tête
13. moi seul, Charley,
14. ai droit de vie et de mort sur
15. qui ai réussi à m'extirper de l'autre âme
16. à volonté
17. lui arracher le dernier souffle de vie
18. son génie allait déconcerter les forces de l'ordre
19. embrouiller
20. dérouter ces gens horripilants

slipper from the foot of each of the dead girls beginning with Nan.

Of course.

There was a way to prove he wasn't a copycat. His body shook with silent, mirthless laughter.[1]

Oh yes, indeed. There was a way.

1. Il fut secoué d'un rire étouffé et forcé.

VII
SATURDAY
February 23
THROUGH
TUESDAY
February 26

THE NEXT WEEK for Darcy passed as though she was a robot who had been wound up[1] and programmed to perform specific tasks.

Accompanied by Vince D'Ambrosio and a detective from the local precinct[2], she went to Erin's apartment on Saturday. There were three more calls that had been received after she'd been[3] in the apartment on Friday morning. Darcy rewound[4] the answering machine. One was from the manager at Bertolini's. "Miss Kelley, we gave your check to your manager, Mr. Stratton. We cannot tell you how pleased we are with the necklace.[5]"

Darcy raised her eyebrows. "I never heard Erin refer to Stratton as her manager[6]."

The second call was from someone who identified himself as Box 2695. "Erin, it's Milton. We went out[7] last month. I've been away[8]. I'd like to see you again. My phone number is 555-3681. And listen, I'm sorry if I came on a little too strong[9] last time."

The third call was from Michael Nash. "He left a message the other night," Darcy said.

Vince copied the names and numbers. "We'll leave the tape on for the next few days."

Vince had told Darcy that forensics experts[10] from the NYPD would arrive shortly[11] to go over[12] Erin's apartment for possible evidence[13]. She had asked

1. un robot mécanique que l'on avait remonté
2. commissariat
3. depuis qu'elle était passée
4. rembobina
5. Nous sommes enchantés du collier.
6. dire que Stratton était son agent
7. On a passé une soirée ensemble
8. absent
9. je me suis montré un peu trop entreprenant
10. l'équipe médico-légale
11. n'allait pas tarder à arriver
12. pour examiner
13. à la recherche d'indices

Vince if she could come with him and get Erin's private papers[1]. "My name is on her bank account[2] and insurance policies as trustee for[3] her father. She told me the papers were in her file under his name."

Erin's instructions were simple and explicit. If anything happened to Erin, as agreed, Darcy would use her insurance to pay nursing home expenses[4]. She had contracted[5] with a funeral director[6] in Wellesley that when the time came[7] he would handle her father's arrangements[8]. Everything in her apartment, all her personal jewelry and clothing, were left to Darcy Scott.

There was a brief note for Darcy: "Darce, this is surely a just-in-case[9]. But I know you'll keep your promise to look after[10] Dad if I'm not around[11]. And if that ever should happen[12], thanks for all the great times we had together, and have fun for both of us."

Dry-eyed[13], Darcy looked at the familiar signature.

"I hope you'll follow her advice[14]," Vince said quietly.

"I will someday," Darcy told him. "But not yet. Would you make a copy for me of that personal ads file I gave you?"

"Sure," Vince said, "but why? We're going to look up[15] the people who placed the ads she circled."

"But you're not going to date them. She answered some ads for both of us. Maybe I'll get calls from people who took her out."

Darcy left as the forensics crew[16] arrived. She went directly home and began to make phone calls. The funeral director in Wellesley. Sympathy[17], then practicality[18]. He would send a hearse[19] to the morgue when Erin's body was released[20]. What about clothing? Open casket?[21]

Darcy thought about the bruises[22] on Erin's throat. Undoubtedly, there'd be media at the funeral parlor.

1. les documents personnels
2. son compte en banque
3. en qualité de tutrice de
4. pour payer les frais de la maison de retraite médicalisée
5. établi un contrat
6. un entrepreneur des pompes funèbres
7. pour que, le moment venu,
8. l'enterrement de son père soit pris en charge
9. juste au cas où
10. t'occuper de
11. si je ne suis plus là
12. si cela devait se produire un jour
13. Sans verser une larme
14. ses conseils
15. se renseigner sur
16. équipe
17. Quelques mots de condoléances
18. les détails pratiques
19. un corbillard
20. on aurait le permis d'inhumer
21. Cercueil ouvert ?
22. les bleus

1. de quoi l'habiller
2. Le recueillement avant la levée du corps est prévu
3. La messe d'enterrement,
4. d'une voix tremblante
5. qu'elle avait en tête
6. si peu à la hauteur
7. mes parents
8. un tailleur griffé
9. avait vachement d'allure
10. ses propres bijoux
11. Vaguement
12. à être plus audacieuse dans ma façon de m'habiller
13. à se fier à son instinct
14. sortit
15. une veste ajustée
16. et une jupe fluide en mousseline de soie rose et argentée
17. une soirée de bienfaisance
18. exécutait les danses de salon à merveille
19. encore une chose que nous avions en commun
20. les pupilles de Darcy soient si dilatées

"Closed casket. I'll bring up clothing for her[1]." Visitation[2] on Monday. Funeral mass[3] on Tuesday at St. Paul's.

St. Paul's. When she'd stayed with Erin and Billy, she had gone to St. Paul's with them.

She went back to Erin's apartment. Vince D'Ambrosio was still there. He accompanied her into the bedroom and watched as she opened the closet door.

"Erin had so much style," Darcy said unsteadily[4] as she searched for the dress she had in mind[5]. "She used to tell me that she felt so out of it[6] when I walked in the room with my folks[7] that first day at college. I was wearing a designer suit[8] and Italian boots my mother had forced on me. I thought she looked smashing[9] in chinos and a sweater and marvelous jewelry. Even then she was designing her own pieces[10]."

Vince was a good listener. Abstractly[11], Darcy was aware that she was glad he was letting her talk. "No one's going to see her," she said, "except maybe I will, just for a minute. But I want to feel that she'd be pleased with what I chose for her. ... Erin urged me to be more daring about clothes[12]. I taught her to trust her own instincts[13]. She had impeccable taste."

She pulled out[14] a two-piece cocktail dress: pale pink fitted jacket[15], delicate silver buttons, flowing pink and silver chiffon skirt[16]. "Erin just bought this to wear to a benefit[17], a dinner dance. She was a wonderful ballroom dancer[18]. That was something else we shared[19]. Nona too. We met Nona in a ballroom dancing class at our health club."

Vince remembered Nona had told him that. "From what you tell me, this dress sounds like something Erin would want to wear now."

He didn't like the fact that Darcy's pupils were so enlarged[20]. He wished he could call Nona Roberts. She had told him she absolutely had to be on a shoot[1] in Nanuet today. Darcy Scott ought not to be alone too much[2].

Darcy realized she could read D'Ambrosio's thoughts. She also realized there was no use[3] reassuring him. The best service she could perform[4] was to get out of here and let the fingerprint experts[5] and God knows who else[6] do their thing[7]. She tried to make her voice and manner matter-of-fact as she asked[8], "What are you doing to find the man Erin was meeting Tuesday night?"

"We've found Charles North. What Erin told you checks out[9]. It was a lucky break[10] you happened to ask her about him. He moved[11] last month from a law firm[12] in Philadelphia to one on Park Avenue. He left yesterday for a trip to Germany. We'll be waiting for him when he gets back Monday. Detectives from this precinct are going around pubs and bars in the Washington Square area with Erin's picture. We want to see if some bartender[13] or waiter[14] can remember seeing her on Tuesday evening and possibly can identify North when we get him."

Darcy nodded. "I'm going to Wellesley. I'll stay there till after the funeral."

"Nona Roberts is going to join you there?"

"On Tuesday morning. She can't get up[15] before then." Darcy tried to smile. "Please don't worry. Erin had loads of[16] friends. I've heard from[17] so many of the Mount Holyoke grads[18]. They'll be there. So will a lot of our buddies[19] from New York. And she lived in Wellesley all her life. I'm staying with[20] the people who used to be her next-door neighbors[21]."

She went home to pack[22]. A call came from Australia. Her mother and father. "Darling, if only we

1. tournage
2. ne devrait pas passer trop de temps toute seule
3. que ça ne servait à rien
4. Ce qu'elle avait de mieux à faire
5. les experts d'empreintes digitales
6. Dieu sait qui d'autre
7. faire ce qu'ils avaient à faire
8. demander d'un air détaché
9. semble coller
10. On a eu la chance
11. a quitté
12. un cabinet d'avocats
13. un barman
14. un serveur
15. ne peut pas venir
16. plein d'
17. J'ai été contactée par
18. diplômés
19. nos potes
20. Je vais être logée par
21. ses plus proches voisins
22. pour faire sa valise

could be with you. You know we thought of Erin as our second daughter."

"I know." *If only we could be with you.* How many times had she heard that over the years? Birthdays. Graduations.[1] But there had been lots of times when they *were* with her. Any other kid would have been so happy to have the golden[2] couple as parents. Why had she been a throwback[3] to the cottage-with-a-picket-fence mentality[4]? "It's so good to talk with you. How's the play going?"

Now they were on safe ground.[5]

The funeral was a media event. Photographers and cameras. Neighbors and friends. Curiosity seekers.[6] Vince had told her that hidden cameras would be recording[7] everyone who came to the funeral parlor, the church, and the interment[8], in case Erin's killer was there.

The white-haired Monsignor[9] who had known Erin all her life. "Who can forget the sight of[10] that little girl pushing her father's wheelchair into this church?"

The soloist[11]. "… All I ask of you is forever to remember me as loving you …"

The interment. "When every tear shall be wiped away[12] …"

The hours she spent with Billy. I'm glad you don't know, she thought. Holding his hand.. If he understands anything, I hope he thinks it's Erin with him.

Tuesday afternoon the Pan Am shuttle[13] back to New York, Nona beside her. "Can you take a couple of days off[14], Darce?" Nona asked. "This has been a pretty awful[15] time for you."

"As soon as I know they have Charles North in custody[16], I will go away for a week. A couple of

1. Remises de diplômes.
2. de rêve
3. pour eux un renvoi
4. à la petite maison Sam'suffit
5. Là on était en terrain moins délicat.
6. Des curieux.
7. filmeraient
8. l'inhumation
9. prêtre
10. pourrait oublier l'image de
11. soliste
12. Dieu essuiera toute larme de leurs yeux [Bible, Apocalypse de saint Jean]
13. navette
14. quelques jours de congé
15. très difficile
16. je saurai que Charles North a été arrêté

my friends have a condo[1] in St. Thomas. They want me to visit."

Nona hesitated. "That's not the way it's going to work[2], Darcy. Vince called me last night. They picked up Charles North.[3] Last Tuesday evening he was in a board meeting[4] at his law firm with twenty partners[5]. Whoever met[6] Erin was using his name[7]."

AFTER HE SAW the broadcast and spoke to Chief Moore, Chris decided to go to Darien for the weekend. He wanted to be around[8] when the FBI talked to his mother.

He knew Greta was planning to attend a black-tie dinner[9] at the club. He stopped to eat at Nicola's, arrived at the house around ten and decided to watch a film. A classic movie buff[10], he put on *Bridge of San Luis Rey* and then wondered at his choice. The idea of lives drawn together to one particular moment in time[11] always intrigued him. How much was fate?[12] How much was happenstance?[13] Was there some kind of inevitable, inexorable plan to it all?

He heard the whirring of[14] the garage door shortly before midnight and walked to the head of the basement stairs[15] to wait for Greta, wishing once again that she had live-in help[16]. He did not like the idea of her coming into this big house alone late at night.

Greta adamantly[17] refused that suggestion. Dorothy, the daily housekeeper of three decades[18], suited her fine[19]. That and the weekly cleaning service. If she had a dinner party, her caterer[20] was excellent. And that was that[21].

1. un appartement
2. comme ça que ça va se dérouler
3. North a été interpellé.
4. à une réunion du conseil d'administration
5. associés
6. Celui qui a rencontré
7. se faisait passer pour lui
8. là
9. d'assister à un dîner habillé
10. Amateur de grands classiques
11. se croisant à un moment précis
12. Quelle était la part du destin ?
13. Quelle était la part du hasard ?
14. s'ouvrir
15. alla en haut de l'escalier du sous-sol
16. ait une aide à domicile à plein temps
17. catégoriquement
18. gouvernante de la maison depuis trente ans
19. lui convenait très bien
20. traiteur
21. voilà tout

As she approached the stairs, he called down, "Hi, Mother."

Her gasp was audible.[1] "What! Oh dear God, Chris. You startled me.[2] I'm a bundle of nerves.[3]" She looked up, trying to smile. "I was so glad to see your car." In the dim light her fine-boned face reminded him of Nan's delicate features[4]. Her hair, shimmering silver, was pulled back in a French knot[5]. A sable[6] jacket fell loosely[7] from her shoulders. She was wearing a long black velvet sheath[8]. Greta would be sixty on her next birthday. An elegant, beautiful woman whose smile never fully removed the sadness from her eyes.

It suddenly struck Chris that his mother always appeared to be poised waiting or listening for something[9], some sort of signal. When he was a kid, his grandfather had told him a World War I story about a soldier who had lost the message warning of an imminent enemy attack. Afterward[10] the soldier always blamed himself[11] for the terrible casualties[12] and went through life[13] looking in gutters[14] and under stones for the lost message.

Over a nightcap[15], he told Greta about Erin Kelley and understood why the simile had occurred to him[16]. Greta always felt that there was something Nan had told her before she died that had set off an instinctive alarm[17]. Last week, once again, she had received a warning and been powerless to prevent a tragedy[18].

"The girl they found had a high-heeled evening shoe on?" Greta asked. "Like Nan? The sort of shoe you would dance in? That note said a dancing girl would die."

Chris chose his words carefully. "Erin Kelley was a jewelry designer. From what I understand[19], the feeling is that[20] this is a copycat murder. Somebody

1. Elle eut un hoquet de surprise.
2. Tu m'as fait peur.
3. J'ai les nerfs en boule.
4. les traits
5. remonté en chignon
6. en zibeline
7. lui tombait
8. fourreau
9. donnait toujours l'impression d'attendre quelque chose ou de tendre l'oreille
10. Plus tard,
11. s'était toujours senti responsable
12. nombre de victimes
13. avait passé sa vie à
14. dans les caniveaux
15. En buvant un petit verre avec elle
16. la comparaison lui était venue
17. qui avait instinctivement suscité son inquiétude
18. mais n'avait rien pu faire pour éviter un drame
19. D'après ce que j'ai compris
20. la police pense que

got the idea from watching that *True Crimes* program. An FBI agent wants to talk to us about it."

Chief Moore phoned on Saturday. An FBI agent, Vincent D'Ambrosio, would like to drop in on[1] the Sheridans on Sunday.

Chris was glad that D'Ambrosio emphasized[2] that no one could have acted on[3] the letter Greta had received. "Mrs. Sheridan," he told her, "we get tips[4] much more specific than that one and still can't prevent a tragedy from happening."

Vince asked Chris to walk outside with him. "The Darien police have the files on your sister's death," he explained. "They're going to copy them for me. Would you mind taking me[5] to the exact place where she was found?"

They walked down the road that led from the Sheridan property to the wooded area with the jogging path. The trees had grown higher, their branches thicker in the fifteen years, but otherwise[6], Chris commented, the place was pretty much the same.

A bucolic scene in a wealthy town, contrasted with[7] an abandoned West Side pier. Nan Sheridan had been a nineteen-year-old kid. A student. A jogger. Erin Kelley was a twenty-eight-year-old career woman[8]. Nan had come from a well-to-do social family[9]. Erin was on her own[10]. The only two similarities were in the manner of death and the footwear[11]. They both had been strangled. They both had been wearing one fancy[12] shoe. Vince asked Chris if while Nan was at school, she did any blind dating through personal ads[13].

Chris smiled. "Believe me, Nan had enough guys flocking around[14] that she didn't need to[15] answer

1. passer voir
2. insiste sur le fait
3. prendre de mesures à la suite de
4. nous recevons des informations
5. ça vous ennuierait de m'emmener
6. à part ça
7. à l'opposé d'
8. jeune professionnelle
9. d'un milieu très aisé
10. seule
11. leurs chaussures
12. chic
13. des rencontres par petites annonces
14. qui lui tournaient autour
15. pour ne pas avoir à

ads to get a date. Anyhow[1], there was none of that personal-ads stuff when we were in college."

"You went to Brown?"

"Nan did. I was at Williams."

"I assume any special boyfriends were checked out[2]?"

They were walking along the path that threaded through the woods[3]. Chris stopped. "This is where I found her." He shoved his hands[4] in the pockets of his windbreaker[5]. "Nan thought anyone who got tied up[6] with one guy was crazy. She was something of a flirt[7]. She liked to have a good time. She never willingly missed a party[8], and she danced every dance."

Vince turned to face him[9]. "This is important. You're sure the fancy slipper your sister was wearing when she was found was not one of her own[10]."

"Absolutely. Nan hated spike heels[11]. She simply wouldn't have bought that shoe. And of course, there was no trace of[12] the mate in her closet."

As he drove back to New York, Vince continued to weigh the comparisons and differences[13] between Nan Sheridan and Erin Kelley. It's got to be a copycat murder, he told himself. *Dancing girl.* That's what was bugging him[14]. The note Greta Sheridan had received. Nan Sheridan had danced every dance. Had that come out[15] on the *True Crimes* program? Erin Kelley had met Nona Roberts in a dancing class. Was it a coincidence?

1. En tout cas
2. ont été interrogés à l'époque
3. s'enfonçait dans les bois
4. fourra les mains
5. coupe-vent
6. se mettre en couple
7. aimait faire du charme
8. ne ratait jamais une fête volontairement
9. se retourna face à lui
10. ne lui appartenait pas
11. détestait les talons pointus
12. on n'a jamais trouvé
13. évaluer les points communs et les différences
14. ce qui le tracassait
15. Cela avait-il été mentionné

ON TUESDAY afternoon, Charles North was interrogated for the second time by Vincent D'Ambrosio. He had been met at Kennedy Airport on Monday evening and his astonishment[1] at being greeted[2] by two FBI agents had been quickly replaced by anger. "I never heard of Erin Kelley. I never answered a personal ad. I think they're ridiculous. I cannot imagine who would use my name."

It was a simple matter[3] to ascertain[4] that North had been in a board meeting at seven o'clock on the previous[5] Tuesday evening, the hour Erin Kelley supposedly planned[6] to meet him.

This time the questioning was[7] in FBI headquarters on Federal Plaza. North was of medium height[8] with a stocky build[9]. A slightly florid face suggested a three-martini drinker.[10] Nevertheless[11], Vince decided, he had a distinct air of authority and sophistication that probably appealed to women[12]. Forty years old, he had been married twelve years prior to[13] his recent divorce. He made it very clear[14] that he deeply resented the request that he drop in[15] at Vince's office for a second interview.

"I think you must understand that I have just become a partner in a prestigious law firm. It certainly will be a great embarrassment[16] if I am in any way linked to that young woman's death. An embarrassment for me personally and most certainly for my firm[17]."

"I'm very sorry to embarrass you, Mr. North," Vince said coldly. "I can assure you that at this moment you are not a suspect in Erin Kelley's death.

1. sa surprise
2. de se voir accueilli
3. Ce ne fut pas compliqué
4. de vérifier
5. de la semaine précédente
6. avait soi-disant eu l'intention
7. l'interrogatoire eut lieu
8. de taille moyenne,
9. assez trapu
10. Vu son visage rougeaud, il ne lésinait pas sur l'apéro.
11. Néanmoins
12. plaisait aux femmes
13. avant
14. ne cacha pas
15. qu'il n'appréciait pas du tout d'être convoqué
16. Ce serait évidemment très gênant
17. mon cabinet

But Erin Kelley is dead, the victim of a brutal[1] homicide. It is possible that she is one of a number of young women who have answered personal ads and disappeared. Someone used your name to place that ad. A very clever someone who knew you would have left your Philadelphia firm by the time he arranged to meet Erin Kelley."

"Will you please tell me why that would matter to anyone[2]?" North snapped.

"Because some women who answer personal ads are smart enough to check out the man they agree to date. Suppose[3] Erin Kelley's killer thought she might be that careful[4]. What better name to use than someone who had just left his law firm in Philadelphia to relocate[5] in New York. Suppose Erin had looked you up[6] in the Pennsylvania Bar Register[7] and called your old office. She would have been told that you just left the firm to relocate in New York. She might even have been able to ascertain that you're divorced. Now she has no qualms about[8] meeting Charles North."

Vince leaned forward across[9] his desk. "Like it or not[10], Mr. North, you are a link to Erin Kelley's death. Someone who knows your activities used your name. We're going to be following up a lot of leads[11]. We're going to contact the people whose ads Erin Kelley may have answered. We're going to pump her friends' memories[12] to see if she mentioned any names we don't have. In each and every case[13], we're going to talk to you to see if that person is someone who somehow is connected to you[14]."

North stood up. "I see that I'm being told, not asked. Just one thing. Has my name been released to the media[15]?"

"No, it has not."

1. horrible
2. pourquoi cela aurait de l'importance
3. Imaginons que
4. possible qu'elle prenne cette précaution
5. s'installer
6. ait pris vos coordonnées
7. annuaire des avocats
8. n'a aucune raison de ne pas vouloir
9. se pencha au-dessus de
10. Que ça vous plaise ou non
11. suivre un certain nombre de pistes
12. inciter ses amis à fouiller dans leur mémoire
13. Et à chaque fois
14. a un lien quelconque avec vous
15. communiqué à la presse

"Then see that it isn't[1]. And when you call at the office, don't identify yourself as FBI, Say," he smiled mirthlessly, "say it's personal business. Not personal *ad* business, of course."

When he left, Vince leaned back in his chair[2]. I don't like wise guys[3], he thought. He picked up the intercom[4]. "Betsy, I want a complete background check[5] on Charles North. I mean everything. And here's another one. Gus Boxer, the superintendent at 101 Christopher Street. That's the apartment building where Erin Kelley lived. His face has been bugging me[6] since Saturday. We've got a file on him[7], I'm sure of it."

Vince snapped his fingers. "Wait a minute. That's not his name. I remember. It's *Hoffman*. He was the super[8] ten years ago in the building where a twenty-year-old woman was murdered."

1. faites en sorte que cela ne change pas
2. se radossa dans sa chaise
3. les petits malins
4. appuya sur l'Interphone
5. un profil complet
6. me dit quelque chose
7. Il est fiché
8. gardien

DR. MICHAEL NASH was not surprised when on his return to Manhattan Sunday night there was a call on his answering machine asking him to contact FBI agent Vincent D'Ambrosio. Obviously, they were following up on[9] the people who had left messages for Erin Kelley.

He returned the call on Monday morning and arranged for Vince to stop by[10] before his first appointment on Tuesday.

Vince arrived at Nash's office promptly[11] at 8:15 Tuesday morning. The receptionist was waiting for him and ushered him in to where[12] Nash was already at his desk.

It was a clubby kind of room[13], Vince decided. Several comfortable chairs, walls a sunny yellow[14],

9. contactaient
10. accepta que Vince passe
11. ponctuel,
12. le conduisit dans la pièce où
13. La pièce avait des allures de club sélect
14. d'un jaune lumineux

curtains[1] that let the daylight in[2] but shielded the occupants[3] from the view of passersby[4] on the sidewalk[5]. The traditional couch[6], a leather version of the chaise longue[7] Alice had bought years ago, was at a right angle to the desk.

A restful[8] room, and the expression in the eyes of the man at the desk was both kind and thoughtful[9]. Vince thought of Saturday afternoons. Confession. "Bless me[10], Father, for I have sinned[11]." The transgressions evolved from disobeying[12] his parents to recitation of more lusty offenses[13] in teenage years[14].

It always bothered him to hear someone say that analysis had replaced confession. "In confession you blame yourself," he'd point out. "In analysis you blame everyone else." His own master's degree in psychology had only strengthened[15] that viewpoint[16].

He had the feeling Nash sensed his gut-level hostility[17] to most shrinks[18]. Sensed it and understood it.

They eyed each other[19]. Well-dressed in an unobtrusive way[20], Vince thought. Vince was aware that he was no good at picking out[21] the right tie for his suit[22]. Alice used to do that for him. Not that he cared.[23] He'd rather wear a brown tie with a blue suit than hear her harping at him[24] all the time. "Why don't you leave the Bureau and get a job where you can earn some real money?" Today he'd grabbed the nearest tie[25] and pulled it on in the elevator. It was brown and green. His suit was a blue pinstripe.

Alice was now Mrs. Malcolm Drucker. Malcolm wore Hermès ties and custom-made[26] suits. Recently, Hank told Vince that Malcolm had blown up to size fifty-two[27]. Fifty-two short.

1. des rideaux
2. laissaient passer la lumière du jour
3. cachaient les personnes assises dans la pièce
4. à la vue des passants
5. trottoir
6. traditionnel divan
7. méridienne
8. paisible
9. réfléchie
10. Bénissez-moi
11. car j'ai péché
12. d'avoir désobéi à
13. l'aveu d'offenses moins chastes
14. à l'adolescence
15. n'avait fait que renforcer
16. cette opinion
17. percevait son hostilité instinctive
18. envers la plupart des psys
19. se regardèrent
20. avec discrétion
21. n'était pas doué pour choisir
22. une cravate qui irait avec son costume
23. Ça ne le gênait pas plus que ça.
24. le houspiller
25. la première cravate venue
26. sur mesure
27. tellement grossi qu'il faisait du 62

Nash was wearing a gray tweed jacket, a red and gray tie. Nicelooking guy, Vince conceded. Strong chin, deep-set eyes. Skin a touch windburned[1]. Vince liked a man to look as though he didn't hide indoors[2] in lousy weather[3].

He got right to the point. "Dr. Nash, you left two messages for Erin Kelley. They suggest that you knew her, had dated her. Is that the case?"

"Yes. I am in the process of writing a book analyzing the social phenomenon of the personal ad situation. Kearns and Brown is my publisher[4]; Justin Crowell, my editor[5]."

Just in case I thought he was really trying to get a date, Vince thought, then warned himself to knock it off[6]. "How did you come to go out with Erin Kelley? Did you answer her ad or did she answer yours?"

"She answered mine." Nash reached in his drawer[7]. "I was anticipating your question. Here is the ad she answered. Here is her letter. I met her for a drink on January thirtieth at the Pierre. She was a lovely young woman. I expressed surprise that anyone so attractive would need to seek companionship[8]. She quite frankly told me that she was answering ads at the behest of a friend[9] who is doing a documentary. I don't usually acknowledge[10] that I'm doing research on these meetings, but I was upfront[11] with her."

"And that was the only time you saw her?"

"Yes. I've been terribly busy. I'm almost at the end of my book and wanted to get it finished. I'd planned to call Erin again when I turned it in[12]. Last week I realized that it's going to take another month to complete[13] and rushing it simply didn't work[14]."

"And so you called her."

"Yes, early in the week. Then again last Thursday. No, it was Friday, just before I left for the weekend."

1. un tout petit peu burinée
2. les hommes qui ne donnaient pas l'impression de rester à l'intérieur
3. dès qu'il faisait mauvais
4. la maison d'édition
5. mon éditeur
6. pensa qu'il devrait arrêter d'être si hostile
7. fouilla dans un tiroir
8. ait besoin de passer une annonce de rencontres
9. à la demande d'un(e) ami(e)
10. n'avoue pas d'ordinaire
11. j'ai été honnête
12. une fois que j'aurais remis le manuscrit
13. il va me falloir encore un mois pour le finir
14. que ça ne servait à rien de bâcler

Vince studied the letter Erin had written to Nash. His ad was clipped to it[1]: DWM[2], Physician[3], 37, 6' 1"[4], attractive, successful, good sense of humor. Enjoys skiing, riding, museums, and concerts. Seeking[5] creative, attractive s/d/wf[6]. Box 3295.

Erin's typewritten note had said,

Hi, Box 3295. Perhaps I'm all of the above. No, not quite[7]. I do have a good sense of humor. I'm twenty-eight, 5' 7", 120 pounds, and my best friend tells me I'm very attractive! I'm a jewelry designer on my way to being successful[8]. I'm a good skier; can ride if the horse is slow and fat[9]. Definitely a museum-goer.[10] In fact, I get a lot of ideas for my jewelry by haunting them[11]. And music is a must. See you? Erin Kelley, 212–555–1432.

"You can understand why I called," Nash said.

"And you never saw her again."

"I never got the chance[12]." Michael Nash stood up. "I'm sorry. I have to cut this short.[13] My first patient is arriving earlier than usual. But I'm here[14] if you want me. If there's any way I can help, please allow me[15]."

"How do you think you can help, Doctor?" Vince got to his feet[16] as he asked the question.

Nash shrugged. "I don't know. I suppose it's the instinctive desire to want a killer brought to justice[17]. Erin Kelley obviously loved life and had much to offer. She was only twenty-eight years old." He held out his hand[18]. "You don't think much of us shrinks[19], do you, Mr. D'Ambrosio? Your version is that neurotic, self-centered[20] people pay good money[21] to come in here and complain[22]. Let me explain how I view my job. My professional life is devoted to[23] trying to help people who for whatever

1. y était agrafée
2. Homme divorcé, blanc
3. médecin
4. 1,85 m
5. Cherche
6. femme blanche célibataire ou divorcée
7. pas tout à fait
8. qui espère réussir
9. lent et gros
10. J'adore aller au musée.
11. en y passant des heures
12. l'occasion
13. Je vais devoir abréger.
14. disponible
15. n'hésitez pas
16. se leva
17. de vouloir qu'un criminel soit amené devant la justice
18. lui tendit la main
19. Vous n'avez pas beaucoup d'estime pour nous autres psys
20. égocentriques
21. cher
22. venir se plaindre
23. Je passe ma vie professionnelle à

reason[1] are in danger of sinking[2]. Some cases are easy. I'm like a lifeguard[3] who swims out[4] because he notices that someone is over his head[5] and simply escorts him back in[6]. Other cases are much tougher[7]. It's as though I'm trying to rescue a shipwreck victim[8] during a hurricane[9]. It takes a long time to get close[10] to him and tidal waves[11] are forcing me back[12]. It's pretty satisfying when I'm able to complete the rescue."

Vince put Erin's letter in his briefcase[13]. "You may be able to help us, Doctor. We're going to be tracking down[14] the people Erin met through personal ads. Would you be willing[15] to interview some of them and give your professional opinion of what makes them tick[16]?"

"Absolutely."

"By any chance, are you[17] a member of AAPL?" Psychiatrists who belonged to the American Association of Psychiatry and the Law, Vince knew, were particularly skilled in dealing with[18] psychopaths.

"No, I'm not. But, Mr. D'Ambrosio, my research has shown that the vast majority of people who place or answer these ads do so because of loneliness or boredom[19]. Others may have more sinister[20] motives."

Vince turned and walked to the door. As he twisted the knob[21], he looked back[22]. "I'd say that was true[23] in Erin Kelley's case."

1. pour une raison ou une autre,
2. risquent de sombrer
3. un sauveteur
4. nage vers le large
5. en train de couler
6. le ramène vers la rive
7. bien plus difficiles
8. un naufragé
9. ouragan
10. arriver près
11. le courant
12. me pousse dans l'autre sens
13. attaché-case
14. essayer de retrouver
15. d'accord
16. sur ce qui les motive
17. Seriez-vous par hasard
18. savaient particulièrement bien s'occuper
19. pour combler leur solitude ou leur ennui
20. inquiétants
21. En tournant la poignée
22. se retourna
23. Je dirais que c'est le cas

ON TUESDAY night, Charley drove to the retreat and went directly to the basement. He took down the stack[1] of shoe boxes and laid them on top of[2] the freezer. Clipped onto each of them was the name of the girl who belonged with them. Not that he needed reminding[3], of course. He remembered every single one[4] in perfect detail. Besides that[5], except for Nan, he had a videotape of each of them. And he had videotaped the *True Crimes* program about Nan's death. They'd done a good job of finding[6] a girl who looked like her.

He opened Nan's box. The scuffed[7] Nike and the black sequined satin slipper. The slipper was garish[8]. His taste had improved since then.[9]

Should he send Nan's and Erin's things back at the same time? Carefully, he considered the idea.[10] It was such an interesting decision.

No. If he did that the police and the media would realize immediately that their theory about a copycat murder was wrong. They'd know that one set of hands[11] had snuffed out both lives[12].

Maybe it would be more fun to toy with them[13] for a while.

Maybe start by returning Nan's shoe and the one from the first of the other girls. That had been Claire, two years ago. An ash-blond[14] musical-comedy actress from Lancaster. She could dance so beautifully[15]. Gifted.[16] Really gifted. Her wallet was in the box with her white sandal and the gold slipper. Surely by now her family had given up her

1. la pile
2. les posa sur
3. Non qu'il ait besoin d'un pense-bête
4. chacune d'entre elles
5. En outre
6. s'étaient bien débrouillés pour trouver
7. éraflée
8. kitsch
9. Il avait plus de goût maintenant.
10. Il y réfléchit posément.
11. c'était les mêmes mains
12. qui avaient supprimé les deux victimes
13. de les faire marcher
14. aux cheveux blond cendré
15. dansait si bien
16. Très douée.

apartment[1]. He'd send the package to the address in Lancaster.

Then every few days[2] he'd send another package. Janine. Marie. Sheila. Leslie. Annette. Tina. Erin.

He'd time it so they'd all be delivered[3] by March thirteenth. Fifteen days from now.[4]

On that night, no matter how he accomplished it[5], Darcy would be here dancing with him.

Charley stared at the freezer. Darcy was going to be the last one. Maybe he'd keep her with him always ...

1. avait dû libérer l'appartement
2. tous les 2 ou 3 jours,
3. Il ferait en sorte qu'ils soient tous arrivés
4. Dans quinze jours.
5. d'une manière ou d'une autre

WHEN DARCY got back to her apartment from the airport Tuesday evening, there were a dozen messages on the answering machine. Condolences[6] from old friends. Seven calls had come in from personal ads Erin must have answered for her. The pleasant-voiced[7] David Weld again. This time he left a number. So did Len Parker, Cal Griffin, and Albert Booth.

A call from Gus Boxer saying he had a tenant[8] for Erin Kelley's apartment. Could Miss Scott get the place cleared out[9] by the weekend? If she did, she wouldn't have to pay the March rent[10].

Darcy rewound the tape, wrote down the names and phone numbers of the personal ad callers, and changed cassettes. Vince D'Ambrosio might want to have a record of those voices[11].

She heated[12] a can of soup[13], ate it on a tray[14] in bed. When she was finished she reached for the phone and the list of men who had called for a date. She dialed the first number. As it began to ring[15] she slammed the phone back in the cradle[16]. Tears gushed down[17] her cheeks as she sobbed[18], "Erin, I want to call *you*[19]."

6. Des condoléances
7. dont la voix était agréable
8. un locataire
9. vider l'appartement
10. loyer
11. en voudrait peut-être un enregistrement
12. réchauffa
13. de la soupe en boîte
14. plateau
15. À la première sonnerie,
16. raccrocha brutalement
17. coulèrent à flots sur
18. sanglotait
19. c'est toi que je voudrais appeler

VIII
WEDNESDAY
February 27

AT NINE O'CLOCK, Darcy went to the office. Bev was already there. She had coffee brewing[1] and fresh juicc and warm bagels. A new plant was on the windowsill. Bev hugged her[2] briefly, her extravagantly mascaraed eyes filled with sympathy[3]. "You can guess everything I want to say."

"Yes, I can." Darcy realized the coffee aroma was enticing[4]. She reached for a bagel. "I didn't know I was hungry."

Bev assumed a businesslike attitude[5]. "We had two calls in yesterday. People who saw the magic you did on the Ralston Arms apartment. Want you to redo[6] for them. Also, would you take on that residential hotel on Thirtieth and Ninth? New owners. Claim they have more taste than money.[7]"

"Before I do anything else, I have to clear out Erin's apartment." Darcy took a gulp[8] of coffee and pushed back her hair. "I dread it.[9]"

It was Bev who suggested she simply move all the furniture[10] to the warehouse[11]. "You told me it was a terrific setup[12]. Could you use Erin's things piece by piece on jobs? One of the women who called wants to redo her daughter's bedroom in a really special way. The kid's sixteen and is coming home from the hospital after a long siege[13]. She'll be laid up[14] for quite a while[15]."

1. avait mis le café en route
2. la serra dans ses bras
3. ses yeux trop fardés pleins de compassion
4. alléchant
5. prit un ton professionnel
6. vous demander de faire une déco
7. Ils disent avoir plus de goût que de moyens.
8. gorgée
9. J'appréhende.
10. que le plus simple serait d'envoyer tous les meubles
11. leur entrepôt
12. un appart super
13. séjour
14. va encore garder la chambre
15. un bon bout de temps

It was good to think of Erin's pewter and brass bed being enjoyed by a girl like that. It made it easier. "I'd better check[1] that it's all right for me to move everything out[2]." She called Vince D'Ambrosio.

"I know the NYPD is finished going over the place[3]," he told her.

Bev arranged for the van[4] to go to Christopher Street the next day. "I'll meet it. Just show me what you want." At noon she went with Darcy to Erin's apartment. Boxer let them in[5].

"Sure appreciate you releasing the place[6]," he whined[7]. "Nice person taking it."

I wonder how much you got under the table[8], Darcy thought. I never want to come here again.

There were a few blouses[9] and scarves[10] that she decided to keep as mementos[11]. The rest of Erin's clothes she gave to Bev. "You're Erin's size. Just please don't wear them to the office[12]."

The jewelry Erin had made. Swiftly[13] she gathered it[14], not wanting to think now about Erin's talent. What else was bothering her? Finally she laid all the jewelry on the worktable. Earrings, necklaces, pins[15], bracelets. Gold. Silver. Semiprecious stones. All imaginative, whether formal or fun pieces. *What was bothering her?*

The new necklace Erin had completed with the chunky gold copies[16] of Roman coins[17]. Erin had joked about it. "It'll retail for[18] about three thousand dollars. I designed it for a fashion show in April. Can't afford[19] to keep it for myself, but until then I'm going to wear it a few times."

Where was that necklace?

Had Erin been wearing it when she went out that last time? That and her initial ring and her watch[20]. Were they with the clothes she'd been wearing when her body was found?

1. Je ferais mieux de vérifier
2. de tout enlever
3. a fini d'examiner l'appartement
4. camionnette
5. leur ouvrit
6. C'est gentil à vous de libérer l'appartement
7. dit-il d'un ton geignard
8. combien tu touches au passage
9. chemisiers
10. des écharpes
11. en souvenir
12. ne les porte pas au travail
13. Rapidement
14. les regroupa
15. des broches
16. grosses reproductions en or
17. de pièces de monnaie romaines
18. Ça se vendra pour
19. Je ne peux pas me permettre
20. montre

Darcy scooped[1] Erin's personal jewelry into a suitcase along with the contents of the safe[2]. She'd have the loose gems appraised[3] and sold for[4] Billy's nursing home expenses. She did not look back when she closed the door of apartment 3B for the last time.

1. fourra
2. le contenu du coffre
3. Elle ferait évaluer les pierres non encore montées
4. les vendrait pour payer

On Wednesday afternoon at four o'clock, a detective from the Sixth Precinct, armed with Erin Kelley's picture, was making the rounds[5] of the pubs in the Washington Square area. So far his search had been fruitless[6]. Several bartenders freely acknowledged knowing[7] Erin. "She'd drop in once in a while. Sometimes with a date.[8] Sometimes meeting someone. Last Tuesday. No. Didn't see her at all last week."

Charles North's picture produced no effect at all[9]. "Never saw that one."

Finally, at Eddie's Aurora on West Fourth Street, a bartender positively stated[10]: "Yeah, that girl was here last Tuesday. I went to Florida Wednesday morning. Just got back. That's why I'm sure about the date. I started talking to her. Told her I was finally getting away for some sun. She said she was a typical redhead[11], her skin always burned[12]. She was expecting to meet someone and waited around for about forty minutes. He never showed up[13]. Nice girl. Finally, she paid her bill[14] and left."

The bartender was sure it was Tuesday; sure Erin Kelley had come in at seven o'clock; sure she had been stood up[15]. He accurately[16] described the clothes she had been wearing, including an unusual[17] necklace that resembled old Roman coins. "Necklace was real different. Looked expensive.[18]

5. faisait le tour
6. il avait fait chou blanc
7. avaient reconnu sans problème qu'ils connaissaient
8. Parfois avec un homme.
9. ne suscita aucune réaction
10. déclara
11. comme toutes les rousses
12. elle avait tout de suite des coups de soleil
13. n'est pas venu
14. a payé l'addition
15. qu'on lui avait posé un lapin
16. minutieusement
17. peu commun
18. Il avait l'air d'avoir de la valeur.

I told her not to wander around outside[1] without pulling her coat collar over it[2]."

The detective reported to Vince D'Ambrosio from the pay phone in the bar. Vince immediately phoned Darcy, who verified[3] that Erin had had a gold coin necklace. "I thought it might have been found on her." She told Vince that Erin's initial ring and watch were also missing.

"She was wearing a watch and earrings when she was found," Vince said quietly, and asked if he could come over[4].

"Sure," Darcy said. "I'll be working late."

When Vince arrived at the office, he was carrying a copy of Erin's personal ad file. "We did an exhaustive examination of all Erin's papers[5]. In them we found a receipt for one of those private safe deposit boxes[6] that are accessible twenty-four hours a day. Erin signed up for that only[7] last week. She told the manager that she was a jewelry designer and was uncomfortable about[8] the value of some of the stones she was keeping[9] in her apartment."

Darcy listened attentively as Vince D'Ambrosio told her that Erin had been stood up on Tuesday night. "She left that bar alone at about quarter of eight. We're leaning to the theory[10] that it was a felony murder[11]. She was wearing the necklace Tuesday night, but not when she was found. We don't know about the ring."

"She always wore that ring," Darcy said.

Vince nodded. "She may have had the pouch of diamonds in her possession[12]." He wondered if he was getting through to Darcy Scott[13]. She was sitting at her desk, a pale yellow sweater accentuating the blond highlights[14] in her brown hair, her expression totally controlled[15], her eyes more green

1. de ne pas se promener avec
2. sans remonter son col de manteau par-dessus
3. confirma
4. s'il pouvait passer la voir
5. a épluché les dossiers d'Erin
6. un reçu pour un de ces coffres-forts personnels
7. n'en a ouvert un que
8. n'était pas très rassurée de
9. garder des pierres d'une telle valeur
10. Nous pensons de plus en plus
11. un vol qui aurait dérapé en homicide involontaire
12. sur elle
13. si Darcy Scott l'écoutait
14. mèches
15. l'air tout à fait calme

than hazel[1] today. He hated to be giving her copies[2] of Kelley's personal ads file. He was sure that she was going to start writing to the ones that were circled.

Unconsciously, his voice deepened[3] as he stressed[4], "Darcy, I know the sense of rage you're feeling at losing a friend like Erin. The point is, I beg you[5] not to answer these personal ads with some crazy idea that[6] you'll find the man who called himself Charles North. We're going to do everything we can to find Erin's killer. But the fact remains that even though Erin may not have been one of his victims, there is a serial murderer using these ads to meet young women, and I don't want you to be his next date[7]."

1. noisette
2. Ça ne lui plaisait pas du tout de lui donner des photocopies
3. il prit une voix plus grave
4. en insistant
5. je vous supplie
6. en vous mettant en tête que
7. je ne veux pas que vous soyez la prochaine

DOUG Fox had not strayed from[8] Scarsdale over the weekend. He'd devoted himself to[9] Susan and the children and been pleasantly compensated[10] for his efforts by having Susan tell him that she'd arranged for[11] a babysitter Monday afternoon. She wanted to do some shopping and proposed that they meet for dinner in New York that night and ride home together[12].

She had not told him that before shopping, she had the appointment with an investigative agency.

Doug had taken her to San Domenico for dinner and made it his business[13] to be especially charming, even telling her that[14] sometimes he forgot how really pretty she was[15].

Susan had laughed.

Tuesday night Doug had arrived home at midnight. "Damn late meetings," he'd sighed.

Wednesday morning he felt secure enough[16] to tell Susan he'd be taking clients out to dinner[17] and

8. n'avait pas quitté
9. Il avait passé tout son temps avec
10. récompensé
11. réservé
12. qu'ils rentrent ensemble
13. avait fait un effort
14. lui disant même que
15. comme elle était jolie
16. il se sentit suffisamment rassuré
17. qu'il devait emmener des clients au restaurant

might as well stay at the Gateway[1]. He was relieved at how understanding she was[2]. "A client is a client, Doug. Just don't wear yourself out.[3]"

Wednesday afternoon when he left the office, he went straight to the apartment in London Terrace. He was meeting a divorced thirty-two-year-old real estate broker[4] in SoHo for drinks at seven-thirty. But first he wanted to change into casual clothes[5] and make a phone call.

He hoped that tonight he'd reach[6] Darcy Scott.

1. qu'il ferait aussi bien de rester au Gateway pour la nuit
2. fut soulagé qu'elle se montre si compréhensive
3. Ne te fatigue pas trop.
4. une femme agent immobilier
5. passer quelque chose de plus décontracté
6. il arriverait à joindre

ON WEDNESDAY AFTERNOON, Jay Stratton received a call from Merrill Ashton of Winston-Salem, North Carolina. Ashton had been thinking long and hard about[7] Stratton's suggestion that he buy Frances an important piece of jewelry for their fortieth wedding anniversary. "If I discuss it with her, she'll talk me out of it[8]," Ashton said, a smile in his voice. "Point is, I have to be in New York next week on business[9]. You got anything to show me[10]? I was thinking maybe a diamond bracelet."

Jay assured him that he most certainly did have[11] something to show him. "I just bought some particularly fine diamonds which are being set in a bracelet right now. It would be perfect on your wife."

"I'd want an appraisal[12]."

"Of course you would. If you like the bracelet, you can take it to a jeweler in Winston-Salem whom you trust[13] and if he doesn't agree that the value is there[14], we don't have a deal[15]. Are you prepared to spend forty thousand dollars? One for each year of your marriage?"

7. avait bien réfléchi à
8. elle va m'en dissuader
9. pour affaire
10. à me montrer
11. bien sûr il avait
12. le faire évaluer
13. en qui vous avez confiance
14. s'il estime que le bracelet a moins de valeur
15. on annule la vente

He heard the hesitation in Ashton's reply. "Well, that's a bit steep[1]."

"A truly exquisite[2] bracelet," Jay assured him. "Something that Frances Junior will proudly leave to her own daughter[3]."

They arranged to meet for a drink next Monday, March fourth.

Was it all going too well[4], Stratton wondered as he laid the portable phone on the coffee table[5]. The twenty-thousand-dollar check for the Bertolini necklace. Would anyone think to come looking for it[6]? The insurance on the pouch of diamonds. With Erin's body found, the chance[7] that she had been robbed[8] could not be disputed[9]. He'd give Ashton the gem-stones at a reasonable but not questionable price[10]. A jeweler in Winston-Salem wasn't going to be looking for stones listed as missing or stolen.

A wave of pure pleasure swept over him. Stratton laughed, remembering what his uncle had said to him twenty years ago. "Jay, I've sent you to an Ivy League school[11]. You've got the brains[12] to get good marks[13] on your own, and you still cheat[14]. Your father will never be dead while you're around[15]."

When he told his uncle that he'd conned the dean[16] at Brown into letting him reapply[17] if he joined the Peace Corps[18] for two years, his uncle had sarcastically snapped, "Be careful. There's nothing to steal in the Peace Corps and you might actually have to do some work."

Not that much work.[19] At twenty he'd started over[20] at Brown as a freshman[21]. Never get caught, his father had warned him. And if you do, no matter how you fix it[22], make sure you don't have a record[23].

He'd of course been older than the other students. They'd all looked like babyfaced kids, even the ones who were obviously rich.

1. un peu beaucoup
2. ravissant
3. sera fière de léguer à sa fille
4. Est-ce que tout se passait trop bien
5. table basse
6. à le réclamer
7. la possibilité
8. qu'elle se le soit fait voler
9. était indéniable
10. à un prix raisonnable qui n'éveillerait pas les soupçons
11. dans une grande école
12. Tu es largement assez intelligent
13. de bonnes notes
14. tu triches quand même
15. n'est pour ainsi dire pas mort, puisque tu es là
16. embobiné le directeur
17. pour qu'il le laisse reposer sa candidature
18. s'il s'engageait dans les Peace Corps
19. Pas tant de boulot que ça.
20. repris à zéro ses études
21. en première année
22. par n'importe quel biais
23. arrange-toi pour ne jamais avoir de casier judiciaire

Except for one.

The phone rang. It was Enid Armstrong. Enid Armstrong? Of course, the teary-eyed[1] widow.

She sounded excited. "I talked to my sister about your suggestion of what I should do to my ring and she said, 'Enid, if that will give you a lift[2], do it. You deserve[3] to pamper yourself[4].' "

1. à la larme facile

2. ça peut te remonter le moral

3. mérites

4. de te dorloter un peu

ON THE CHANNEL 4 six o'clock news, reporter John Miller had an ongoing report about[5] Erin Kelley. It had been learned that[6] a quarter of a million dollars in diamonds was missing from her safe. Lloyd's of London had posted[7] a fifty-thousand-dollar reward[8] for their return[9]. The police still believed that she had been the victim of a copycat murderer who might not have known that she was carrying valuables[10]. The report ended with a reminder that the *True Crimes* dramatization[11] of Nan Sheridan's death was being repeated[12] at eight o'clock.

Darcy snapped the off button on the remote control[13]. "It had nothing to do with a robbery[14]," she said aloud. "It had nothing to do with a copycat murder. No matter what they say[15], it had everything to do with a personal ad."

Vince D'Ambrosio would undoubtedly learn the identity of some of the people Erin had dated. But Erin had been meeting for the first time the man who called himself Charles North, and he hadn't shown up. Suppose he'd been just coming into the bar and met her at the door[16]? Suppose he'd been one of the ones to whom she'd sent a picture? Suppose he'd said, "Erin Kelley, I'm Charles North. I got

5. donnait le bulletin quotidien sur le meurtre d'

6. On avait appris que

7. offert

8. récompense

9. à qui les rapporterait

10. des objets de valeur

11. reconstitution à l'écran

12. repasserait

13. éteignit rageusement avec la télécommande

14. Ça n'a rien à voir avec un vol

15. Ils ont beau dire

16. qu'il l'ait croisée à l'entrée

stuck in traffic.[1] This place looks crowded.[2] Let's go somewhere else."

It makes sense[3], Darcy thought. If there is a serial killer out there and if he's been responsible for other deaths, he won't stop now. If only she knew which ads Erin had actually[4] answered, which ads she'd answered for both of them.

It was seven o'clock, a good time to try returning the calls that had been left on her machine[5]. In the next forty minutes she reached three people, left messages for the other four. Now she had a date for drinks with Len Parker at McMullen's on Thursday, drinks with David Weld at Smith and Wollensky's Grill on Friday, and brunch with Albert Booth at the Victory Café on Saturday.

What about the guys who had left messages on Erin's machine? A couple of them had given phone numbers that she'd taken down[6]. Maybe she'd call them back, tell them about Erin in case they didn't already know[7], and try to get a date[8] with them. If they were meeting a lot of girls, they might have heard someone talk about a date who turned out to be[9] weird[10].

The first two didn't answer. The next one picked up immediately. "Michael Nash."

"Michael, I'm Darcy Scott, a good friend of Erin Kelley's. I imagine you know what happened to her."

"Darcy Scott." The pleasant voice deepened with concern[11]. "Erin told me about you. I'm so terribly sorry. I spoke with an FBI agent yesterday and assured him I'd like to help in any way I can[12]. Erin was a lovely girl."

Darcy realized her eyes were filling with tears[13]. "Yes, she was."

1. J'étais bloqué dans un embouteillage.
2. Il y a trop de monde ici.
3. C'est logique
4. effectivement
5. la bonne heure pour rappeler ceux qui avaient laissé des messages sur son répondeur
6. notés
7. au cas où ils ne seraient pas déjà au courant
8. rendez-vous
9. qui s'était révélé
10. un peu étrange
11. se fit plus grave et prit un ton soucieux
12. si je peux faire quoi que ce soit
13. se gonflaient de larmes

Obviously, he caught the catch in her voice[1]. "This is terribly rough[2] for you. Can I take you out for dinner[3] some night soon? Talking about it may help."

"I'd like that."

"Tomorrow?"

Darcy thought swiftly. She was meeting Len at six. "If eight o'clock is all right with you[4]."

"It's fine. I'll make a reservation at Le Cirque. Incidentally[5], how will I know you[6]?"

"Medium brown hair, five eight. I'll wear a blue wool[7] dress with a white collar."

"I'll be the most average-looking[8] guy in the place. I'll be waiting at the bar."

Darcy hung up feeling somehow comforted[9]. At least I'll get some use out of[10] the Rodeo Drive clothes, she thought, and realized that instinctively she was making a mental note[11] to call Erin and tell her that.

She got up and massaged the back of her neck[12]. A dull headache[13] made her realize she hadn't eaten since noon. It was now quarter of eight. A quick, hot shower, she decided. Then I'll heat some soup and watch that program.

The soup, appetizing enough when piping hot[14], slumped into[15] a thick concoction[16] of bits of vegetables swimming in tomato stock[17] as Darcy stared at the screen. The photograph of the dead nineteen-year-old, her one foot in a scuffed Nike, the other in a sequined black satin pump, was horrifying. Was that the way Erin had looked[18] when she'd been found? Hands folded on her waist, the tips of the mismatched shoes[19] pointing in the air? What kind of sick brain could[20] see that picture and want to duplicate it[21]? The program closed with a refer-

1. perçut le tremblement dans sa voix
2. C'est un moment très difficile
3. Est-ce que je peux vous emmener dîner
4. vous convient
5. Au fait
6. comment est-ce que je vous reconnaîtrai
7. en laine
8. le plus ordinaire
9. se sentant un peu réconfortée
10. ça me donne une occasion de mettre
11. par habitude elle se promettait
12. se massa la nuque
13. migraine sourde
14. assez appétissante tant qu'elle était bien chaude
15. s'effondra en
16. masse
17. du jus de tomate
18. Est-ce qu'Erin avait ressemblé à ça
19. le bout des chaussures dépareillées
20. Qui avait l'esprit assez tordu pour
21. la reproduire

ence to the fact that a copycat murderer might be responsible for the death of Erin Kelley.

When it was over, she snapped off the set and buried her face in her hands[1]. Maybe the FBI was right about the copycat murder. It could not have been sheer coincidence[2] that a few weeks after that program was shown, Erin had died in the same way.

But why Erin? And did the slipper she was wearing fit[3]? If it did, how did her killer know her size[4]? Maybe I'm crazy, she thought. Maybe I should back off[5] and leave this to people who know what they're doing.

The phone rang. She was tempted not to answer it. Suddenly she felt too tired to talk to anyone. But it might be news about Billy. The nursing home had her number to call for emergencies[6]. She picked up the receiver. "Darcy Scott."

"In person. Well, *at last*[7]. I've been trying you every few days.[8] I'm Box 2721. Doug Fields."

1. se cacha le visage dans les mains
2. être par simple coïncidence
3. la chaussure qu'elle portait était-elle à la bonne pointure
4. sa pointure
5. laisser tomber
6. en cas d'urgence
7. enfin
8. Ça fait plusieurs jours que j'essaie de vous joindre.

IX
THURSDAY
February 28

On Thursday morning, Nona, working with her assistant producer, Liz Kroll, completed the planning of the documentary. Liz, a thin-faced, sharp-featured[1] young woman, had interviewed the potential guests[2], culling the duds as she put it[3].

"We've got a nice mix," she assured Nona. "Two couples who ended up married[4]. The Cairones fell in love at first sight[5] and are mushy enough[6] to satisfy the romantic slobs[7]. The Quinlans answered each other's ads and are pretty funny telling how their letters crossed in the mail[8]. We've got someone who looks like young Abe Lincoln confiding how shy he[9] is and that he's still hunting for[10] the perfect girl. We've got a gal[11] whose ad mistakenly read[12] that she was a wealthy divorcée. She got seven hundred answers and has dated fifty-two of them so far[13]. We've got a woman who had dinner with her date and at the end he picked a fight with her[14], stalked off[15], and stuck her with the check[16]. The next guy practically attacked her when he drove her home. Now he hangs around her house[17]. She woke up one morning and saw him looking in her bedroom window. If your friend Erin Kelley had actually met her date[18] that night, we'd have a heck of a terrific wrap-up[19]."

1. aux traits anguleux
2. invités
3. elle appelait ça « éliminer les nuls »
4. se sont mariés
5. ont eu le coup de foudre
6. suffisamment niais
7. pour plaire aux romantiques à l'eau de rose
8. quand ils racontent que leurs lettres se sont croisées
9. qui avoue être très timide
10. il cherche encore
11. une nana
12. dont l'annonce disait par erreur
13. pour l'instant
14. s'est mis à l'engueuler
15. est parti furieux
16. en lui laissant l'addition
17. traîne autour de chez elle
18. le type avec qui elle avait rendez-vous
19. une conclusion d'enfer

"Wouldn't we ever[1]," Nona said quietly, and realized that she had never liked Liz.

Kroll did not seem to notice[2]. "That FBI agent, Vince D'Ambrosio, is cute[3]. I talked to him yesterday. He's going to show pictures of those missing girls on the program and warn people that they all answered personal ads. Then he'll ask if anybody has any information, that kind of thing. That worries me[4] a little. We don't want to sound like *True Crimes*, but what can you do[5]?" She got up to go. "One more thing. You know that Barnes woman from Lancaster whose daughter Claire has been missing for two years? I had a brainstorm[6] yesterday. What about having her on the show? Just a brief segment. I bumped into[7] Hamilton and he thought it was a great idea but said to check with you[8]."

"Nobody bumps into Austin Hamilton." Nona felt anger cut through the dull lethargy[9] that had been encompassing her with each passing day[10]. Not for a single minute could she get Erin out of her mind.[11] That face, always ready to break into a smile[12], that slender, graceful body. Like the others in the waltz class where they'd met, Nona was a pretty good dancer, but both Erin and Darcy were outstanding[13]. Particularly Erin. Everyone else stopped to watch when she waltzed with the instructor[14]. And I got friendly with them and told them about this great idea I had for a personal ad documentary. If only Vince D'Ambrosio were right[15]. He believed Erin had been the random victim[16] of a copycat murderer. Please God, let it be that[17], Nona prayed. Let it be that.

But if Erin had died because she'd answered personal ads, let this program help to[18] save someone else. "I'll call Mrs. Barnes in Lancaster," she told Kroll, her tone a clear dismissal[19].

1. Ben tiens
2. s'en apercevoir
3. mignon
4. Ça m'inquiète
5. que peut-on y faire
6. une idée de génie
7. suis tombée par hasard sur
8. voir ça avec vous
9. sentit la colère monter et la sortir de l'apathie
10. qui chaque jour l'abattait un peu plus
11. Elle ne pouvait un seul instant s'enlever Erin de la tête.
12. à sourire
13. d'un niveau exceptionnel
14. valsait avec le professeur
15. pouvait avoir raison
16. la victime fortuite
17. faites que ce soit le cas
18. au moins que cette émission serve à
19. d'un ton sans appel

Darcy sat on the windowsill of the bedroom she was redecorating for the teenager who would soon be coming home from the hospital. Erin's pewter and brass bed would be perfect. The charming turn-of-the-century[1] lady's vanity[2] that she'd picked up in Old Tappan last week had deep drawers. It really was like a small dresser[3] and wouldn't crowd the room[4]. The present double dresser, a battered mahogany veneer object[5], was a horror. More overhead shelves[6] in the closet would take care of bulky items[7] like sweaters.

She was aware that the girl's mother, a weary look on her pleasant face[8], was studying her anxiously. "Lisa's been in a dreary[9] room in the hospital for such a long time that I thought having her room done over[10] might give her a lift. She's in for so much therapy[11], but she's spunky[12]. She told the doctors she'll be back in dancing class in another couple of years. Ever since she could toddle[13], the minute she heard music she'd start to dance."

Lisa had been run over[14] by a messenger[15] on a bike who'd been cycling at top speed against the traffic[16] on a one-way street[17]. He'd smashed into her[18], breaking her legs, ankles, and foot bones. "She loves to dance," her mother added wistfully[19].

"Loves music, loves to dance." Darcy smiled, thinking of the framed poster with that title that had been in Erin's bedroom. Erin always said that it was the first thing she saw in the morning and it brightened her day[20]. She firmly squelched the[21] instinctive desire to keep it as a memoir[22]. "I have just

1. style Belle Époque
2. coiffeuse
3. commode
4. n'encombrerait pas la pièce
5. un meuble tout abîmé en faux acajou
6. Quelques étagères de plus
7. vêtements encombrants
8. l'air las malgré son visage avenant
9. triste
10. faire refaire sa chambre
11. en a encore pour des semaines de soins
12. elle a beaucoup de cran
13. Depuis qu'elle est toute petite
14. renversée
15. un coursier
16. qui pédalait à toute vitesse en sens inverse
17. dans une rue à sens unique
18. Il l'avait heurtée de plein fouet
19. d'un air triste et songeur
20. que ça illuminait sa journée
21. avait réfréné son
22. le garder en souvenir

the thing[1] for that wall," she said, and felt the constant pain ease a little[2]. It was almost as though Erin was nodding in approval[3].

THE HARKNESS AGENCY on East Forty-fifth Street was the discreet investigative firm Susan Fox retained to probe into[4] the nocturnal wanderings[5] of her husband, Douglas. The retainer[6] of fifteen hundred dollars had seemed symbolic to her. That was just what she had squirreled away[7] in a personal account, saving for Doug's August birthday. She'd smiled sadly as she wrote the check[8].

On Wednesday she had called Carol Harkness. "My husband has one of his famous nonmeetings[9] tonight."

"We'll have Joe Pabst, one of our best people, following him," she was assured[10].

On Thursday, Pabst, jovial-featured, heavy-set[11], reported[12] to his boss. "This guy's a piece of work[13]. He leaves his office, cabs up to[14] London Terrace. He's got an apartment there; been subletting from the[15] owner, an engineer[16] named Carter Fields, for two years. He's registered as Douglas Fields. Pretty neat. That way, nobody questions an illegal sublet and he don't run into anyone tracking him down[17] at work or at home. Same initials, too. That's lucky. Don't have to worry about his monogrammed cuff links[18]."

Pabst shook his head in reluctant admiration[19]. "The neighbors think he's an illustrator. Super[20] tells me he's got a lot of signed pen-and-ink stuff[21] framed in the apartment. I gave the super the garbage[22] about him being up for a government

1. exactement ce qu'il vous faut
2. cette douleur qui ne la quittait pas s'apaiser un peu
3. était là pour l'approuver
4. avait choisie pour enquêter sur
5. les équipées nocturnes
6. L'acompte
7. ce qu'elle avait économisé sou par sou
8. en remplissant le chèque
9. une de ses fameuses réunions bidon
10. lui avait-on assuré
11. costaud
12. venait faire son rapport
13. un sacré numéro
14. prend un taxi pour
15. il sous-loue au
16. ingénieur
17. il risque pas d'être retrouvé par quelqu'un
18. des initiales sur ses boutons de manchette
19. tout de même admiratif
20. Le gardien
21. dessins à l'encre
22. Je lui ai sorti les sornettes habituelles

assignment[1]. Slipped the usual twenty bucks[2] to keep the mouth shut[3]."

At thirty-eight, Carol Harkness looked like one of the women executives in the AT&T commercials[4]. Her well-cut black suit[5] was brightened only by a gold lapel pin[6]. Her ash-blond hair was shoulder length[7]. Her hazel eyes had a cool, impersonal expression. The daughter of a New York City detective[8], the love of police work was in her blood.

"Did he stay there or go out?" she asked.

"Went out. About seven o'clock. You should have seen the difference in him. Hair combed so it looked real curly.[9] Turtleneck sweater.[10] Jeans. Leather jacket. Don't get me wrong[11], not cheap-looking[12]. Kind of the way the arty types with money dress.[13] He met some gal in a bar in SoHo. Attractive. Thirty or so. Classy. I got the table behind them. They had a coupla drinks, then she said she had to leave."

"Anxious to dump him?[14]" Harkness asked quickly.

"No way.[15] She had big eyes for him[16]. He's a good-looking guy and can turn on the charm[17]. They have a date Friday night. They're going dancing at some nightclub downtown."

HIS FOREHEAD CREASED in concentration[18], Vince D'Ambrosio studied the autopsy report on Erin Kelley. It stated that she had eaten approximately an hour before she died. Her body showed no sign of decomposition. Her clothing had been soaked through[19]. These facts were initially attributed to the sleet and cold the day she was found. The autopsy revealed that her organs were partially thawed[20].

1. comme quoi il bossait pour le gouvernement
2. Je lui ai filé les 20 $ de rigueur
3. pour qu'il se la ferme
4. ces femmes cadres des pubs pour télécoms
5. tailleur noir bien coupé
6. une broche en or sur le revers
7. lui arrivaient aux épaules
8. policier
9. Il s'était fait une belle mise en plis.
10. Un col roulé.
11. Attention
12. pas bas de gamme
13. Le genre de choses que portent les artistes friqués.
14. Pour le planter là ?
15. Pas du tout.
16. avait l'air emballée
17. il sait y faire
18. Le front plissé par la concentration
19. étaient trempés
20. à moitié décongelés

The medical examiner[1] concluded that her body had been frozen[2] immediately after her death.

Frozen! Why? Because it was too dangerous for the killer to dispose of the body[3] immediately? Where had she been kept? Had she died on Tuesday night? Or was it possible that she had been held captive somewhere and died as late as Thursday[4]?

Had she been planning to put the pouch of diamonds in the security vault[5]? From all accounts, Erin Kelley was a levelheaded[6] young woman. Certainly, she didn't seem like the kind who would confide to a stranger[7] that she was carrying a fortune in jewels in her purse.

Or would she?

They'd been running down[8] the identity of the people who'd placed some of the ads they believed Erin answered. So far they'd all been like that lawyer, North. Absolute proof of where they'd been Tuesday night.[9] Some of them picked up their own mail at the magazines or newspapers where they'd run the ads. Three of the forwarding addresses for the others[10] turned out to be mail drops[11]. Probably married guys who didn't want to take any chance[12] of their wives opening the mail[13].

It was nearly five when Vince received a call from Darcy Scott. "I've been wanting to talk to you all day, but I've been out of the office on jobs[14]," she explained.

Best thing for her[15], Vince thought. He liked Darcy Scott. After Kelley's body was found, he'd asked Nona Roberts about Scott's family and had been astonished[16] to learn that she was the offspring[17] of two superstars. Nothing Hollywood about that girl. Genuine.[18] It was amazing some guy hadn't snapped her up yet[19]. He asked her how it was going.

"It's going okay," Darcy said.

1. médecin légiste
2. congelé
3. se débarrasser du corps
4. ne soit morte que jeudi
5. au coffre
6. pleine de bon sens
7. à raconter à un inconnu
8. vérifié
9. Ils pouvaient prouver où ils étaient mardi soir.
10. Trois des adresses auxquelles les autres faisaient suivre leur courrier
11. s'étaient avérées être des boîtes postales
12. risquer
13. que leur femme ouvre leur courrier
14. j'étais chez des clients
15. C'est encore ce qu'elle peut faire de mieux
16. stupéfait
17. la fille
18. Très naturelle.
19. qu'aucun type ne l'ait encore trouvée à son goût

Vince tried to analyze what he was hearing in her voice[1]. The first time he met her in Nona's office her low, strained tone[2] suggested acute worry[3]. At the morgue, until she'd broken down[4], she'd spoken in the emotionless monotone[5] of a person in shock[6]. Now there was a certain briskness[7]. Determination. Vince knew instantly that Darcy Scott was still convinced that Erin's death was the result of answering personal ads.

He was about to talk to her about that when she asked, "Vince, something has been bothering me. Did that high-heeled shoe Erin was wearing fit? I mean, was it her size?"

"It was the same size as her boot, seven and a half narrow."

"Then how did whoever put it on her happen to have[8] a shoe exactly her size?"

Smart girl, Vince thought. Carefully, he weighed his words[9]. "Miss Scott, that's something we're working on now. We're trying to trace that shoe through the manufacturer[10] to learn where it was purchased[11]. It's not cheap, in fact the pair probably cost several hundred dollars. That narrows[12] considerably the number of outlets[13] in the New York area that might carry it[14]. I promise I'll keep you posted[15] on developments[16]." He hesitated, then added, "I hope you've given up the idea[17] of following up any personal ads Erin Kelley answered for you."

"As a matter of fact[18]," Darcy told him, "I have my first date with one of them in an hour."

1. le ton de sa voix
2. sa voix basse, son ton forcé
3. qu'elle était extrêmement inquiète
4. elle s'effondre
5. du ton monocorde
6. en état de choc
7. vivacité
8. ait justement eu
9. pesa ses mots
10. en contactant le fabricant
11. achetée
12. réduit
13. boutiques
14. susceptibles de les avoir en stock
15. que je vous tiendrai au courant
16. de nos progrès
17. que vous avez laissé tomber l'idée
18. En fait

LEN PARKER at six. They were meeting at McMullen's on Seventy-sixth and Third. A trendy place[1], Darcy thought, and certainly safe[2]. A favorite with the New York "in" crowd.[3] She'd been there on dates a few times and liked the owner, Jim McMullen. She was only going to have a glass of wine with Parker. He'd told her he was meeting some friends at the Athletic Club to play basketball.

She had told Michael Nash that she would be wearing a blue wool dress with a white collar. Now that she had it on, she felt overdressed[4]. Erin always teased her[5] about the clothes her mother showered on her[6]. "When you get around to wearing them[7], you make the rest of us look as though we shop in John's Bargain Store[8]."

Not true, Darcy thought as she applied another smidgen of[9] midnight-gray[10] eye shadow[11]. Erin always looked great, even in college when she had so little money to buy clothes.

She decided to wear the silver and azurite pin Erin had given her for her birthday. "Funky but fun[12]," Erin had pronounced it[13]. The pin was shaped like a bar of music[14]. The notes were lined in azurite, exactly the sea-blue shade[15] of the dress. Silver bracelets and earrings and narrow suede[16] boots completed the outfit[17].

Carefully, Darcy appraised herself[18] in the mirror. On the trip to California, her mother had bullied her into going[19] to her personal hairdresser[20]. He'd changed her part[21], cut off a few inches[22], then accentuated the natural blond highlights in her hair.

1. Un endroit à la mode
2. très sûr
3. Un des endroits préférés des New-Yorkais branchés.
4. un peu trop habillée
5. la taquinait toujours
6. que sa mère lui offrait sans arrêt
7. acceptes enfin de les porter
8. on a toutes l'air de se fringuer dans une solderie
9. encore une touche de
10. gris souris
11. fard à paupières
12. Branchée et rigolote à la fois
13. avait jugé Erin
14. avait la forme d'une portée de musique
15. couleur
16. en daim
17. sa tenue
18. se regarda
19. avait insisté pour qu'elle aille
20. coiffeur
21. sa raie de côté
22. coupé quelques centimètres

She had to admit that she liked the results. She shrugged[1]. Okay, I look good enough that Len Parker probably won't walk out on me[2] when I show up.

Parker was tall, bone-thin[3], but not unattractive. A college teacher[4], he told her he had recently moved to New York from Wichita, Kansas, and didn't know many people. Over a glass of wine[5] he confided that a friend had suggested he place a personal ad. "They're really expensive. You'd be surprised.[6] It makes a lot more sense to answer other people's ads, but I'm sure glad you answered mine." His eyes were light brown but large and expressive. He stared at Darcy. "I really have to say this. You're very pretty."

"Thank you." Why was it that something about him made her uncomfortable?[7] Was he really a teacher, or was he like the one date she'd had before she went to California? That guy had claimed[8] to be an advertising executive and didn't know the first thing[9] about the agencies she brought up with him[10].

Parker fidgeted[11] on the bar stool, rocking it slightly[12]. His voice was low and with the hubbub of conversation from the people nearby[13], Darcy had to lean over to hear him[14].

"Very pretty," he emphasized. "You know, not all the girls I've met are pretty. When you read the letters they send, you'd think they were[15] Miss Universe. And who shows up? Olive Oyl.[16]"

He signaled for another glass of wine. "You?"

"I'm fine." Carefully, she chose her words. "Surely all of them weren't that bad. I bet you've met some really pretty girls."

He shook his head emphatically[17]. "Not like you. No way."

1. haussa les épaules
2. ne parte pas en courant
3. très maigre
4. Professeur d'université
5. Pendant qu'ils buvaient un verre de vin,
6. Vous n'avez pas idée.
7. Pourquoi y avait-il quelque chose chez lui qui la mettait mal à l'aise ?
8. prétendu
9. ne savait strictement rien
10. des agences qu'elle avait mentionnées
11. gigotait
12. en se balançant légèrement
13. brouhaha
14. devait se pencher pour l'entendre
15. on s'attend à
16. La femme de Popeye !
17. vigoureusement

It was a long hour. Darcy heard about Parker's trouble finding an apartment. The prices, wow. Some girls think you should take them out for fancy dinners[1]. Come on.[2] Who can keep that up?[3]

Finally, Darcy was able to get Erin's name in[4]. "I know. My friend and I both met some strange people through these ads. Her name was Erin Kelley. Did you meet her by any chance[5]?"

"Erin Kelley?" Parker swallowed convulsively[6]. "Wasn't that the girl who got murdered last week? No, I never met her. And she was your friend? Gee[7], I'm sorry. That's lousy.[8] Did they find the killer yet?"

She did not want to discuss Erin's death. There was no way, even if Erin met this man once, that she'd have gone out with him a second time. She looked at her watch. "I have to run.[9] And you'll be late for your basketball game."

"Oh, that's all right. I'll skip it.[10] Stay for dinner. They have good hamburgers here. Expensive, but good."

"I really can't. I'm meeting someone."

Parker frowned. "Tomorrow night? I mean, I know I'm not much to look at[11] and teachers are famous for not making much money[12], but I'd really like to see you again."

Darcy slipped her arms into her coat[13]. "I really can't. Thank you."

Parker stood up and punched[14] the bar. "Well, you can pay for the drinks. You think you're too good for me. I'm too good for you."

She was relieved[15] to see him stalk out[16] of the restaurant. When the bartender came with the check[17], he said, "Miss, don't bother with that nut[18]. Did he pull his college-professor stuff?[19] He's on the maintenance staff[20] at NYU[21]. He gets more free drinks

1. dans des restaurants chics
2. Allons !
3. Qui peut se permettre ce genre d'endroits sans arrêt ?
4. glisser le nom d'Erin
5. par hasard
6. déglutit péniblement
7. Mince
8. C'est un coup dur.
9. Il faut que je me sauve.
10. Je peux ne pas y aller.
11. que je ne paye pas de mine
12. que les profs sont connus pour être mal payés
13. enfila son manteau
14. tapa du poing sur
15. soulagée
16. sortir à pas pressés
17. l'addition
18. ce taré
19. Il s'est fait passer pour un prof de fac comme d'hab ?
20. Il fait partie du personnel d'entretien
21. l'université de New-York

and meals through those ads he places. You got off cheap.[1]"

Darcy laughed. "I think I did, too." A thought struck her. She reached in her purse for Erin's picture. "By any chance, did he ever show up with this girl?"

The bartender, who looked as though he might be an actor[2], studied the picture carefully, then nodded. "He sure did. Around two weeks ago. She was a knockout[3]. She walked out on him[4]."

At six o'clock, Nona was surprised and pleased to receive a call from Vince D'Ambrosio. "You're obviously another one who doesn't keep regular hours[5]," he said. "I'd like to talk to you about your program. Are you free for dinner in about an hour?"

She was.

"Okay, make a reservation at a good steak place in your neighborhood[6]."

Smiling, she hung up. D'Ambrosio was clearly a meat-and-potatoes[7] man, but she'd bet her bottom dollar[8] that his cholesterol level[9] was fine. She realized that she was unreasonably glad[10] that she'd worn[11] her new Donna Karan jumpsuit today. The cranberry shade[12] suited her[13] and the gold belt with the clasped[14] hands accentuated her small waist[15]. Nona knew that her waistline[16] was her one vanity[17]. Then she had a flash of overwhelming sadness[18]. Erin had made that belt for her for Christmas.

Shaking her head as though to negate the reality of Erin's death, she got up and walked around her desk, rotating her shoulders[19]. She'd spent the entire day working on the documentary and felt as

1. Vous en êtes quitte à bon compte.
2. avait un physique d'acteur
3. super belle
4. l'a planté là
5. vous aussi, du genre à horaires irréguliers
6. quartier
7. aux goûts simples
8. elle mettrait sa main à couper
9. son taux de cholestérol
10. un peu trop contente
11. d'avoir mis
12. rouge grenat
13. lui allait bien
14. entrelacées
15. taille fine
16. tour de taille
17. le seul point dont elle soit vraiment fière
18. la tristesse l'envahit
19. en roulant les épaules

though her body was a mass of knots[1]. At three o'clock, Gary Finch, the Hudson Cable anchorman, had reviewed it with her. At the end of the session, Finch, a notorious perfectionist[2], smiled and said, "It's going to be great."

"Approbation from Sir Hubert is praise indeed[3]." Nona stretched[4] and tried to decide whether or not to call Emma Barnes in Lancaster again. She'd already tried three or four times. Admittedly,[5] Liz was smart to suggest having Barnes appear on the program to talk about her missing daughter who had answered personal ads. Liz was bright and imaginative. But she was trying to skunk me[6] when she discussed Barnes with Hamilton, Nona decided. She wants my job. Let her try.[7]

She gave one last, long stretch[8], sat at her desk, and dialed the Lancaster number. Once more the Barnes household did not answer[9].

Vince arrived promptly at seven. He was wearing a well-cut gray pinstriped suit accompanied by a brown and beige tie. It's for sure no woman picks out his ties[10], Nona thought, remembering how fussy Matt had been[11] about what tie went with which shirt and what suit.

The restaurant was on Broadway, a few blocks from[12] Nona's apartment. "Let's save the serious stuff[13] for dessert," Vince suggested. Over salads they briefly sketched their personal lives[14]. "If you were placing a personal ad, what would you say about yourself?" he asked.

Nona reflected. "Divorced White Female, age 41, cable television producer."

He sipped his scotch. "Go on.[15]"

1. tout noué
2. connu pour être ultra perfectionniste
3. est un véritable compliment
4. s'étira
5. Il fallait admettre que
6. m'écraser
7. Qu'elle essaye donc !
8. s'étira une dernière fois, longuement
9. personne ne répondit chez les Barnes
10. En tout cas, ce n'est pas une femme qui lui choisit ses cravates
11. à quel point Matt était difficile
12. à quelques rues de
13. Gardons les choses sérieuses
14. ils évoquèrent brièvement leur vie privée
15. Continuez.

"Manhattan born and bred.[1] Think anyone who lives anywhere else is mentally ill[2]."

He laughed. She noticed that caused friendly creases in the corners of his eyes[3].

Nona sipped her wine. "This is terrific burgundy[4]," she commented. "I hope you're planning to have some when the steak comes."

"I am. Finish your ad, please."

"Barnard graduate.[5] I didn't even leave Manhattan for college[6], you see. I did have a year abroad, and I do like to travel as long as I'm not gone more than three weeks."

"Your ad's getting expensive."

"I'll wind it up.[7] Clean but not particularly tidy[8]. You've noticed my office. Do not have green thumb[9]. Good cook but hate fussy food[10]. Love jazz. And oh, yes, I'm a good dancer."

"That's how you got friendly with Erin Kelley and Darcy Scott, in a dance class," D'Ambrosio commented, and then watched as pain darkened Nona's eyes[11]. Hurriedly he added, "My ad's a little shorter. I work for the government. Divorced White Male, 43 years old, FBI agent, brought up in Waldwick, New Jersey, graduated from NYU. Can't dance without tripping over my own feet.[12] Like to travel as long as it isn't Vietnam. Three years there was enough. And last, but certainly not least,[13] I have a fifteen-year-old son, Hank, who's a swell[14] kid."

As she had promised, the steaks were superb. Over coffee they talked about the program. "We're taping it[15] in two weeks," Nona said. "I'd like to save you for last[16] so people are left with a sobering warning about[17] the potential danger of answering these ads[18]. You're going to show the pictures of the missing girls, aren't you?"

1. New-Yorkaise invétérée.
2. ne va pas bien dans sa tête
3. que le rire lui mettait des pattes d'oie sympathiques au coin des yeux
4. Ce bourgogne est délicieux
5. Diplômée de Barnard.
6. mes études supérieures
7. J'arrive au bout.
8. ordonnée
9. la main verte
10. les plats sophistiqués
11. remarqua la douleur dans le regard de Nona
12. Incapable de danser sans me prendre les pieds.
13. pour finir, mais c'est sans doute le plus important,
14. sensass
15. Nous l'enregistrons
16. vous garder pour la fin
17. pour que votre intervention ait plus d'impact sur les gens et leur signale
18. les risques qu'ils prennent en répondant à ces annonces

"Yes. There's always the chance a viewer[1] may have information about one of them."

It was biting cold[2] when they left the restaurant. A frosty winter wind made Nona gasp.[3] Vince took her arm as they crossed the street. He did not remove it the rest of the way to her apartment.

He accepted her invitation to come up for a nightcap. Nona remembered happily that her cleaning lady[4], Lola, had been in[5]. The place would look presentable.

The seven-room apartment was in a prewar building[6]. She could see D'Ambrosio's eyebrows raise[7] as he took in the large foyer[8], the high ceilings[9], the long windows on Central Park West, the paintings in the living room, the massive Jacobean furniture[10]. "Very nice," he commented.

"My folks gave it to me as is when they moved to Florida. I'm an only child[11], and this way when they come up to New York, my father feels comfortable. He hates hotels." She went to the bar. "What'll it be?[12]"

She poured Sambuca for both of them, then paused. "It's only quarter past nine. Do you mind if I take a minute to phone someone?" She reached in her purse. As she looked up the Barnes's number, she explained why she was calling them.

This time the phone was picked up immediately. Nona froze[13] as she realized the sound she was hearing was a woman screaming[14]. A man's voice gave a distracted greeting[15]. In shocked bewilderment[16] he said, "Whoever this is, please get off the phone[17]. I must call the police immediately. We've been away all day and just opened the mail. There was a package addressed to my wife."

1. spectateur
2. Il faisait un froid pénétrant
3. Nona eut le souffle coupé par le vent d'hiver glacé.
4. femme de ménage
5. était passée
6. un immeuble d'avant-guerre
7. le haussement de sourcils de D'Ambrosio
8. en voyant la grande entrée
9. les hauts plafonds
10. mobilier XVIIe
11. enfant unique
12. Qu'est-ce que vous prenez ?
13. se figea
14. les cris d'une femme
15. répondit d'un air absent
16. Visiblement sous le choc,
17. merci de raccrocher

The screams were now a shrieking crescendo[1]. Nona motioned to[2] Vince to pick up the portable telephone[3] on the table beside him.

"Our daughter," the bewildered voice went on[4]. "She's been missing for two years. That package has one of Claire's own shoes and a high-heeled satin slipper in it." He began to shout, "Who sent this? Why did they send it? Does this mean Claire is dead?"

1. se muaient en hurlements qui allaient crescendo
2. fit signe à
3. de décrocher le téléphone sans fil
4. continua la même voix perplexe

DARCY WAS handed out of the cab by the doorman[5], entered Le Cirque, and felt herself begin to unwind[6]. She had not realized how much energy she had put into the meeting with Len Parker. Her head was still buzzing[7] with the realization that[8] he had met Erin. Why had he denied it?[9] Erin had walked out on him. Certainly, she'd never dated him again. Was it simply that he didn't want to be questioned and have to admit the lies about his background[10]?

Every time her mother and father were in New York they dined at Le Cirque. It was a wonderful restaurant. Darcy found herself wondering why she didn't come here more often. *How ever did two such stunning people manage to produce that mousy-looking child?* And how could one sentence remain so imbedded in memory[11]?

The bar was to the left[12]. Small and charming, it was not a hangout[13] but a place to wait for a guest or a table. A young couple was standing near it, chatting animatedly[14]. A single man[15] was at the end. *The most ordinary-looking person you'll see.*

Michael Nash had not been kind to himself[16]. Dark blond hair, a face that was saved from being conven-

5. sortit du taxi avec l'aide du portier
6. sentit qu'elle se détendait
7. Elle avait encore l'esprit troublé
8. d'avoir compris qu'
9. Pourquoi l'avait-il nié ?
10. qu'il avait menti sur sa profession
11. si ancrée dans sa mémoire
12. sur la gauche
13. n'était pas un endroit où l'on passait la soirée
14. discutant avec animation
15. Un homme seul
16. avait été un peu dur avec lui-même

tionally handsome[1] by a rather sharp chin[2], a long, trim[3] body, dark blue suit with faint pinstripes, silver and blue tie. As he looked at her with obvious recognition and pleasure[4], Darcy was aware that Michael Nash's eyes were an unusual shade[5], somewhere between sapphire and midnight blue[6].

"Darcy Scott." It was a statement[7], not a question. He signaled to the maître d'[8] and put his hand under her elbow[9].

They were seated at a prime table[10] in full view of the entrance[11]. Michael Nash must be a frequent and valued[12] customer[13] of Le Cirque.

"A drink? Wine?"

"White wine, please. And a glass of water."

He ordered a bottle of Pellegrino with the Chardonnay, then smiled. "Now that for the moment we've taken care of the necessaries[14], as an old friend puts it[15], Darcy, it's good to meet you."

For the next half hour, she realized that he was deliberately steering the conversation away from[16] Erin. It was only after she had begun to sip the[17] wine and pick at a roll[18] that he said, "Mission accomplished. I think you are finally starting to feel safe."

Darcy stared at him. "Whatever do you mean?"

"I mean that I was watching for you[19]. I saw the way you hurried in. Everything about you suggested a high level of tension. What happened?"

"Nothing. I'd really like to talk about Erin."

"I would too. But Darcy ..." He stopped. "Look, I can't get out of the business of doing what I do all day[20]. I'm a psychiatrist." His smile was apologetic.[21]

She felt herself at last begin to relax. "I'm the one who should apologize.[22] You're absolutely right. I did feel pretty tense coming here.[23]" She told him about Len Parker.

1. d'une beauté originale
2. grâce à un menton anguleux
3. svelte
4. l'air de la reconnaître avec plaisir
5. d'une couleur peu commune
6. d'un bleu entre saphir et bleu nuit
7. une affirmation
8. maître d'hôtel
9. sous son coude
10. à une bonne table
11. face à l'entrée
12. apprécié
13. client
14. nous avons réglé l'aspect pratique
15. comme dit un vieil ami à moi
16. faisait exprès de détourner la conversation pour ne pas évoquer
17. siroter son
18. à grignoter un peu de pain
19. je guettais votre arrivée
20. j'ai du mal à faire abstraction de ce que je fais toute la journée
21. Il sourit pour s'excuser.
22. C'est moi qui devrais m'excuser.
23. J'étais un peu tendue en arrivant.

He listened attentively, his head slightly tilted[1]. "You'll of course report this man to the police."

"The FBI, actually."

"Vincent D'Ambrosio? As I told you when you called, he came to my office on Tuesday. Unfortunately[2], I could tell him very little[3]. I met Erin for a drink several weeks ago. I had the immediate feeling that a girl like her had no need to answer[4] personal ads. I challenged her with that[5] and she told me about the program her friend is putting together[6]. She mentioned you. Said her best friend was answering ads with her."

Darcy nodded, hoping that her eyes were not going to fill with tears.

"I don't usually explain[7] that the reason I'm going this route[8] is because of a book I'm working on, but I did tell Erin. We exchanged some stories about our various dates. I've tried to remember everything she said, but she didn't give any names and they were funny stories[9]. Certainly, I had no hint that anyone worried her[10]."

" 'Close encounters of the worst kind[11],' she used to call them."

Nash laughed. "She told me that. I asked if we could plan dinner soon, and she agreed. I was trying to wrap up[12] my book and she was completing[13] a necklace she had designed. I said I'd get back to her[14]. When I tried, there was no answer. From what Vincent D'Ambrosio said, it was already too late."

"That was the night she thought she was meeting someone named Charles North. I still think that even though he didn't show up, her death has to do with a personal ad she answered."

"Thinking that[15], why are you answering personal ads now?"

1. la tête légèrement inclinée
2. Malheureusement
3. je n'ai pas pu lui dire grand-chose
4. n'avait nul besoin de répondre à
5. Je le lui ai dit sans ambages
6. est en train de mettre sur pied
7. Je n'explique généralement pas
8. pour laquelle je fais ça
9. des anecdotes amusantes
10. je n'ai pas eu l'impression que quiconque l'ait tracassée
11. Rencontres du pire type [allusion à un film de Spielberg]
12. finir
13. terminait
14. que je la recontacterais
15. Si c'est ce que vous pensez

"Because I'm going to find that man."

He looked troubled but did not comment. They studied the menu, both selecting the Dover sole[1]. As they ate, Nash seemed to be deliberately trying to keep her mind off[2] Erin's death. He told her about himself. "My father made his money in plastics. Literally lived out[3] that famous line[4] from *The Graduate*[5]. Then bought a rather garishly ornate mansion[6] in Bridgewater. He was a decent, fine man, and every time I wonder why three of us needed twenty-two rooms, I remember how happy he was showing them off[7]."

He touched on his divorce. "I married the week after I graduated from college. Terrible mistake for both of us. It wasn't a financial problem, but medical school[8], especially when it involves the continuing study of psychoanalysis, is a long, hard road[9]. We didn't have time for each other. By the end of four years, she'd had enough[10]. Sheryl lives in Chicago now and has three children."

It was Darcy's turn. Carefully, she steered around giving the names[11] of her famous parents, jumping quickly to leaving[12] the advertising agency and setting up her budget decorating business. "Somebody once told me I'm a new version of Sanford and Son[13], and I guess it's true[14], but I love it." She thought of the room she was decorating for the recuperating sixteen-year-old[15].

If he noticed gaps in the background[16], he did not comment. The salads arrived just as a producer friend of her parents stopped at the table. "Darcy!" A warm kiss[17], a hug[18]. He introduced himself to Michael Nash. "Harry Curtis." He turned back to Darcy. "You get prettier every day. I hear your parents are touring in Australia. How's it going?"

"They just got there."

1. et choisirent tous deux la sole
2. de la distraire de
3. Il a suivi exactement le conseil donné par
4. réplique
5. le Lauréat
6. une grande demeure assez voyante
7. de les faire visiter
8. les études de médecine
9. sont longues et prenantes
10. elle avait eu sa dose
11. réussit à ne pas dévoiler le nom
12. en arrivant vite à son départ de
13. [série télé dont les héros sont brocanteurs]
14. c'est sans doute vrai
15. convalescente de 16 ans
16. Même s'il avait remarqué quelques blancs dans son histoire
17. Embrassades chaleureuses
18. accolade

"Well, give them my love[1]." Another hug and Curtis left for his own table.

Nash's eyes did not signal curiosity[2]. That's the way it works with shrinks[3], Darcy thought. They wait for you to tell them. She did not offer an explanation[4] of what Curtis had said.

It was a pleasant dinner. Nash confessed to[5] two passions, riding and tennis. "They're what keep me[6] in Bridgewater." Over espresso, he returned to the subject of Erin's death. "Darcy, I don't usually offer advice to people, even free advice, but I wish you'd drop[7] the idea of answering these ads. That FBI fellow[8] seemed perfectly competent to me and if I'm any judge[9], he's not going to rest until[10] whoever murdered Erin is paying the price[11]."

"He told me that in so many words.[12] I guess we all do what we have to do." She managed a smile. "The last time I spoke to Erin, she said she'd met one nice guy and wouldn't you know it,[13] he hadn't called back. I'd bet my bottom dollar it was you."

He took her home in a cab, told the driver to wait, and walked her[14] to the door. The wind was sharp[15] and he turned so that he was protecting her from its full blast[16] as she turned the key. "May I call you again?"

"I'd like that." For a moment she thought he was going to kiss her cheek, but he simply pressed her hand and went back to the waiting cab.

The wind pulled at[17] the door, causing it to close slowly[18]. As the lock clicked[19], the sound of footsteps made her turn[20]. Through the glass[21] she could see the figure[22] of a man rushing up the steps[23]. An instant sooner and he would have been in the vestibule with her. As she stared at him, her mouth too dry to scream[24], Len Parker pounded[25] at the door, kicked it[26], then turned and ran down the block[27].

1. embrasse-les pour moi
2. ne montrèrent aucune curiosité
3. C'est comme ça, avec les psys
4. ne fournit aucune explication
5. avoua
6. C'est pour ça que je continue à aller
7. que vous abandonniez
8. Ce type du FBI
9. si je ne me trompe pas
10. il n'aura de cesse que
11. n'en paye le prix
12. Il me l'a dit explicitement.
13. que, bien sûr,
14. l'accompagna
15. vif
16. pour la protéger des plus grosses rafales
17. tira sur
18. et la ferma doucement
19. la serrure claqua
20. un bruit de pas la fit se retourner
21. À travers la vitre,
22. la silhouette
23. montant les marches en courant
24. la gorge trop sèche pour crier
25. tambourina
26. donna des coups de pied dedans
27. décampa

X
FRIDAY
March 1

Greta Sheridan debated[1] between getting up or trying to sleep for another hour. A gusty March wind[2] was rattling the windowpanes[3] and she remembered that Chris had been after her[4] to have these windows replaced[5].

The early-morning light[6] filtered through the drawn draperies[7]. She loved a cold room for sleeping. The quilt[8] and blankets[9] were warm and the blue and white moire canopy[10] gave the bed a comforting enclosed feeling[11].

She had been dreaming of Nan. The anniversary of her death, March thirteenth, was two weeks away. Nan had turned nineteen the day before. This year she would have been celebrating her thirty-fourth birthday.

Would have been.

Impatiently, Greta tossed back the covers[12], reached for her velour robe[13], and got up. Pulling on her slippers[14], she went into the hallway[15] and down the winding staircase[16] to the main floor. She understood why Chris was concerned[17]. It was a large house and it was generally known that[18] she lived alone. "You don't know how easy it is for a professional to disarm a security system[19]," he had warned several times.

"I love this house." Every room held so many happy memories. Somehow, Greta felt that to leave this

1. hésitait
2. rafale de mars
3. faisait trembler les vitres
4. n'arrêtait pas d'insister
5. pour qu'elle fasse changer les fenêtres
6. La lumière du petit matin
7. passait à travers les rideaux
8. couette
9. les couvertures
10. le baldaquin en tissu bleu et blanc moiré
11. lui donnait la sensation d'être à l'abri dans son lit
12. repoussa les couvertures
13. peignoir
14. Après avoir enfilé ses chaussons
15. sortit dans le couloir
16. descendit l'escalier en colimaçon
17. inquiet
18. tout le monde savait que
19. de neutraliser un système d'alarme

place would be to leave them as well. And, she thought with an unconscious smile, if Chris would finally settle down[1] one of these days and give me some grandchildren, it will be a wonderful place for them to visit[2].

The *Times* was at the side door[3]. As the coffee perked[4], Greta began to read. There was a brief item on an inside page[5] about that girl who'd been found dead in New York last week. Copycat murder. What a horrible thought. How could there be two such evil people[6], the one who had snuffed out Nan's life and the one who had killed Erin Kelley? Would Erin Kelley still be alive[7] if that program had not been aired[8]?

And what was it that she had been trying to remember[9] when she insisted on watching it? Nan. Nan, she thought. You told me something that I should have realized was important[10].

Nan, chatting about school, her classes, her friends, her dates. Nan looking forward to[11] the summer program in France. Nan who loved to dance. "I Could Have Danced All Night[12]." The song could have been written for her.

Erin Kelley had also been found wearing one high-heeled shoe. High heel? What was it about those two words? Impatiently, Greta opened the *Times* to the crossword puzzle[13].

The phone rang. It was Gregory Layton. She'd met him at the club dinner the other night. In his early sixties, he was a federal judge and lived in Kent about forty miles away[14]. "An attractive widower[15]," Priscilla Clayburn had whispered to her. He *was* attractive, and he was asking her to have dinner with him tonight. Greta accepted and replaced the receiver, realizing that she was looking forward to the evening.

1. se décidait à se marier

2. ce serait merveilleux pour eux de pouvoir lui rendre visite ici

3. devant la porte de service

4. passait

5. un court article dans le journal

6. deux personnes aussi diaboliques

7. Erin Kelley serait-elle toujours en vie

8. diffusée

9. de quoi essayait-elle de se souvenir

10. dont j'aurais dû saisir l'importance

11. se réjouissant à l'idée de

12. [L'une des chansons du film Le Roi et moi]

13. à la page du mots croisés

14. à une soixantaine de kilomètres de chez elle

15. Un veuf très séduisant

Dorothy came in at the stroke of nine[1]. "Hope you don't have to go out this morning, Mrs. Sheridan. That wind is mean.[2]" She was carrying the mail[3], including a bulky package under her arm. She laid everything on the table and frowned. "That's a funny-looking thing. I mean, no return address[4]. I hope it's not a bomb or something."

"Probably more of that awful crank mail[5]. Damn that program." Greta started to pull at the string[6] on the package and had a sudden sense of panic. "It does look funny.[7] Let me call Glenn Moore."

Police Chief Moore had just arrived in his office at headquarters. "Don't touch that package, Mrs. Sheridan," he told her crisply[8]. "We'll be right over.[9]" He called the state police. They promised to rush a portable security surveillance unit[10] to the Sheridan household.

At ten o'clock, handling[11] the package with infinite caution[12], an officer in the bomb squad[13] positioned it to be X-rayed[14].

From the living room to which she and Dorothy had been banished[15], Greta heard the man's relieved laughter. Dorothy at her heels[16], she hurried back to the kitchen.

"These won't blow up[17], ma'am," she was assured. "Nothing in there except a pair of mismatched shoes."

Greta saw Moore's startled expression, felt the blood drain from her face[18] as the package was ripped open[19], revealing a shoe box with the sketch of an evening slipper on the cover. The lid came off.[20] Inside, nestled together in tissue[21], were a high-heeled sequined slipper and a scuffed running shoe.

"Oh, Nan! Nan!" Greta did not feel Moore grab her as she fainted[22].

1. à neuf heures tapantes
2. Il y a un de ces vents.
3. avait apporté le courrier
4. il n'y a pas l'adresse de l'expéditeur
5. encore du courrier malveillant
6. tirer sur la ficelle
7. C'est vrai que ça a l'air bizarre.
8. fermement
9. On arrive tout de suite.
10. d'envoyer d'urgence une équipe de sécurité
11. en manipulant
12. très délicatement
13. de l'équipe de déminage
14. le plaça dans la machine à rayons X
15. où Dorothy et elle avaient été cantonnées
16. sur les talons
17. Ça risque pas d'exploser
18. se sentit blêmir
19. pendant qu'on ouvrait le paquet
20. Le couvercle glissa.
21. emballées ensemble dans du papier de soie
22. quand elle s'évanouit

AT THREE O'CLOCK on Friday morning, Darcy was yanked from restless sleep[1] by the insistent ringing[2] of the phone. Reaching for it, she saw the time on the clock radio[3]. Her "hello" was quick and breathless.[4]

"Darcy." Her name was whispered. The voice sounded familiar[5], but she couldn't place it[6].

"Who is this?"

The whisper became a shout. "Don't you ever close the door in my face again![7] Hear me? Hear me?"

Len Parker. She slammed down the phone[8], pulled the covers around her. A moment later the phone began to ring again. She did not pick it up. The ringing continued. Fifteen, sixteen, seventeen rings. She knew she should take the receiver off the hook[9] but could not bear to touch it, knowing that Parker was on the other end[10].

Finally it stopped. She yanked the jack from the wall[11], rushed into the living room, and put the answering machine on automatic pickup[12], then hurried back to bed, slamming[13] the bedroom door behind her.

Had he done this to Erin? Followed her when she walked out on him? Maybe followed her to the bar where she was supposed to meet someone named Charles North? Maybe forced her into a car[14]?

She'd call Vince D'Ambrosio in the morning.

1. tirée d'un sommeil agité

2. par les sonneries insistantes

3. radioréveil

4. Elle fit « allô » le souffle court.

5. ne lui était pas inconnue

6. avait du mal à l'identifier

7. Ne me refermez plus jamais la porte au nez !

8. raccrocha brutalement

9. décrocher en posant le combiné

10. au bout du fil

11. débrancha d'un coup sec

12. téléphone sur messagerie

13. en claquant

14. à monter dans sa voiture

For the next two hours she lay awake[1], finally falling into a sleep that once again was troubled with vague, restless dreams.

At seven-thirty, she awakened with an instant sense of fear[2], then remembered the reason for it[3]. A long, hot shower relieved some of the tension[4]. She pulled on jeans, a turtleneck sweater, her favorite boots.

The answering machine showed only hangups[5].

Juice and coffee at the table by the window. Staring down into the lifeless[6] garden. At eight o'clock the phone rang. Not Len Parker, please. Her "hello" was guarded[7].

"Darcy, I hope it's not too early to call. I just wanted to tell you how much I enjoyed being with you last night."

She exhaled, a relieved sigh[8]. "Oh, Michael, I can't tell you how much I enjoyed being with you too."

"Something happened. What was it?"

The concern in his voice was comforting. She told him about Len Parker, the episode on the steps[9], the phone call.

"I blame myself that[10] I didn't see you upstairs[11]."

"Please don't."

"Darcy, call that FBI agent and report this Parker character[12], and can I implore you to stop answering those ads?"

"I'm afraid not. But I will call Vince D'Ambrosio right away."

When she said good-bye, she hung up feeling oddly consoled[13].

She called Vince from the office. A wide-eyed Bev[14] stood by her desk as she spoke to another agent. Vince had flown to[15] Lancaster. The other agent took the information. "We're working with the po-

1. ne put se rendormir
2. prise d'une peur irraisonnée
3. pourquoi
4. l'aida à se détendre un peu
5. des appels avortés
6. sans vie
7. prudent
8. eut un long soupir de soulagement
9. l'incident de l'escalier
10. Je m'en veux de
11. ne pas vous avoir accompagnée en haut des marches
12. signalez les agissements de ce Parker
13. étrangement réconfortée
14. Bev, incrédule,
15. avait pris l'avion pour

lice department. We'll get right onto that character.[1] Thanks, miss."

Nona phoned and told her why Vince had gone to Lancaster. "Darce, this is so scary[2]. It's one thing if someone saw that *True Crimes* episode and was perverted enough to repeat it[3], but this means someone may have been doing this for a long time. Claire Barnes has been missing for two years. She and Erin were so alike[4]. She was just about to get her first big break[5] in a Broadway musical[6]. Erin had just gotten her first big break[7] with Bertolini's."

Her first big break with Bertolini's. The words rippled through Darcy's mind[8] as she made and received phone calls, went through Connecticut and New Jersey papers[9] for notices of estate and moving sales[10], made a quick trip to the rental apartment she was furnishing, and finally stopped for a sandwich and coffee at a lunch counter[11].

That was where she[12] realized what had been bothering her[13]. *Her first big break with Bertolini's.* Erin had told her she was to receive twenty thousand dollars for designing and executing the necklace[14]. In the rush of events[15], she forgot about the strange message on Erin's answering machine. She'd call them as soon as she got back to the office to confirm.

Aldo Marco came to the phone. Was this a family member making inquiries[16]?

"I'm executor of Erin Kelley's estate[17]." The words sounded appalling to her ears.[18]

Payment had already been made to[19] Miss Kelley's manager, Jay Stratton. Was there a problem?

"I'm sure there isn't." So Stratton presumed to act as[20] Erin's manager.

1. On va s'occuper de ce type.
2. c'est si terrifiant
3. ait été assez pervers pour reproduire le meurtre
4. avaient tant de points communs
5. décrocher son premier rôle important
6. comédie musicale
7. venait de décrocher son premier gros contrat
8. résonnaient dans sa tête
9. les journaux
10. à la recherche d'avis de vente de meubles
11. dans un petit salon de thé
12. C'est là qu'elle
13. ce qui la tracassait
14. pour la conception et la réalisation du collier
15. Avec tout ce qui s'était passé
16. voulant se renseigner
17. l'exécutrice testamentaire d'Erin Kelley
18. La phrase la faisait frémir.
19. Un règlement avait déjà eu lieu à l'ordre de
20. s'était fait passer pour

He was not home. The message she left was brusque[1]. Please call her immediately about Erin's check.

Jay Stratton phoned just before five o'clock. "I'm sorry. Of course I should have gotten to you sooner[2]. I've been away. How shall I make out the check?[3]" He told Darcy that while he was out of town[4] he'd thought of nothing but Erin. "That beautiful, talented girl. I firmly believe that someone knew about that jewelry, killed her for it, and then tried to make it look like a copycat murder."

You of all people knew about the jewelry.[5] It was an effort to listen to Stratton, to respond pleasantly to his sympathetic comments. He would be out of town again for a few days. She agreed to meet him Monday evening.

For minutes after she said good-bye to him, Darcy stared straight ahead[6], lost in thought[7], then said aloud, "After all, as you say, Mr. Stratton, two of Erin's closest friends[8] really ought to know each other better." She sighed. She'd better get some work done[9] before it was time to dress[10] for her date with Box 1527.

1. sec
2. j'aurais dû vous faire signe plus tôt
3. À quel ordre dois-je établir le chèque ?
4. en déplacement
5. Si quelqu'un était au courant pour les bijoux, c'est bien toi.
6. regarda dans le vague
7. perdue dans ses pensées
8. amis les plus proches
9. Elle ferait mieux de travailler un peu
10. avant de devoir se préparer

VINCE FLEW to Lancaster on the earliest flight[11] Friday morning. He had urged[12] Claire Barnes's father not to tell anyone outside the family about the package of shoes. But when he arrived at the airport the local paper[13] had the story in headlines[14]. He phoned the Barnes's home and learned from the maid[15] that Mrs. Barnes had been rushed to the hospital last night.

11. par le premier vol
12. prié
13. journal
14. en avait fait sa une
15. appris par l'employée de maison

Lawrence Barnes was a heavy-set executive type[1] who, Vince decided, in other circumstances would have a commanding presence[2]. Seated at the bedside, a young woman next to him, he was anxiously looking down at his heavily sedated wife[3]. Vince showed him his card and was followed out into the corridor[4].

Barnes introduced the young woman as his other daughter, Karen. "A reporter happened to be[5] in the emergency room[6] when we got here," Barnes said tonelessly[7]. "He heard Emma screaming about the package and that Claire was dead."

"Where are the shoes now?"

"At home."

Karen Barnes drove him to get them. A corporate lawyer[8] in Pittsburgh, she had never shared her parents' hope that[9] one day Claire would suddenly show up[10]. "There was no way, if she were alive, she would have given up the chance[11] to be in Tommy Tune's show[12]."

The Barnes's home was a large Colonial in an impressive neighborhood. Zoning[13] at least an acre[14], Vince thought. There was a television mobile unit[15] on the street. Karen drove quickly past it[16], into the driveway, and around to the back of the house. A policeman prevented the reporter from stopping her[17].

The living room was filled with framed family pictures[18], many of them showing Karen and Claire in their growing-up years[19]. Karen picked one of them off the piano. "I took this one of Claire the last time I saw her. We were in Central Park just a few weeks before she disappeared."

1. un homme d'affaires corpulent
2. aurait eu une présence imposante
3. son épouse sous forte dose de calmants
4. il le suivit dans le couloir
5. Il y avait un journaliste qui se trouvait par hasard
6. aux urgences
7. d'un ton morne
8. Avocate en droit des affaires
9. n'avait jamais partagé l'espoir de ses parents
10. de voir Claire réapparaître un jour
11. ait renoncé à l'occasion
12. spectacle
13. Le terrain devait faire
14. plus de 4 000 m²
15. un camion de télévision
16. le dépassa sans ralentir
17. empêcha un journaliste de la harponner
18. photos de famille encadrées
19. enfants puis ados

Slender. Pretty. Blond. Mid-twenties. Joyous smile. You can pick 'em[1], Buster[2], Vince thought bitterly[3]. "May I take this? I'll make copies and get the original right back to you."

The package was on the foyer table[4]. Ordinary brown wrapper[5], address label[6] you could buy anywhere, block printing[7]. Postmarked[8] New York City. The box had no markings[9] except for a delicately drawn sketch of a high-heeled slipper on the lid. The mismatched shoes. One a white Bruno Magli sandal, the other a gold slingback[10] with an open toe and narrow high heel. They were the same size, six narrow.

"You're sure this sandal is hers?"

"Yes. I have an identical pair. We bought them together that last day in New York."

"How long had your sister been responding to personal ads?"

"About six months. The police checked out anyone whose ad she had answered, at least anyone they could find[11]."

"Did she ever place any?"

"Not that I know of.[12]"

"Where did she live in New York?"

"On West 63rd Street. An apartment in a brownstone. My father paid the rent for nearly a year after she disappeared, then gave it up[13]."

"Where did you put her belongings[14]?"

"The furniture wasn't worth shipping.[15] Her clothes and books and whatever[16] are upstairs in her old room."

"I'd like to see them."

There was a cardboard file box[17] on a shelf in the closet. "I packed that[18]," Karen told him. "Her address book, date book[19], stationery[20], some mail, that sort of

1. J'as l'œil
2. mon gars
3. avec amertume
4. sur la table de l'entrée
5. Un papier d'emballage
6. une étiquette
7. écriture majuscule
8. Avec le cachet de la poste de
9. Il n'y avait rien sur la boîte
10. une chaussure dorée à talon ouvert
11. en tout cas, tous ceux dont ils avaient retrouvé la trace
12. Pas que je sache.
13. puis il a libéré l'appartement
14. ses affaires
15. Les meubles ne méritaient pas qu'on les fasse revenir.
16. et autres
17. une boîte à archives en carton
18. C'est moi qui ai rempli cette boîte
19. son agenda
20. son papier à lettres

thing. When we reported her missing, the New York police went through all her personal papers."

Vince lifted down the box[1] and opened it. A date book now two years old was on top[2]. He skimmed through it[3]. From January till August the pages were filled with appointments. Claire Barnes had not been seen after August fourth.

"What makes it hard is that Claire had her own kind of shorthand[4]." Karen Barnes's voice quavered[5]. "You see where it says 'Jim.' That meant Jim Haworth's studio, where she took dancing lessons. See, August fifth, 'Tommy.' That meant rehearsal[6] for the Tommy Tune show, *Grand Hotel*. She'd just been hired.[7]"

Vince turned the pages back[8]. On July fifteenth at five o'clock he saw "Charley."

Charley!

In a noncommittal tone[9] he pointed to the entry[10]. "Do you know who this one is?"

"No. Although she did mention a Charley who took her dancing once. I don't believe the police were able to locate him." Karen Barnes's face paled[11]. "That slipper. It's the sort of thing you'd wear to a dance[12]."

"Exactly. Miss Barnes, keep that name between the two of us, please. By the way[13], how long had your sister lived in her apartment?"

"Just about a year. Before that she had a place in the Village."

"Where?"

"Christopher Street. At 101 Christopher Street."

1. descendit la boîte de l'étagère
2. sur le dessus
3. le feuilleta
4. propre façon de noter les choses
5. tremblait
6. une répétition
7. Elle venait d'être engagée.
8. revint en arrière de quelques pages
9. Il demanda d'un ton neutre,
10. en pointant le nom du doigt
11. pâlit
12. qu'on porte pour aller danser
13. Au fait

1. factures à payer
2. impulsivement
3. un type jovial qui se faisait des sous comme vigile
4. s'était déjà mis au travail
5. La chambre sera prête
6. d'ici
7. Heureusement
8. que j'ai pensé
9. avec un décolleté arrondi
10. en soie
11. mi-longue
12. une étole assortie
13. C'était une idée un peu folle mais
14. de porter les armes d'Erin
15. en partant au combat
16. enleva la barrette qui retenait ses cheveux
17. les brossa puis les laissa détachés
18. ne pas vous mettre en valeur
19. me tannait
20. pour que je me maquille plus
21. que je porte les habits chics

AT QUARTER OF FIVE, Darcy handed Bev the last of the bills to be paid[1], and on impulse[2] phoned the mother of the recuperating teenager. The girl was coming home at the end of next week. The painter Darcy hired, a cheerful moonlighting security guard[3], was already on the job[4]. "We'll have the room all set[5] by[6] Wednesday," Darcy assured the woman.

Thank heaven[7] I had the brains[8] to bring some clothes with me this morning, she thought as she changed from her sweater and jeans to an oval-necked[9], long-sleeved black silk[10] blouse, a calf-length[11] Italian silk skirt in tones of green and gold, a matching stole[12]. Gold chain, a narrow gold bracelet, gold earrings—the jewelry all designed by Erin. In a crazy way[13] she felt as though she was donning Erin's coat of arms[14] as she rode into battle[15].

She released her hair from the clip[16] and brushed it loose[17] around her face.

Bev came back just as she finished applying eyeshadow. "You look fabulous, Darcy." Bev hesitated. "I mean, it always seemed to me that you kind of tried to play down your looks[18] and now, I mean, oh God, I'm not saying it right. I'm sorry."

"Erin pretty much said the same thing," Darcy reassured her. "She was always bullying me[19] to use more makeup[20] or wear some of the fancy duds[21] my mother sends me."

Bev was wearing a skirt and sweater Darcy had seen on her frequently. "By the way, how do Erin's clothes fit?"

"Perfect. I'm so glad to get them. The tuition[1] just jumped again[2] and I swear, with today's prices, I was getting ready to do a[3] Scarlett O'Hara and make a dress out of curtains[4]."

Darcy laughed. "That's still my favorite scene in *Gone With the Wind*[5]. Look, I know I asked you to avoid wearing[6] Erin's things[7] to the office, but she'd be the first to say enjoy them[8]. So feel free.[9]"

"Are you sure?"

Darcy reached past the faithful leather jacket[10] for her cashmere cape[11]. "Of course I'm sure."

She was meeting Box Number 1527, David Weld, at the grill at Smith and Wollensky's at five-thirty. He'd said he'd be at the last seat[12] at the bar, "or standing near it." Brown hair. Brown eyes. About six feet tall. Wearing a dark suit.

It was easy to pick him out[13].

A pleasant guy, Darcy decided fifteen minutes later as they sat across from each other[14] at one of the small tables. Born and raised in Boston. Worked for Holden's, the department store chain[15]. Had been coming back and forth[16] for the last few years as they expanded[17] into the Tri-State Area[18].

She judged him to be in his mid-thirties, then wondered if there was something about that age that sent unattached singles scurrying to the[19] personal ads.

It was easy to direct the conversation. He'd gone to Northeastern. His father and grandfather had been executives with Holden's. He'd worked there from the time he was a kid[20]. After school. Saturdays. Summer vacations.[21] "Never occurred to me[22] to do anything else," he confided. "Retailing runs in the family.[23]"

1. Les frais de scolarité
2. ont encore augmenté
3. comme
4. à prendre les rideaux pour me faire une robe
5. Autant en emporte le vent
6. d'éviter de porter
7. les affaires
8. d'en profiter
9. Alors, n'hésite pas.
10. sa bonne vieille veste en cuir
11. pour attraper sa cape en cachemire
12. sur le dernier tabouret
13. de le repérer
14. assise en face de lui
15. la chaîne de grands magasins
16. Il avait fait pas mal d'allées et venues
17. avaient ouvert de nouveaux magasins
18. dans le secteur des 3 États New York-New Jersey-Connecticut
19. poussaient les célibataires à se ruer sur les
20. depuis qu'il était gamin
21. Aux vacances d'été.
22. Il ne m'est jamais venu à l'idée
23. On est commerçants de génération en génération.

He had never met Erin. He'd read about her death. "That's what makes you feel funny placing these ads. I mean, all I want is to meet some nice people." Pause. *"You're nice."*

"Thank you."

"I'd be very pleased to have dinner with you if you can stay." He looked hopeful but the request was made with dignity.

No ego problem here[1], Darcy thought. "I honestly can't, but I bet you've met some nice people answering these ads, haven't you?"

He smiled. "A couple of very nice ones. One of them, if you can believe it, just started to work for Holden's in the Paramus, New Jersey, store. She's a buyer[2]. Same kind of job I had before I went into the management end[3]."

"Oh? What was that?"

"I was shoe buyer for our New England stores."

VINCE GOT BACK to his office at Federal Plaza at three o'clock Friday afternoon. There was an urgent message for him to call Police Chief Moore in Darien. From him, Vince learned about the package that had arrived at the Sheridan home.

"You're sure they're the mates of the ones[4] Nan Sheridan was wearing?"

"We've compared them. We have both sets[5] now."

"Has the press gotten hold of this?[6]"

"Not so far.[7] We're trying to keep it quiet[8], but no guarantees. You've met Chris Sheridan. That was his first concern.[9]"

"It's mine, too," Vince said quickly. "What we now know is that this killer started fifteen years ago, if

1. Aucun problème d'ego chez celui-là
2. responsable des achats
3. que je ne devienne directeur
4. qu'elles font la paire avec celles que
5. les deux paires
6. La presse est au courant ?
7. Pas encore.
8. ne pas l'ébruiter
9. Ça a été sa première préoccupation.

not sooner[1]. He has to have a reason for sending those shoes back at this time[2]. I want to talk to one of our psychiatrists to get his opinion. But if anyone questioned[3] about Nan Sheridan's death also can be linked to[4] Claire Barnes, we've got something positive to go on[5].

"How about Erin Kelley? Don't you include her?"

"I'm still keeping an open mind.[6] Her death may have been connected to the missing jewelry[7] and made to look like a copycat murder." Vince arranged to pick up the shoes the next day and hung up.

His assistant, Ernie Cizek, a new young agent from Colorado, briefed him on[8] Darcy's call about Len Parker.

"This guy's a weirdo[9]," Cizek said. "Works in maintenance at NYU. An electrical whiz.[10] Can fix[11] anything. Loner.[12] Paranoid about money.[13] But get this! The family is loaded[14]. Parker's got a hefty income[15]. A trustee banks an allowance for him.[16] He only made one large withdrawal[17], some years ago. The trustee thinks he bought property. Seems to live on his maintenance salary in a cheap walkup[18] on Ninth Avenue. Has an old station wagon. No garage. He parks it on the street."

"Police record?[19]"

"Same sort of thing that the Scott girl complained about. Following girls home. Shouting at them. Banging on doors.[20] He's a great one for placing personal ads. Everybody brushes him off[21]. So far no physical attacks. Restraining orders[22] but no convictions[23]."

"Bring him in now.[24]"

"I've talked to his shrink. He says he's harmless[25]."

1. si ce n'est avant
2. maintenant
3. interrogé par la police
4. a aussi un lien avec
5. ça nous fera quelque chose de tangible pour avancer
6. Je ne veux pas faire de conclusions hâtives.
7. est peut-être liée aux bijoux volés
8. le mit au courant de
9. barge
10. Un électricien hors pair.
11. réparer
12. Solitaire.
13. Obsédé par l'argent.
14. pleine aux as
15. des revenus conséquents
16. Un administrateur légal lui verse sa pension.
17. n'a retiré une grosse somme qu'une fois
18. dans un immeuble modeste
19. Il a un casier ?
20. Tambouriner à la porte.
21. l'envoie balader
22. Des injonctions d'éloignement
23. aucune condamnation
24. Fais-le interpeller.
25. qu'il est inoffensif

"Sure he's harmless. Just like Peeping Toms supposedly never act out their fantasies.[1] We both know better[2], don't we?"

1. Tout comme les voyeurs qui ne passent soit-disant jamais à l'acte.
2. Toi et moi, on sait bien que si

Susan's announcement that she was planning to take the children to visit her father in Guilford, Connecticut, for the weekend was received with eager agreement by[3] her husband. Doug had made the date to go dancing with the divorced real estate broker and was wondering if he should break it[4]. He had been late two nights this week and even though Susan had seemed to enjoy their New York dinner on Monday night, there was something about her attitude[5] that he could not put his finger on[6].

Susan's visiting her father with the kids till Sunday gave him two nights off[7]. He did not offer[8] to go with her. It would have been an empty gesture.[9] Susan's father had never liked him, always made cracks about how important Doug must be that he worked so many nights[10]. "Funny, with all that hard work[11], you needed to borrow so much from me to buy the house, Doug. I'd be glad to go over your budget with you[12] and see where the problem is."

Sure you would.

"Have a good time, honey," Doug told Susan when he was leaving on Friday morning. "And give my best to your Dad[13]."

That afternoon, while the baby slept, Susan phoned the investigative agency for a report. Calmly she took down the information they gave her. The meeting with the woman in the SoHo bar. The date they'd made to go dancing. The apartment in London Terrace under the name Douglas Fields. "Carter

3. fut très bien prise par
4. s'il ne devrait pas annuler
5. dans son comportement
6. qui lui paraissait bizarre
7. lui permettait de passer deux nuits seul
8. ne proposa pas
9. Ça n'aurait eu aucun sens.
10. blaguait toujours sur le grand chef que devait être Doug pour travailler tard si souvent
11. que même en travaillant si dur
12. J'aimerais jeter un œil à ton budget
13. mes amitiés à ton père

Fields is his old buddy[1]," she told the investigator. "They're two of a kind.[2] Don't bother to follow him again. I don't want to hear any more.[3]"

Her father lived year-round[4] in the pre-Revolutionary house that had been their summer home. Several heart attacks had left him with a permanent pallor that tore at Susan's heart[5]. But there was nothing fragile about his demeanor or voice[6]. After dinner, Beth and Donny went next door to visit friends. Susan put Trish and the baby to bed, then fixed demitasse[7] and brought it into the library[8].

She knew her father was studying her as she prepared his cup with sweetener[9] and a lemon peel[10].

"Exactly when do I hear the reason for[11] this unexpected, although most welcome, visit[12]?"

Susan smiled. "Now, I guess. I'm going to divorce Doug."

Her father waited.

Promise not to say "I told you so"[13], Susan prayed silently, then went on, "I've had an investigative agency following him. He has a sublet in New York under the name Douglas Fields. Calls himself a freelance illustrator. Doug does sketch very well as you know. Has plenty of dates. In the meantime[14], he rants on[15] to me about how hard he works, 'all those night meetings.' Donny can see through his lies[16] and is angry and contemptuous[17]. He'll be better off to expect nothing from his father[18] than to keep on hoping that it will change."

"Would you like to move in[19] here, Susan? There's plenty of room."

She flashed him a grateful smile[20]. "You'd go crazy in a week. No. The Scarsdale house is too large. Doug insisted we buy it to impress the people at the club. We couldn't afford it then, and I'm beginning

1. un vieux copain à lui
2. Ils ne valent pas mieux l'un que l'autre.
3. J'en ai assez entendu.
4. toute l'année
5. qui peinait beaucoup Susan
6. dans son allure ou dans sa voix
7. prépara deux cafés serrés
8. bibliothèque
9. du sucre de synthèse
10. zeste de citron
11. Quand comptes-tu me dire le pourquoi de
12. cette visite inattendue, quoique fort agréable
13. « je te l'avais bien dit »
14. Pendant ce temps-là
15. n'arrête pas de se plaindre
16. n'est pas dupe de ses mensonges
17. le méprise
18. Ce sera mieux pour lui de ne plus rien attendre de son père
19. emménager
20. lui adressa un bref sourire reconnaissant

to understand why we can't afford it now. I'll sell it, get a smaller place, put the baby in a day care center[1] next year—there's a terrific one[2] in town. Then I'll get a job."

"It won't be easy."

"It'll be a lot better than it is now."

"Susan, I'm trying not to say, 'I told you so,' but there it is. That fellow is a born womanizer[3] and he's got a vicious streak[4]. Remember your eighteenth birthday? That night he was so drunk[5] when he brought you home that I threw him out[6]? The next morning every window in my car was broken."

"You still can't be sure it was Doug.[7]"

"Come on, Susan. If you're going to start facing facts[8], face them all. And tell me this. Weren't you covering for him[9] when he was questioned in that girl's death?"

"Nan Sheridan?"

"Of course, Nan Sheridan."

"Doug simply isn't capable—"

"Susan, what time did he pick you up the morning she died?"

"Seven o'clock. We wanted to get back to Brown for a hockey game."

"Susan, before she died I got the truth out of Grandma[10]. You were in tears because you thought Doug had stood you up again[11]. He got to our place after nine. At least grant me the satisfaction[12] of telling the truth now."

The front door banged shut.[13] Donny and Beth came in. Donny's face looked relaxed and happy. It was becoming a carbon copy of Doug's face at that age. She'd had a crush on[14] Doug from their sophomore year in high school[15].

Susan felt a stab of pain[16]. I'll never get over him completely[17], she acknowledged[18]. *Doug pleading*

1. à la crèche
2. il y en a une très bien
3. un dragueur impénitent
4. il a un mauvais fond
5. si soûl
6. je l'ai mis à la porte
7. Rien ne prouve que c'était lui.
8. Si tu es décidée à faire enfin face à la réalité
9. Ne l'as-tu pas couvert
10. ta grand-mère m'a dit la vérité
11. t'avait encore posé un lapin
12. fais-moi le plaisir
13. La porte d'entrée claqua.
14. le béguin pour
15. la seconde [au lycée]
16. une douleur aiguë
17. J'aurai toujours des sentiments pour lui
18. reconnut

with her, "Susan, my car broke down. They're trying to accuse me. They want to blame somebody. Please say I was here at seven."

Donny came over to kiss her. She reached back and smoothed his hair[1], then turned to her father. "Dad, come on. You know how confused Grandma was. Even back then[2] she didn't know one day from another[3]."

1. lui caressa les cheveux

2. Déjà à l'époque,

3. confondait les jours

XI
SATURDAY
March 2

IT WAS 2:30 A.M. Saturday morning when he got to the place[1]. By then his need to be there was overwhelming.[2] When he was in the place, Charley could be his own person[3]. No more skulking[4] behind the other one. Able to dance in synch[5] with Astaire, smiling down at the phantom in his arms, crooning in her ear[6]. The wonderful solitude of the place, the draperies drawn against the unseemly gaze[7] of a casual interloper[8], the bolts securing him[9] from the outside world, the limitless sense of self, unrestrained by listeners or observers[10], free to roam in the[11] delicious memories.

Nan. Claire. Janine. Marie. Sheila. Leslie. Annette. Tina. Erin. All of them smiling at him, so glad to be with him, never getting the chance to turn on him[12], sneer at him[13], look at him with contempt[14]. In the end, when they understood, it had been so wonderfully satisfying. He regretted that he hadn't given Nan a chance to realize what was happening, to beg[15]. Leslie and Annette had pleaded for their lives[16]. Marie and Tina had cried.

Sometimes the girls came back to him one by one[17]. Other times they appeared together. *Change partners and dance with me.*

By now the first two packages would have arrived. Oh, if only one could be the proverbial fly

1. ce lieu
2. Son besoin d'y être était devenu irrésistible.
3. lui-même
4. Plus besoin de se cacher
5. en rythme
6. lui chantonnant à l'oreille
7. le regard inconvenant
8. d'un passant indiscret
9. les verrous le protégeant
10. le sentiment de liberté sans l'entrave de se sentir écouté ni observé
11. de s'abandonner aux
12. de s'en prendre à lui
13. de se moquer de lui
14. mépris
15. de le supplier
16. l'avaient supplié de les laisser vivre
17. lui revenaient à l'esprit une par une

on the wall[1], watching the moment when they were opened, when the puzzled expression changed to[2] comprehension.

Copycat.

They wouldn't call him that anymore. Now had Janine been next, or Marie? Janine. September twentieth, two years ago. He'd send her package now.

He went to the basement. The boxes with the shoes were such an amusing sight[3]. Pulling on the plastic gloves he always used when he handled[4] anything that belonged to the girls[5], he reached for the one behind the place card[6] marked "Janine." He'd send it to her family in White Plains.

His eye lingered[7] on the last place card. "Erin." He began to giggle[8]. Why not send hers now? That would really put their copycat notion in the gutter[9]. She'd told him her father was in a nursing home. He'd send them to her New York address.

But suppose no one in her apartment building was smart enough to[10] give the package to the police? What a waste[11] to have it gathering dust in some storeroom[12].

What about sending the shoes care of[13] the morgue? After all, that was her last address in New York. How funny that would be.

First, make sure to wipe[14] the shoes and boxes thoroughly[15] just to make sure there were absolutely no prints on them[16]. Get out the identification[17]. He'd plucked[18] their wallets from their purses, then buried the purses.

Wrap fresh tissue around the mismatched sets.[19] Close the lids[20]. He admired his sketches[21]. He was getting better. The one on Erin's box was as good as any professional could do[22].

1. si seulement il pouvait être une petite souris
2. la perplexité laisserait place à
3. si drôles à voir
4. manipulait
5. ayant appartenu aux filles
6. étiquette
7. Son regard s'attarda
8. à ricaner
9. ficherait en l'air leur théorie du meurtre à l'identique
10. n'ait l'intelligence de
11. Quel gâchis
12. s'il finissait dans un débarras
13. aux bons soins de
14. bien essuyer
15. à fond
16. qu'il n'y ait aucune empreinte dessus
17. Sortir les papiers d'identité
18. retiré
19. Envelopper les chaussures désassorties dans du papier de soie neuf.
20. couvercles
21. croquis
22. était digne d'un professionnel

Brown wrapping paper[1], sealing tape[2]. Address label. Any one of them could have been bought anywhere in the United States.

He addressed[3] Janine's package first.

Now it was Erin's turn. The New York telephone book would give the address of the morgue.

Charley frowned. Suppose some dumb klutz[4] in the mailroom[5] didn't open it, just gave it back to the postman[6]. "Nobody with that name works here." Without a return address the package would go into the dead-letter office[7].

There was one other possibility. Would it be a mistake? No. Not really. He giggled[8] again. This will certainly keep them guessing![9]

He began to print[10] the name of the person he had chosen to receive Erin's boot and special slipper.

DARCY SCOTT …

1. Papier kraft
2. ruban adhésif
3. inscrivit l'adresse sur
4. Mais si un gros balourd
5. du service du courrier
6. et se contente de le rendre au facteur
7. au service des lettres non distribuées
8. ricana
9. Ça devrait les intriguer !
10. écrire en majuscules

ON SATURDAY, Darcy met Box 1143, Albert Booth, for brunch at the Victory Café. She judged him to be about forty. In their telephone conversation she'd managed to learn that his ad claimed[11] he was a computer expert, enjoyed reading, skiing, golfing, waltzing, leisurely strolls through[12] museums, and listening to records. He also said he had a good sense of humor[13].

That, Darcy decided, after Booth asked her "if meeting a box number made her feel boxed in,[14]" stretched truth to the breaking point[15]. By the time she had finished her first cup of coffee, she also doubted just about everything else he'd claimed except computer expert. He had a soft couch-

11. d'après son annonce,
12. flâner dans
13. qu'il avait le sens de l'humour
14. après que Booth lui eut demandé si elle aimait être mise en boîte... postale,
15. n'était pas la stricte vérité

potato look[1] that did not hint of a[2] skier, golfer, waltzer, or walker.

His conversation consisted solely of the[3] past, present, and future of computers. "Forty years ago a computer took two big rooms of heavy equipment[4] to do what the one on your desk is doing now."

"I finally bought one just last year."

He looked shocked.

Over eggs Benedict[5], he shared his disgust with[6] the way clever students were manipulating school records[7] by breaking into computer systems[8]. "They should go to jail[9] for five years. And pay a big fine[10] too."

Darcy was sure that desecration of the sanctuary[11] or ark of the temple[12] would not have been any more serious to him.

Over the last cup of coffee, he finally finished expounding[13] his theory that future wars would be won or lost by experts able to crack enemy computers[14]. "Change all the figures[15], see what I mean. You think you have two thousand nuclear warheads[16] in Colorado. Somebody changes it to two hundred. You have armies deployed.[17] The statistics change. Where's the Fifth Division? The Seventh? You don't know anymore. Right?"

"Right."

Booth smiled suddenly. "You're a good listener[18], Darcy. Not many girls are good listeners."

It was the opening she needed.[19] "I've just started to answer personal ads. You certainly meet a variety of people. What are most of them like?"

"Most of them are pretty boring[20]." Albert leaned across the table. "Listen, you want to know who I took out[21] just two weeks ago[22]?"

"Who?"

"That girl who was murdered. Erin Kelley."

1. un air pépère
2. qui n'indiquait pas vraiment le
3. se bornait au
4. remplissait deux salles d'une lourde installation
5. En mangeant ses œufs pochés à la sauce hollandaise
6. lui fit part de son dégoût pour
7. trafiquaient leur dossier scolaire
8. en piratant les systèmes électroniques
9. en prison
10. amende
11. la profanation d'un sanctuaire
12. de l'arche d'alliance
13. d'exposer
14. capables d'infiltrer les ordinateurs de l'ennemi
15. chiffres
16. ogives nucléaires
17. On envoie les troupes.
18. Vous savez écouter
19. C'était la perche qu'elle attendait.
20. ennuyeuses
21. qui j'ai invité à dîner
22. il n'y a pas deux semaines

Darcy hoped she would not overreact[1]. "What was *she* like?"

"Pretty girl. Nice. She was worried about something."

Darcy gripped[2] her coffee cup. "Did she tell you what was worrying her?"

"She sure did.[3] She told me she was finishing some necklace and it was her first really big job and as soon as she was paid she was going to look for a new apartment."

"Any reason?"

"She said the superintendent was always brushing against her[4] when she passed him[5] and making excuses to be[6] in her apartment. Looking for a water leak[7], a heat blockage[8], that kind of thing. She said she supposed he was harmless, but it was kind of creepy[9] to walk into her bedroom and find him there. I guess it had just happened again[10] the day before I met her."

"Don't you think you ought to let the police know about this[11]?"

"No way.[12] I work for IBM. They don't want any of their employees ever to be mentioned in the papers unless they're getting married or buried. I tell the police and they start checking on me[13]. Right? But I wonder. Do you think I ought to drop them an anonymous note[14]?"

The vast resources of the FBI swung into high gear for the search for[15] the retail outlet[16] where the high-heeled evening slipper that had been returned to the home of Claire Barnes and the one found on Erin Kelley's body had been purchased[17].

1. qu'elle n'allait pas réagir de façon trop appuyée
2. serra
3. Tout à fait.
4. à l'effleurer
5. près de lui
6. à trouver des prétextes pour aller
7. une fuite d'eau
8. un problème de chauffage
9. quand même flippant
10. que ça venait de se reproduire
11. devriez en parler à la police
12. Pas question.
13. vont commencer à me soupçonner
14. leur envoyer une lettre anonyme
15. furent mobilisées pour trouver
16. la boutique
17. achetées

In the case of Nan Sheridan, fifteen years ago the police had traced the slipper to[1] a shoe outlet[2] on Route 1 in Connecticut. No one then had had any memory of[3] who had bought it.

The Claire Barnes slipper was expensive, a Charles Jourdan, sold in fine department stores[4] all over the country. Two thousand pairs, to be exact. Impossible to trace. Erin Kelley's was a Salvatore Ferragamo, a current model[5].

Agents and NYPD detectives began to fan through[6] department stores, shoe salons[7], discount outlets[8].

Len Parker was brought in for questioning[9]. He began immediately to rant about[10] how rude Darcy had been to him[11]. "I just wanted to apologize. I knew I'd been mean[12]. Maybe she did have a dinner date. I followed her and she wasn't lying. I waited outside in the cold while she ate in that fancy restaurant[13]."

"You just stood there?"

"Yes."

"And then?"

"She got right in a cab[14] with some guy. I took one too. Got out down the block[15]. The guy walked her to the door and left. I ran up.[16] After all I went through[17] to apologize, she slammed the door in my face[18]."

"How about Erin Kelley? Did you follow her?"

"Why should I? She walked out on me. Maybe that was my fault. I was in a bad mood[19] when I saw her. I told her all women were rotten gold diggers[20]."

"Then why didn't you admit that to Darcy Scott? When she asked you, you denied meeting Erin."

"Because I knew I'd end up here[21]."

1. était remontée jusqu'à
2. un magasin de chaussures
3. Personne à l'époque ne s'était rappelé
4. les grands magasins de luxe
5. un modèle de la collection actuelle
6. quadriller
7. les chausseurs chics
8. les solderies
9. conduit au poste pour interrogatoire
10. à se plaindre
11. de la grossièreté de Darcy à son égard
12. que j'avais été vache
13. ce restaurant chic
14. a sauté dans un taxi
15. au coin de la rue
16. Je suis arrivé en courant.
17. Après tous mes efforts
18. m'a claqué la porte au nez
19. de mauvaise humeur
20. ne couraient qu'après le fric
21. qu'alors je me retrouverais ici

"You live on Ninth Avenue and Forty-eighth Street?"

"Yes."

"Your trustee at the bank thinks you have another residence. You withdrew[1] a large sum of money five or six years ago."

"It was my money to spend as I please.[2]"

"Did you buy another residence?"

"Prove it."

On Saturday afternoon when he was finished with Len Parker, Vince D'Ambrosio drove to 101 Christopher Street and rang the bell. Gus Boxer, his face set in surly lines[3], came to the door. He was wearing a long-sleeved[4] undershirt[5]. Tattered suspenders[6] held up shapeless[7] trousers. He acted unimpressed[8] by the FBI badge. "I'm off duty.[9] What do ye want?"

"I want to talk to you, Gus. Your place or headquarters?[10] And drop the righteous indignation[11]. I have your file on my desk, Mr. Hoffman."

Boxer's eyes darted nervously[12]. "Come on in. And keep your voice down[13]."

"I wasn't aware I'd raised it.[14]"

Boxer led the way to[15] his ground-floor apartment. As Vince had expected from the way the man dressed, the apartment was a further extension of his personality[16]. Shabby, stained upholstery.[17] Remnants of a once-beige rug.[18] A rickety[19] table piled with porn magazines[20].

Vince riffled through them[21]. "Quite a collection you have here.[22]"

"Any law against it?"

Vince slapped down[23] the magazines. "Listen, Hoffman, we've never gotten anything on you, but your name has an unhealthy way of coming up[24] on the computer. Ten years ago you were the super

1. avez retiré
2. C'était mon argent, je pouvais en faire ce que je voulais.
3. l'air renfrogné
4. à manches longues
5. maillot de corps
6. De vieilles bretelles
7. informe
8. fit comme s'il n'était pas impressionné
9. J'ai fini mon service.
10. Chez toi ou au QG ?
11. arrête de monter sur tes grands chevaux
12. regarda nerveusement à droite et à gauche
13. ne parlez pas si fort
14. Je ne m'étais pas rendu compte que j'avais levé la voix.
15. le conduisit à
16. était à son image
17. Des sièges élimés et tachés.
18. Les restes d'un tapis qui avait été beige.
19. branlante
20. des revues porno
21. les feuilleta
22. Jolie collection !
23. reposa violemment
24. revient un peu trop souvent

of an apartment where a twenty-year-old girl was found dead in the basement."

"I had nothing to do with that."

"She'd filed a complaint with the management[1] that she found you in her apartment going through her closet[2]."

"I was looking for a water leak. There was a water-pipe[3] in the wall behind that closet."

"That's the same story you gave[4] Erin Kelley two weeks ago, isn't it?"

"Who said that?"

"She told someone that she was going to move as soon as possible because she'd found you in her bedroom."

"I was—"

"Looking for a water leak. I know. Now let's talk about Claire Barnes. How many times did you drop in on her[5] unexpectedly[6] when she lived here?"

"Never."

When he left Boxer, Vince went directly to his office, arriving there just in time to get a call from Hank. Was it okay if he didn't get in until eight or so? There was a basketball game at school and some of the gang[7] were going out for pizza afterward[8].

A great kid, Vince told himself again as he assured Hank that was fine. Worth all the years of trying[9] to make a go of[10] his marriage to Alice. Well at least she was happy now. The pampered[11] wife of a guy whose wallet was as fat as his waistline[12]. And he? I'd like to meet someone, Vince admitted to himself, then realized that Nona Roberts's face was suddenly filling his mind[13].

His assistant Ernie told him there'd been a break[14]. A detective from the Midtown North Precinct had picked up Petey Potters, the derelict[15] who lived on

1. s'était plainte au gérant
2. en train de fouiller dans son placard
3. conduite d'eau
4. les mêmes bobards que vous avez racontés à
5. êtes-vous passé la voir
6. à l'improviste
7. certains de ses copains
8. après le match
9. Ça justifiait toutes les années passées à essayer
10. de faire marcher
11. choyée
12. aussi rembourré que sa bedaine
13. lui était soudain venu à l'esprit
14. qu'il y avait un élément nouveau
15. clochard

the pier where Erin Kelley's body was found. They were bringing Petey into the precinct for questioning. Vince turned and ran for the elevators[1].

Petey was having trouble with his vision[2]. Seeing double. That happened sometimes after he'd had a coupla[3] bottles of dago red. That meant that instead of three cops he was seeing three sets of twin cops[4]. Nobody's eyes were friendly.[5]

Petey thought about the dead girl. How cold she'd felt[6] when he'd lifted[7] the necklace.

What was the cop saying? "Petey, there are fingerprints[8] on Erin Kelley's throat. We're going to compare them with yours."

Through a haze[9], Petey thought of one of his friends who'd happened to stab[10] a guy. He was in prison for five years now and the guy he stabbed had hardly been scratched[11]. Petey had never been in trouble with the cops. Never. He wouldn't hurt a fly[12].

He told them that. He could tell[13] they didn't believe him.

"Look," he volunteered[14] in a burst of confidence[15]. "I found that girl. I didn't have enough money to buy even a cuppa coffee." Tears formed in his eyes at the memory of how thirsty he'd been[16]. "I could tell the necklace was real gold. It had a long chain with lots of fancy coins[17] attached. Figured if I didn't take it[18], the first guy who found her would[19]. Including some cops I've heard about." He was sorry he'd added that[20].

"What'd you do with the necklace, Petey?"

"Sold it for twenty-five bucks[21] to that big dude[22] who works Seventh Avenue around Central Park South."

1. fit demi-tour et se précipita vers l'ascenseur
2. n'avait pas les yeux en face des trous
3. deux
4. trois couples de policiers jumeaux
5. Aucun n'avait l'air bienveillant.
6. Comme elle était froide
7. il lui avait pris
8. des empreintes digitales
9. brouillard
10. poignardé
11. avait eu à peine une égratignure
12. ne ferait pas de mal à une mouche
13. voyait bien
14. ajouta spontanément
15. avec plus d'assurance
16. ce qu'il avait eu soif
17. jolies pièces de monnaie
18. Je m'suis dit que si moi je le prenais pas
19. le premier qui la trouverait le prendrait
20. regretta d'avoir dit ça
21. dollars
22. mec

"Buy-and-Sell Bert," one of the cops remarked. "We'll pick him up.[1]"

"When did you find the body, Petey?" Vince asked.

"When I woke up late morning." Petey squinted[2]. His eyes took on a crafty expression.[3] Everything was coming into focus.[4] "But real early[5], I mean when it was still pitch dark[6], I heard a car drive onto the pier, pass my place, and stop. I figured it might be a drug deal so I stayed inside. Honest.[7]"

"Even when you knew it was driving away?" one of the detectives asked. "You didn't even peek[8]?"

"Well, when I was sure it was going ..."

"Did you get a look at it, Petey?"

They believed him. He knew it. If he could only tell them something else to make them feel like he was trying to cooperate. Petey forced the alcoholic haze to retreat[9] for a split second[10] from his brain. All the days of standing with a bottle of sudsy[11] water and a squeegee[12] at the Fifty-sixth Street exit of the West Side Highway rushed through his mind[13]. He'd had plenty of chance to know[14] what the backs of cars looked like.

Again he could see the taillights[15] of the car disappearing off the pier. Something about the rear window[16]. "It was a station wagon[17]," he said with a triumphant wheeze[18]. "On Birdie's grave[19], it was a station wagon."

As the haze rushed back[20], Petey had to force himself not to cackle[21]. Birdie was probably still alive.

1. On va l'interpeller.
2. plissa les yeux
3. Il prit un air roublard.
4. Il commençait à avoir les idées plus claires.
5. super tôt
6. il faisait encore nuit noire
7. Juré !
8. n'avez même pas jeté un coup d'œil
9. s'efforça de chasser les vapeurs d'alcool
10. pendant une fraction de seconde
11. savonneuse
12. raclette
13. lui revinrent soudain
14. Ce ne sont pas les occasions qui lui avaient manqué de voir
15. feux arrière
16. la lunette arrière
17. break
18. d'un ton rauque triomphant
19. Je le jure sur la tombe de Birdie
20. L'esprit à nouveau embrouillé
21. pour ne pas glousser

1. n'était pas d'humeur pour l'instant
2. avait gardé
3. Quelle tristesse !
4. filles
5. qui soient entrées ici
6. Dieu ait son âme
7. tapota
8. avez été une amie formidable pour elle
9. pour manger un morceau
10. je m'asseyais pour lui tenir compagnie
11. de faire attention
12. Bien sûr que j'étais contre !
13. pour prendre un mouchoir
14. ça a attiré mon attention
15. que vous ne vous livrez pas à ces sottises
16. pas très douée pour les traces écrites
17. résolut de ne pas avouer

Darcy and Nona had planned to have dinner together on Saturday night. Other friends were calling, inviting her to join them, but Darcy was in no mood yet[1] to see anyone.

They arranged to meet at Jimmy Neary's Restaurant on East Fifty-seventh Street. Darcy arrived first. Jimmy had saved[2] the left back corner table for them. "A damn shame[3]," he said as he greeted Darcy. "Erin was one of the prettiest lasses[4] ever to walk through this door[5], God rest her[6]." He patted[7] Darcy's hand. "You were a grand friend to her[8]. And don't think I don't know it. Sometimes when she'd come in for a quick bite[9], I'd sit with her for the moment[10]. I told her to watch her step[11] answering those crazy ads."

Darcy smiled. "I'm surprised she told you about them, Jimmy. She'd have known you wouldn't approve."

"Be sure I didn't.[12] She reached in her jacket pocket for a handkerchief[13] last month and pulled out one that she'd torn from a magazine. It fell to the floor and when I picked it up, it caught my eye[14]. I said to her, 'Erin Kelley, I hope you're not into that foolishness[15].' "

"That's what I'm afraid of," Darcy told him. "Erin was a fabulous jewelry designer but not much of a record keeper[16]. The FBI is trying to trace anyone Erin wrote to or met, but I'm sure the list isn't complete." Darcy decided against saying[17] that she was also answering personal ads. "Do you remember what that ad said?"

Neary's brow furrowed in thought[1]. "No, but I got a fair glance at it[2], and I will[3]. Something about singing or—ah, it'll come. Look, here's Nona and she has someone with her."

Vince followed Nona to the table. "I'm only going to stop by for a minute," he told Darcy. "I don't want to interfere with[4] your dinner, but I was trying to reach you, phoned Nona, and found out you were here."

"It's fine, and I wish you'd stay." Darcy noticed that Nona's eyes had a brightness[5] she had never seen in them before[6]. "You got the message about Erin's telling one of her dates that she'd found the superintendent in her apartment again?"

"I saw Boxer today." Vince raised an eyebrow. *"Again?"*

"Erin told me he pulled that[7] last year, but she always dismissed him as being harmless[8]. Apparently as of two weeks ago[9] she changed her mind."

"We're following up on him[10] as well as other people. I'd like to hear about the guy from last night."

"He was a nice guy ..."

Liz came to take their orders[11]. She gave Darcy a quick, sympathetic smile. She always took such good care of us[12], Darcy thought. She had told Erin that growing up[13] in Ireland she'd been a redhead too[14].

Dubonnet for Darcy and Nona. A beer for Vince.

Darcy and Nona decided on[15] the red snapper[16]. Nona said crisply[17] to Vince, "You've got to eat sometime."

He ordered the corned beef[18] and cabbage[19].

Vince got back to Darcy's other date. "I want to know about everybody you met. You've already

1. fronça les sourcils pour se concentrer
2. l'ai assez bien vue
3. ça va me revenir
4. interrompre
5. un éclat
6. qu'elle ne leur connaissait pas
7. qu'il avait sorti le même prétexte
8. se disait toujours qu'il n'était pas dangereux
9. il y a deux semaines
10. On le surveille
11. commandes
12. s'est toujours si bien occupée de nous
13. quand elle était petite
14. elle aussi avait été rousse
15. choisirent
16. vivaneau [poisson tropical]
17. d'un ton autoritaire
18. [viande de bœuf en conserve]
19. avec du chou

seen two who admitted knowing Erin. Please let me decide on who is or isn't important."

She told him about David Weld. "He's an executive[1] from Boston with the Holden chain. I gather[2] he's been back and forth to[3] New York for the last few years as they opened new stores." She felt as though she could[4] read Vince D'Ambrosio's mind[5]. *Back and forth to New York for the last two years.* Darcy said, "The one thing[6] that did strike me[7] is that he's been a shoe buyer."

"Shoe buyer! What's this guy's name?" Vince made a note in his book. "David Weld, Box 1527. Believe me, we'll check him out[8]. Darcy, Nona told you about the shoes that were returned[9] to the parents of the girl from Lancaster?"

"Yes."

He hesitated, glanced around[10], and saw that the people at the next table were absorbed in their own conversation. "We're trying to keep this one quiet[11]. Another pair of mismatched shoes were delivered yesterday. They were the mates of the ones Nan Sheridan was found wearing fifteen years ago."

Darcy gripped[12] the table. "Then Erin's death may not be a copycat crime."

"We just don't know. We're digging to see[13] if anyone who knew Claire Barnes also knew Nan Sheridan."

"And Erin?" Nona asked.

"That would of course clinch the fact[14] we have another Ted Bundy[15] who's been getting away with serial murders for years." Vince put down his fork. "I've got to tell it to you straight[16]. A lot of people who answer these ads turn out to be a far different cry from the way they describe themselves[17]. All the young women our computer targeted as being possible serial-killer victims[18] are in your age bracket[19],

1. cadre supérieur
2. D'après ce que j'ai compris,
3. il a fait la navette entre Boston et
4. eut l'impression de pouvoir
5. lire dans les pensées de Vince
6. seul détail
7. qui m'ait frappée
8. on va se renseigner sur lui
9. renvoyées
10. regarda autour de lui
11. de ne pas l'ébruiter
12. s'agrippa à
13. On creuse pour savoir
14. Ça confirmerait bien sûr que
15. [réel tueur en série]
16. vous le dire carrément
17. n'ont en fait rien à voir avec le portrait qu'ils font d'eux-mêmes
18. identifiées par notre ordinateur comme victimes éventuelles du tueur
19. tranche d'âge

in your intelligence bracket, in your looks bracket[1]. In other words, our killer may date fifty girls and then one turns him on[2]. I know I can't dissuade you from answering these ads. Frankly, you've turned up[3] some mighty[4] interesting people for us to investigate. Nevertheless, you're not trained to[5] be a decoy[6]. You're a thoroughly[7] nice, vulnerable young woman who doesn't have the ability to protect herself if she suddenly finds that she's painted into a corner[8]."

"I don't intend to let myself get painted into a corner."

Vince had a quick coffee and left. He explained that his son, Hank, was coming in on a train from Long Island and he wanted to be in the apartment when he arrived.

Nona's eyes followed him as he stopped to pay the check[9]. "Did you notice his tie?" she asked. "Today it was a blue and black check[10] with a brown tweed jacket."

"So? Surely that doesn't bother you[11]."

"No, I like it. Vince D'Ambrosio is so determined to find whoever killed these girls that I swear he blocks out anything unimportant[12]. I happened to call the Barnes home in Lancaster just after they opened the package with the shoes and I tell you, hearing them broke my heart[13]. Today I called Nan Sheridan's brother to ask him to be on the program. I could hear that same pain in his voice. Oh, Darcy, please God, be careful."

1. ont votre genre d'intelligence et votre genre de beauté
2. mais une seule lui fera de l'effet
3. vous nous avez mis sur la piste de
4. très
5. n'avez pas la formation pour
6. jouer les appâts
7. extrêmement
8. elle se retrouve acculée
9. l'addition
10. à carreaux bleus et noirs
11. ne te dérange pas
12. il fait l'impasse sur tout ce qui est secondaire
13. ça m'a fendu le cœur de les entendre

XII
SUNDAY
March 3

On Sunday morning at nine o'clock, Michael Nash phoned. "I've been thinking about you, even worrying about you. How's it going?"

She had slept reasonably well. "Okay, I guess."

"Up to a drive to[1] Bridgewater, New Jersey, and an early dinner?" He did not wait for her to answer. "In case you haven't looked out the window, it's a beautiful day. Really feels like spring.[2] My housekeeper is a great cook[3] and has to be treated for frustration[4] if I don't bring company home[5] at least once over the weekend[6]."

Somehow, she had dreaded this day.[7] If they didn't have other plans, she and Erin had often met for brunch on Sundays and spent the afternoon at Lincoln Center or in a museum. "That sounds fine." They arranged that he'd pick her up[8] at eleven-thirty.

"And don't get all gussied up[9]. In fact, if you like to ride[10], wear a pair of jeans. I've got a couple of darn good[11] horses."

"I love to ride."

His car was a two-seater[12] Mercedes. "Very fancy," Darcy said.

1. Vous seriez d'attaque pour une balade à
2. On dirait que c'est déjà le printemps.
3. très bonne cuisinière
4. souffre de frustration aiguë
5. ne ramène pas d'invités
6. une fois pendant le week-end
7. C'était le jour de la semaine qu'elle appréhendait.
8. convinrent qu'il passerait la prendre
9. ne vous mettez pas sur votre trente et un
10. monter à cheval
11. supers
12. un coupé

Nash was wearing a turtleneck sport shirt[1], jeans, a herringbone[2] jacket. The other night at dinner, she'd had the impression of how kind his eyes were. Today they were still kind, but there was something else. Maybe, she told herself, just the look a guy got when he was interested in a woman. Darcy realized that the thought pleased her.

The drive was pleasant. As they progressed south[3] on Route 287, the suburbs[4] disappeared. Houses that could be glimpsed from[5] the road were now farther and farther apart[6]. Nash talked with affectionate warmth[7] about his parents. "To paraphrase that old commercial[8], 'My father made his money the old-fashioned way[9], he earned it[10].' He was just starting to hit it big[11] when I was born. For ten years we moved every year, one house larger than the other, until he bought the present place when I was eleven. As I told you, my tastes are somewhat simpler[12], but God he was so proud the day we moved in. Carried my mother over the threshold.[13]"

Somehow it was easy to talk with Michael Nash about her famous parents and the Bel-Air mansion. "I always felt like a changeling[14] there, as though the princess daughter of the royal couple must be living in a cottage[15] and I was an impostor in her place." *How ever did two such stunning people manage to produce that mousy-looking child?*

Erin was the only one who knew about that. Now Darcy found herself telling[16] Michael Nash. Then she added, "Hey, this is Sunday. You're off duty[17], doctor. Be careful, you've got a way of being too good a listener[18]."

He glanced at her. "And when you grew up, you never looked in the mirror and realized what an outrageous statement that was[19]?"

"Should I have?"

1. un sous-pull à col roulé
2. à chevrons
3. avançaient vers le sud
4. la banlieue
5. l'on distinguait depuis
6. de plus en plus éparses
7. avec chaleur et affection
8. publicité
9. à l'ancienne
10. l'a gagné à la sueur de son front
11. faire fortune
12. j'ai des goûts plus simples
13. Il a pris ma mère dans ses bras pour franchir le seuil.
14. [enfant substitué par les fées à l'enfant réel d'un couple]
15. une chaumière
16. se surprit à le raconter à
17. C'est votre jour de repos
18. tendance à tendre une oreille trop attentive
19. quelle remarque scandaleuse c'était

"I would say so." He was steering the car off[1] the highway, through the quaint[2] town, along a country road. "The fence starts the property.[3]"

It was a full minute before they turned into the gate. "My God, how many acres do you have?"

"Four hundred."

At the Le Cirque dinner he had said the house was too ornate[4]. Darcy silently agreed but nevertheless[5] decided that it was an imposing and substantial mansion. The trees and plants were still bare of[6] leaves and flowers, but the evergreens[7] that edged[8] the long driveway were full and luxuriant[9]. "If you decide you've enjoyed yourself and come back next month, the grounds will be worth the trip[10]," Nash commented.

Mrs. Hughes, the housekeeper, had prepared a light lunch. Sandwiches quartered[11] with the crusts cut off[12]—chicken, ham and cheese—then cookies, coffee. She looked approvingly at Darcy, severely at Michael. "I hope this is enough, miss. Doctor said that since you'll be having an early dinner I mustn't overdo now[13]."

"It's perfect," Darcy told her sincerely. They ate in the breakfast room off[14] the kitchen. Michael then gave her a quick tour[15] of the house.

"Interior-decorator picture perfect[16]," he said. "Don't you agree? Antiques that cost a fortune. I suspect half of them are fakes[17]. Someday I'll change everything, but for now[18] it just isn't worth the effort[19]. Unless I'm having guests I live in the study[20]. Here we are.

"Now this is a comfortable room," Darcy said with real pleasure. "Warm. Lived-in. Wonderful view. Good lighting[21]. It's the kind of look I try to give a place when I refurbish[22]."

1. quittait
2. au charme désuet
3. La propriété commence derrière cette barrière.
4. avait une déco trop chargée
5. néanmoins
6. dénués de
7. arbustes persistants
8. bordaient
9. somptueux
10. le domaine méritera le voyage
11. [en pain de mie] coupés en quatre
12. sans la croûte
13. ne devais pas préparer trop de choses pour maintenant
14. qui donnait sur
15. lui fit faire une visite rapide
16. La déco intérieure sublime comme pour une photo
17. des faux
18. pour l'instant,
19. ça n'en vaut pas la peine
20. bureau
21. éclairage
22. que je redécore

"You really haven't told me much about your job. I want to hear, but how about that ride now? John has the horses ready."

Darcy had begun riding when she was three. It was one of the few activities she had not shared[1] with Erin. "She was afraid of horses," Darcy told Michael as she swung onto[2] the coal-black mare[3].

"Then riding won't be memory lane for you[4] today. That's good."

The air, fresh and clean, seemed to at last cleanse[5] the scent[6] of funeral flowers from her nostrils[7]. They cantered across Michael's property[8], slowed the horses to a walk as they went across town[9], joined other riders whom he introduced as his neighbors[10].

At six o'clock, they had dinner in the small dining room. The temperature had dropped[11]. A fire was blazing[12], the white wine chilling[13], a decanter[14] of red wine on the sideboard[15]. John Hughes, now in uniform, served the beautifully prepared meal. Crabmeat cocktail. Veal medallions. Tiny asparagus.[16] Roast[17] potatoes. Green salad with pepper cheese. Sherbet.[18] Espresso.

Darcy sighed as she sipped the coffee. "I can't thank you enough. If I'd been home by myself all day, it would have been pretty rough[19]."

"If I'd been here alone all day, it would have been pretty boring."

She could not help overhearing[20] Mrs. Hughes comment to her husband as they were leaving, "Now there is one lovely girl. I hope Doctor brings her back."

1. qu'elle n'avait pas partagées
2. en enfourchant
3. la jument anthracite
4. ne vous rappellera pas le bon temps passé ensemble
5. chasser enfin
6. l'odeur
7. qui subsistait dans ses narines
8. traversèrent la propriété de Michael au petit galop
9. une fois en ville
10. qu'il présenta comme étant ses voisins
11. nettement baissé
12. Un bon feu flambait
13. était au frais
14. carafe
15. sur le buffet
16. De petites asperges.
17. au four
18. Du sorbet.
19. éprouvant
20. ne put s'empêcher d'entendre

XIII
MONDAY
March 4

1. dans une ravissante monture de style victorien
2. plut immédiatement à Ashton
3. s'écria, enthousiaste
4. Je suis bien content
5. rendra très bien
6. qu'il vaut ne serait-ce qu'un centime de moins que
7. sûrement
8. avez bien marchandé
9. c'est votre produit d'appel
10. rit benoîtement
11. en sortant son chéquier
12. eut le frisson d'excitation que lui donnait toujours la prise de risque
13. Tout bijoutier digne de ce nom
14. aurait encore été une affaire
15. avait hâte de mettre la main

ON MONDAY EVENING, Jay Stratton met Merrill Ashton in the Oak Bar of the Plaza. The bracelet, a band of diamonds in a charming Victorian setting[1], won Ashton's instant approval[2]. "Frances is just going to love that," he enthused[3]. "I'm sure glad[4] you convinced me to order it for her."

"I knew you'd be pleased. Your wife is a very pretty woman. That bracelet will look lovely[5] on her arm. As I told you, I want you to have it appraised when you get home. If the jeweler tells you it's worth one cent less than[6] forty thousand dollars, the deal is off. In fact, he'll undoubtedly[7] tell you that you drove a hard bargain[8]. But the fact is that I'm hoping that next Christmas you'll think of another piece for Frances. A diamond necklace? Diamond earrings? We'll see."

"So this is your loss leader for me[9]?" Ashton chuckled[10] as he reached for his checkbook[11]. "That's good business."

Jay felt the peculiar thrill that came with taking risks[12]. Any decent jeweler[13] would tell Ashton that at fifty thousand the bracelet would still be a bargain[14]. Tomorrow he had a lunch date with Enid Armstrong. He couldn't wait to get his hands[15] on her ring.

Thank you, Erin, he thought as he accepted the check.

Ashton invited Jay to have a quick bite[1] before he left for the airport. He was taking a 9:30 plane home to Winston-Salem. Stratton explained that he was meeting a client at seven. He did not add[2] that Darcy Scott was hardly the kind of client[3] he wanted. He had a check in his pocket for seventeen thousand five hundred dollars; the twenty thousand from Bertolini less his commission.

Effusive good-byes.[4] "Give my very best to[5] Frances. I know how happy you'll make her."

Stratton did not notice another man quietly leave a nearby table[6] and follow Merrill Ashton into the lobby.

"If I may have a word with you[7], sir."

Ashton accepted the card that was offered to him[8]. *Nigel Bruce, Lloyd's of London.*

"I don't understand," Ashton sputtered[9].

"Sir, if Mr. Stratton comes out, I don't want to be observed. Would you mind if we step[10] into the jewelry shop right over there? One of our experts will meet us. We'd like to have a look at the jewelry you just purchased[11]." The investigator took pity[12] on Ashton's bewildered expression[13]. "It's routine[14]."

"Routine! Are you suggesting that the bracelet I just bought was stolen?"

"I'm not suggesting anything, sir."

"The hell you're not.[15] Well, if there's anything funny[16] about this bracelet, I want to know right now[17]. That check isn't certified[18]. I can have payment stopped[19] in the morning."

1. à manger un morceau
2. ne précisa pas
3. n'était vraiment pas le type de cliente
4. Au revoir chaleureux.
5. Mes amitiés à
6. quitter discrètement une table voisine
7. Si vous aviez un instant à m'accorder
8. qu'on lui tendit
9. bafouilla
10. nous entrons
11. que vous venez d'acquérir
12. eut pitié
13. de l'air ébahi d'Ashton
14. une simple formalité
15. Mon œil !
16. quoi que ce soit de louche
17. tout de suite
18. n'a pas été certifié [par ma banque]
19. faire opposition

THE INVESTIGATIVE REPORTER for the *New York Post* had done his job well. Somehow he managed to learn[1] that a package had been delivered to Nan Sheridan's home and that it contained the mates of the mismatched shoes she'd been wearing when her body was found. Nan Sheridan's picture; Erin's picture; Claire Barnes's picture. Splashed side by side on the front page.[2] SERIAL KILLER ON THE LOOSE[3].

Darcy read the paper[4] in a cab on the way to the Plaza.

"Here we are, miss."

"What? Oh, all right. Thank you."

She was glad that she had had wall-to-wall appointments[5] that day. Once again, she had brought clothes to the office. This time she changed into the red wool Rodeo Drive ensemble. As she got out of the cab, she remembered that she'd worn this outfit[6] the last time she spoke to Erin. If only I'd seen her just once more, she thought.

It was ten of seven[7], a bit early for her meeting with Jay Stratton. Darcy decided to pop into[8] the Oak Room. Fred, the maître d'[9] of the restaurant, was an old friend. Ever since she could remember[10], when she and her parents had come to New York they had stayed at the Plaza.

Something Michael Nash had said yesterday was gnawing at her[11]. Hadn't he been suggesting that she was still harboring[12] a child's resentment[13] at a careless, even cruel remark[14] that had no present validity[15]? She found herself looking forward[16] to

1. Il avait découvert on ne sait trop comment
2. Leurs photos faisaient la une.
3. en liberté
4. le journal
5. rendez-vous sur rendez-vous
6. c'était la tenue qu'elle portait
7. 18 h 50
8. passer à
9. maître d'hôtel
10. D'aussi loin qu'elle se souvienne
11. la travaillait
12. nourrissait toujours
13. une rancœur d'enfant
14. blessé par une remarque inconsidérée, voire cruelle
15. n'avait plus rien de fondé
16. réalisa qu'elle attendait avec impatience

the next time she saw Nash. I suppose it's like getting a free consultation, but I'd like to ask him about it, she acknowledged[1] as a beaming Fred[2] rushed to greet her[3].

Promptly at seven she went next door to the bar. Jay Stratton was at a corner table. The only other time she had met him had been at Erin's apartment. Her first impression had been distinctly unfavorable[4]. He'd been angry about the missing Bertolini necklace, then after it was found switched to a display of anxiety over[5] the missing pouch of diamonds. He'd been infinitely more concerned[6] about the necklace than about the fact that Erin was missing. Tonight it was like being with a different person. He was really trying to turn on the charm[7]. Somehow, she was sure she'd seen the real Jay Stratton the first time.

She asked him where he had met Erin.

"Don't laugh. She happened to answer[8] a personal ad I placed. I knew her casually[9] and called her. One of those serendipity things.[10] Bertolini had asked me about resetting those jewels and when I read Erin's letter I remembered that wonderful piece she did that won[11] the N.W. Ayer award[12]. And so we got together. It was strictly business[13], although she did ask me to escort her[14] to a benefit[15]. A client had given her the tickets. We danced the night away[16]."

Why had he felt it necessary to add "strictly business"? Darcy wondered. And would it have been strictly business for Erin? Only six months ago Erin had said almost wistfully[17], "You know, Darce, I'm at the point where I'd really like to meet some nice guy and fall madly in love."

1. s'avoua-t-elle
2. Fred, radieux,
3. accourait pour lui dire bonjour
4. nettement défavorable
5. avait eu l'air de s'inquiéter de
6. inquiet
7. lui faisait un vrai numéro de charme
8. Il se trouve qu'elle avait répondu à
9. avais vaguement entendu parler d'elle
10. Un heureux hasard.
11. ce merveilleux bijou qui lui avait valu
12. prix
13. purement professionnel
14. l'accompagner
15. un gala de bienfaisance
16. toute la soirée
17. presque avec mélancolie

The Jay Stratton who was sitting across the table, attentive[1], handsome, able to understand Erin's talent, might well have fit the bill[2].

"What ad of yours did she answer?"

Stratton shrugged. "Frankly, I place so many of them I forget." He smiled. "You look shocked, Darcy. I'll explain to you what I explained to Erin. I will marry a very rich woman someday[3]. I haven't met her yet, but be assured I will[4]. I meet many women through these ads. It is not very difficult to persuade older women, ever so gently[5], to relieve their loneliness[6] by treating themselves to[7] a particularly beautiful piece of jewelry or by resetting their own rings, necklaces, or bracelets. They're happy. I'm happy."

"Why are you telling me this?" Darcy asked. "I hope it's not your way of letting me down easily[8]. I didn't think of tonight as a date. For me, it's 'strictly business.' "

Stratton shook his head. "God forbid[9] I should be so presumptuous[10]. I'm telling you exactly what I told Erin after she explained to me her purpose in answering the ads[11]. Your producer friend's documentary, isn't it?"

"Yes."

"What I'm trying to say and probably not doing it very well is that there was no romantic spark[12] between Erin and me. The next point I'd like to make is[13] to profoundly apologize for my behavior[14] the first time we met. Bertolini is a valued client of mine[15]. I'd never worked with Erin before. I didn't know her well enough to be totally sure that she wouldn't go away on a whim[16] and forget the deadline for delivery[17]. Believe me, I've had very uncomfortable moments[18] of communing with myself[19] and realizing the impression I must have

1. attentionné
2. aurait bien pu faire l'affaire
3. un jour
4. vous pouvez être sûre que ça va arriver
5. avec beaucoup de délicatesse
6. d'alléger leur solitude
7. en s'offrant
8. de me rejeter tranquillement
9. Dieu me préserve
10. d'avoir cette prétention
11. son but en répondant à ces annonces
12. déclic
13. La deuxième chose importante, c'est
14. mon comportement
15. l'un de mes clients les plus importants
16. sur un coup de tête
17. la date de la livraison
18. j'ai été très mal à l'aise
19. en m'interrogeant sur mes actions

made on you when you were heartsick with worry[1] about your missing friend and I was talking client deadlines."

A wonderful speech, Darcy thought. I should warn him I've lived most of my life with two of the best actors in this country. She wondered if it would be appropriate[2] to burst into applause[3]. Instead she said[4], "You do have the check for the necklace?"

"Yes. I didn't know how to make it out[5]. Do you think 'Estate of Erin Kelley[6]' will be appropriate[7]?"

Estate of Erin Kelley. All the years Erin had cheerfully done without the things[8] that most of their friends considered essential. So proud that she could[9] keep her father in a private nursing home. Just on the threshold of[10] major success. Swallowing over a lump in her throat[11], Darcy said, "That will do[12]."

She looked down at the check. Seventeen thousand five hundred dollars made out to the Estate of Erin Kelley, drawn on[13] Chase Manhattan Bank, and signed by Jay Charles Stratton.

1. morte d'inquiétude
2. si elle devait
3. se mettre à applaudir
4. Elle se contenta de dire
5. à quel ordre le libeller
6. Succession Erin Kelley
7. conviendrait
8. s'était volontiers passé des choses
9. Si fière de pouvoir
10. À la veille de
11. La gorge serrée
12. Ça fera l'affaire
13. provenant d'un compte de la

XIV
TUESDAY
March 5

1. qu'on ne le conduise à l'étage, au

2. qu'il avait toujours eu envie de faire

3. des cours sur l'art

4. La formation du FBI contre les vols d'œuvres d'art

5. n'avait fait que lui donner envie d'y revenir

6. il s'était lassé d'attendre

7. qu'elle se montre fair-play

8. Elle l'avait bien pris au mot.

9. fit signe à Vince de s'asseoir

10. suivit

11. largement surévaluée

12. somme

13. ils ne tiendront pas parole

14. de proposer des enchères de départ raisonnables

15. à patienter

16. encore

17. estimations

ON TUESDAY MORNING when Agent D'Ambrosio entered Sheridan Galleries, he took a quick look around before he was ushered upstairs to[1] Chris Sheridan's office. The furniture reminded him of the contents of Nona Roberts's living room. Funny. One of the things that had always been on his list[2] was to take courses in art[3] and antique furniture. The Bureau's Art Theft program[4] had only whetted his appetite in that area[5].

In the meantime, Vince thought as he followed a secretary down the corridor, I live with Alice's mistakes. At the time of the divorce he'd gotten tired of expecting[6] a fair shake from her[7]. "Take what you want if it's so important to you," he'd offered.

She'd certainly taken him at his word.[8]

Sheridan was on the phone. He smiled and waved Vince to a seat[9]. Without appearing to be paying attention, Vince took in[10] the conversation. Something about a collection being wildly overvalued[11].

Sheridan was saying, "Tell Lord Kilman that they may promise him that amount[12] but they can't deliver[13]. We'll be happy to set reasonable opening bids[14]. The market isn't as strong as it was a few years ago, but is he prepared to wait it out[15] another[16] three to five years? Otherwise, I think if he looks carefully at our estimates[17] he'll realize that many of the pieces he acquired fairly recently will still turn him a handsome profit[1]."

Confident.[2] Knowledgeable.[3] Innate warmth.[4] That was the way Vince had sized up[5] Chris Sheridan last week when he'd gone to Darien. At that time, Sheridan had been wearing a sports shirt and windbreaker. Today he was dressed in a charcoal gray[6] suit, white shirt, red and gray tie, very much the executive[7].

Chris hung up and reached across the desk[8] to shake hands[9]. Vince apologized for giving him such short notice[10] and got right to the point[11]. "When I saw you last week, I was pretty sure that Erin Kelley's death was a copycat murder because of the *True Crimes* program about your sister. I'm not sure about that anymore.[12]" He told him about Claire Barnes and the package that had been returned to her home.

Chris listened attentively. "Another one."

It seemed to Vince that all the residual pain of[13] his sister's murder was in those two words.

"Is there anything I can do to help?" Chris asked.

"I don't know," Vince said frankly. "Whoever[14] killed your sister must have known her. The matching shoe size can't be a coincidence. We have three possibilities. The same murderer has continued to kill young women all through these years. The same murderer stopped killing and started again several years ago. The third possibility is that Nan's murderer confided his modus operandi to[15] someone else who decided to take over[16]. The last one is the least likely[17]."

"Then you're going to try to connect[18] someone whom Nan knew to someone these other women knew?"

1. lui feraient tout de même un joli bénéfice
2. Sûr de lui.
3. Connaissant son affaire.
4. Chaleureux.
5. avait perçu
6. anthracite
7. le look du cadre supérieur
8. se pencha au-dessus du bureau
9. pour lui serrer la main
10. de l'avoir prévenu si tard
11. entra tout de suite dans le vif du sujet
12. Je n'en suis plus très sûr.
13. toute la douleur qu'il éprouvait encore à la suite de
14. Celui qui
15. ait confié ses méthodes à
16. de prendre la suite
17. la moins probable
18. relier

"Exactly. Although in Erin Kelley's case, because of the missing diamonds, there is still a possibility that we have a different culprit[1]. That's why we're planning to explore both avenues[2]. The reason I'm here is that I'm going to try to link one person with Nan, Erin Kelley, and Claire Barnes."

"Someone who knew my sister fifteen years ago and recently met those girls through personal ads?"

"You've got it.[3] Darcy Scott was Erin Kelley's closest friend. They'd been answering the ads only because a television producer friend is doing a documentary and asked them to take part in the research. Darcy was out of town for a month[4]. She gave Erin a sample[5] of the letter she was sending, and some photographs. We know Erin answered some of those ads for both of them. Darcy Scott is hoping that whoever killed Erin will contact her."

Chris frowned. "You mean, you're allowing[6] another young woman to be set up as a possible victim[7]?"

Vince raised his hand[8] as though to wave away the suggestion[9]. "You don't know Darcy Scott. I'm not allowing anything. It's what she's determined to do. The one thing I have to grant her is[10] she's already met some pretty interesting characters and come up with information[11] that might be helpful."

"I still think it's a lousy idea[12]," Chris said flatly[13].

"So do I and now that we've established that[14], here's how I hope you can help. The faster we get[15] this guy, the less chance[16] Darcy Scott or some other young woman might get hurt. We're going to Brown to get a roster[17] of everyone who was in the student body[18] or on the faculty[19] when your sister was there. We'll check those names against anyone we know Erin met[20] or Darcy meets on these dates. I also think it would be a good idea if, besides the

1. un autre coupable
2. suivre les deux pistes
3. Exactement.
4. s'est absentée un mois
5. copie
6. vous permettez qu'
7. serve d'appât
8. leva la main
9. comme pour balayer l 'accusation
10. Je dois avouer qu'
11. nous a fourni des informations
12. c'est une très mauvaise idée
13. d'un ton catégorique
14. que nous sommes d'accord là-dessus
15. Plus vite nous arrêterons
16. moins il y aura de risques que
17. une liste
18. faisaient partie des étudiants
19. du personnel enseignant
20. Nous comparerons avec tous ceux dont nous savons qu'Erin les a rencontrés

school yearbooks[1] that we can get ourselves, you dig out any snapshots[2], albums, whatever[3], of your sister's friends or acquaintances[4]. You've got to understand that not everybody who answers a personal ad uses his own name. I want Darcy Scott to look over Nan's pictures to see if she can spot[5] anyone she meets along the way."

"Of course we've got endless[6] snapshots of Nan," Chris said slowly. "Ten years ago, after my father died, I managed to persuade my mother to pack up most of them[7] and put them in the attic[8]. Mother admitted that Nan's room was getting to be a shrine[9]."

"Good for you," Vince said. "You must have been pretty persuasive[10]."

Chris smiled quickly. "I pointed out that[11] it was one of the brightest rooms in the house and would be great for a visiting grandchild someday. The problem is, as my mother frequently reminds me, I haven't delivered[12]." The smile disappeared. "I can't get up to Connecticut until the weekend. I'll bring everything down[13] on Sunday."

Vince stood up. "I appreciate this.[14] I know how tough this has been on your mother, but if it turns out that we find[15] the guy who was responsible for your sister's death, believe me, in the long run[16] it will give her a lot of peace[17]."

As he turned to go, his beeper sounded[18]. "Do you mind if I call my office?"

Sheridan handed him[19] the phone, watched as D'Ambrosio's forehead furrowed[20]. "How is Darcy?"

Chris Sheridan felt a cold wave of apprehension. He didn't know this girl but experienced a sudden unreasoning fear for her[21]. He had never told anyone that when Nan went for a jog the morning after their birthday party, he had heard her go out. Still half asleep[22], he'd started to get up. Some instinct

1. en plus des albums de sa promo à la fac
2. vous pouviez retrouver des photos
3. n'importe
4. connaissances
5. remarque
6. une multitude de
7. d'en ranger une grande partie
8. au grenier
9. commençait à ressembler à une chapelle du souvenir
10. plutôt convaincant
11. Je lui ai fait remarquer
12. je n'ai pas rempli ma part du marché
13. Je rapporterai tout ça
14. Je vous en suis très reconnaissant.
15. si on finit par trouver
16. à long terme
17. ce sera un apaisement pour elle
18. son bip sonna
19. lui passa
20. vit D'Ambrosio froncer les sourcils
21. s'inquiéta soudain pour elle d'une façon irrationnelle
22. Encore à moitié endormi

was urging him[1] to follow her. He'd shrugged it off[2] and gone back to sleep.

Vince hung up the phone and turned back to Chris. "Is there any way you could possibly get[3] those pictures immediately? The White Plains police phoned. The father of Janine Wetzl, another one of the missing girls, just received the sort of package your mother and the Barnes family got. Her own shoe and a high-heeled white satin slipper." He slapped his hand on the table. "And while one agent was taking that call, Darcy Scott phoned. She had just opened a package that came in the morning mail[4]. The mates of the shoes found on Erin Kelley's body were sent to her."

Chris knew that the frustrated anger he saw on Agent D'Ambrosio's face mirrored his own expression[5]. "Why the hell[6] is he doing this?" Chris blurted[7]. "To prove the girls are dead? To taunt?[8] What makes him tick?[9]"

"When I know that, I'll know who he is," Vince said quietly. "And now, do you mind if I use your phone again? I have to call Darcy Scott."

1. Un instinct lui avait soufflé
2. Il l'avait ignoré
3. Pourriez-vous mettre la main sur
4. avec le courrier du matin
5. reflétait la sienne
6. Pourquoi diable
7. laissa échapper
8. pour railler la police
9. Qu'est-ce qui le motive ?

FROM THE MOMENT Darcy saw the package, she'd known. The mailman arrived just as she was leaving for work. He'd handed her the package and the letters and magazines and junk mail[10]. Afterward, Darcy remembered that he'd looked puzzled[11] when she did not respond to his greeting[12].

Like an automaton she'd walked stiffly upstairs to[13] her apartment and laid the package on the table by the window. Deliberately keeping her gloves

10. des prospectus
11. eu l'air perplexe
12. n'avait pas répondu à son bonjour
13. Elle était remontée avec un pas raide d'automate dans

on[1], she opened it, unknotting the twine[2] and slitting the sealing tape[3] at the flaps[4].

The sketch of the slipper on the lid[5]. Remove the lid. Separate the tissue. Look down at Erin's boot and a pink and silver slipper nestled together[6].

The slipper is so pretty, she thought. It would have gone beautifully with the dress Erin was buried in[7].

She did not have to look up[8] Vince D'Ambrosio's number, her brain produced it effortlessly[9]. He was not there but they promised to locate him[10]. "Can you wait for him?"

"Yes."

He called a few minutes later, was at the apartment within half an hour[11]. "This is rough for you."

"I touched the heel of the slipper with my glove," she confessed[12]. "I simply had to know[13] if it was Erin's size. It was."

Vince looked at her compassionately. "Maybe you should take it easy[14] today."

Darcy shook her head. "That would be the worst thing in the world for me to do." She attempted a smile[15]. "I've got a big project scheduled[16], and then, guess what? I have a date tonight."

WHEN VINCE left with the package, Darcy went directly to the newly purchased[17] hotel on West Twenty-third Street. Small, a total of thirty guest rooms, rundown[18], badly in need of paint[19], it still had tremendous possibilities[20]. The owners, a couple in their late thirties[21], explained that the cost of basic repairs[22] would leave very little for refurbishing[23]. They were delighted with her suggestion that they decorate in the style of an English

1. Faisant exprès de garder ses gants
2. en dénouant la ficelle
3. coupant le ruban adhésif
4. sur les rabats
5. chaussure dessinée sur le couvercle
6. pressées l'une contre l'autre
7. portait dans son cercueil
8. chercher
9. il lui vint automatiquement à l'esprit
10. le joindre
11. dans la demi-heure
12. avoua-t-elle
13. Il fallait que je sache
14. que vous devriez lever le pied
15. essaya de sourire
16. à mon agenda
17. que ses clients venaient d'acheter
18. délabré
19. ayant bien besoin d'une couche de peinture
20. offrait toutefois beaucoup de possibilités
21. qui avaient entre 35 et 40 ans
22. le coût des réparations essentielles
23. laisserait très peu d'argent pour la décoration

country inn[1]. "I can get plenty of sofas and upholstered chairs and lamps and tables in very good condition at private sales," she'd told them. "We can give this place a lot of charm. Look at the Algonquin. The most intimate bar in Manhattan and you'd be hard put to[2] find a chair that isn't threadbare[3]."

She walked through the rooms with them, making notes on their various sizes and shapes[4], and marking what furniture was usable[5]. The day passed quickly. She had intended to go home and change for her date, but then decided against it[6]. When Doug Fields called to reconfirm, he'd told her that he dressed casually[7]. "Slacks and a sweater are pretty much a uniform for me."

They were meeting at six at the Twenty-third Street Bar and Grill. Darcy got there exactly on time. Doug Fields was fifteen minutes late[8]. He burst[9] into the bar, clearly irritated and filled with apologies[10]. "I swear I've never seen this block so messed up[11]. So many cars, you'd swear it was an assembly line[12] in Detroit[13]. I'm so sorry, Darcy. I never keep people waiting. It's a thing with me.[14]"

"It really doesn't matter." He's good-looking, Darcy thought. Attractive.[15] Why had he found it necessary to immediately insist that he never kept people waiting?

Over a glass of wine, she listened to him on two levels. He was amusing, self-confident, well-spoken[16]. Extremely likable. He'd been raised in Virginia, went to the University there, dropped out of law school[17]. "I'd have made a lousy lawyer[18]. Don't have enough of the 'go for the jugular.'[19] "

Go for the jugular. Darcy thought of the bruises[20] on Erin's throat.

"Switched to art school.[21] Pointed out to[22] my father that instead of cracking the books[23], I was do-

1. auberge
2. on aurait du mal à
3. élimé
4. leurs formes
5. listant les meubles réutilisables
6. estima que ce n'était pas la peine
7. de façon décontractée
8. avait 15 minutes de retard
9. fit irruption
10. se confondant en excuses
11. de tels embouteillages dans ce quartier
12. on aurait dit une chaîne de montage
13. [industrie automobile]
14. Je déteste ça.
15. Séduisant.
16. il s'exprimait bien
17. avait laissé tomber ses études de droit
18. un très mauvais avocat
19. Je ne suis pas dans le trip « Prendre l'autre à la gorge ».
20. les bleus
21. J'ai opté pour les beaux-arts.
22. J'ai fait remarquer à
23. au lieu de me plonger dans les bouquins

ing caricatures of the profs. It was a good decision. I love illustrating and do well at it[1]."

"There's an old saying[2], 'If you want to be happy for a year, win the lottery. If you want to be happy for life, love what you do.' " Darcy hoped she sounded relaxed. This was the kind of guy Erin would have enjoyed meeting, the kind who after a date or two she would have trusted[3]. An artist? The sketch? Was everybody suspect?

The inevitable question came. "Why would a pretty girl like you need to answer personal ads?"

This time the question was easy to parry[4]. "Why would a good-looking, successful guy like you need to place personal ads?"

"That's easy," he said promptly. "I was married for eight years and now I'm not. I'm not interested in getting serious[5]. You get introduced to somebody at a friend's house, take her out a few times, and bingo[6], everybody's looking at the two of you waiting for the big announcement[7]. This way, I meet a lot of nice women. Lay the cards on the table[8] just like this and see if it clicks[9]. Tell me, how many dates from ads have you had this week?"

"You're the first one."

"Last week, then. Starting with Monday."

Monday I was standing over Erin's casket, Darcy thought. Tuesday I was watching that casket being lowered[10]. Wednesday I was home watching the reenactment[11] of Nan Sheridan's murder. Thursday she had met Len Parker. Friday, David Weld, the mild-mannered[12], rather shy[13] man who described himself as a department store executive and claimed not to have known[14] Erin. Saturday, Albert Booth, a computer analyst who was enthralled with[15] the wonders of[16] desktop publishing[17] and who knew Erin was frightened of her superintendent.

1. je ne suis pas mauvais
2. un vieux dicton
3. à qui elle aurait fait confiance après un ou deux rendez-vous
4. facile à éluder
5. par une relation sérieuse
6. paf !
7. en s'attendant à ce que vous leur annonciez la grande nouvelle
8. Je la joue cartes sur table
9. je vois si ça marche
10. la mise en terre
11. la reconstitution
12. doux
13. timide
14. affirmait n'avoir jamais rencontré
15. passionné par
16. les merveilles de
17. la microédition

"Oh, come on, admit you had dates last week," Doug urged[1]. "I called you Wednesday and you weren't free until tonight[2]."

Startled[3], Darcy realized that a number of times recently, someone had to repeat a question. "I'm sorry. Yes, I did go out a couple of times last week."

"And had fun?"

She thought of Len Parker pounding on the door[4]. "You could call it that.[5]"

He laughed. "That speaks volumes.[6] I've met some winners[7] too. Now you've gotten my life history[8], how about telling me about yourself?"

She gave a carefully edited version[9].

Doug raised one eyebrow. "I sense a lot of omissions but maybe when you get to know me a bit better, you'll fill me in[10]."

She refused a second glass of wine. "I really have to be going."

He did not argue[11]. "Actually, I do too. When am I going to see you again, Darcy? Tomorrow night? Let's make it dinner."

"I really am busy."

"Thursday?"

"I'm working on a job that's going to tie me up[12]. Will you call in a few days?"

"Yes. And if you keep turning me down[13], I promise I won't persist. But I hope you don't."

He really is nice, Darcy thought, or else he's a heck of a good actor[14].

Doug put her in a cab, then quickly waved one down for himself[15]. In the apartment, he tore off[16] the sweater and slacks and rushed into[17] the suit he'd worn to the office. At quarter of eight he was on the train to Scarsdale. At quarter of nine he was reading a bedtime story to Trish[18] while Susan broiled a

1. insista
2. n'étiez pas libre avant ce soir
3. Surprise
4. tambourinant à sa porte
5. Si on peut dire.
6. Ça en dit long !
7. des cas spéciaux
8. que vous connaissez mon passé
9. en donna une version prudemment revue et corrigée
10. vous m'en direz plus
11. ne protesta pas
12. qui va être très prenant
13. vous continuez à décliner mes invitations
14. ou alors c'est un très bon acteur
15. en arrêta un autre pour lui
16. quitta en vitesse
17. se dépêcha d'enfiler
18. une histoire à Trish pour l'endormir

steak for him[1]. She certainly understood how maddening these late meetings were[2]. "You work too hard, Doug, dear," she had said soothingly[3] when he stamped[4] into the house, ranting about missing[5] the earlier train by a hairbreadth[6].

Through hours of intense questioning[7], Jay Stratton remained calm. His only explanation for the diamonds in the bracelet that he had sold to Merrill Ashton was that it must have been a ghastly[8] error. Erin Kelley had been commissioned to create settings for a number of fine diamonds. Stratton claimed that somehow he had made a mistake and inadvertently substituted other fine stones for some of the ones that were meant to[9] be in the diamond pouch he had given Kelley. That was not to say[10] that those others were not of equal value[11]. Take a look at his various insurance policies.

A search warrant[12] revealed no other missing diamonds in his apartment or in his safety deposit box[13]. He was booked[14] on suspicion of receiving stolen goods[15] and bail was set[16]. Disdainfully[17], he strode from the precinct[18] with his lawyer.

Vince had shared the interrogation with detectives from the Sixth Precinct. They all knew he was guilty, but as Vince said, "There goes one of the most convincing con men[19] I've ever come across[20] and believe me, I've run into a lot of them[21]."

The crazy thing, Vince thought as he left for his office, is that Darcy Scott ends up being a witness[22] *for* Stratton. She'd opened the safe for him and would swear that the pouch wasn't there. And of course the big question was, would Stratton have

1. lui faisait griller un steak
2. comme ces réunions tardives étaient pénibles
3. d'un ton apaisant
4. déboula
5. se plaignant avec colère d'avoir raté
6. d'un cheveu
7. Après plusieurs heures d'interrogatoire
8. terrible
9. de celles qui auraient dû
10. Cela ne voulait pas dire
11. n'avaient pas tout autant de valeur
12. mandat de perquisition
13. son coffre à la banque
14. arrêté
15. pour recel présumé
16. puis libéré sous caution
17. D'un air dédaigneux
18. quitta le poste à grands pas
19. un des escrocs les plus convaincants
20. que j'aie jamais rencontrés
21. j'en ai croisé un paquet
22. se retrouve témoin

1. le culot

2. ne serait plus là pour

3. aboya ses ordres

had the nerve[1] to claim those diamonds were missing unless he knew that Erin Kelley would never show up to[2] say what happened to them?

In the office, Vince snapped out orders[3]. "I want to know everything, and I mean *everything*, about Jay Stratton. Jay Charles Stratton."

XV
WEDNESDAY
March 6

Chris Sheridan studied Darcy Scott, liking what he saw. She was wearing a leather jacket belted at the waist[1], tan[2] slacks that disappeared into scuffed[3] but fine leather boots, a knotted silk scarf[4] that accentuated the hollow in the nape of her neck[5]. Her brown hair, darted with[6] blond highlights, was soft and loose around her face. Hazel eyes, soft brown flecked with[7] green, were framed by dark lashes[8]. Charcoal brows accentuated her porcelain complexion[9]. He judged her to be in her late twenties.

She reminds me of Nan. The realization shocked him. But they don't look alike, he thought. Nan had been the typical Nordic beauty with her pink and white skin, vivid blue eyes, hair the color of daffodils[10]. Then where was the resemblance? It was in the absolute grace with which Darcy moved. Nan had walked like that, as though[11] if music began to play, she would glide into a dance step[12].

Darcy was aware of Chris Sheridan's scrutiny[13]. She had been making some observations of her own. She liked his strong features[14], the slight bump[15] on the bridge of his nose[16], probably the result of a break[17]. The width of his shoulders[18] and an overall impression of disciplined fitness[19] suggested athletic prowess[20].

1. ceinturée à la taille
2. marron clair
3. un peu râpées
4. un foulard en soie noué
5. le creux de sa nuque
6. parsemés de
7. avec des pointes de
8. des cils foncés
9. son teint de porcelaine
10. de la couleur des jonquilles
11. comme si
12. allait se mettre à danser
13. sentait bien que Chris Sheridan la regardait
14. traits
15. la légère bosse
16. à la naissance de l'arête du nez
17. à la suite d'une chute
18. Sa largeur d'épaules
19. une impression générale de forme physique
20. l'athlète

A few years ago, her mother and father had both had plastic surgery[1]. "A nip here, a tuck there[2]," her mother had said, laughing. "Don't look so disapproving, darling Darcy. Remember, our looks are an important part of our stock in trade[3]."

How totally irrelevant[4] to remember that now, Darcy thought. Was she simply trying to escape the delayed shock of opening the package with Erin's boot and the dancing slipper? She'd been composed[5] all day yesterday, then woke up this morning at four o'clock to find her face and pillow wet with tears[6]. She bit her lip at the memory[7], but could not prevent new tears from welling in her eyes[8]. "I'm sorry," she said quickly, and tried to sound brisk[9]. "It was good of you to go to Connecticut for the pictures last night. Vince D'Ambrosio told me you had to change your plans."

"They weren't important." Chris sensed that Darcy Scott wanted him to ignore her distress[10]. "There's an awful lot of stuff[11]," he said matter-of-factly[12]. "I have it laid out[13] on a table in the conference room. My suggestion is that you take a look at it. If you want to bring everything home or to your office, I can have it delivered[14]. If you want part of it, we can arrange that too. I know most of the people in the pictures. Some, of course, I don't. Anyhow[15], let's take a look."

They went downstairs. Darcy realized that in the fifteen minutes she'd been in Chris Sheridan's office, the crowd[16] inspecting the items[17] for the next auction had increased substantially[18]. She loved auctions. Growing up she had regularly gone to them with the dealer representing her parents. They never could go themselves. If either one of them was known to be interested in acquiring[19] a painting or antique, the price shot up instantly[20]. It was hearing

1. eu recours à la chirurgie esthétique
2. Un petit coup de bistouri par-ci par-là
3. la plastique est importante dans notre branche
4. C'était totalement incongru
5. gardé son calme
6. trempés de larmes
7. en y repensant
8. empêcher l'afflux de nouvelles larmes
9. reprendre un peu d'allant
10. qu'il fasse comme si de rien n'était
11. des tonnes de photos
12. d'un ton neutre
13. tout mis
14. vous les faire livrer
15. En tout cas
16. le nombre de personnes
17. les articles proposés
18. considérablement augmenté
19. Si l'on savait que l'un d'eux était intéressé par
20. grimpait tout de suite

her mother and father recite the history of their acquisitions that made her uncomfortable[1].

She was walking next to Sheridan toward the rear of the building[2] when she spotted[3] a cylinder writing desk[4] and darted over to it[5]. "Is this really a Roentgen?"

Chris ran his hand over[6] the mahogany[7] surface. "Yes, it is. You know your antiques.[8] Are you in the business[9]?"

Darcy thought of the Roentgen in the library of the Bel-Air house. Her mother loved to tell the story of how Marie Antoinette had sent it to Vienna as a gift to her mother, the Empress[10], which was why it had escaped being sold during the French Revolution. This one had obviously been shipped out of France as well[11].

"Are you in the business?" Chris repeated.

"Oh, I'm sorry." Darcy smiled, thinking of the hotel she was refurbishing with garage sale trappings[12]. "In a way you could say that.[13]"

Chris raised his eyebrows but did not ask for an explanation. "Down this way.[14]" A wide foyer[15] led to a double-doored room[16]. Inside, a protective cloth[17] covered a Georgian banquet table. Albums, yearbooks, framed pictures, snapshots, and carousels of slides[18] were neatly placed rowlike[19] on the table.

"Don't forget, these were all taken somewhere[20] between fifteen and eighteen years ago," Sheridan warned.

"I know." Darcy considered the mass of material[21]. "How much do you use this room?"

"Not that often.[22]"

"Then would it be possible to leave everything here and let me come in and out[23]? The thing is, when

1. la mettait mal à l'aise
2. vers le fond du bâtiment
3. remarqua
4. un secrétaire à cylindre
5. courut le voir de plus près
6. passa la main sur
7. en acajou
8. Vous vous y connaissez en antiquités.
9. du métier
10. impératrice
11. venait aussi de France, de toute évidence
12. en puisant dans les vide-greniers
13. En quelque sorte.
14. Par ici.
15. grand vestibule
16. une pièce dans laquelle on entrait par une porte à deux battants
17. une housse
18. des paniers de diapositives
19. soigneusement alignés
20. plus ou moins
21. photos
22. Rarement.
23. me laisser venir de temps en temps

I'm in the office I'm always busy. My apartment isn't large, and anyhow[1] I'm not there very much."

Chris knew it was none of his business[2] but could not stop himself. "Agent D'Ambrosio told me you were answering personal ads." He watched the withdrawal in Darcy Scott's expression[3].

"Erin didn't want to answer those ads," Darcy said. "I persuaded her. The only way I can possibly atone for that[4] is to try to help find her killer. Is it all right if I come back and forth[5]? I promise I won't bother you or your staff."

Chris realized what Vince D'Ambrosio had meant when he said that Darcy Scott was going to do what she wanted about the personal ads. "You won't be any bother[6]. One of the secretaries is always here by eight. The cleaning staff[7] is around until ten at night. I'll leave word for them[8] to let you in. Better yet[9], let me give you a key."

Darcy smiled. "I promise not to make off[10] with a Sèvres. Is it okay if I stay for a while now? I have a few hours free."

"Of course. And remember, I know many of those people. Try me if[11] you want a name."

At three-thirty Sheridan returned, followed by a maid[12] carrying a tea tray[13]. "I thought you might need a break. I'll join you if I may.[14]"

"That would be fine." Darcy realized she had a vague headache[15] and remembered she had skipped lunch[16]. She accepted a cup of tea, poured a few drops of milk from the delicate Limoges pitcher[17], and tried not to look too anxious as she reached for a sugar cookie. She waited until the maid left, then commented, "I know how hard it must have been for you to put all this together. Memory Lane is pretty shattering.[18]"

1. de toute façon
2. que ça ne le regardait pas
3. vit Darcy Scott se murer
4. La seule façon pour moi de réparer ma faute
5. passe quand je peux
6. ne nous dérangerez pas du tout
7. personnel de nettoyage
8. Je leur donnerai l'instruction
9. Mieux encore
10. de ne pas disparaître
11. N'hésitez pas à demander si
12. hôtesse d'accueil
13. une collation
14. Ça ne vous gêne pas si je me joins à vous ?
15. mal de tête
16. sauté le déjeuner
17. pot à lait
18. C'est douloureux de remuer les vieux souvenirs.

"My mother did most of it. She surprises me. She fainted[1] when that package of shoes arrived, but now, whatever she can do[2] to track down[3] Nan's killer and to stop him from harming anyone else[4] is all she cares about[5]."

"And you?"

"Nan was six minutes older than I. She never let me forget it. Called me 'little brother.' She was outgoing[6]. I was shy. We kind of balanced each other.[7] Long ago I gave up the hope of seeing her killer in court[8]. Now that hope is within reach again[9]." He looked at the stack[10] of pictures she had separated. "Anyone you know?"

Darcy shook her head. "Not so far.[11]"

At quarter of five, she poked her head[12] in his office. "I'm running along now.[13]"

Chris jumped up[14]. "Here's the key. I meant to give it to you when I came down."

Darcy pocketed it[15]. "I'll probably come back early in the morning."

Chris could not resist. "Have you got one of those dates now? I'm sorry. I have no right to ask.[16] I'm only concerned[17] because I think it's so dangerous."

This time he was glad to see Darcy Scott did not stiffen[18]. She simply said, "I'll be fine," and with a half-wave[19] left him.

He stared after her[20], remembering the one time he had gone hunting[21]. The doe[22] had been drinking water from a stream[23]. Sensing danger, it had lifted its head, listening, poised for flight[24]. An instant later it sank to the ground[25]. He had not joined in the exultant cheers[26] the others in the party[27] accorded the marksman[28]. His instinct had been to

1. s'est évanouie
2. faire tout ce qui est en son pouvoir
3. pour aider à retrouver
4. l'empêcher de nuire,
5. c'est tout ce qui l'intéresse
6. extravertie
7. On se complétait.
8. sur le banc des accusés
9. cet espoir renaît
10. pile
11. Pas pour l'instant.
12. passa la tête
13. Je me sauve.
14. se leva d'un bond
15. la mit dans sa poche
16. Je n'ai aucun droit de poser la question.
17. inquiet
18. ne se raidissait pas
19. en esquissant un au revoir
20. la regarda partir
21. était allé à la chasse
22. biche
23. un ruisseau
24. prête à fuir
25. s'effondra au sol
26. n'avait pas pris part aux félicitations enthousiastes
27. que les autres participants
28. avaient adressées au tireur

shout a warning to[1] the deer[2]. That same instinct was crying out to him[3] now.

1. d'alerter
2. la biche
3. se manifestait

"HOW'S THE PROGRAM GOING?" Vince asked Nona as he tried to find a comfortable spot[4] on the green love seat in her office.

"It is and it isn't." Nona sighed. Wearily[5], she ran a hand through her hair. "The hardest thing is to find a balance[6]. When you wrote and asked me to include a segment about the possible dangers of answering those ads, I had no idea what the next week would bring[7]. I still think my original concept is right. I want to give an overall picture[8] and then end with a warning." She smiled at him. "I'm glad you called and suggested pasta."

4. position
5. D'un air las
6. de trouver le bon équilibre
7. de ce qui allait se passer la semaine suivante
8. vue d'ensemble

It had been a long day. At four-thirty, Vince had had a brainstorm[9]. He'd had a list made[10] of the dates the eight young women had disappeared and ordered researchers to start collecting[11] personal ads from New York area newspapers and magazines that had appeared three months previous to those dates[12].

A sense of accomplishment at the new possible lead[13] had made him realize that he was gut-level tired[14]. The thought of going back to the apartment and finding some food in the neglected refrigerator had been depressing. Instead, almost inadvertently[15], he'd reached for the phone and dialed Nona.

Now it was seven o'clock. He'd just arrived at her office and Nona was ready to pack it in[16].

The phone rang. Nona raised her eyes to heaven[17], reached for it, and identified herself. Vince watched as her expression changed.

9. une idée de génie
10. fait faire une liste
11. à rassembler
12. avant
13. Le sentiment de progresser, dû à la nouvelle piste
14. lessivé
15. presque sans réfléchir
16. partir
17. leva les yeux au ciel

"You're right, Matt. Always a safe bet that[1] you'll find me here. What can I do for you?" She listened. "Matt, get it straight[2]. I'm not in the market[3] to buy you out[4]. Not today. Not tomorrow. If you'll remember, last year when we had a buyer you didn't think it was enough. The usual.[5] Now I can wait. You can wait. What the heck is the rush?[6] Does Jeanie need braces[7] or something?"

Nona laughed as she hung up. "That was the man I promised to love, honor, and cherish all the days of my life. Trouble is, he forgot to remember."

"It's been known to happen.[8]"

They went to Pasta Lovers on West Fifty-eighth Street. "I duck in here a lot[9] when I'm by myself[10]," Nona told him. "Wait till you taste the pasta. It would drive anyone's blues away[11]."

A glass of red wine. The salad. Warm bread. "It's the connection," Vince heard himself saying. "There's got to be a connection between one man and all those girls."

"I thought you were convinced that except for Nan Sheridan the connection is the personal ads."

"It is. But don't you see? He can't just *happen* to have[12] the right-sized slipper[13] for each one of them. Granted[14], he could have bought the slippers after he killed the girls, but he certainly had the one he left on Nan Sheridan's foot with him when he attacked her. This type of killer usually follows a pattern.[15]"

"So you're talking about someone who met these girls, somehow managed to learn their shoe size without any of them getting bad vibes[16], and then was able to get them in a situation[17] where they disappeared without a trace."

"You've got it.[18]" Over linguine with clam sauce[19], he told her about his plan to analyze personal

1. Tu peux être sûr que
2. que ce soit bien clair
3. Je n'ai aucune intention
4. de racheter ta part
5. Comme toujours.
6. C'est quoi l'urgence ?
7. d'un appareil dentaire
8. Il n'est pas le seul.
9. me réfugie souvent ici
10. je suis seule
11. remonterait le moral à n'importe qui
12. Ce n'est pas possible qu'il ait comme par hasard
13. la bonne pointure
14. D'accord
15. Il y a en général des constantes dans le comportement de ce type de tueur.
16. sans qu'elles se méfient
17. a réussi à faire en sorte
18. C'est ça.
19. aux palourdes

ads that had been placed in the New York area in the three months before each of the women disappeared, to see if the same one showed up[1]. "And of course that could be another dead end[2]," he acknowledged[3]. "For all we know[4], the same guy is placing a dozen different ads."

They both ordered decaf cappuccino. Nona began talking about the documentary. "I still haven't settled on a psychiatrist[5]," she said. "I certainly don't want to get one of those professional showbiz experts who pop up[6] whenever you turn the dial[7]."

Vince told her about Michael Nash. "Very articulate guy.[8] Writing a book about personal ads. He'd met Erin."

"Darcy told me about him. A very good idea, Agent D'Ambrosio."

Vince took Nona home in a cab, and had it wait[9] while he saw her[10] inside her building. "I have a hunch[11] we're both pretty beat[12]," he said in answer to her suggestion of a nightcap[13]. "But please give me a raincheck[14]."

"You've got it." Nona grinned. "I am tired, and anyhow, my cleaning woman hasn't been around since last Friday. I don't think you're ready for the real me."

It was all Vince could do[15] to remember that he was technically on the job[16]. That did not stop him from wondering how it would feel to hold Nona Roberts in his arms.

Back at his apartment, there was a message on his answering machine. Ernie, his assistant. "No emergency[17], but I thought you'd be interested in hearing this, Vince. We have the roster of students[18] from Brown for the time Nan Sheridan was there. Guess

1. si la même annonce revenait
2. ne pas aboutir non plus
3. admit
4. Si ça se trouve
5. n'ai pas encore décidé quel psy inviter
6. qu'on ressort
7. sur tous les plateaux
8. C'est un type qui s'exprime bien.
9. fit attendre le chauffeur
10. le temps qu'il la raccompagne
11. J'ai comme l'impression
12. nazes
13. quand elle l'invita à monter boire un dernier verre
14. une autre fois, je ne dis pas non
15. Vince dut faire effort
16. qu'en théorie, il était de service
17. Rien d'urgent
18. la liste des étudiants

who was a returning[1] student and in some of her classes? None other than our friend the jeweler[2], Jay Stratton."

1. reprenant ses études
2. Notre ami le bijoutier en personne

DARCY's five-thirty date was to meet Box 4307, Cal Griffin, in the bar at Tavern on the Green. He's not in his early thirties, was her first impression. Griffin was closer to fifty[3]. A beefy[4] man who combed his hair across the top of his head[5] to conceal[6] his bald spot[7], he was expensively and conservatively dressed[8]. He was from Milwaukee, but, as he explained, got into New York regularly.

A suggestive wink followed.[9] Don't get him wrong[10], he was a happily married man, but when he came in on business it would sure be good to have a friend. Another wink. Believe you me[11], he knew how to treat a woman. What show haven't you seen? He knew how to get house seats[12]. What's your favorite restaurant? Lutèce? Expensive, but worth every penny[13].

Darcy managed to ask him the last time he'd been in New York.

Too long. Last month he'd taken the wife and kids—great teenagers but you know teenagers—skiing in Vail. They had a house there. They were building a bigger place. Money's no object.[14] Anyhow, the kids brought their friends and it was bedlam[15]. That rock and roll stuff. Drive you crazy[16], wouldn't it? They had a great stereo system in the house.

Darcy had ordered a Perrier. Halfway through it[17], she made a business of glancing at her watch[18]. "My

3. plus proche de la cinquantaine
4. grassouillet
5. qui rabattait des mèches de cheveux sur son crâne
6. cacher
7. sa calvitie
8. il portait des vêtements chers et très classiques
9. Il lui fit aussitôt un clin d'œil suggestif.
10. Attention, hein
11. Aucun doute
12. des places de théâtre gratuites
13. ça valait le coup
14. L'argent n'était pas un problème.
15. ça avait été l'anarchie
16. C'est à vous rendre fou
17. Quand elle en eut bu la moitié
18. regarda ostensiblement sa montre

boss was real mad at me for leaving[1]," she said. "I'm going to have to cut this short.[2]"

"Forget him," Griffin ordered. "You and I are going to have a nice night."

They were sitting at a banquette. A beefy arm went around her. A moist kiss was planted on her ear.[3]

Darcy did not want to make a scene. "Oh, my God," she said, pointing to a nearby table where a man was sitting alone, his back to them[4]. "That's my husband. I've got to get out of here."

The arm disappeared from around her waist. Griffin looked shaken[5]. "I don't want trouble[6]."

"I'll just slip away[7]," Darcy whispered.

On the way home in the cab, she tried not to laugh out loud[8]. Well, one thing's for sure[9]—it's not that one.

The phone was ringing as she turned her key in the lock[10]. It was Doug Fields. "Hi, Darcy. Why are you so unforgettable[11]? I know you said you were busy tonight, but my plans changed and I decided to take a chance[12]. How about a hamburger at P.J. Clarke's or something?"

Darcy realized that she had forgotten to tell Vince D'Ambrosio about Doug Fields. A nice guy. Attractive. An illustrator. The kind Erin might easily have been interested in. "That sounds great," she answered. "What time?"

HOW STUPID does Doug think I am? Susan wondered as she sat at the kitchen table with Donny and went over his geometry homework[13]. The guidance counseler[14] had phoned her this after-

1. furieux que je parte
2. Il va falloir que j'abrège.
3. Il lui planta un baiser humide sur l'oreille.
4. leur tournant le dos
5. eut l'air secoué
6. d'ennuis
7. Je vais filer discrètement
8. de ne pas éclater de rire
9. une chose était sûre
10. serrure
11. inoubliable
12. de tenter ma chance
13. regardait ses exercices de géométrie
14. conseiller d'éducation

noon. Was there a problem at home? Donny, always a good student[1], was slipping[2] in all his subjects[3]. He seemed distracted[4] and depressed.

"Well, that's it," she said cheerfully[5]. "As *my* geometry teacher used to say, 'It shows what you can do, Miss Frawley, when you put your mind to it[6].' "

Donny smiled and gathered up[7] his books. "Mom ..." He hesitated.

"Donny, you've always been able to talk to me. What is it?"

He looked around[8].

"The little kids are in bed. Beth is taking one of her thirty-minute showers. We can talk," Susan assured him.

"And Dad is in one of his meetings," Donny said bitterly[9].

He suspects, Susan thought. There was no use trying to protect him. This was as good a time as any[10] to be straight with him[11]. "Donny, Dad isn't in a meeting."

"You know?" Relief flooded[12] the troubled face.

"Yes, I do. But how did you find out[13]?"

He looked down. "Patrick Driscoll, one of the guys on the team, was in New York Friday night when we were visiting Grandpa. Dad was in a restaurant with some woman. They were holding hands[14] and kissing. Patrick said it was gross[15]. His mother wants to tell you. His dad won't let her[16]."

"Donny, I'm planning to divorce your father. It's not something I want, but living like this isn't great for any of us. This way we won't always be waiting for him to come home, always putting up with his lies[17]. I hope he makes it his business[18] to see you kids, but I can't guarantee it. I'm sorry. I'm terribly, terribly sorry." She realized she was crying.

1. bon élève
2. avait des mauvaises notes
3. dans toutes les matières
4. déconcentré
5. d'un ton enjoué
6. quand vous faites un effort
7. rassembla
8. regarda autour de lui
9. d'un ton amer
10. un moment comme un autre
11. pour lui dire la vérité
12. Un grand soulagement se lut sur
13. toi, comment tu l'as su
14. se tenaient la main
15. que c'était immonde
16. l'en empêche
17. à supporter ses mensonges
18. qu'il fera un effort

Donny patted her shoulder. "Mom, he doesn't deserve you[1]. I promise I'll help with the other kids. I swear I'll do a better job[2] than he did with us."

Donny may look like Doug, but thank God, Susan thought, he's got enough of my genes in him[3] that he'll never act[4] like his father. She kissed Donny's cheek. "Let's keep this between us[5] for now[6]. Okay."

Susan went to bed at eleven o'clock. Doug was still not home. She turned on the late news[7] and watched horrified as the anchorman[8] updated the story of[9] the missing young women and the packages of mismatched shoes that were being returned to their families.

The announcer[10] was saying, "Although the FBI refuses to comment, inside sources tell us[11] that the latest shoes to be returned are the mates of the ones Erin Kelley was wearing when her body was found. If true[12], she is probably linked to the disappearance of two young women originally from Lancaster and White Plains, who had been living in Manhattan, and the long-unsolved murder of Nan Sheridan."

Nan Sheridan. Erin Kelley.

"Oh my God," Susan moaned[13]. Her hands clenched in fists[14], she stared at the screen.

Pictures of Claire Barnes, Erin Kelley, Janine Wetzl and Nan Sheridan were flashed on the screen[15].

The announcer was saying, "The trail of death[16] seems to have begun on that cold March morning, fifteen years ago next week, when Nan Sheridan was strangled[17] on the jogging path near her home."

Susan felt her own throat close[18]. Fifteen years ago she had lied for Doug when he was questioned about Nan's death. If she hadn't, would these other young women not have disappeared? That night almost two weeks ago when the announcement came

1. il ne te mérite pas
2. que je me débrouillerai mieux
3. il tient suffisamment de moi
4. pour ne jamais faire
5. Gardons ça pour nous
6. pour l'instant
7. alluma le journal de la nuit
8. présentateur
9. donnait les dernières nouvelles sur
10. présentateur
11. nous savons par nos informateurs
12. Si c'est le cas
13. gémit
14. Les poings serrés
15. défilèrent à l'écran
16. La série de meurtres
17. étranglée
18. en eut elle-même la gorge serrée

about Erin Kelley's death[1], Doug had had a nightmare[2]. Called out[3] *Erin* in his sleep[4].

"... The FBI is cooperating with the New York Police Department in an attempt to trace the evening shoes back to the purchaser[5]. The file on Nan Sheridan's death has been reopened ..."

Suppose they questioned Doug again? Suppose they question *me*, Susan thought. Did she have a duty[6] to tell the police she had lied fifteen years ago?

Donny. Beth. Trish. Conner. What would their lives be like if they grew up as[7] the children of a serial killer?

The police commissioner[8] of New York was being interviewed. "We believe we're dealing with[9] a vicious[10] serial killer."

Vicious.

"What shall I do?" Susan whispered to herself. Her father's words rang in her ears[11]. "Vicious *streak*[12] ..."

Two years ago when she challenged him about[13] his relationship with the *au pair*, his face had contorted with rage[14]. The fear she had experienced at that moment swept through her again[15]. As the news ended, Susan finally faced[16] the fact she had never allowed herself to consider[17]. "I thought he was going to hurt me that night."

1. la mort d'Erin Kelley avait été annoncée
2. un cauchemar
3. Il avait crié
4. dans son sommeil
5. l'acheteur
6. Était-ce son devoir
7. s'ils grandissaient en se sachant
8. préfet
9. nous avons affaire à
10. terrible
11. résonnaient encore
12. Un fond violent
13. l'avait interrogé
14. s'était révulsé
15. l'envahit à nouveau
16. admit enfin
17. ce qu'elle n'avait jamais osé s'avouer

SHALL WE DANCE? Shall we dance? Shall we dance? On a bright cloud of music shall we fly? ... Shall we still be together with our arms around each other, shall we dance? Shall we dance? Shall we dance?

Charley laughed aloud at the sheer exultation of the music.[18] Whirling[19] and stepping in synch[20] with Yul

18. La musique transportait Charley d'allégresse et le faisait rire aux éclats.
19. Tournoyant
20. dansant en rythme

Brynner, he stamped his foot[1], twisted[2], twirled[3] an imaginary Darcy in his arms. They'd dance to this next week! Then Astaire! What joy! What joy! It was only seven days away: Nan's fifteenth anniversary!

On the clear understanding[4] that this kind of thing can happen, shall we dance? Shall we dance? Shall we dance?

The music stopped. He reached for the remote control and snapped off the video[5]. If only he could spend the night[6]. But that would be foolish[7]. Do what he had come to do.

The basement stairs creaked[8] and he frowned. Must take care of that.[9] Annette had fled down these stairs. Listening to the frantic tapping[10] of the heels on the bare wood[11] had enthralled him[12]. If Darcy tried to escape him that same way, he didn't want a creaking noise to interfere with the sound of her slippers on their futile flight[13].

Darcy. How hard it had been to sit across the table from her.[14] He had wanted to say "Come with me" and bring her here. Like the Phantom of the Opera inviting his beloved[15] to the netherworld[16].

The shoe boxes. Five of them now. Marie and Sheila and Leslie and Annette and Tina. Suddenly he realized he wanted to send them all back at once. Be finished with it.[17] And then there would be only one.

Only Darcy's package would be here next week. Maybe he'd never return it.

He opened the latch[18] of the freezer, lifted the heavy door, and stared down into the empty space. Awaiting[19] a new ice maiden, Charley thought. This one he wouldn't give back.[20]

1. tapait du pied
2. tournait
3. faisait virevolter
4. En étant bien d'accord
5. coupa la cassette vidéo
6. passer la nuit ici
7. idiot
8. craquèrent
9. Faudrait s'occuper de ça.
10. le tapotement frénétique
11. sur le bois nu
12. l'avait captivé
13. alors qu'ils tenteraient vainement de s'enfuir
14. Comme ça avait été difficile d'être à table en face d'elle !
15. sa bien-aimée
16. dans l'autre monde
17. Qu'il en soit débarrassé.
18. le loquet
19. Prêt pour
20. Celle-là, il ne la rendrait pas.

XVI
THURSDAY
March 7

"How well did you know Nan Sheridan?" Vince snapped. He and a detective from the Midtown North precinct were taking turns questioning Jay Stratton[1].

Stratton remained unruffled[2]. "She was a student at Brown when I was there."

"You dropped out of Brown and came back the year she was a sophomore[3]?"

"That's right. I wasn't much of a student[4] my freshman year[5]. My uncle, who was my guardian[6], thought it would do me a lot of good[7] to mature a bit[8]. I went into the Peace Corps for two years."

"I repeat: How well did you know Nan Sheridan?"

How well indeed, Stratton thought. Lovely Nan. *To dance with her was to feel a will-o'-the-wisp[9] in your arms.*

D'Ambrosio's eyes narrowed.[10] He had seen something in Stratton's face. "You haven't answered me."

Stratton shrugged. "There's no answer to give. Certainly I remember her. I was there when the whole student body[11] was talking endlessly about the tragedy[12]."

"Were you invited to her birthday party?"

"No, I was not. Nan Sheridan and I happened to be in several classes together[13]. Period.[14]"

1. interrogeaient Stratton à tour de rôle
2. imperturbable
3. en 2e année
4. n'ai pas beaucoup travaillé
5. en 1re année
6. tuteur
7. que ça me ferait beaucoup de bien
8. de mûrir un peu
9. un feu follet
10. Le regard de D'Ambrosio se fit perçant.
11. tous les étudiants
12. ne parlaient que du drame
13. on avait plusieurs cours en commun
14. Un point, c'est tout.

"Let's talk about Erin Kelley. You were in an awfully big hurry[1] to report those missing diamonds[2] to the insurance company."

"As Miss Scott can certainly verify[3], my first response when I spoke with her was irritation. I really didn't know Erin well. It was her work I knew. When she didn't keep the appointment[4] to turn over[5] the necklace to Bertolini, I convinced myself that she simply lost track of time[6]. The moment I met Darcy Scott I realized how foolish that was. Her terrible concern made me see the situation clearly."

"Do you often mix up[7] valuable gemstones[8]?"

"Certainly not."

Vince tried another tack[9]. "You didn't know Nan Sheridan well, but did you know anyone who had a crush on her[10]? Besides you[11], of course," he added deliberately.

1. drôlement pressé
2. de signaler la disparition des diamants
3. pourra vous le confirmer
4. ne s'est pas présentée au rendez-vous
5. pour remettre
6. avait tout bonnement perdu la notion du temps
7. Ça vous arrive souvent de mélanger
8. des pierres précieuses
9. une autre approche
10. qui était amoureux d'elle
11. À part vous

XVII
FRIDAY
March 8

1. convalescente
2. des coussins décoratifs
3. coiffeuse
4. le poster qu'Erin aimait tant
5. fauteuil à bascule
6. Le papier peint à rayures de couleur acidulée
7. un manège
8. avec embrasses
9. le couvre-lit
10. Un cache-sommier à volants de coton blanc empesé
11. rehaussait
12. le blanc brillant
13. des plinthes
14. représentait
15. œuvres de jeunesse, moins connues
16. s'élançant
17. tendus
18. la pointe des pieds tendue
19. enfonça des crochets

On Friday afternoon, Darcy went to the West Side apartment where she'd redecorated the room for Lisa, the recuperating[1] teenager. She brought with her plants for the windowsill, some throw pillows[2], a porcelain vanity set[3] that she'd picked up at a house sale. And Erin's much-loved poster[4].

The large pieces were already in; the pewter and brass bed, the dresser, the night table, the rocker[5]. The Indian rug that had been in Erin's living room was perfect in this space. Candy-striped wallpaper[6] gave the room a feeling of movement. Almost like a carousel[7], Darcy thought. The tieback[8] curtains and spread[9] were the same candy stripe as the paper. A starched white cotton dust ruffle[10] picked up[11] the glistening white[12] of the ceiling and trim[13].

Carefully, Darcy positioned the poster. It depicted[14] an Egret painting, one of his early, lesser known works[15]: a young dancer soaring through the air[16], her arms extended[17], her toes pointed[18]. He'd called it, "Loves Music, Loves to Dance."

She drove picture hooks[19] into the wall, thinking of all the dance classes she and Erin had taken. "Why jog in the freezing rain when you can get just as much exercise dancing?" Erin would ask. "There's an old slogan, 'To put a little fun in your life, try dancing.' "

Darcy stepped back[1] to be sure the poster was hanging straight[2]. It was. Then what was gnawing at her[3]? *The personal ads.* But why now? Shrugging, she closed her toolbox[4].

She went directly to Sheridan Galleries. So far, all the poring over the pictures[5] had proven useless[6]. She had come across Jay Stratton's picture, but Vince D'Ambrosio had already picked his name from[7] the student roster. Yesterday, Chris Sheridan had pointed out that she probably had a better chance of[8] winning the lottery than of having a familiar face jump out at her[9].

She'd been afraid that he might have regretted his decision to let her use his conference room, but that wasn't the case. "You look wiped out[10]," he'd said to her late yesterday afternoon. "I understand you've been here since eight o'clock this morning."

"I was able to rearrange some appointments[11]. This seems more important."

Last night had been Box 3823, Owen Larkin, an internist from[12] New York Hospital. He'd been pretty full of himself[13]. "Trouble with being an unattached doctor is that all the nurses[14] keep offering to have you over for a home-cooked meal[15]." He was from Tulsa and hated New York. "The minute I finish my residency[16] I'm on my way back[17] to God's country[18]. You can keep these crowded[19] cities."

Casually[20], she'd brought up[21] Erin's name. His tone confidential[22], he'd told her, "I didn't meet her, but one of my friends at the hospital who answers these ads did. Just once. He's keeping his fingers crossed[23] that she didn't keep records[24]. The last thing he needs is to be questioned in a murder investigation."

1. recula
2. bien droit
3. la turlupinait
4. boîte à outils
5. tout le temps passé à regarder les photos
6. n'avait servi à rien
7. déjà repéré son nom sur
8. plus de chances de
9. que de tomber sur une tête connue
10. épuisée
11. déplacer des rendez-vous
12. interne à
13. plutôt frimeur
14. infirmières
15. vous invitent tout le temps à dîner chez elles
16. internat,
17. je retourne
18. par chez moi
19. surpeuplées
20. Mine de rien
21. glissé
22. À voix basse
23. Il espère fortement
24. qu'elle ne l'a noté nulle part

"When did he see her?"

"Early February."

"I wonder if I've ever met him."

"Not unless you met him around that time[1]. He'd broken up[2] with his girlfriend and they got back together[3]."

"What's his name?"

"Brad Whalen. Say, is this some kind of inquisition[4]? Let's talk about you and me."

Brad Whalen. Another name for Vince D'Ambrosio to check out.

Chris was standing at his office window when he saw the cab pull up[5] and Darcy get out of it. He shoved his hands[6] in his pockets. It was windy[7] and he watched as Darcy closed the door of the cab and turned to the building. She pulled her jacket around her neck[8] and bent forward slightly[9] as she crossed the sidewalk.

Yesterday had been busy. He had some important Japanese clients examining the silver[10] from the von Wallens estate to be auctioned[11] next week. He'd spent the better part of the afternoon[12] with them.

Mrs. Vail, the housekeeper for the gallery, had made sure that morning coffee, a light lunch, and tea were brought to Darcy Scott. "That poor girl is going to ruin her eyes[13], Mr. Sheridan," Vail had fussed[14].

At four-thirty, Chris had gone to the conference room. He'd realized what a blunder he'd made[15] when he suggested the task was hopeless[16]. He hadn't meant it to come out like that.[17] It was just that when you analyzed it, the chances of Darcy Scott's meeting someone who had known Nan, and recognizing him in a picture fifteen years old, were, to say the least[18], very slim[19].

1. à ce moment-là
2. rompu
3. se sont remis ensemble
4. un interrogatoire ou quoi
5. s'arrêter
6. fourra les mains
7. Il y avait du vent
8. remonta son col autour de son cou
9. se pencha légèrement en avant
10. l'argenterie
11. qui serait vendue aux enchères
12. presque tout l'après-midi
13. s'abîmer les yeux
14. s'était inquiétée
15. qu'il avait fait une gaffe
16. la tâche était désespérée
17. Ce n'est pas ce qu'il avait voulu dire.
18. c'était le moins qu'on puisse dire
19. très minces

Yesterday she'd asked him if Nan had ever dated anyone named Charles North.

Not to his knowledge.[1] When he came to Darien, Vince D'Ambrosio had asked him and his mother the same question.

Chris realized that he wanted to go downstairs now and talk to Darcy. He wondered if she would get the feeling again[2] that he was anxious to be rid of her[3].

The phone rang. He let his secretary pick it up[4]. A moment later she buzzed through[5]. "It's your mother, Chris."

Greta came directly to the point. "Chris, you know that business about someone named[6] Charles. As long as we had to get all those pictures down, I decided to go through[7] the rest of Nan's things. No use leaving the job to you someday.[8] I reread her letters. There's one from the September before ... before we lost her. She'd just started the fall semester[9]. She wrote about dancing with a fellow named Charley who teased her about wearing[10] Capezios.

"Here's exactly the way she put it[11]: 'Can you believe that a guy in my generation thinks girls should wear spike heels[12]?' "

1. Pas à sa connaissance.

2. si elle aurait une fois de plus l'impression

3. avait hâte qu'elle soit partie

4. répondre

5. l'appela sur l'Interphone

6. ces questions sur quelqu'un qui s'appellerait

7. de parcourir

8. Pas la peine que tu aies à faire ça un jour.

9. premier trimestre

10. s'était moqué d'elle parce qu'elle portait

11. sa formulation exacte

12. des talons aiguilles

"I WAS FINISHED with my patients at three o'clock and thought it would be a lot easier to come over[13] and talk with you than discuss this on the phone." Michael Nash shifted slightly[14], trying to find a comfortable position on the green love seat in Nona's office. He could not help analyzing why an obviously bright[15] and outgoing person like Nona

13. de venir vous voir

14. changea légèrement de position

15. manifestement intelligente

Roberts would submit her visitors to this torturous object[1].

"Doctor, I'm sorry." Nona yanked files from the one comfortable chair[2] next to her desk. "Please."

Nash moved willingly[3].

"I really should get rid of that thing," Nona apologized. "It's just I never get around to it[4]. There's always something more interesting to do than fool around with arranging furniture[5]." Her smile was guilty[6]. "But for heaven's sake[7], don't tell Darcy that."

He returned the smile. "In my profession, I'm sworn to secrecy[8]. Now, how can I help you?"

A really attractive man, Nona thought. Late thirties. A maturity that probably comes with the territory of being a psychiatrist[9]. Darcy had told her about the visit to his place in New Jersey. Don't marry for money, as Nona's old aunts used to say, but it's just as easy to love a rich man as a poor one. Not, God knows, that Darcy needed to marry money[10]. Her folks had been making millions since before she was born. But Nona had always sensed a loneliness in[11] Darcy, a little girl lost[12]. Without Erin, that was bound to get worse[13]. It would be wonderful if she met the right guy[14] now.

She realized that Dr. Michael Nash was looking at her with an amused expression. "Will I pass?[15]" he asked.

"Absolutely." She fished for[16] the documentary file. "Darcy probably told you why she and Erin got into answering personal ads."

Nash nodded.

"We've got the program pretty much together[17], but I want to have a psychiatrist do an overall viewpoint[18] about the kind of people who place or answer ads and what motivates them. Maybe it would

1. imposerait à ses visiteurs un siège aussi peu confortable
2. enleva des dossiers de la seule chaise confortable
3. sans se faire prier
4. que je n'ai jamais le temps de m'en occuper
5. que de s'amuser à changer les meubles
6. coupable
7. par pitié
8. tenu à la confidentialité
9. probablement due à sa profession de psychiatre
10. ait besoin de faire un mariage d'argent
11. remarqué une profonde solitude chez
12. une petite fille esseulée
13. ça ne ferait qu'empirer
14. l'homme idéal
15. Est-ce que je fais l'affaire ?
16. chercha
17. L'émission est quasiment au point
18. qui fasse une présentation générale

be possible to give some hints[1] as to what kind of behavior[2] should raise warning signals[3]. Am I saying it right?"

"You're saying it very explicitly. I gather that the FBI agent will concentrate on the serial killer aspect."

Nona felt herself tense[4]. "Yes."

"Ms. Roberts, Nona, if I may[5], I wish you could see the expression on your face right now. You and Darcy are alike[6]. You must stop torturing yourselves. You are no more responsible for Erin Kelley's death than the mother who takes her child for a walk and sees it crushed by an out-of-control car[7]. Some things must be considered acts of fate[8]. Grieve for[9] your friend. Do anything you can to alert others that there is a madman out there[10]. But don't try to play God[11]."

Nona tried to keep her voice steady[12]. "I wish I could hear that about five times a day. If it's bad for me, it's ten times worse for Darcy. I hope you've told her that."

Michael Nash's smile reached his eyes. "My housekeeper has called three times this week with suggested menus if I'll only bring Darcy back[13]. She's going to drive to Wellesley to see Erin's father on Sunday, but she will have dinner with me on Saturday."

"Good! And now how about the program. We tape[14] next Wednesday. It will be aired[15] Thursday night."

"I usually shy away from[16] this sort of thing. Too many of my colleagues rush to be on television panels[17] or in the witness box[18] at criminal trials[19]. But maybe I can contribute something here. Count me in.[20]"

1. conseils
2. sur le type de comportement
3. dont on devrait se méfier
4. se raidit
5. si vous le permettez
6. tellement semblables
7. le voit se faire écraser par un chauffard
8. comme des actes du destin
9. Pleurez la disparition de
10. il y a un fou dans les rues de New York
11. ne vous prenez pas pour Dieu
12. de ne pas trembler en parlant
13. si je lui ramène Darcy
14. enregistrons l'émission
15. Elle sera diffusée
16. Normalement, j'évite
17. se précipitent sur les plateaux de télévision
18. à la barre des témoins
19. lors de procès [au pénal]
20. Je suis partant.

"Terrific." They stood up together. Nona waved her hand at the desks[1] in the open area[2] outside her office. "I understand you're writing a book about personal ads. If you need any more research, most of the uncommitted people[3] out there[4] have been playing the game."

"Thanks, but my own file is pretty thick. I'll be turning my book in[5] by the end of the month."

Nona watched Nash's long, easy stride as he made his way[6] to the elevator. She closed the door of her office and dialed Darcy's apartment.

When the answering machine came on, she said, "I know you're not home yet, but I had to tell you. I just met Michael Nash and he's a doll[7]."

1. lui indiqua d'un geste les bureaux
2. de l'open space
3. des célibataires
4. qui travaillent là
5. Je vais rendre mon manuscrit
6. se diriger de son pas souple
7. adorable

DOUG'S WARNING ANTENNA was signaling him[8]. When he phoned Susan this morning, saying he didn't want to wake her up by calling when he knew he couldn't get home last night, she'd been warm and pleasant.

"That was sweet of you[9], Doug. I did get to bed early."

The warning signal had come after he'd hung up and realized that she didn't ask him if he'd be on time[10] tonight. Up till a couple of weeks ago, she'd always pulled that martyred, anxious routine[11]. "Doug, those people have to realize you have a family. It's not fair[12] to expect you to stay[13] for meetings night after night[14]."

She'd seemed pretty happy when she'd met him for dinner in New York. Maybe he should call back and suggest she meet him again tonight.

8. sentait quelque chose d'anormal dans l'air
9. Comme c'est gentil de ta part
10. rentrerait à l'heure
11. jouait toujours les martyres angoissées
12. Ce n'est pas juste
13. de s'attendre à ce que tu restes
14. tard pour des réunions tous les soirs

Or maybe he'd better get home early, make a fuss over the kids[1]. They had been away last weekend.

If Susan ever got mad, really mad[2], especially with the way the personal ad murders were getting played up[3] and all the interest in Nan ...!

Doug's office was on the forty-fourth floor of the World Trade Center. Unseeingly, he stared down at[4] Lady Liberty[5].

It was time to play the role of devoted[6] husband and father.

Something else. He'd better stop using the apartment for a while. His clothes. His sketches. The ads. When he got a chance[7] next week, he'd bring them up to the cottage.

Maybe he'd better think about[8] leaving the station wagon there too.

1. cajoler les mômes
2. se fâchait vraiment
3. vu tout ce battage autour des meurtres des petites annonces
4. Il regardait sans la voir
5. la statue de la Liberté
6. dévoué
7. Dès qu'il en aurait l'occasion
8. Il ferait peut-être mieux aussi de

WAS IT POSSIBLE? Darcy blinked[9] and reached for the magnifying glass[10]. This five-by-seven[11] snapshot of Nan Sheridan and her friends on the beach[12]. The maintenance[13] man in the background[14]. Did he look familiar or was she crazy?

She did not hear Chris Sheridan come in. His quiet greeting[15], "I don't want to interrupt you, Darcy," made her jump[16].

Chris rushed to apologize. "I knocked.[17] You didn't hear me. I'm terribly sorry."

Darcy rubbed her eyes[18]. "You shouldn't have to knock. It's your place.[19] I guess I'm getting jumpy.[20]"

He looked at the magnifying glass in her hand. "Do you think you've come across[21] something?"

"I can't be sure. It's just this guy ..." She pointed to the figure behind the cluster[22] of girls, "looks a little

9. cligna des yeux de surprise
10. la loupe
11. de 13 x 18 cm
12. à la plage
13. d'entretien
14. à l'arrière-plan
15. Quand il dit doucement
16. il la fit sursauter
17. J'ai frappé.
18. se frotta les yeux
19. Vous êtes chez vous.
20. Je suis sans doute un peu nerveuse.
21. avoir trouvé
22. le groupe

like someone I know. Do you remember where this picture was taken?"

Chris studied it[1]. "On Belle Island. That's a few miles from Darien. One of Nan's best friends has a summer home[2] there."

"May I take this?"

"Of course." Concerned[3], Chris watched as Darcy slipped the snapshot[4] into her carrying case[5] and began to stack[6] the pictures she had perused[7] into orderly[8] piles. Her movements were slow, almost mechanical, as though she were terribly tired.

"Darcy, do you have one of your dates tonight?"

She nodded.

"Drinks, dinner?"

"I try to keep them to[9] a glass of wine. By then, I think I can get a handle on whether or not[10] they either met Erin or sound funny if[11] they deny knowing her."

"You don't drive off with them[12] or go to their homes?"

"Lord[13], no."

"That's good. You look as though you wouldn't have much strength to fight back[14] if someone made a pass at you[15]." Chris hesitated. "Believe it or not, I'm not here to ask questions about something that isn't my business. I just wanted you to know that my mother came across a letter from Nan, written six months before she died. In it she refers to a[16] Charley who thought girls ought to wear spike heels."

Darcy looked up at him. "Have you told Vince D'Ambrosio?"

"Not yet. I will, of course. But I'm wondering if it would be a good idea for you to talk to my mother. It was digging out[17] all these pictures that made her go through Nan's letters. No one had asked her to do that. I just think that if there is anything my

1. regarda de près
2. résidence d'été
3. Inquiet
4. ranger la photo
5. sa sacoche
6. empiler
7. qu'elle avait déjà examinées
8. bien nettes
9. de m'en tenir à
10. avoir une idée de si, oui ou non,
11. s'ils ont l'air bizarres quand
12. ne partez pas en voiture avec eux
13. Mon Dieu
14. guère la force de vous défendre
15. devenait trop entreprenant
16. Elle y parle d'un certain
17. C'est le fait d'avoir ressorti

mother knows, it might come to the surface faster[1] if she talks to another woman who understands the kind of pain she's been living with all these years."

Nan was six minutes older than I. She never let me forget it. She was outgoing. I was shy.

Chris Sheridan and his mother had probably come to terms with[2] Nan Sheridan's death, Darcy thought. The *True Crimes* program, Erin's murder, the returned shoes, and now me. They've been forced to rip open[3] whatever scars[4] had healed[5]. For them as well as me, there'll be no peace[6] until this is over.

The distress in Chris Sheridan's face for the moment robbed it of[7] the aura of sophistication and executive confidence[8] that had been so noticeable[9] a few days ago.

"I'd like to meet your mother," Darcy said. "She lives in Darien, doesn't she?"

"Yes. I'll drive you."

"I'm going up to Wellesley early Sunday morning to visit Erin Kelley's father. If it's all right, I'll stop late Sunday afternoon on my way home."

"Sounds like a long day for you. Tomorrow wouldn't be better?"

Darcy thought it was ridiculous at her age to blush[10]. "I have plans for tomorrow."

She got up to go. Robert Kruse was meeting her at Mickey Mantle's at five-thirty. As of now,[11] no one else[12] had called. She had run out of[13] personal ad dates.

Next week she'd start writing to the ads Erin had circled.

1. lui revenir plus vite
2. accepté
3. rouvrir
4. les plaies
5. qui avaient cicatrisé
6. Ni eux ni moi ne connaîtrons la paix
7. lui ôta un instant
8. son air distingué et son assurance,
9. si palpables
10. de rougir à son âge
11. Pour l'instant,
12. personne d'autre
13. était arrivée au bout de ses

Len Parker had been angry at work. A maintenance man at NYU, there was nothing he couldn't fix[1]. Not that he'd studied much.[2] It was just the feel[3] of wires[4] in his hands, the feel of a lock and key, doorjambs[5], switches[6]. He was supposed to do only routine maintenance, but often when he saw something wrong, he'd fix it without talking about it. It was the one thing that gave him peace[7].

But today, his thoughts had been confused[8]. He'd yelled at[9] his trustee for hinting[10] that he might have a house somewhere. Whose business?[11] Whose?

His family? What about them? His brothers and sisters. Never even invited him to visit. Glad to wash their hands of him[12].

That girl, Darcy. Maybe he'd been mean to[13] her, but she didn't realize how cold it had been standing waiting outside that fancy restaurant to apologize to her.

He'd told Mr. Doran, the trustee, about that. Mr. Doran said, "Lenny, if you'd only understand that you have enough money to eat in Le Cirque or anywhere else every night of your life."

Mr. Doran just didn't understand.

Lenny could remember his mother yelling at his father all the time. "You'll put your children in the streets[14] with your crazy investments[15]." Lenny used to cower in bed[16]. He hated to think of being out in the cold.

Was that when he started going outside in his pajamas so he'd be used to it when it really happened? No one knew he did that. By the time his father

1. il n'y avait rien qu'il ne sache réparer
2. Il n'avait pourtant pas vraiment eu de formation.
3. plaisir de toucher
4. fils électriques
5. des montants de porte
6. des interrupteurs
7. qui le calmait
8. il avait l'esprit embrouillé
9. crié après
10. parce qu'il avait suggéré
11. Qui ça regardait ?
12. de ne plus rien avoir à faire avec lui
13. méchant avec
14. Tes enfants finiront à la rue
15. avec tes investissements douteux
16. se recroqueviller dans son lit

made all that money[1], he was used to being in the cold[2].

It was hard to remember. He got so confused[3]. Sometimes he imagined things that didn't happen.

Like Erin Kelley. He'd looked up[4] her address. She'd told him she lived in Greenwich Village and there she was: Erin Kelley, 101 Christopher Street.

One night he'd followed her, hadn't he?

Was he wrong?[5]

Was it just a dream that she went to that bar and he stood outside? She sat and had[6] something. He didn't know what it was. Wine? Club soda?[7] What difference? He'd tried to decide whether or not to go in and join her.

Then she'd come out. He'd been about to go up and talk to her when the station wagon pulled up.

He couldn't remember if he'd gotten a look at the driver[8]. Sometimes he dreamed about a face.

Erin got in.

That was the night they say she disappeared.

The thing was that Lenny wasn't sure if he'd just dreamed that. And if he told that to the cops, would they try to say he was crazy and make him go back to the place[9] where they locked him up[10]?

1. Le temps que son père fasse fortune
2. il s'était habitué au froid
3. était parfois si désorienté
4. avait cherché
5. Est-ce qu'il se trompait ?
6. avait commandé
7. De l'eau gazeuse ?
8. s'il avait vu le conducteur
9. l'obligeraient à retourner là
10. où on l'avait déjà enfermé

XVIII
SATURDAY
March 9

AT NOON on Saturday, FBI agents Vince D'Ambrosio and Ernie Cizek sat in a dark-gray Chrysler across the street from the entrance to 101 Christopher Street.

"There he goes[1]," Vince said. "All dressed up[2] for his day off[3]."

Gus Boxer was exiting[4] from the building. He was wearing a red and black check[5] lumber jacket[6] over loose-fitting[7] dark brown polyester pants, heavy laced boots[8], a black cap[9] with a rim that[10] half-covered his face.

"You call that dressed up?" Ernie exclaimed. "In that getup[11] I thought he was paying off a bet[12]."

"You just never saw him in his underwear and suspenders[13]. Let's go." Vince opened the driver's door.

They had checked with the building managers. Boxer was off from noon every other Saturday[14] till Monday morning. In his absence, a substitute super[15], Jose Rodriguez, handled complaints[16] and did minor repairs.

Rodriguez answered their ring. A sturdy[17] man in his mid-thirties with a direct manner, Vince wondered why the management[18] didn't keep him full-time[19]. He and Ernie showed their Bureau

1. Le voilà
2. Bien habillé
3. de congé
4. sortait
5. à carreaux
6. veste de bûcheron
7. ample
8. de grosses chaussures à lacets
9. casquette
10. dont la visière
11. cet accoutrement
12. que c'était son gage pour avoir perdu un pari
13. en sous-vêtements et bretelles
14. un samedi sur deux
15. remplaçant
16. s'occupait des réclamations
17. robuste
18. la direction
19. à temps plein

credentials[1]. "We're going from apartment to apartment questioning the tenants[2] about Erin Kelley. A number of them[3] were not in[4] the last time we went through."

Vince did not add that today he was going to get very specific about[5] what the tenants thought of Gus Boxer.

On the fourth floor, he hit gold[6]. An eighty-year-old woman answered the door, taking care not to remove the security chain[7]. Vince showed his badge. Rodriguez explained, "It's all right, Miss Durkin. They just want to ask a few questions. I'll stay right here where you can see me."

"Can't hear," the old woman yelled.

"I just want to ..."

Rodriguez touched D'Ambrosio's arm. "She can hear better than you or me," he whispered[8]. "Come on, Miss Durkin, you liked Erin Kelley. Remember how she always asked you if you needed anything from the store and how she'd take you to church[9] sometimes? You want the cops to get the guy who did that to her, don't you?"

The door opened the length of the chain. "Ask your questions." Miss Durkin looked severely at Vince. "And don't shout[10]. It gives me a headache.[11]"

For the next fifteen minutes, the two agents got an earful[12] of what a native New York octogenarian[13] thought of how the city was being run[14]. "I've lived here all my life," Miss Durkin informed them crisply[15], her wavy gray hair bobbing as she spoke[16]. "We never used to lock our doors[17]. Why would you? Who'd bother you? But now, all this crime and no one doing a thing about it. Disgusting.[18] I tell you, they should ship all those drug dealers[19] to the ends of the earth[20] and let them sail off[21]."

1. badges du FBI
2. locataires
3. Un certain nombre
4. absents
5. poser des questions très précises sur
6. mit dans le mille
7. prenant bien soin de ne pas retirer la chaîne de sécurité
8. lui souffla
9. qu'elle vous emmenait à l'église
10. ne criez pas
11. Ça me fait mal à la tête.
12. durent subir l'exposé
13. de ce qu'une octogénaire, new-yorkaise de souche,
14. de la façon dont la ville était gérée
15. vivement
16. en secouant ses cheveux gris bouclés
17. ne fermions jamais nos portes à clé
18. C'est une honte.
19. on devrait expédier ces trafiquants de drogue
20. au bout du monde
21. qu'on ne les revoie plus

"I agree with you, Miss Durkin," Vince said wearily[1]. "Now about Erin Kelley."

The old woman's face saddened[2]. "A sweeter girl you'd never find.[3] I'd like to get my hands on whoever[4] did that to her. Now a few years ago, I happened to be sitting at the window looking at that apartment building across the street[5]. A woman was murdered. They came around asking questions but May and I—she lives next door[6]—decided to keep our mouths shut[7]. We saw it. We know who did it. But that woman was no better than she ought to be[8], and there was good reason[9]."

"You witnessed a murder[10] and didn't tell the police?" Ernie asked incredulously.

She snapped her lips closed[11]. "If I said that, I didn't say it the way I meant[12]. What I meant was, I have my suspicions[13] and so does May. But that's as far as it goes."

Suspicions! She saw that murder, Vince thought. He also knew that no one would ever get her or her friend May to testify[14]. With an inward sigh[15], he said, "Miss Durkin, you sit by the window. I have a feeling you're a good observer[16]. Did you see Erin Kelley leave with anyone that evening?"

"No. She left alone."

"Was she carrying anything?"

"Only her shoulder bag."

"Was it large?"

"Erin always carried a large shoulder bag. She often carried jewelry and didn't want anything that could be yanked from her hand[17]."

"Then it was generally known she carried jewelry?"

"I guess so. Everyone knew she was a designer. From the street, you could see her sitting at her worktable."

"Did she date much?"

1. avec lassitude
2. s'assombrit
3. Il n'y avait pas plus gentille.
4. mettre la main sur celui qui
5. d'en face
6. l'appartement voisin
7. on a décidé de ne rien dire
8. n'était pas quelqu'un de bien
9. elle l'avait bien mérité
10. avez été témoin d'un meurtre
11. se referma comme une huître
12. je me suis mal exprimée
13. que j'avais des soupçons
14. témoigner
15. Prenant sur lui
16. que vous êtes très observatrice
17. qu'on pourrait lui arracher de la main

"She dated. But I wouldn't say much. Of course, she might have been meeting people outside. That's the way young people do it now. In my day,[1] a young man picked you up at your home or you didn't set foot out the door[2]. It was better then."

"I'm inclined to agree.[3]" They were still standing in the hall. "Miss Durkin, I wonder if we might just step inside[4] for a moment. I don't want to be overheard[5]."

"Your feet aren't muddy[6], are they?"

"No, ma'am."

"I'll wait right here, Miss Durkin," Rodriguez promised.

The apartment had the same layout[7] as the one where Erin Kelley had lived. It was meticulously neat[8]. Overstuffed horsehair[9] furniture protected with antimacassars[10], standing lamps[11] with elaborate silk shades[12], polished end tables[13], framed family pictures of bewhiskered[14] men and severe women. Vince was carried back to the memory of[15] his grandmother's parlor[16] in Jackson Heights.

They were not invited to sit down.

"Miss Durkin, tell me, what do you think of Gus Boxer?"

A ladylike snort.[17] "That one! Believe me, this is one of the few apartments he doesn't barge into[18] looking for one of his famous water leaks. And this is the one that has it.[19] I don't like that man. I don't know why the management keeps him on[20]. Goes around[21] in those disgusting clothes. Surly.[22] The only thing I can figure[23] is that they get him cheap[24]. Just a week before she disappeared, I heard Erin Kelley tell him that if she found him in her apartment again, she'd call the police."

"Erin told him that?"

"You bet she did.[25] And she was right."

1. De mon temps,
2. sinon vous ne sortiez pas
3. J'aurais tendance à être d'accord.
4. auriez-vous l'obligeance de nous laisser entrer
5. qu'on m'entende
6. Vous n'avez pas de boue aux pieds
7. était agencé
8. propre et bien rangé
9. excessivement rembourrés de crin de cheval
10. par des têtières
11. des lampadaires
12. des abat-jour
13. des guéridons
14. à favoris
15. Cela rappela à Vince
16. salon
17. Elle lança un « pff ! » distingué.
18. où il ne débarque pas à l'improviste
19. le seul où il y en ait une !
20. le garde
21. Il se balade
22. Il est grincheux.
23. Ma seule hypothèse
24. il ne leur coûte pas cher
25. Mais certainement.

"Was Gus Boxer aware of the amount of jewelry Erin Kelley handled?[1]"

"Gus Boxer is aware of everything that goes on in this place."

"Miss Durkin, you've been very helpful[2]. Is there anything else you can think of to tell us?"

She hesitated. "For a few weeks before Erin disappeared, from time to time a young fellow used to hang out across the street[3]. Always when it was getting dark[4] so you couldn't see him clearly. Now I don't know what he was up to[5]. But that Tuesday night that Erin left here for the last time, I could make out that[6] she was alone and carrying that big shoulder bag. My glasses[7] had fogged up[8] and I'm not sure if it was that same fellow across the street, but I think it was, and when Erin started walking down the block[9], he went in the same direction."

"You didn't see him clearly that night, but you saw him other times. What did he look like, Miss Durkin?"

"Beanpole.[10] Collar up.[11] Hands in his pockets, kind of hugging his arms against his body[12]. Thin face. Dark, messy hair.[13]"

Len Parker, Vince thought. He glanced at Ernie, who obviously had the same idea.

"I've been looking forward to this.[14]" Darcy leaned back[15] in the passenger seat of the Mercedes and smiled at Michael. "It's been quite a week.[16]"

"So I gathered[17]," he said dryly[18]. "It was all I could do to catch you in[19] at home or at your office."

"I know. I'm sorry."

1. Boxer savait-il qu'Erin pouvait avoir autant de bijoux chez elle ?
2. d'une grande aide
3. traînait sur le trottoir d'en face
4. à la tombée de la nuit
5. ce qu'il fichait là
6. j'ai bien vu qu'
7. Mes lunettes
8. étaient embuées
9. est partie dans la rue
10. Grand et maigre.
11. Le col remonté.
12. les bras collés au corps
13. Des cheveux foncés, en bataille.
14. J'attendais ce moment avec impatience.
15. s'adossa
16. Quelle semaine !
17. C'est ce que j'ai cru comprendre
18. d'un ton sec
19. la croix et la bannière pour vous joindre

"Don't be sorry about anything. It's a great day for a ride, isn't it?"

They were on Route 202 nearing Bridgewater. "I never knew very much about New Jersey," Darcy commented.

"Except comedians' jokes[1]. Everyone judges it by that turnpike strip[2] with all the refineries[3]. Believe it or not, it has a longer coastline[4] than most other states on the eastern seaboard[5] and has among the highest number of horses per capita[6] in the nation."

"So there![7]" Darcy laughed.

"So there. Who knows? With my missionary zeal[8], maybe I'll make you a convert[9]."

Mrs. Hughes was bathed in smiles[10]. "Oh, Miss Scott, I've been planning the nicest dinner since Doctor said you were coming."

"How nice of you."

"The guest room[11] at the head of the stairs[12] is all ready. You can just freshen up there[13] after your ride."

"Great."

If anything, the day was even[14] more perfect than last Sunday. Cool. Sunny. A hint of spring[15] in the air. Darcy managed to give herself[16] completely to the enjoyment of the canter[17].

When they stopped to let the horses rest, Michael said, "I don't have to ask if you're having a good time. It shows.[18]"

The late afternoon[19] turned sharply cooler[20]. A fire had been laid[21] in Michael's study. The draft from the chimney[22] was brisk, causing the flames to leap up[23].

1. des blagues d'humoristes
2. cette autoroute à péage
3. bordée de raffineries
4. un bord de mer plus long
5. de la côte est
6. par personne
7. D'accord !
8. À force de prosélytisme
9. vais-je réussir à vous convertir
10. était tout sourire
11. chambre d'amis
12. en haut de l'escalier
13. y faire un brin de toilette
14. Le temps était même encore
15. Un parfum de printemps
16. s'abandonner
17. au plaisir de galoper
18. Ça se voit.
19. En fin d'après-midi,
20. la température baissa brusquement
21. allumé
22. L'appel d'air de la cheminée
23. faisant jaillir les flammes

Michael poured wine for her, made an old-fashioned[1] for himself, sat beside her on the comfortable leather couch, stretched his feet[2] on the coffee table. His arm went around the back of the sofa. "Do you know," he said, "I've spent more time this week thinking about what you told me. It's terrible that a chance[3] remark can hurt a child so much[4]. But Darcy, can you honestly say that sometimes you don't look in the mirror and see the fairest of all[5]?"

"I certainly do not." Darcy hesitated. "God forbid I should angle for[6] a free[7] consultation, but I've been meaning to talk to you about that. No, never mind."

His hand ruffled her hair.[8] "What? Shoot.[9] Spit it out.[10]"

She looked directly at him, concentrating on the kindness in his eyes. "Michael, I get the feeling that you understand how devastating that remark was for me, but that you think I've been—how can I put this[11]—subconsciously blaming my mother and father all these years."

Michael whistled[12]. "Hey, you'd put me out of business[13]. Most people take a year of therapy before they come to that kind of conclusion."

"You haven't answered me."

He kissed her cheek. "And I don't intend to. Come on, I think Mrs. Hughes has the fatted calf on the table[14]."

They got back to her apartment at ten o'clock. He parked the car and walked her to the door. "This time I don't leave until I make sure you're safely inside[15]. I wish you'd let me drive you to Wellesley tomorrow. That's a heck of a long round-trip for one day.[16]"

"I don't mind it. And I have to make a stop on the way back[17]."

1. [cocktail au whisky]
2. allongea les jambes
3. fortuite
4. puisse blesser un enfant à ce point
5. que vous ne voyez pas la plus belle en ce royaume
6. Loin de moi l'idée d'avoir
7. gratuite
8. Il lui passa la main dans les cheveux.
9. Allez !
10. Crachez le morceau !
11. comment dire
12. siffla
13. vous allez me mettre au chômage
14. tué le veau gras
15. que vous êtes à l'abri chez vous
16. Ça fait vraiment long comme aller et retour dans la journée.
17. au retour

"More garage sales?[1]"

She did not want to talk about the Nan Sheridan pictures. "Something like that. Another fishing expedition.[2]"

He put his hands on her shoulders, tilted up her face[3], brought his lips down to hers. His kiss was warm but brief. "Darcy, call me when you get home tomorrow night. I just want to be sure you're safe."

"I will. Thank you."

She stood inside the door[4] until the car disappeared down the block[5]. Then, humming[6], she ran up the stairs.

1. Encore des vide-greniers ?
2. Une recherche de plus.
3. lui inclina la tête
4. resta debout derrière la porte
5. au coin de la rue
6. en chantonnant

HANK WAS COMING in early Saturday evening. We have so little time together, Vince fretted[7] as he opened the door to his apartment. When they were married, he and Alice had been living in Great Neck[8]. There hadn't been much point[9] in his commuting[10] after they split up[11], so when they sold the house he'd taken this apartment at Second Avenue and Nineteenth Street[12]. The Gramercy Park area. Not Gramercy Park, of course. Not on his salary.

But he liked his apartment. On the ninth floor, his windows offered a typical midtown view. To the right a peek of the Park[13] with its elegant brownstones, straight down the murderous traffic[14] on Second Avenue, across the street a blend[15] of residential and office buildings with storefront restaurants[16], delis[17], Korean produce[18] markets, a video store.

He had two bedrooms, two baths[19], a fair-sized[20] living room, a dinette[21], a minuscule kitchen. The second bedroom was for Hank, but he'd put book-

7. songea, soucieux
8. [à Long Island]
9. Ça ne servait plus à grand-chose
10. qu'il fasse l'aller et retour quotidien
11. après leur séparation
12. [à Manhattan]
13. on apercevait le parc
14. la circulation infernale
15. mélange
16. des petits restaurants
17. des traiteurs
18. de fruits et légumes
19. salles d'eau
20. assez grand
21. un coin repas

shelves[1] and a desk in it and it also served as a study.

The living room and dinette were furnished in Alice-in-Mistakeville decor[2]. The year before they broke up, she'd gone pastel modern in the living room[3]. Pale peach and white sectional[4], pale peach carpet, peach and teal[5] no-arms easy chair[6]. Glass tables. Lamps that looked like bones[7] in a desert. She'd wished that stuff on him[8], taking all the traditional furniture that he liked. One of these days, when he got around to it[9], Vince was going to get rid of everything and buy good old-fashioned, comfortable furniture. He was sick of feeling as though he'd stumbled into Barbie's Dream House[10].

Hank hadn't arrived yet. Vince stripped[11], stood under a hot shower, pulled on underwear, a sweater, chinos, and loafers[12]. He opened a beer, stretched out[13] on the sectional, and reviewed the case.

This was one baffling investigation[14]. Look under any rock and you'll find a new clue.[15]

Boxer. Erin had threatened to go[16] to the police about him. Yesterday, Darcy Scott had called saying she thought she had a picture of Nan Sheridan at Belle Island with a maintenance man in the background who might have been Boxer. They'd picked up the picture[17] and were checking it out.

Miss Durkin had seen someone who sure as blazes[18] sounded like that looney[19], Len Parker, hanging around Christopher Street, and she thought he had followed Erin Kelley the night she disappeared.

There was a direct connection between that con man[20] Jay Stratton and Nan Sheridan. A direct connection between Jay Stratton and Erin Kelley.

Vince heard the turn of a key in the latch[21]. Hank bounded in[22]. "Hi Dad." Dropped his overnight bag[23]. Quick hug.

1. des étagères
2. selon le goût déplorable d'Alice
3. avait refait le salon en moderne et tons pastel
4. canapé modulaire
5. bleu canard
6. fauteuil sans accoudoirs
7. des ossements
8. lui avait laissé tout ça
9. quand il aurait le temps
10. entrait dans la maison de rêve de Barbie
11. se déshabilla
12. des mocassins
13. s'étendit
14. une enquête sacrément déroutante
15. Un nouvel indice à chaque coin de rue.
16. menacé d'aller se plaindre
17. récupéré la photo
18. il en mettrait sa main au feu,
19. dingue
20. escroc de
21. dans la serrure
22. entra d'un bond
23. son sac pour la nuit

Vince felt the tousled[1] hair brush his cheek. He always had to check himself from showing[2] the fierce[3] love he felt for his son. The kid would be embarrassed[4]. "Hi, pal. How's it going?"

"Great. I think. I aced the chemistry.[5]"

"You studied hard enough."

Hank took off his school jacket[6], flung it into space[7]. "Boy, it's great to have midterms over.[8]" He took long steps[9] into the kitchen and opened the refrigerator door. "Dad, it looks as though you could use Meals-on-Wheels[10]."

"I know. It's been quite a week." Inspiration seized Vince.[11] "I found a terrific new pasta restaurant the other night. It's on West Fifty-eighth Street. We can take in a movie[12] after."

"Great." Hank stretched[13]. "Oh boy, it's good to be here. Mom and Blubber[14] are sore at each other[15]."

It's none of my business, Vince thought, but couldn't help himself[16]. "Why?"

"She wants a Rolex for her birthday. A sixteen, five Rolex."

"Sixteen thousand five hundred dollars? And I thought she was expensive[17] when I was married to her."

Hank laughed. "I love Mom, but you know her. She thinks big[18]. What's going on with the serial murder case?"

The phone rang. Vince frowned. Not again on Hank's night, he thought, observing that Hank's reaction was to look interested. "Maybe there's been a break[19]," Hank said as Vince picked up the phone.

It was Nona Roberts. "Vince, I hate to call you[20] at home, but you did give your number. I was out on location[21] all day and stopped by the office just now[22]. There's a message from Dr. Nash. His editor doesn't want him talking about personal ads

1. ébouriffés
2. se retenir de montrer
3. profond
4. gêné
5. J'ai cartonné en chimie.
6. son blazer d'uniforme
7. le lança en l'air
8. Faut dire que ça fait du bien d'avoir fini les exams.
9. fut en deux enjambées
10. te faire livrer des repas à domicile
11. Vince fut pris d'une inspiration.
12. aller voir un film
13. s'étira
14. Gros Lard
15. se font la gueule
16. ne put se retenir
17. avait des goûts de luxe
18. voit les choses en grand
19. une piste
20. je suis désolée de vous appeler
21. sur un tournage
22. je viens juste de passer au bureau

now when his own book is scheduled for fall publication[1]. Have you any other ideas about a shrink[2] who might be particularly tuned in to[3] this subject?"

"I deal with[4] a few who are members of AAPL. That's an organization of shrinks who are specialists in psychiatry and law. I'll try and get one of them for you[5] by Monday."

"Thanks a lot. Again, forgive me for bothering you. I'm off to[6] Pasta Lovers for another bowl of that spaghetti."

"If you get there first, ask for a table for three. Hank and I are just leaving." Vince realized he sounded presumptuous[7]. "Unless, of course, you're with your own friends." Or *friend*, he thought.

"I'm by myself[8]. That sounds great. See you there." The phone clicked in his ear.[9]

Vince looked at Hank. "Is that okay with you, Chief?" he asked. "Or would you have preferred just the two of us[10]?"

Hank reached for the jacket that had landed on[11] the armless easy chair. "Not at all. It's my duty to check out your dates.[12]"

1. vu que la parution de son livre est prévue pour l'automne
2. psy
3. branché sur
4. J'en fréquente
5. de vous en trouver un
6. Je file à
7. que c'était un peu prétentieux de sa part
8. toute seule
9. Il entendit le clic à l'autre bout de la ligne.
10. qu'on soit que tous les deux
11. atterri
12. C'est mon devoir de voir avec qui tu sors.

XIX
SUNDAY
March 10

DARCY LEFT for Massachusetts at seven o'clock Sunday morning. How many times had she and Erin driven up together to see Billy, she wondered as she steered the car onto[1] the East River Drive. Sharing the driving[2], stopping midway[3] for carry-out coffee[4] at McDonald's, always deciding they really ought to get around to[5] buying a thermos like the one they had had in college[6].

The last time they'd agreed on that, Erin had laughed. "Poor Billy will be dead and buried before we ever get that thermos."

Now it was Erin who was dead and buried.

Darcy drove straight through[7] and got to Wellesley at eleven-thirty. She stopped at St. Paul's and rang the doorbell of the rectory[8]. The monsignor[9] who had celebrated Erin's funeral mass[10] was there. She had coffee with him. "I left word[11] at the nursing home," she told him, "but I wanted you to know as well. If Billy needs anything, if he starts sinking[12], or if he becomes conscious and aware[13], please send for me[14]."

"He's not going to become aware anymore," the monsignor said quietly. "I think that's a special mercy[15] for him."

She attended[16] the noon mass and thought of the eulogy[17] less than two weeks ago. "Who can

1. tournait sur
2. Conduisant à tour de rôle
3. à mi-chemin
4. pour acheter un café à emporter
5. se décider à
6. à la fac
7. sans s'arrêter
8. presbytère
9. prêtre
10. messe
11. J'ai laissé des instructions
12. s'il est au plus mal
13. reprend conscience
14. surtout appelez-moi
15. une délivrance
16. assista à
17. l'éloge funèbre

forget the sight of that little girl pushing her father's wheelchair into this church?"

She went to the cemetery. The ground had not yet settled over[1] Erin's grave. The dark brown soil[2] was still uneven[3]; a glaze of frost[4] over it shimmered[5] in the slanting rays[6] of the weak[7] March sun. Darcy knelt, removed her glove, and placed her hand on the grave. "Erin. Erin."

From there she went to the nursing home and sat by Billy's bed[8] for an hour. He did not open his eyes, but she held his hand and kept up a steady stream of small talk[9]. "Bertolini's is crazy about the necklace Erin designed. They want her to do a lot more work for them."

She talked about her own business[10]. "Honestly, Billy, if you saw Erin and me rummaging through attics[11] looking for goodies[12], you'd think we were crazy. She has a great eye[13] and has picked out some furniture that I would have missed[14]."

As she left, she leaned over and kissed his forehead. "God bless,[15] Billy."

There was a faint pressure[16] on her hand. He does know I'm here, she thought. "I'll be back soon," she promised.

Her car was a Buick station wagon with a cellular built-in phone[17]. The traffic was slow heading south[18], and at five o'clock she called the Sheridan home in Darien. Chris answered. "I'm running later than I expected[19]," she explained. "I don't want to interfere with your mother's plans—or your plans, for that matter[20]."

"No plans," he assured her. "Just come along.[21]"

...

1. ne s'était pas encore tassée sur
2. La terre brune
3. encore irrégulière
4. une couche de givre
5. scintillait
6. sous les rayons obliques
7. faible
8. au chevet de Billy
9. lui fit la conversation
10. parla de son entreprise
11. en train de fouiller dans les greniers
12. choses récupérables
13. a l'œil
14. que je n'aurais pas remarqués
15. Au revoir, cher
16. légère pression
17. téléphone cellulaire intégré
18. vers le sud
19. Je suis un peu en retard
20. d'ailleurs
21. Vous pouvez passer.

She pulled into the Sheridan property at quarter of six. It was almost dark, but outside lights illuminated the handsome Tudor mansion. The long driveway had a roundabout at[1] the main entrance. Darcy parked just past the bend[2].

It was obvious that Chris Sheridan had been watching for her[3]. The front door opened and he came out to greet her. "You made good time[4] at that[5]," he said. "It's nice to see you, Darcy."

He was wearing an oxford cloth shirt[6], corduroy[7] pants[8], and loafers. As he extended his hand to assist her[9] from the car, she was again aware of the breadth of his shoulders[10]. She was also glad to see that he was not in a jacket and tie. On the way down it had occurred to her that she was arriving at dinnertime and her own corduroy pants and wool sweater might not be suitable garb[11].

The interior of the house had the charming combination of lived-in comfort[12] and exquisite taste. Persian carpets were scattered in[13] the high-ceilinged foyer[14]. A Waterford[15] chandelier[16] and matching sconces[17] enhanced[18] the magnificent carving[19] on the curving staircase. Paintings Darcy longed to[20] study covered the stairway wall[21].

"Like most people, my mother uses the den[22] more than any other room," Chris told her. "Through here."

Darcy glanced at the living room as they passed. Chris noticed and said, "The whole house is done in American antiques. Anywhere from early Colonial to Greek Revival. My grandmother was hooked on[23] antiques and I guess we learned by osmosis[24]."

Greta Sheridan was sitting in a comfortable armchair by the fireplace. *The New York Times* was scattered[25] around her. The Sunday magazine

1. La longue allée finissait en rond-point devant
2. après le virage
3. guettait son arrivée
4. avez bien roulé,
5. finalement
6. chemise de gros coton
7. en velours côtelé
8. un pantalon
9. tendait la main pour l'aider à sortir
10. remarqua une fois de plus sa carrure
11. la tenue adéquate
12. aspect pratique
13. ornaient çà et là
14. vestibule haut de plafond
15. [fabrique de cristal irlandaise]
16. lustre
17. des appliques assorties
18. accentuaient
19. bois sculptés
20. que Darcy aurait aimé
21. le mur de la cage d'escalier
22. petit salon
23. passionnée par
24. osmose
25. de tous côtés

section[1] was open to the puzzle page[2] and she was studying a crossword[3] dictionary. She got up gracefully. "You must be Darcy Scott." She took Darcy's hand. "I'm so sorry about your friend."

Darcy nodded. What a beautiful woman, she thought. Many of the film stars who were her mother's intimates[4] would enjoy Greta Sheridan's high cheekbones, patrician features[5], slender frame. She was wearing pale blue wool slacks, a matching cowl neck[6] sweater, diamond earrings, and a diamond pin in the shape of a horseshoe[7].

To the manner born[8], Darcy thought.

Chris poured sherry. A platter[9] of cheese and crackers was on the coffee table[10]. He poked at[11] the fire. "By the end of the day[12], you know it's still March."

Greta Sheridan asked about the trip[13]. "You have more courage than I to go up in the morning to Massachusetts and back a few hours later."

"I'm in the car a lot.[14]"

"Darcy, we've known each other for five days," Chris commented. "Will you please tell me exactly what you do?" He turned to Greta. "The first time I took Darcy through the main floor of the gallery, she spotted the Roentgen writing desk out of the corner of her eye[15]. Then she told me she was 'sort of in the business[16].'"

Darcy laughed. "You won't believe, but here goes[17]."

Greta Sheridan was fascinated. "What a sensational idea. If you're interested, I'll be a scout for you[18]. You'd be amazed at the wonderful furnishings people discard[19] or sell for next to nothing[20] in this area[21]."

1. supplément du dimanche
2. à la page des jeux
3. de mots croisés
4. des amies proches de sa mère
5. ses traits aristocratiques
6. à col boule
7. en forme de fer à cheval
8. L'élégance naturelle
9. plateau
10. table basse
11. tisonna
12. En fin de journée
13. si le trajet s'était bien passé
14. Je fais beaucoup de voiture.
15. du coin de l'œil
16. plus ou moins du métier
17. voici ce que je fais
18. j'irai en éclaireur
19. jettent
20. pour une bouchée de pain
21. par ici

At six-thirty, Chris said, "I'm the chef[1]. I hope you're not a vegetarian, Darcy. We're having steaks, baked potato[2], salad. Gourmet delight time.[3]"

"I'm not a vegetarian. It sounds wonderful."

When he had left, Greta Sheridan began to talk about her daughter and the reenactment[4] of her murder on the *True Crimes* television series. "When I received that letter telling me a dancing girl was going to die in New York in Nan's honor, I thought I would go mad. There's nothing worse than not being able to prevent a tragedy[5] you know is going to happen."

"Except to feel you had a hand in causing it[6]," Darcy said. "I know that the only way I can make up to[7] Erin for urging her to answer those cursed ads[8] is to stop her killer from hurting anyone else. You obviously feel the same way. I understand how it must be tearing you apart[9] to go through Nan's letters and pictures, and I'm grateful[10]."

"I've found some others. They're here." Greta pointed to a stack of small albums on the raised hearth[11]. "These were on a high shelf of the library and missed getting put away[12]." She reached for the top one[13]. Darcy pulled up a chair beside her[14] and together they bent over it[15]. "Nan got interested in photography that last year," Greta said. "We gave her a Canon for Christmas, so these were all taken between late December and early March."

The salad days, Darcy thought. She had albums like this of the Mount Holyoke crowd[16]. The only difference was Mount Holyoke was a women's college. In these pictures there were as many guys as coeds[17]. They began to go through them.

...

1. chef cuisinier
2. pommes de terre au four
3. Un vrai régal.
4. reconstitution
5. éviter un drame
6. se dire qu'on en est, en partie, responsable
7. me racheter envers
8. foutues annonces
9. être déchirant
10. je vous en suis reconnaissante
11. au bord de la cheminée
12. n'ont pas été rangés avec les autres
13. celui du dessus
14. approcha une chaise pour s'asseoir à côté d'elle
15. elles se penchèrent ensemble sur l'album
16. des étudiants de Mount Holyoke
17. que de filles

Chris appeared in the doorway[1]. "Five-minute warning."

"You're a good cook," Darcy said approvingly as she ate the last bite[2] of steak.

They began talking about Nan's reference to someone named[3] Charley who had liked girls to wear spike heels. "That's what I was trying to remember," Greta said. "On the program and in the newspapers they were talking about high-heeled slippers. It was the letter from Nan about spike heels that was gnawing at me. Unfortunately[4], it really hasn't helped much[5], has it?"

"Not yet," Chris said.

Chris carried a tray with coffee into the study.

"You make a marvelous butler[6]," his mother said affectionately.

"Since you refuse[7] to have live-in help[8], I've had to learn."

Darcy thought of the Bel-Air mansion with its permanent staff of three live-ins[9].

When she finished the coffee, she got up to go. "I hate to break this up[10], but it will be over an hour before I get home[11] and if I relax too much, I'll end up falling asleep at the wheel[12]." She hesitated. "Can I just look at that first book again?"

In that first album, on the next to the last[13] page, there was a group scene[14]. "The tall fellow in the school sweater," Darcy said. "The one with his face turned from the camera[15]. There's something about him." She shrugged. "I just have a feeling I may have met him somewhere."

Greta and Chris Sheridan studied the picture. "I can pick out[16] some of the kids," Greta said, "but not that one. How about you, Chris?"

1. sur le seuil
2. bouchée
3. du fait que Nan avait parlé d'un certain
4. Malheureusement
5. ça n'a pas servi à grand-chose
6. majordome
7. Puisque tu refuses
8. d'avoir du personnel à demeure
9. son personnel de trois personnes à demeure
10. suis désolée d'écourter la soirée
11. ça va me prendre plus d'une heure pour rentrer
12. je risque de m'endormir au volant
13. l'avant-dernière
14. une photo de groupe
15. presque de dos
16. reconnais

"No. But look, Janet is in it. She was one of Nan's big buddies[1]," he explained to Darcy. "She lives in Westport." He turned to his mother. "She loves to visit you. Why not ask her to drop in soon[2]?"

"She's so busy with the children. I could drive down there."

As Darcy said good-bye, Greta Sheridan smiled and said, "Darcy, I've been studying you all night[3]. Except for the color of your hair, has anyone ever told you[4] that you have a striking resemblance to[5] Barbara Thorne?"

"Never," Darcy said honestly. It was not the moment to say that Barbara Thorne was her mother. She smiled back. "But I have to tell you, Mrs. Sheridan, that's a very nice thing to say."

Chris walked her to the[6] car. "You're not too tired to drive?"

"Oh no. You should see the long treks I take[7] when I'm out on one of my hunts for[8] furniture."

"We really are in the same business[9]."

"Yes, but you take the high road[10] ..."

"Will you be coming to the gallery tomorrow?"

"I'll be there. Good night, Chris."

Greta Sheridan was waiting at the door. "She's a lovely girl, Chris. Lovely."

Chris shrugged. "I think so too." He remembered how Darcy had blushed when he'd asked her about coming up yesterday.

"But don't start matchmaking[11], Mother. I've got a hunch she's taken.[12]"

1. grandes copines
2. de passer te voir
3. je vous ai observée toute la soirée
4. est-ce qu'on vous a déjà dit
5. vous ressemblez comme deux gouttes d'eau à
6. la raccompagna à sa
7. les expéditions que je fais
8. je pars à la recherche de
9. dans la même branche
10. êtes un cran au-dessus
11. à jouer les entremetteuses
12. J'ai l'impression qu'elle est déjà prise.

OVER THE WEEKEND Doug had been everything any woman could ask of a devoted husband and father. Even knowing his behavior[1] was all a sham[2], Susan managed to assuage her fear[3] that Doug might be a serial killer.

He went to Donny's basketball practice, then got together[4] a scrimmage[5] in the outdoor court[6] with the kids who could stay. He took everyone out to Burger King for lunch. "Nothing like health food[7]," he'd joked[8].

The place was full of young families. This is the sort of togetherness[9] we've been lacking[10], Susan thought. But now it's too late. She looked across the table at Donny, who had hardly said a word.

Back home, Doug played with the baby, helping him build a castle of interlocking blocks[11]. "Let's put the little prince inside." Conner squealed with delight[12].

He took Trish for a ride[13] on her scooter[14]. "We can beat anyone on the block, can't we, toots[15]?"

He had a friendly father-daughter conversation with Beth. "My little girl is getting prettier every day. I'm going to have to build a fence[16] around this house to keep away[17] all the boys who'll be coming after you."

While she was getting dinner, he nuzzled Susan's neck[18]. "We should go dancing some night, honey. Remember how we used to dance in college?"

Like a cold wind, that ended the fantasy that maybe she had[19] been ridiculous in suspecting him

1. Même si elle savait que son comportement
2. n'était qu'une mascarade
3. apaiser sa crainte
4. organisa
5. match
6. le terrain extérieur
7. Y a rien de mieux qu'une nourriture saine !
8. plaisanté
9. ce type d'activités en famille
10. qui nous a manqué
11. avec des cubes à emboîter
12. poussa un cri de joie
13. emmena Trish faire un tour
14. trottinette
15. hein, ma chérie
16. une barrière
17. te protéger de
18. enfouit son nez dans le cou de Susan
19. cela chassa tout espoir d'avoir

of anything stronger than womanizing[1]. *Dancing shoes found on dead bodies.*

Later, in bed, Doug reached for her. "Susan, have I ever told you how much I love you?"

"Many times, but one stands out in my mind.[2]" *When I lied for you after Nan Sheridan died.*

Doug pulled up on one elbow[3], stared down at her in the dark. "Now when was that?" he asked teasingly[4].

Don't let him know what you're thinking. "The day we were married, of course." She laughed nervously. "Oh, Doug, no. Please, I'm really tired." She could not bear his touch[5]. She realized she was afraid of him.

"Susan, what the hell is the matter with you[6]? You're trembling."

Sunday was more of the same[7]. Family togetherness. But Susan could spot the wary[8] expression in Doug's eyes, the lines of worry[9] around his mouth. *Do I have an obligation to report my suspicions[10] to the police? And if I admit that I lied for him fifteen years ago, could I go to prison too? And if that happened, what would become of the children? And if he suspected I was going to tell the police that I lied for him about the morning Nan died, how would he try to stop me?*

1. d'être plus qu'un simple coureur de jupons
2. Souvent, mais une fois surtout m'est restée.
3. se redressa sur un coude
4. taquin
5. qu'il la touche
6. mais qu'est-ce que tu as
7. fut assez semblable à la veille
8. méfiante
9. les rides d'inquiétude
10. faire part de mes soupçons

XX
MONDAY
March 11

On Monday morning, Vince called Nona. "I've got a shrink for your program. Dr. Martin Weiss. A nice guy. Sensible.[1] A member of AAPL and very knowledgeable[2]. He says it straight[3] and he's willing to[4] do the show. Want to take down[5] his number?"

"Absolutely." Nona repeated it, then added, "I like Hank, Vince. He's terrific."

"He wants to know if you'd like to see him pitch[6] when baseball starts."

"I'll bring the Cracker Jacks[7]."

1. Plein de bon sens.
2. compétent
3. parle franchement
4. veut bien
5. noter
6. aller le voir jouer
7. le pop-corn

Nona phoned Dr. Weiss. He agreed to come to the studio at four o'clock on Wednesday. "We tape at five. It will be aired Thursday night at eight."

Darcy spent a good part of Monday in the warehouse[8] tagging[9] furniture for the hotel. At four o'clock she arrived at Sheridan Galleries. An auction was taking place. She saw Chris standing on the side[10] of the first row[11], his back to her. She slipped down the corridor to[12] the conference room.

8. à l'entrepôt
9. à étiqueter
10. debout à côté
11. rang
12. prit discrètement le couloir qui menait à

Many of the snapshots were dated[1]. She wanted to find others in that same time frame[2]. Maybe she'd come across[3] another picture of the student who had seemed vaguely familiar.

At six-thirty she was still at it[4]. Chris came in. She looked up, smiling. "The bidding out there sounded hot and heavy.[5] Was it a good day?"

"Very. No one told me you were here. I noticed the light was on[6]."

"I'm glad you did. Chris, does this fellow look like the one I pointed out yesterday?"

He studied it. "Yes, it does. My mother left a message a few minutes ago. She saw Janet today. That guy was one of the many questioned in Nan's death. He had a crush on her[7], I gather[8]. His name was Doug Fox." At[9] Darcy's shocked expression he asked, "You know him then?"

"As Doug Fields. Through a personal ad."

1. portaient une date
2. de la même période
3. tomberait sur
4. n'avait pas fini
5. Les enchères avaient l'air d'être animées.
6. qu'il y avait de la lumière
7. avait le béguin pour elle
8. d'après ce que j'ai compris
9. Devant

HONEY, THEY called an emergency meeting[10]. I can't talk, but a company we've recommended to our biggest client is going under[11]."

Somehow Susan got through[12] the evening. She gave the baby and Trish a bath and helped Donny and Beth with their homework[13].

At last she was able to turn out the lights and go to bed. For hours she lay sleepless[14]. He'd managed to stay home for a weekend. Now he was on the loose[15] again. And if he was responsible for the deaths of those girls, she was equally guilty[16].

It would be so easy if she could only run away. Bundle the kids[17] in the car and drive as far as they could go.

10. ont organisé une réunion en urgence
11. est sur le point de faire faillite
12. réussit à tenir le coup toute
13. à faire leurs devoirs
14. ne ferma pas l'œil
15. dans la nature
16. tout aussi responsable
17. Coller les enfants

But it didn't work like that.

The next afternoon when she'd seen Trish off on the school bus[1] and put Conner down for his nap[2], Susan picked up the phone and asked information for[3] the number of the FBI headquarters in Manhattan.

She dialed[4] and waited. A voice said, "Federal Bureau of Investigation."

It was not too late to disconnect[5]. Susan shut her eyes, forced her voice above a whisper[6]. "I want to talk to someone about the dancing-shoe murders. I may have some information."

1. après avoir mis Trish dans le car de ramassage scolaire
2. mis Conner au lit pour la sieste
3. aux renseignements
4. composa le numéro
5. pour raccrocher
6. s'obligea à ne pas murmurer

On Monday evening, Darcy met Nona for dinner at Neary's and filled her in[7] about Doug Fox. "Vince was out when I tried to reach him," she said. "I left word with his assistant." She broke off a piece of roll[8] and lightly buttered it[9]. "Nona, Doug Fox, or Doug Fields as he introduced himself to me, is exactly the kind of guy Erin would have enjoyed and trusted. He's good-looking, bright, artistic, and he's got one of those boyish faces[10] that would appeal to[11] a nurturer[12] like Erin."

Nona looked grave[13]. "It's pretty scary[14] that he was questioned in Nan Sheridan's death. You'd better not see him again. Of course, Vince did say that a lot of guys don't give their right names[15] when they answer these ads."

"But how many others were questioned in Nan Sheridan's death?"

"Just don't get your hopes up.[16] So far, it isn't really more of a lead[17] than the fact that Jay Stratton also

7. la mit au courant
8. rompit un morceau de petit pain
9. étala un peu de beurre dessus
10. visages enfantins
11. attirerait
12. quelqu'un de maternant
13. prit un air sérieux
14. Ça fait peur
15. vrai nom
16. N'en attends pas trop.
17. ce n'est pas plus une piste

went to Brown or that Erin's superintendent worked near Nan Sheridan's home fifteen years ago."

"I just want it to be over," Darcy sighed.

"Let's not talk about it anymore. You've been eating and breathing it.[1] How's work going?"

"Oh, I've been neglecting it, of course. But I did have a nice call[2] today about a room I did for a sixteen-year-old girl who had a terrible accident. I used some of Erin's things to furnish it. The mother wanted me to know that her daughter Lisa came home from the hospital Saturday and loves the room. And you know what the mother said really got Lisa excited?"

"What?"

"Remember the poster Erin had on the wall opposite her bed? The one of the Egret painting?"

"Sure I do. 'Loves Music, Loves to Dance.' "

They hadn't noticed that Jimmy Neary had come up to their table. *"That's it,"* he said vehemently. "By heaven[3], that's it. That's the way the ad began that fell out[4] of Erin's pocket, right here on this very spot[5]."

1. Tu baignes trop dedans.
2. un gentil coup de fil
3. Bon Dieu
4. C'est comme ça que commençait l'annonce qui est tombée
5. par terre, juste là

XXI
TUESDAY
March 12

SUSAN HIRED a babysitter on Tuesday and took the train down to[1] New York. Vince had asked her to come in. "I can understand how difficult this is for you, Mrs. Fox," he'd said carefully. He did not tell her that they already had a connection to her husband[2]. "We'll do everything to keep our investigation from the media[3], but the more we know, the easier that will be[4]."

At eleven o'clock, Susan was in FBI headquarters. "You can contact the Harkness Agency," she told Vince. "They've been trailing[5] Doug. I would like to think he's just a philanderer[6], but if it's more than that, I can't let it go on[7]."

Vince saw the agony[8] in the face of the pretty young woman opposite him. "No, you can't let it go on," he said quietly. "However, it's a long jump from[9] knowing your husband is playing around[10] to thinking that he might be a serial killer. How did you make that jump?[11]"

"I was only twenty and I was so in love with him." It was as though Susan was talking to herself.

"How long ago was that?"

"Fifteen years."

Vince kept his face impassive[12]. "What happened at that time, Mrs. Fox?"

1. prit le train pour
2. son mari était déjà impliqué
3. pour garder les médias en dehors de tout ça
4. plus ce sera facile
5. filé
6. coureur de jupons
7. je ne peux pas laisser faire
8. lut la douleur
9. il y a un grand pas entre
10. n'est pas fidèle
11. Qu'est-ce qui vous a menée à cette conclusion ?
12. resta impassible

Her eyes fixed somewhere on the wall behind him, Susan told Vince about lying for[1] Doug when Nan Sheridan died and how Doug had called out Erin's name in his sleep the night her body was discovered.

When she was finished, Vince said, "The Harkness Agency knows where his apartment is?"

"Yes." After she revealed everything she knew or suspected, Susan felt a vast weariness[2]. Now all she had to do was live with herself for the rest of her life.

"Mrs. Fox, this is one of the hardest things you'll ever have to do. We need to check with the Harkness Agency. The fact that they were following your husband could be of great value[3]. Can you act normally with him[4] for the next day or two? Don't forget, our investigation may clear him[5]."

"It isn't hard to keep up appearances[6] with my husband. Most of the time he doesn't notice me except to complain[7]."

When she left, Vince called in Ernie. "We have our first big break and I don't want to blow it[8]. This is what we'll do. ..."

1. qu'elle avait menti pour protéger
2. se sentit très lasse
3. d'un grand secours
4. faire comme si de rien n'était
5. l'innocentera peut-être
6. de faire semblant
7. pour se plaindre
8. tout faire rater

ON TUESDAY AFTERNOON, Jay Charles Stratton was booked for grand theft[9]. The NYPD detectives, in conjunction with[10] the Lloyd's of London security staff[11], had found the jeweler who fenced[12] some of his stolen diamonds. The rest of the gems that were listed as being in the missing pouch were traced to[13]

9. fut arrêté pour vol caractérisé
10. avec l'aide du
11. personnel de sécurité
12. écoulait
13. retrouvés dans

a private safe deposit box rented under the name[1] Jay Charles.

1. loué au nom de

IT HAD BEEN a long meeting and the tension in the office all day was brutal[2]. How do you explain to your best clients that a company's accountants[3] pulled the wool over your eyes[4]? That sort of thing wasn't supposed to happen anymore[5].

Doug called home several times and was surprised to hear the babysitter pick up the phone. Something was definitely up.[6] He'd make it his business to[7] get home tonight. It wasn't that hard[8] to straighten Susan out[9]. His confidence oozed away.[10] She wasn't beginning to suspect … Or was she?

2. extrême
3. les comptables
4. vous ont berné
5. n'était plus censé se produire
6. Il y avait vraiment quelque chose de louche.
7. Il ferait le nécessaire pour
8. si dur
9. de tout arranger avec Susan
10. Il perdit sa belle assurance.

ON TUESDAY EVENING, Darcy went straight home from work. All she wanted to do was heat a can of soup and go to bed early. The tension of the last two weeks was catching up with her[11]. She knew it.

At eight o'clock Michael phoned. "I've heard tired voices[12], but yours just might win first prize[13]."

"I'm sure it would."

"You've been driving yourself too hard[14], Darcy."

"Don't worry. I intend to come straight home from the office for the rest of the week."

"That's a good idea. Darcy, I'll be out of town for a few days, but keep Saturday for me, won't you? Or Sunday? Or better still[15], both days?"

11. se faisait sentir
12. J'ai déjà entendu des voix fatiguées
13. la vôtre gagne haut la main
14. Vous vous surmenez
15. mieux encore

Darcy laughed. "Let's plan on Saturday. Have fun."

"It isn't fun. It's a psychiatric convention[1]. I've been asked to fill in for[2] a friend who's had to cancel[3]. You want to know what it's like to have four hundred shrinks in one room at the same time?"

"I can't imagine."

1. congrès

2. On m'a demandé de remplacer

3. qui a dû annuler

XXII
WEDNESDAY
March 13

D DAY[1], NONA thought as she slipped off[2] her cape and tossed it[3] on the love seat. It was not quite eight A.M. She was grateful to see that Connie was already there and the coffee brewing[4].

Connie followed her in. "It's going to be a great program, Nona." She was carrying freshly washed mugs[5].

"I think Cecil B. DeMille did one of his epics[6] faster than I handled this one," Nona said wryly[7].

"You've been doing all your regular shows while putting this together," Connie pointed out.

"I suppose. Let's be sure to reconfirm all the guests by phone. You did send them a follow-up letter[8]?"

"Of course." Connie looked astonished that she'd ask[9].

Nona grinned[10]. "I'm sorry. It's just that Hamilton has been such a pain[11] about this program, and Liz is determined to take the credit[12] for what's good in it and leave me holding the bag[13] if there are any snafus[14] ..."

"I know."

"Sometimes I wonder who runs this office, Connie, you or me. There's only one area[15] where I wish we weren't alike[16]."

Connie waited.

1. C'est le jour J
2. en ôtant vivement
3. la lança
4. qu'elle avait mis le café en route
5. des tasses qui venaient d'être lavées
6. ses films à grand spectacle
7. avec ironie
8. une lettre de confirmation
9. stupéfaite qu'elle pose la question
10. lui fit un grand sourire
11. a été si pénible
12. s'attribuer tout le mérite
13. à me laisser porter le chapeau
14. des pépins
15. domaine
16. j'aimerais que tu ne sois pas comme moi

"I wish you talked to plants. You're like me. You never even see them." She pointed to the plant on the windowsill. "That poor thing is gasping[1]. Pour something liquid on it[2], will you[3]?"

1. meurt de soif
2. Abreuve-la un coup
3. tu veux bien

LEN PARKER WAS tired Wednesday morning. Yesterday he hadn't been able to stop thinking about Darcy Scott. When he left work he'd hung[4] around her apartment building and seen her step out[5] of a cab around six-thirty or seven. He'd waited until ten, but she hadn't come out. He really wanted to talk to her. Other times he was mad at her[6] for being so mean[7] to him. There was something he had thought about the other day that had been important, but now it was gone[8]. He wondered if he'd remember again.

He put on his maintenance uniform. Nice thing about wearing a uniform,[9] it didn't cost you anything for work clothes[10].

4. traîné
5. sortir
6. furieux contre elle
7. méchante
8. il avait oublié ce que c'était
9. L'avantage avec les uniformes, c'est que
10. en vêtements de travail

VINCE'S SECRETARY had taken a message from Darcy Scott before he got to the office on Wednesday morning. She'd be out[11] all day on different jobs but wanted him to know that Erin had probably answered an ad that began *"Loves Music, Loves to Dance."* That certainly sounded like the kind of ad those missing girls would have answered too, Vince thought.

11. absente

Following up on the[1] personal ads was a grueling job[2]. Anyone who didn't want his real identity known[3] could fake a few ID's[4], open a checking account[5], and rent a private box where magazines and newspapers could forward[6] the responses to the nameless[7] ads. No home address to trace. The people who ran those private box services were in the business of offering secrecy to[8] their clients.

It was going to be a long haul.[9] But this ad had a ring to it[10]. He got on the phone to the researchers[11]. They were closing in on[12] Doug Fox, also known as Doug Fields. The Harkness Agency's file on him was an FBI investigator's dream[13].

Fields had been subletting[14] the apartment for two years, starting just about the time Claire Barnes disappeared.

Joe Pabst, the Harkness man, had sat near Fox in the SoHo restaurant. It was clear he had met the woman through a personal ad.

He'd made a date to take her dancing.

He had a station wagon.

Pabst was sure that Fox had some sort of hideout[15]. He'd overheard him telling the real estate broker[16] in SoHo that he had a retreat he'd love to have her visit[17].

He was passing himself off as[18] an illustrator. The super of the London Terrace building had been in and out of[19] Fields's apartment and said that there were sketches lying around[20] that were really good.

And he had been questioned in Nan Sheridan's death.

But it was all circumstantial[21], Vince reminded himself. Did Fox place ads, or answer them, or both? Would it be better to tap[22] his London Terrace phone for a while, see what that turned up[23]?

1. Remonter la piste des
2. une tâche ingrate
3. ne voulant pas révéler sa véritable identité
4. se faire de fausses pièces d'identité
5. un compte en banque
6. faire suivre
7. anonymes
8. assuraient la confidentialité à
9. Ça allait prendre du temps.
10. lui disait quelque chose
11. les enquêteurs
12. en savaient de plus en plus sur
13. le fichier rêvé pour tout enquêteur du FBI
14. sous-louait
15. une planque
16. la conseillère en immobilier
17. une maison tranquille qu'il aimerait lui faire visiter
18. se faisait passer pour
19. était entré plusieurs fois dans
20. çà et là dans l'appart
21. tout ça ne faisait que des présomptions
22. mettre sur écoute
23. et voir ce que ça leur apprendrait

Should they bring him in for questioning? It was a tough one to call.[1]

Well, at least[2] Darcy Scott was already alerted to the possibility that Fox was the one[3]. She wouldn't let herself get painted into a corner[4] by him.

And wouldn't it be a bonus if it turned out[5] that Fox had placed the ad they knew Erin Kelley had been carrying around? *"Loves Music, Loves to Dance."*

At noon, Vince got a VICAP alert from headquarters in Quantico. Calls had come in from police departments all over the country.[6] Vermont. Washington, D.C. Ohio. Georgia. California. Five more packages of mismatched shoes had been returned. All of them contained a shoe or boot and a high-heeled slipper. All of them were sent to families of the young women who had turned up in[7] the VICAP file, the young women who had lived in New York and been reported missing in the last two years.

At three-thirty, Vince was ready to leave his office for Hudson Cable Network. His secretary stopped him as he passed[8] her desk and handed him[9] the phone. "Mr. Charles North. He says it's important."

Vince felt his eyebrows go up[10]. Don't tell me that stuffy[11] ambulance chaser[12] is starting to cooperate, he thought. "D'Ambrosio," he said crisply[13].

"Mr. D'Ambrosio, I have been doing a great deal of thinking[14]."

Vince waited.

"There is only one possible explanation I can come up with[15] to account for[16] how my plans may have fallen on the wrong ears[17]."

Vince felt a stir[18] of interest.

"When I came to New York in early February to make final living arrangements, I attended a

1. Ce n'était pas une décision facile.
2. au moins
3. était prévenue que Fox pourrait bien être le tueur
4. ne se ferait pas coincer
5. s'il s'avérait
6. Ils avaient reçu des appels venant des quatre coins du pays.
7. déjà repérées par
8. passait devant
9. lui passa
10. leva les sourcils d'étonnement
11. guindé
12. d'avocat rapace
13. d'un ton sec
14. j'ai bien réfléchi
15. Je ne vois qu'une hypothèse
16. pour expliquer
17. comment quelqu'un de mal-intentionné a pu avoir vent de mes projets
18. début

benefit[1] at the Plaza as the guest of my senior partner[2]. The 21st Century Playwrights'[3] Festival Benefit. It was quite a glittery crowd.[4] Helen Hayes, Tony Randall, Martin Charnin, Lee Grant, Lucille Lortel. I was introduced to a great many people during the cocktail hour. The senior partner at my firm was anxious that I become known[5]. I spoke to a group of four or five people right[6] before dinner was announced. One of them asked me for my card, but I can't think of his name."

"What did he look like?"

"You're speaking to someone with a very poor[7] memory for both faces and names, which I am sure must be puzzling to[8] someone in your profession. I'm vague about him[9]. About six feet.[10] Late thirties or early forties. Late thirties, I would think. Well-spoken."

"Do you think that if we got a roster of the people who attended that benefit it might stir your memory[11]?"

"I don't know. It might."

"Okay, Mr. North. I'm grateful for this. We'll get the list and perhaps you can ask your senior partner if he recognizes the names of any of the people you spent time with."

North sounded alarmed. "And how would I explain the need for that information?"

The faint stirring of gratitude[12] that Vince had felt for the man's attempt to be helpful[13] disappeared. "Mr. North," he snapped, "you're a lawyer. You should be used to getting[14] information without giving it." He hung up and yelled for[15] Ernie. "I need the guest list for the[16] 21st Century Playwrights' Benefit at the Plaza in early February," he said. "Shouldn't be hard to get. You know where I'll be[17]."

1. soirée de bienfaisance
2. en tant qu'invité de l'associé principal de mon cabinet
3. des auteurs dramatiques
4. Il y avait du beau monde.
5. voulait me présenter à tout le monde
6. juste
7. mauvaise
8. ce qui est sûrement un mystère pour
9. Je n'ai qu'un vague souvenir de lui.
10. Environ 1,80 m.
11. vous rafraîchir la mémoire
12. Le semblant de gratitude
13. devant l'effort du monsieur pour se rendre utile
14. avoir l'habitude d'obtenir
15. cria à
16. la liste des invités au
17. où me joindre

IT WAS MARCH thirteenth, Nan's anniversary[1]. Yesterday had been their thirty-fourth birthday.

Long ago[2] Chris had started to celebrate his[3] on the twenty-fourth, Greta's birthday. It was easier for both of them. His mother had phoned yesterday before he left for work. "Chris, I thank my stars every day that I have you[4]. Happy birthday, dear."

This morning he'd phoned her. "The tough[5] day, Mother."

"I guess it always will be. Are you sure you want to be on that program?"

"Want to? No. But I think if it does anything to help solve this case[6], it's worth it[7]. Maybe someone watching it will remember something about Nan."

"I hope so." Greta sighed. Her tone changed. "How's Darcy? Chris, she is so dear[8]."

"I think this whole business is wearing her down[9]."

"Will she be on the program as well?"

"No. And she doesn't want to watch it being taped[10]."

It was a quiet day at the gallery. Chris had a chance to catch up on paperwork[11]. He'd left instructions that if Darcy came in he was to be notified[12]. But there was no sign of her. Maybe she wasn't well[13]. At two he phoned her office. Her secretary said she was working on some outside job all day and then planned to go directly home.

At three-thirty, Chris was hailing a cab[14] to go to Hudson Cable.

Let's get this over with[15], he thought grimly[16].

1. l'anniversaire de la mort de Nan
2. Il y a bien longtemps
3. fêter le sien
4. chaque jour, je rends grâce au ciel de t'avoir
5. difficile
6. que si ça peut aider à résoudre l'affaire
7. ça en vaut la peine
8. adorable
9. que toute cette affaire la mine
10. assister à l'enregistrement
11. d'écluser quelques paperasses
12. on le prévienne
13. était-elle souffrante
14. arrêtait un taxi
15. finissons-en
16. l'air sombre

The guests for the program gathered[1] in the greenroom[2]. Nona introduced them. The Corras, a couple in their mid-forties. They'd separated. Each had placed a personal ad. They'd answered each other's ad. That had been the catalyst[3] that brought them back together[4].

The Daleys, a serious-looking couple in their fifties. Neither had ever married. They'd both been embarrassed about placing and answering ads. They'd met three years ago. "It was good from the very beginning[5]," Mrs. Daley said. "I've always been much too reticent. I was able to put on paper[6] what I couldn't say to anyone." She was a research scientist. He was a college professor.

Adrian Greenfield, the vivacious divorcée in her late forties. "I'm having more fun," she told the others. "Actually, they made a printing error[7]. They were supposed to say that I was well-liked[8]. Instead, they put down[9] that I was wealthy. I swear, you need a U-Haul[10] for the mail I've gotten."

Wayne Harsh, the shy[11] president of a toy manufacturing company[12]. In his late twenties. Every mother's dream of the kind of guy her daughter will bring home[13], Vince decided. Harsh was enjoying his dates. In his ad he'd written that it frustrated him to see the toys he manufactured being enjoyed by kids all over the world while he is childless[14]. Anxious to[15] meet sweet, bright woman in her twenties who wants a nice guy who'll be home on time and won't drop his laundry[16] on the floor.

1. se rassemblèrent
2. foyer
3. le catalyseur
4. de leur réconciliation
5. dès le début
6. écrire
7. une faute de frappe
8. très appréciée
9. ont écrit
10. faudrait un camion
11. timide
12. usine de jouets
13. Le gendre idéal
14. alors qu'il n'avait pas d'enfant
15. Désireux de
16. ne laissera pas traîner son linge sale

The lovebirds[1], the Cairones. They fell in love on their first personal ad date. At the end of the evening he had gone over to the piano at the[2] bar where they met and played "Get Me to the Church on Time." They were married a month later.

"Until they came along[3], I was worried that we didn't have any young couples," Nona had confided to Vince when he arrived. "Those two make you believe in romance[4]."

Vince saw the psychiatrist, Dr. Martin Weiss, come in and got up to greet him[5].

Weiss was a man in his late sixties with a strong face, a good head of silver hair[6], penetrating blue eyes. They went over to the coffeepot[7].

"Thank you for doing this on short notice[8], Doctor," Vince said.

"Hello, Vince."

Vince turned as Chris came up to them[9]. He remembered that this was the anniversary of Nan Sheridan's death. "Not the best day for you," he said.

AT QUARTER OF FIVE, Darcy leaned back in the cab, her eyes closed. At least today she'd made up for lost time[10]. The painters would start next Monday at the hotel. This morning she'd brought down a brochure from the Pelham Hotel in London. "This is an absolutely elegant and intimate hotel. It's like your place in the sense that the rooms aren't large, the reception area is small, the parlor[11] off it[12] is perfect for receiving visitors. Notice the little bar in the corner. You can have the same thing. And study

1. tourtereaux
2. il s'était installé au piano du
3. Jusqu'à ce qu'ils se manifestent
4. croire à l'amour
5. se leva pour l'accueillir
6. une belle chevelure grise
7. se dirigèrent vers la cafetière
8. au pied levé
9. venait vers eux
10. rattrapé le temps perdu
11. salon
12. juste à côté

the rooms. We're not going to be nearly that grand[1], of course, but we can give it the effect."

It was obvious they were delighted[2].

Now, Darcy thought, I've got to get in touch with[3] the window designer[4] at Wilston's. She'd been shocked to realize that when a window display was taken down[5], the fabrics[6] were often sold for peanuts[7]. Yards and yards[8] of top-quality goods.

She shook her head, trying to dislodge a nagging headache[9]. I don't know whether I'm getting a bug[10] or if I just ache[11], but it's another early night for me[12]. The cab was pulling up to her building.

In the apartment her answering machine was blinking[13]. Bev had left a message. "Darcy, you got the craziest call[14] about twenty minutes ago. Call me right away.[15]"

Quickly, Darcy dialed[16] her office. "Bev, what's the message?"

"It was some woman. Spoke real low.[17] I could hardly hear her[18]. She wanted to know where she could get in touch with you. I didn't want to give your home number so I said I'd give you a message. She said she was in the bar the night Erin disappeared, afraid to admit it because her date[19] wasn't her husband. She saw Erin meet someone who was coming in just as Erin was leaving[20]. They walked away together. She got a good look at him."

"How can I get back to her?[21]"

"You can't. She wouldn't leave[22] her name. She wants you to meet her at that bar. It's Eddie's Aurora on West Fourth Street off[23] Washington Square. She said to come alone and sit at the bar. She'll be there by six unless she can't get away[24]. Don't wait any longer than that. She'll call tomorrow if you don't get together[25] tonight."

1. faire tout à fait aussi grandiose
2. ravis
3. contacter
4. l'étalagiste
5. une vitrine était démontée
6. les tissus
7. pour une bouchée de pain
8. Des métrages à n'en plus finir
9. se débarrasser d'une migraine
10. si je couve quelque chose
11. si c'est juste un mal de tête
12. je vais encore me coucher tôt
13. clignotait
14. un appel complètement insensé
15. Rappelez-moi dès que vous serez rentrée.
16. appela
17. Elle parlait tout bas.
18. l'entendais à peine
19. elle était avec un homme qui
20. parler en partant à quelqu'un qui entrait
21. Où puis-je la joindre ?
22. a refusé de laisser
23. au coin de
24. à moins qu'elle ne puisse pas s'éclipser
25. si ça ne marche pas

"Thanks, Bev."

"Listen, Darcy, I'm going to stay late. I have an exam to study for and there's no peace and quiet[1] in my apartment with my roommate's friends always hanging around[2]. Call me back, won't you? I'd just like to know that you're okay."

"I'll be fine. But yes, I'll call you back."

Darcy forgot that she was tired. It was five of five. She had just time to freshen her face[3], brush her hair, and change from her dusty jeans to a skirt[4] and sweater. Oh, Erin, she thought. Maybe it's ending.

1. il y a trop de bruit
2. vu que ma colocataire a toujours des copains à la maison
3. se repoudrer
4. de quitter son jean poussiéreux pour enfiler une jupe

NONA WATCHED THE CREDITS[5] roll[6] as the guests chatted[7] quietly, still on-camera[8] but off-mike[9]. "Amen," she said as the screen went dark. She jumped up and ran down the steps to the set[10]. "You were wonderful," she said. "Every one of you. I can't thank you enough."

A relaxed smile from some of the participants. Chris, Vince, and Dr. Weiss got up together.

"I'm glad it's over," Chris said.

"Understandable," Martin Weiss said. "From what I've heard today, both you and your mother have shown remarkable strength[11] through all this[12]."

"You do what you have to do[13], Doctor."

Nona came up to them. "The others are leaving, but I wish you people[14] would come back to my office for a cocktail. You've certainly earned it.[15]"

"Oh, I don't think ..." Weiss shook his head, then hesitated. "I must check in with[16] my office. If I can do it from there?"

"Of course."

5. le générique
6. défiler
7. discutaient
8. toujours à l'écran
9. micros coupés
10. vers le plateau
11. avez fait preuve de beaucoup de courage
12. depuis le début
13. On n'a pas le choix
14. que vous trois
15. Vous l'avez bien mérité.
16. Il faut que j'appelle

Chris debated[1]. He realized how low he was feeling[2]. Darcy's secretary had said she was going straight home. He wondered if he could talk her into a quick dinner[3]. "Can I get on line for[4] the phone too?"

"Dial away.[5]"

The beeper went off[6] on Vince's belt[7]. "I hope you have a lot of phones around here, Nona."

Vince dialed from the secretary's desk and received a message to call Ernie at the 21st Century Playwrights' Festival office. When he reached him, Ernie was brimming with news[8].

"I've got the guest list. Guess[9] who was there that night?"

"Who?"

"Erin Kelley and Jay Stratton."

"Holy smoke.[10]" He thought of the description North had given him of the man who had taken his card. Tall. Late thirties or early forties. Well-spoken. But Erin Kelley! That afternoon in Kelley's apartment Darcy had selected a pink and silver dress for Erin to be buried in[11]. Darcy had told him Erin bought it to wear *to a benefit*. Then when he'd picked up the package of shoes that had been mailed[12] to Darcy's apartment, she'd said that the evening slipper in the package went better with Erin's pink and silver dress than the ones Erin had bought herself. He suddenly knew[13] why the shoes went so well with it. Her killer had been at the benefit and seen her wearing that dress.

"Meet me in Nona Roberts's office," he told Ernie. "We might as well go downtown together."

In the office Dr. Weiss seemed more relaxed. "No problems. I was concerned[14] that one patient might need to see me tonight. Ms. Roberts, I'm going to

1. hésita
2. qu'il avait le cafard
3. la persuader de dîner en vitesse avec lui
4. Je peux faire la queue pour
5. Mais oui, je vous en prie.
6. Le bip sonna
7. ceinture
8. débordait de nouvelles
9. Devine
10. Juste ciel !
11. pour Erin dans son cercueil
12. qui avait été envoyé
13. comprit
14. Je craignais

take advantage of your kindness[1]. My youngest son is a communications major[2] and will be graduating from college[3] in June. How does he get a foothold[4] in this business?"

Chris Sheridan had moved the phone from Nona's desk to the windowsill. Absently[5], he fingered the dusty plant[6]. Darcy wasn't home. When he'd called her office, her secretary had been evasive[7]. Something about expecting to hear from her later.[8] "A very important meeting had come up[9]."

His intuition was pounding at him[10]. Something was wrong.

He knew it.

DARCY WASN'T SUPPOSED to wait any longer than six o'clock. She stayed until six-thirty, then decided to give up[11] for tonight. Obviously[12] the woman who called hadn't been able to meet her. She paid for the Perrier and left.

She stepped out onto[13] the street. The wind had stirred up again[14] and seemed to cut through her body[15]. I hope I can get a cab, she said to herself.

"Darcy. I'm so glad I caught you[16]. Your secretary said you'd be here. Hop in.[17]"

"Oh, you're a lifesaver[18]. What luck.[19]"

Len Parker huddled in a doorway[20] across the street and watched the vanishing taillights[21]. It was just like last time[22] when Erin Kelley came out and someone called her from that station wagon.

Suppose this was[23] the same person who had killed Erin Kelley? Should he call that FBI agent? His name was D'Ambrosio. Len had his card.

1. abuser de votre gentillesse
2. fait des études en communication
3. devrait avoir son diplôme
4. Comment peut-il mettre un pied
5. Distraitement
6. tripota la plante poussiéreuse
7. était restée évasive
8. Disant juste qu'elle devait rappeler.
9. avait surgi
10. le taraudait
11. laisser tomber
12. Il était évident que
13. sortit dans
14. s'était à nouveau levé
15. était terriblement pénétrant
16. de vous avoir trouvée
17. Montez !
18. vous me sauvez la vie
19. Quelle chance !
20. se blottit sous un porche
21. les feux arrière disparaître
22. exactement comme la dernière fois
23. Et si c'était

Would they think he was crazy?

Erin Kelley had walked out on him and Darcy Scott had refused to have dinner with him.

But he'd been mean to them.

Maybe he should call.

He'd spent a lot of money on cabs following[1] Darcy Scott these last couple of days.

And the phone call would only cost a quarter[2].

1. en taxis, à force de suivre
2. 25 cents

CHRIS TURNED FROM the window. He had to ask. Vince D'Ambrosio had just come back into the room. "Do you know if Darcy is answering another one of those damn ads[3] tonight?" he demanded[4].

Vince saw the concern on Sheridan's face and ignored the belligerent[5] tone. He knew it was not directed at him[6]. "I understood from Nona that Darcy was planning an early night."

"She was." The smile vanished from Nona's face. "When I called her office, her secretary said she was going straight home from that hotel she's redoing[7]."

"Well, something changed her mind[8]," Chris retorted[9]. "Her secretary sounds very mysterious."

"What's her office number?" Vince grabbed[10] the phone. When Bev answered, he identified himself. "I'm concerned about Miss Scott's plans.[11] If you know what they are, I want to hear them."

"I'd really rather let her get back to you[12]—" Bev began, but was interrupted.

"Listen, miss, I have no intention of interfering with[13] her private life, but if this has to do[14] with a personal ad, I want to know. We're getting very close to solving this case[15] but no one is in custody[16]."

"Well, promise not to interfere—"

3. ces satanées annonces
4. s'enquit abruptement
5. agressif
6. que ce n'était pas dirigé contre lui
7. qu'elle est en train de retaper
8. l'a fait changer d'avis
9. rétorqua
10. saisit
11. Les projets de Mlle Scott m'inquiètent.
12. Je préférerais vraiment qu'elle vous rappelle
13. me mêler de
14. concerne
15. près d'aboutir
16. n'avons encore arrêté personne

"Where is Darcy Scott?"

Bev told him. Vince gave her Nona's number. "Ask Miss Scott to call me immediately when you hear from her[1]." He hung up. "She's meeting a woman who claims she saw[2] Erin Kelley leave Eddie's Aurora in the Village the night she disappeared, and can describe the man she met outside. This woman hasn't come forward[3] because she was with a guy who wasn't her husband."

"Do you believe it?" Nona asked.

"I don't like the sound of it.[4] But if Darcy meets her in that bar, it should be okay. What time is it?"

"Six-thirty," Dr. Weiss said.

"Then Darcy should be phoning her office any minute[5]. She was only supposed to wait until six for that caller to show up[6]."

"Didn't the same thing happen to Erin Kelley?" Chris demanded. "As I understand it, she went to Eddie's Aurora, was stood up[7], left, and disappeared."

Vince felt the skin on the back of his neck start to crawl[8]. "I'll phone there." When he reached the bar, he fired rapid questions[9], listened, then slammed down the receiver[10]. "The bartender says a young woman answering Darcy's description walked out a few minutes ago. Nobody showed up to meet her."

Chris swore under his breath[11]. The moment when he'd found Nan's body fifteen years ago today filled his mind[12] with sickening clarity[13].

An escort from reception[14] tapped on the half-open door[15]. "Mr. Cizek from the FBI says you're expecting him[16]," she told Nona.

Nona nodded. "Show him in.[17]"

Cizek was pulling the thick guest list for the Playwrights' gala from a bulging manila envelope[18] as he came through the door. It was stuck.[19] When he tried to yank it out[20], the clip[21] fell off[22] and the

1. dès qu'elle vous recontacte
2. qui dit avoir vu
3. ne s'était pas manifestée
4. Ça ne me dit rien qui vaille.
5. d'une minute à l'autre
6. pour voir cette femme
7. avait attendu en vain
8. un frisson d'appréhension
9. mitrailla son interlocuteur de questions
10. reposa violemment le combiné
11. jura tout bas
12. lui revint
13. avec une clarté dérangeante
14. Une hôtesse d'accueil
15. frappa à la porte entrouverte
16. qu'il est attendu
17. Faites-le entrer.
18. une enveloppe kraft volumineuse
19. La liste coinçait.
20. la tirer d'un coup sec
21. le trombone
22. tomba

pages scattered. Nona and Dr. Weiss helped to retrieve them[1].

Chris was clenching and unclenching his fists[2], Vince noticed. "We have two strong suspects," he told Chris, "and we have a tail on[3] both of them."

Dr. Weiss was examining one of the pages he picked up. As though he was thinking aloud[4] he commented, "I'd have thought[5] he was too busy with his personal ads to go to parties."

Vince looked up quickly. "Who are you talking about?"

Weiss seemed embarrassed[6]. "Dr. Michael Nash. Forgive me. That was an unprofessional comment.[7]"

"Nothing is unprofessional at this point[8]," Vince said sharply. "It could be very important that Dr. Nash was at the benefit. You sound as if you don't like him. Why?"

All eyes were on[9] Martin Weiss. He seemed to be debating with himself, then said slowly, "This must go no farther than this room.[10] One of Nash's former patients[11], who now consults with me, noticed him in a restaurant with a young woman she knew. The next time she saw that young woman she teased her[12] about it."

Vince felt his nerves tingling the way they always did[13] when he sensed a break in the case[14]. "Go on, Doctor."

Weiss looked uncomfortable[15]. "My patient's young friend said that she had met the man when she answered his personal ad and wasn't surprised to learn that he had lied about his name and background. She felt distinctly uneasy[16] with him."

Vince sensed that Dr. Weiss was deliberately[17] choosing his words. "Doctor," he said, "you know what we're up against[18]. You've got to level with

1. à les ramasser
2. ne cessait de serrer et de desserrer les poings
3. les faisons suivre
4. pensait tout haut
5. j'aurais cru
6. gêné
7. Ce n'était pas très pro de ma part de dire ça.
8. à ce stade
9. Tous les regards se tournèrent vers
10. Cela doit rester entre nous.
11. ex-patientes
12. l'a taquinée
13. le picotement caractéristique
14. qui lui venait devant l'indice décisif
15. gêné
16. s'était sentie très mal à l'aise
17. avec soin
18. la situation

me[1]. What is your candid opinion of[2] Dr. Michael Nash?"

"I consider it unethical[3] for him to do research for a professional book under false pretenses[4]," Weiss said cautiously[5].

"You're hedging[6]," Vince told him. "If you were on the witness stand[7], how would you describe him?"

Weiss looked away. "Loner[8]," he said flatly. "Repressed.[9] Pleasant on the surface but basically antisocial. Probably has deep-rooted[10] problems that began to manifest themselves in childhood[11]. However, he's a natural dissembler[12] and could fool[13] most professionals."

Chris felt blood pounding in his temples[14]. "Has Darcy been seeing this guy?"

"Yes," Nona whispered.

"Doctor," Vince continued rapidly, "I want to get in touch with that young woman immediately and find out what ad he placed."

"My patient brought it in to show me[15]," Weiss said. "I have it in my office."

"Would you remember if it began *'Loves Music, Loves to Dance'?"* Vince asked.

As Weiss said, "Why yes[16], that's right," Vince's beeper went off. He grabbed the phone, dialed, and barked[17] his name. Nona, Chris, Dr. Weiss, and Ernie waited in absolute silence as they saw the lines on Vince D'Ambrosio's forehead deepen[18]. Still holding the receiver he told them, "That Len Parker looney[19] just phoned in[20]. He was following Darcy. She came out of that bar and got into the same station wagon Erin Kelley drove off in[21] the night she disappeared." He paused, then said tersely[22], "It's a black Mercedes registered to[23] Dr. Michael Nash of Bridgewater, New Jersey."

1. me parler en toute franchise
2. Que pensez-vous sincèrement de
3. contraire à la déontologie
4. qu'il prétende faire de la recherche incognito
5. prudemment
6. Vous tournez autour du pot
7. parliez en tant que témoin à un procès
8. Solitaire
9. Refoulé.
10. profondément enracinés
11. dès l'enfance
12. a un sens inné de la dissimulation
13. duper
14. le sang battre ses tempes
15. me l'a apportée pour me la montrer
16. Mais oui !
17. aboya
18. se creuser
19. maboul de Len Parker
20. vient d'appeler
21. le même break dans lequel est partie
22. avec brusquerie
23. immatriculée au nom de

"YOU HAVE a different car."

"I mostly use this one in the country[1]."

"You got back early from the convention."

"The speaker[2] I was to replace[3] felt well enough to come after all[4]."

"I see. Michael, you're sweet[5], but I think I'd just as soon[6] go home tonight."

"What'd you have for dinner last night?"

Darcy smiled. "A can of soup."

"You lean your head back and rest. Sleep if you can. Mrs. Hughes is going to have a fire blazing, a terrific dinner, and then you can sleep all the way home[7]." He reached over and gently stroked her hair[8]. "Doctor's orders[9], Darcy. You know I like taking care of you."

"It's nice to be taken care of.[10] Oh!" She reached for the car phone. "Is it all right if I call my secretary? I promised to check in with her."

He placed his hand over hers and squeezed it[11]. "I'm afraid it will have to wait until we get to the house. The phone is broken. Now you just relax."

Darcy knew Bev would be there at least a few more hours. She closed her eyes and began to drift off[12]. She was asleep by the time they went through the Lincoln Tunnel.

1. à la campagne
2. L'intervenant
3. que je devais remplacer
4. finalement
5. gentil
6. que je préférerais
7. pendant le trajet de retour
8. lui caressa délicatement les cheveux
9. Ordre du médecin
10. C'est agréable de se faire dorloter.
11. la serra
12. s'assoupir

"WE'LL HAVE NASH'S apartment checked," Vince said. "But he'd never take her there or to his office. The doorman would see them."

"Darcy told me his place in Bridgewater is a four-hundred-acre estate. She's been there a couple of times." Nona was gripping the sides of the desk[1] to steady herself[2].

"Then if he suggested going there with him tonight, she wouldn't be suspicious." Vince felt growing anger at himself[3].

Ernie returned from the next office. "I've checked surveillance.[4] Doug Fox is home in Scarsdale. Jay Stratton is at the Park Lane with some old broad[5]."

"That lets them out.[6]" It makes sense[7], Vince thought furiously. Nash left word on Erin's answering machine to call him at his apartment the night he drove off with her[8]. I never thought to check that out[9]. He leaves a phony message[10] with[11] Darcy's secretary and probably acts as though the secretary told him where to find Darcy. We know Darcy trusts him[12]. Sure, she gets into his car. And if that weirdo[13] Parker hadn't been trailing her[14], she'd have vanished into thin air too[15].

"How are we going to find Darcy?" Chris asked desperately[16]. Agonizing fear[17] that made it hard to breathe was crushing his chest[18]. He knew that sometime in this past week, he had fallen hard for[19] Darcy Scott.

Vince was on the line[20] snapping orders[21] to headquarters[22]. "Alert the Bridgewater police," he was saying. "Have them meet us there."

1. se cramponnait au bureau
2. pour ne pas perdre l'équilibre
3. était de plus en plus en colère contre lui-même
4. J'ai vérifié auprès des équipes de surveillance.
5. une vieille rombière
6. Donc, ils n'y sont pour rien.
7. C'est logique
8. l'a emmenée dans sa voiture
9. vérifier ça
10. un message bidon
11. à
12. lui fait confiance
13. ce taré de
14. collé à ses basques
15. elle se serait, elle aussi, volatilisée
16. d'un ton désespéré
17. Une peur incontrôlable
18. l'oppressait
19. était tombé très amoureux de
20. au téléphone
21. en train d'aboyer des ordres
22. au QG

"Be careful, Vince," Ernie warned. "We have absolutely no proof of anything, and the only witness is certifiably nuts[1]."

Chris spun on him[2]. "*You* be careful.[3]" He felt Weiss grip his arm.

"Get directions to Nash's place[4]," Vince was saying. "And have a chopper[5] at the Thirtieth Street pad[6] in ten minutes."

Five minutes later, they were in a patrol car, lights flashing, sirens screaming[7], racing down Ninth Avenue. Vince was in the front seat with the driver, Nona, Chris, and Ernie Cizek in the back. Chris had flatly declared[8] that he was going with Vince. Nona had looked at Vince, her eyes begging[9].

Vince did not share the chilling information[10] received from the Bridgewater police. Nash's estate had a number of outer buildings[11] scattered over[12] the four hundred acres, including some in wooded areas[13]. A search could take a long time.[14]

And every minute we lose, the clock is running out[15] for Darcy, he thought.

"WE'RE HERE, sweetheart[16]."

Darcy stirred[17]. "I did fall asleep, didn't I?" She yawned[18]."Forgive me for being such boring[19] company."

"I was glad you were sleeping. Rest heals the spirit[20] as well as the body."

Darcy looked out[21]. "Where are we?"

"Only ten miles from the house. I have a little retreat where I get my writing done and I forgot my manuscript the other day. You don't mind if we stop

1. est un dingue notoire
2. se tourna brutalement vers lui
3. Vous, faites gaffe !
4. Trouvez le chemin pour aller chez Nash
5. hélicoptère
6. aire de décollage
7. la sirène à fond
8. dit tout net
9. l'implorant du regard
10. l'information glaçante
11. un certain nombre de dépendances
12. disséminées parmi
13. des bois
14. Trouver le bon risquait de prendre longtemps.
15. chaque minute perdue est une minute de moins
16. ma chérie
17. remua
18. bâilla
19. si piètre
20. Le sommeil est réparateur pour l'esprit
21. regarda dehors

for it? As a matter of fact[1], we can have a glass of sherry here."

"As long as[2] we don't stay too long. I do want to get home early, Michael."

"You will. I promise. Come on in.[3] Sorry it's so dark."

His hand was under her arm. "How did you ever find this place?" Darcy asked as he opened the door.

"Pure luck. I know it doesn't look like much outside[4], but the interior is quite nice."

He pushed the door open and reached for the light switch[5]. Beneath it[6], Darcy noticed a button marked "Panic."

She looked around the large room. "Oh, this is handsome," she said, taking in[7] the seating area by the fireplace, the open kitchen, the polished floors[8]. Then she noticed the big-screen television and elaborate stereo speakers. "That's magnificent equipment. Isn't it wasted[9] in a writing retreat?"

"No, it isn't." He was removing her coat. Darcy shivered[10] even though[11] the room was comfortably warm[12]. There was a bottle of wine in a silver holder[13] on the coffee table by the sofa.

"Does Mrs. Hughes take care of this place?"

"No. She doesn't know it exists." He walked the length of the room[14] and switched on the stereo.

The opening bars[15] of "Till There Was You" sounded from the wall speakers[16].

"Come here, Darcy." He poured sherry into a glass and handed it to her. "On a cold night this tastes wonderful[17], doesn't it?"

He was smiling at her affectionately. Then what was wrong? Why did she suddenly sense something different? His voice seemed slightly blurred[18], almost as though he'd been drinking. His eyes. That was it. There was something about his eyes.

1. En fait
2. Du moment que
3. Venez, entrez !
4. que l'extérieur ne paie pas de mine
5. l'interrupteur
6. Juste en dessous
7. devant
8. le parquet ciré
9. Ce n'est pas un peu du gâchis
10. frissonna
11. bien que
12. soit bien chauffée
13. seau en argent
14. traversa la pièce
15. premières mesures
16. enceintes murales
17. c'est délicieux
18. pâteuse

Her instinct was to run for the door, but that was ridiculous. She searched frantically for[1] something to say. Her eyes rested on[2] the staircase. "How many rooms do you have upstairs?" To her own ears the question sounded abrupt.[3]

He didn't seem to notice. "Just a smallish[4] bedroom and bath. This is one of those really old-fashioned[5] cottages."

The smile was still there, but his eyes were changing, the pupils widening[6]. *Where were his computer and printer and books and all the usual trappings[7] of a writer?*

Darcy felt perspiration form[8] on her forehead. What was the matter with her? Was she going crazy suspecting … what? It was just nerves[9]. This was Michael.

Holding his sherry, he settled[10] in the large chair opposite the sofa and stretched out his legs[11]. His eyes never left her face.

"Let me look around." She walked aimlessly[12] through the room, pausing as though to examine one of the few pieces of bric-a-brac, running her hand over[13] the countertop[14] that separated the kitchen area from the rest of the room. "What beautiful cabinets."

"I had them made, but I installed them myself."

"You did!"

His voice was genial[15] but a hard edge came into it[16]. "I told you my father was a self-made man. He wanted me to be able to turn my hand to anything[17]."

"He did a good job teaching you[18]." There was no way she could stand here any longer.[19] She turned, walked toward the sofa, and stepped on something solid[20] that was almost covered by the fringe of the rug in the seating area.

1. chercha désespérément
2. regard tomba sur
3. Elle trouva son propre ton un peu brusque.
4. assez petite
5. très vieillottes
6. ses pupilles se dilataient
7. tout le matériel habituel
8. de la transpiration perler
9. ses nerfs
10. s'installa
11. allongea les jambes
12. sans but
13. passant la main sur
14. bar
15. Le ton était chaleureux
16. devenait cassant
17. toucher un peu à tout
18. a été bon professeur
19. Impossible de rester là plus longtemps.
20. sentit quelque chose de dur sous son pied

Ignoring it, Darcy sat down quickly. Her knees were shaking so much she felt as though they would buckle under her.[1] *What was the matter? Why was she so afraid?*

This was Michael, kind, considerate[2] Michael. She did not want to think about Erin now, but Erin's face was looming in her mind[3]. She took a quick sip[4] of sherry to relieve the dryness in her mouth[5].

The music stopped. Michael looked annoyed[6], got up and went to the stereo. From the shelf above it, he took a pile of cassettes and began to examine them. "I didn't realize that tape was so close to the end[7]."

It was as though he was talking to himself. Darcy gripped the stem[8] of the glass. Now her hands were trembling. A few drops[9] of sherry spilled on the floor[10]. She grabbed the cocktail napkin[11] and bent to pat it dry[12].

As she began to straighten up,[13] she noticed that something was actually caught in the fringe[14] of the rug, something that glinted in the light from the lamp beside the sofa[15]. That's what she must have stepped on.[16] It was probably a button. She reached for it[17]. The tips[18] of her thumb[19] and index finger slipped into hollow space[20] and met[21]. It wasn't a button, it was a ring. Darcy picked it up and stared unbelieving[22].

A gold *E* on an onyx background in an oval setting. *Erin's ring.*

Erin had been in this house. Erin had answered Michael Nash's personal ad.

Sheer horror washed over Darcy.[23] Michael had lied when he claimed he'd only met Erin once for a drink at the Pierre.

1. Elle avait cru que ses genoux allaient se dérober tellement ils tremblaient.
2. prévenant
3. l'image d'Erin l'obsédait
4. gorgée
5. pour avoir la bouche un peu moins sèche
6. contrarié
7. que la cassette était presque finie
8. serra le pied
9. gouttes
10. tombèrent sur le parquet
11. sa serviette en papier
12. pour tamponner la tache
13. En se redressant,
14. pris dans les franges
15. qui brillait à la lumière de la lampe près du canapé
16. C'était sans doute ce qu'elle avait senti sous son pied.
17. tendit le bras pour le prendre
18. Le bout
19. pouce
20. ne rencontrèrent rien
21. se rejoignirent
22. la fixa, incrédule
23. Darcy fut saisie de terreur.

The stereo suddenly started to blare.[1] "Sorry," Michael said. His back was still to her.[2]

"Change Partners and Dance." He was humming the opening bars with the orchestra as he lowered the volume[3] and turned to her.

Help me, Darcy prayed. Help me. He must not see the ring. He was staring at her. She clasped her hands together[4], managed to slip the ring on her finger[5] as Michael came to her, his arms outstretched[6].

"We've never danced together, Darcy. I'm good, and I know you are."

Erin's body had been found with a dancing slipper on her foot. Had she danced with him here in this room? Had she died in this room?

Darcy leaned back on the sofa. "I didn't think you cared about dancing[7], Michael. When I talked about the classes Nona and Erin and I took together, I didn't think you were very interested."

He dropped his arms[8], reached for his glass of sherry. He perched[9] on the chair this time, so much on the edge[10] that it seemed as though his legs, planted on the floor, were preventing him from falling[11].

Almost as though any moment he might spring at her[12].

"I love dancing," he said. "I didn't think it would be healthy[13] for you to be thinking about the fun you had taking those classes with Erin."

Darcy tilted her head[14] as though considering his answer. "You don't stop riding in cars[15] because someone you cared about[16] was in an automobile accident, do you?" She did not wait for a response, but tried to change the subject. She examined the stem of the glass. "Lovely glassware[17]," she commented.

"I bought a set of these[18] in Vienna," he said. "I swear they make the sherry taste even better.[19]"

1. La chaîne HIFI se mit à tonitruer.
2. Il lui tournait toujours le dos.
3. baissait le son
4. joignit les mains
5. glisser la bague à son doigt
6. bras tendus
7. que vous aimiez danser
8. baissa les bras
9. se jucha
10. tellement au bord
11. l'empêchaient de tomber
12. lui sauter à la gorge
13. très sain
14. inclina la tête
15. On n'arrête pas de monter dans une voiture
16. qu'on aime
17. Très jolis verres
18. J'en ai acheté un service
19. Je suis sûr qu'ils donnent encore meilleur goût au sherry.

She smiled with him. Now he sounded like the Michael she knew. The strange look in his eye vanished for an instant. *Keep him like that, her intuition warned. Talk to him. Make him talk to you.*

"Michael." She made her voice hesitant, confidential. "Can I ask you something?"

"Of course." He looked interested.

"The other day, I think you were suggesting that I've been making my parents pay for that remark that hurt me so much when I was a kid. Can I possibly be[1] that selfish[2]?"

1. Est-il possible que je sois
2. aussi égoïste

DURING THE TWENTY-MINUTE helicopter ride, no one spoke. His mind racing[3], Vince had gone over[4] every detail of the investigation. Michael Nash. I sat in his office, thinking he sounded like one of the few shrinks who make sense[5]. Was this a wild-goose chase?[6] What was to say[7] that someone with Nash's money hadn't some sort of retreat in Connecticut or upstate[8] New York?

Maybe he did, but with all his property, the odds were[9] that he would bring his victims here. Over the whir of the propeller[10] Vince could hear in his head the names of serial killers who buried their victims in the attics or basements[11] of their own homes.

The chopper circled over[12] the country road. "There!" Vince pointed to the right where twin high beams[13] were gleaming upward[14], making paths through the darkness[15]. "The Bridgewater police said they'd park right outside Nash's place. Put it down."

3. L'esprit en ébullition
4. passé en revue
5. disent des choses sensées
6. Serait-ce une fausse piste ?
7. Comment être sûrs
8. au nord de l'État de
9. il était probable
10. Malgré le bruit de l'hélice,
11. au sous-sol
12. vola en cercle au-dessus de
13. deux faisceaux lumineux
14. pointaient vers le ciel
15. trouant l'obscurité

The mansion was outwardly tranquil[1]. There were lights shining from several windows on the main floor. Vince insisted that Nona stay outside with the pilot. Ernie and Chris at his heels, he ran from the side lawn up the long driveway[2] and rang the bell. "Leave the talking to me.[3]"

A woman answered, using the intercom[4]. "Who is it?"

Vince clenched his teeth[5]. If Nash was in there, they were giving him plenty of warning[6]. "FBI agent Vincent D'Ambrosio, ma'am. I must speak to Dr. Nash."

A moment later the door opened slightly. The security chain was still in place. "May I see your identification, sir?" The courteous[7] tone of a trained servant[8], this time a man.

Vince passed it through[9].

"Hurry them[10]," Chris urged.

The security chain was released,[11] the door opened. Housekeeping couple, Vince thought. They had that look. He asked them to identify themselves[12].

"We're John and Irma Hughes. We work for Dr. Nash."

"Is he here?"

"Yes, he is," Mrs. Hughes answered. "He's been in all evening. He's completing[13] his book and doesn't wish to be disturbed[14]."

1. avait l'air paisible
2. quitta la pelouse en courant, remonta la longue allée
3. C'est moi qui parle.
4. à l'Interphone
5. serra les dents
6. il avait largement le temps d'être alerté
7. courtois
8. d'un domestique très professionnel
9. la fit passer dans l'entrebaillement
10. Dites-leur de se dépêcher
11. fut enlevée,
12. leur demanda de se présenter
13. finit
14. souhaite qu'on ne le dérange pas

DARCY, YOU REALLY have great introspection," Michael said. "I told you that last week. You're feeling a little guilty[15] about your attitude toward your parents, aren't you?"

15. coupable

"I think I am." Darcy could see that his pupils were closer to normal size[1]. The blue-gray color was visible in his eyes.

The next song on the tape began to play. "Red Roses for a Blue[2] Lady." Michael's right foot began to move in synch with the music.

"*Should* I feel guilty?" she asked quickly.

"WHERE IS DR. NASH'S room?" Vince demanded. "I'll take responsibility for disturbing him."

"He always locks the door when he wants privacy[3], and won't answer. He's very firm about not being interrupted when he's in his room. We haven't even seen him since we got home from shopping late this afternoon[4], but his car is in the driveway."

Chris had had enough[5]. "He's not upstairs. He's driving around in a station wagon doing God knows what[6]." Chris started for the staircase[7]. "Where the hell is his room?"

Mrs. Hughes looked pleadingly[8] at her husband, then led them up the stairs[9]. Her repeated knocking brought no response.[10]

"Have you a key?" Vince demanded.

"Doctor has forbidden me[11] to use it when he leaves his door locked."

"Get it."

As Vince had expected, the massive bedroom was empty. "Mrs. Hughes, we have a witness who saw Darcy Scott get into the doctor's station wagon tonight. We believe she is in imminent danger. Does Dr. Nash have a studio or a cottage on this property or some other place he might have taken her[12]?"

1. reprenaient une taille normale
2. triste
3. être seul
4. en fin d'après-midi
5. en avait assez
6. en train de faire Dieu sait quoi
7. se dirigea vers l'escalier
8. d'un air implorant
9. les conduisit à l'étage
10. Elle eut beau frapper, il n'y eut pas de réponse.
11. m'a interdit
12. où il aurait pu l'emmener

"You must be mistaken[1]," the woman protested. "He's brought Miss Scott here twice. They're great friends."

"Mrs. Hughes, you haven't answered my question."

"On this estate there are barns[2] and a stable[3] and some storage facilities[4]. There's no other building where he'd bring a young lady. He also has an apartment and office in New York."

Her husband was nodding in agreement[5]. Vince could see they were telling the truth[6].

"Sir," Mrs. Hughes said timidly, "we've worked for Dr. Nash for fourteen years. If Miss Scott is with him, I can assure you you have nothing to worry about[7]. Dr. Nash wouldn't hurt a fly[8]."

HOW LONG HAD they been talking? Darcy didn't know. The music was soft in the background. "Begin the Beguine" was playing. How often had she seen her mother and father dance to this music?

"Mother and Daddy were the ones who really taught me to dance," she told Nash. "Sometimes they'd just put on records[9] and fox-trot or waltz[10]. They're really good[11]."

His eyes were still kind. They were the eyes she'd seen the other times she'd been with him. As long as he[12] didn't suspect that she knew about him, maybe he would leave with her, take her to the house for dinner. I've got to make him want to keep talking to me.

Mother had always said, "Darcy, you have a real talent for acting[13]. Why do you keep resisting it?[14]"

If I have it, let me prove it[15] now, she prayed.

1. vous tromper
2. des granges,
3. une écurie
4. des entrepôts
5. acquiesçait de la tête
6. disaient la vérité
7. que vous n'avez aucune raison de vous inquiéter
8. ne ferait pas de mal à une mouche
9. mettaient des disques
10. dansaient le fox-trot ou des valses
11. doués
12. Tant qu'il
13. ferais une très bonne actrice
14. Pourquoi t'obstines-tu à l'ignorer ?
15. faites que je le prouve

All her life she'd heard her mother and father discussing how a scene should be played[1]. She must have learned something[2].

I can't let him see how scared I am[3], Darcy thought. Channel my nervousness into[4] the performance[5]. How would her mother play this scene, a woman trapped[6] in the home of a serial killer? Mother would stop thinking about Erin's ring on her finger and do exactly what Darcy was trying to pull off[7]. She'd play it as though Michael Nash was a psychiatrist and she was a patient confiding in him.

What was Michael saying?

"Have you noticed, Darcy, that when you let yourself[8] talk about your parents you become animated[9]? I think you enjoyed your childhood much more than you realized."

People always clustered around them[10]*. Remember the time the crowd was so great*[11] *that she lost her mother's hand?*

"Tell me, Darcy, what are you thinking? Say it. Let it out.[12]"

"I was so frightened. I couldn't see them. I knew that moment that I hated ..."

"What did you hate?"

"The crowds. Being torn from them[13] ..."

"It wasn't their fault."

"If they weren't so famous ..."

"You've resented that fame[14] ..."

"No." It was working. His voice was his own.[15] I don't want to talk about this, she thought, but I must. I've got to be honest with him. It's my only[16] chance. Mother. Daddy. Help me. Be here for me. "They're so far away." She didn't know she'd said it aloud[17].

"Who are?"

"My mother and father."

1. de la meilleure façon de jouer une scène
2. devait bien en avoir tiré quelque chose
3. à quel point j'ai peur
4. Me calmer en mettant ma nervosité dans
5. mon interprétation
6. prise au piège
7. s'efforçait de faire
8. vous autorisez à
9. vous animez
10. s'attroupaient toujours autour d'eux
11. la fois où il y avait tant de monde
12. Exprimez-vous.
13. Que la foule nous sépare
14. Vous leur en voulez de leur célébrité
15. Il avait sa voix normale.
16. seule
17. à haute voix

"You mean now?"

"Yes. They're touring[1] in Australia with their play[2]."

"You sound so forlorn[3], frightened even[4]. Are you frightened, Darcy?"

Don't let him think that. "No, I'm just sorry that I won't see them[5] for six months."

"Do you think the time you were separated from them that day was the first time you felt abandoned?"

She wanted to shout, "I feel abandoned now." Instead, she turned her mind to[6] the past. "Yes."

"You hesitated. Why?"

"There was another time, when I was six. I was in the hospital and they didn't think I was going to live[7] ..." She tried not to look at him. She was so afraid the eyes would become empty and dark again[8].

She was reminded of the character[9] in "One Thousand and One Nights"[10] who had told stories to stay alive[11].

Chris was engulfed[12] with a sense of helplessness[13]. Darcy had been in this house a few days ago with the man who had killed Nan and Erin Kelley and all those other girls, and she was going to be his next victim.

They were in the kitchen, where Vince had an open line on one phone to the Bureau[14], a second one to the state police[15]. More copters were on the way.[16]

Nona was standing near Vince, looking as though she was about to pass out[17]. The Hugheses, their expressions bewildered and frightened, were sit-

1. en tournée
2. pièce de théâtre
3. avez l'air si triste
4. effrayée, même
5. triste de ne pas les voir
6. regarda résolument vers
7. que j'allais m'en sortir
8. que son regard redevienne froid et sombre
9. se rappela le personnage
10. des Mille et Une Nuits
11. pour rester en vie
12. paralysé
13. par un sentiment d'impuissance
14. était en contact permanent avec le FBI sur une ligne
15. avec la police du New Jersey sur une autre
16. Il y avait d'autres hélicoptères en route.
17. s'évanouir

ting, shoulders touching[1], at the long refectory table. A local cop was talking to them, questioning them about Nash's activities. Ernie Cizek was in the chopper, which was flying low over the grounds[2]. Chris could hear the sound of the engine[3] through the closed window. They were looking for Michael Nash's black Mercedes station wagon. Local squad cars were fanning out[4] across the property checking the outer buildings.

Grimly,[5] Chris remembered how lucky he'd been when he bought a Mercedes station wagon last year. The salesman[6] had talked him into[7] having the Lojack system installed. "It's built right into the wiring[8]," he'd explained. "If your car is ever stolen, it can be located[9] within minutes. You phone in[10] your Lojack code number to the police, it's fed into a computer[11], and a transmitter[12] activates the system in your vehicle. Many police cars are equipped to follow the signal."

Chris had owned the station wagon only one week before it was stolen outside the gallery with a one hundred thousand dollar painting in the back. He'd dashed back inside his office[13] for[14] his briefcase[15], and when he came out the car was gone. He'd phoned to report the theft, and within fifteen minutes the station wagon had been traced and recovered[16].

If only Nash had picked up Darcy in a stolen car that could be traced.

"Oh my God!" Chris ran across the room[17] and grabbed Mrs. Hughes's arm. "Does Nash keep his personal files[18] here or in New York?"

She looked startled[19]. "Here. In a room off the library[20]."

"I want to see them."

1. collés l'un à l'autre
2. survolait la propriété à basse altitude
3. moteur
4. avaient été déployées
5. Sombre,
6. vendeur
7. l'avait convaincu de
8. intégré dans le circuit électronique
9. localisée
10. donnez par téléphone
11. on le rentre dans un ordinateur
12. un émetteur
13. Il était retourné en vitesse dans son bureau
14. rechercher
15. attaché-case
16. repérée et retrouvée
17. traversa la pièce en courant
18. dossiers
19. surprise
20. qui donne sur la bibliothèque

Vince said, “Hold it[1],” into the phone. “What have you got, Chris?”

Chris didn’t answer. “How long has the doctor owned the station wagon?”

“About six months,” John Hughes replied. “He trades in regularly[2].”

“Then I’ll bet he has it[3].”

The files were contained in a row of handsome mahogany cabinets[4]. Mrs. Hughes knew where the key was hidden.

The Mercedes file was easy to find. Chris grabbed it. His exultant cry[5] brought the others running[6]. From the folder he pulled[7] the Lojack pamphlet[8]. The code number for Nash’s black Mercedes was listed[9].

The Bridgewater cop realized what Chris had found. “Give me that,” he said. “I’ll phone it in.[10] Our squad cars have the system[11].”

“You were in the hospital, Darcy.” Michael’s voice was calm.

Her mouth was so dry. She wanted a glass of water, but she didn’t dare distract him[12]. “Yes, I had spinal meningitis[13]. I remember feeling so sick[14]. I thought I was going to die. My parents were at the bedside. I heard the doctor say he didn’t think I’d make it[15].”

“How did your mother and father react?”

“They were hugging each other[16]. My father said, ‘Barbara, we have each other.’ ”

“And that hurt you[17], didn’t it?”

“I knew they didn’t need me,” she whispered.

1. Un instant
2. en change régulièrement
3. je parierais qu’il en a un
4. dans une rangée d’élégants placards en acajou
5. cri de joie
6. fit accourir les autres
7. Il sortit du dossier
8. brochure
9. y figurait
10. Je vais transmettre le code par téléphone.
11. sont équipées
12. n’osait pas le distraire
13. une méningite cérébro-spinale
14. m’être sentie si mal
15. que j’allais m’en sortir
16. se tenaient embrassés
17. ça vous a blessée

"Oh, Darcy, don't you know that when you think you're going to lose someone you love, the instinctive reaction is to look for someone or something to hang on to[1]? They were trying to cope[2], or more accurately[3], preparing to cope. Believe it or not, that's healthy[4]. And ever since then, you've been trying to shut them out[5], haven't you?"

Had she? Always resisting the clothes her mother bought for her, the gifts they showered on her[6], scorning their lifestyle[7], something they'd worked all their lives to achieve[8]. Even her job. Was that one-upmanship to prove something?[9] "No, it isn't."

"What isn't?"

"My job. I really do love what I do."

"Love what I do." Michael repeated the words slowly, in cadence. A new song had begun on the tape. "Save the Last Dance for Me." He stood up. "And I love to dance. *Now*, Darcy. But first I have a present for you."

Horrified, she watched as he got up and reached behind the chair. He turned to her, a shoe box in his hand. "I bought you pretty slippers to dance in, Darcy."

He knelt in front of the sofa and pulled off her boots. Every instinct warned Darcy not to protest. She dug her nails[10] into her palms[11] to keep from screaming[12]. Erin's ring had turned and she could feel the impression of the raised *E*[13] against her skin.

Michael was opening the shoe box and parting the tissue[14]. He took one shoe out and held it up for her to admire[15]. It was an open-toed[16], high-heeled satin slipper. Gossamer ankle straps[17] were almost transparent bands of gold and silver. Michael took Darcy's right foot in his hand and eased it[18] into the shoe, double-knotting the long straps[19]. He reached

1. à qui se raccrocher
2. tenir le coup
3. plus exactement
4. c 'est une réaction saine
5. prendre vos distances
6. refusant les cadeaux dont ils la couvraient
7. méprisant leur mode de vie
8. pour lequel ils avaient travaillé dur toute leur vie
9. par volonté de prouver qu'elle était la meilleure ?
10. enfonça ses ongles
11. dans ses paumes
12. pour se retenir de crier
13. l'empreinte du E en relief
14. écartait le papier de soie
15. la lui montra pour qu'elle l'admire
16. à bouts ouverts
17. Des lanières en voile léger
18. le glissa
19. avant de faire un double nœud avec les lanières

into the box, removed the other slipper, and caressed her ankle as he guided her foot along the insole[1].

When she had both shoes on, he looked up and smiled. "Do you feel like Cinderella[2]?" he asked.

She could not answer.

1. le long de la semelle intérieure
2. Cendrillon

"THE RADAR INDICATES the wagon is parked about ten miles away in a northwest direction," the Bridgewater cop said tersely as the squad car raced down the country road[3]. Vince, Chris, and Nona were with him.

3. filait sur la route de campagne

"The signal's getting stronger," he said a few minutes later."We're getting closer.[4]"

"Until we're there, we're not close enough," Chris exploded. "Can't you go faster?"

They rounded a curve[5]. The driver slammed on the brakes[6]. The squad car skidded[7], then straightened. "Oh hell!"

"What's the matter?" Vince snapped.

"They're digging up the road down here. We can't get through[8]. And the damn detour will waste time[9]."

4. On approche.
5. prirent un tournant
6. freina brutalement
7. dérapa
8. On ne peut pas passer
9. va nous faire perdre du temps

MUSIC FILLED THE ROOM but could not drown out[10] his maniacal[11] laugh. Darcy's footsteps were flying in synch with his. "I don't often do a Viennese waltz," he shouted, "but tonight it was what I

10. ne couvrait pas
11. de fou

planned for you." Twirling, bobbing, turning.[1] Darcy's hair flew around her face. She was gasping[2] but he seemed not to notice.

The waltz ended. He did not remove his arms from around her. His eyes were glittering[3], dark, empty holes again.

"Can't Get Started with You." Easily, he slipped into a graceful fox-trot.[4] Effortlessly[5], she followed him. He was holding her tightly[6], crushing her[7]. She couldn't breathe. Is this what he did to the others? Got them to trust him. Brought them to this desolate[8] house. Where were their bodies? Buried around here somewhere?

What chance did she have to get away from him[9]? He'd catch her before she could get to the door. When they came in, she'd noticed the panic button. Was it hooked up[10] to a security system? Knowing that someone was on the way[11], he might not kill her.

Now there was a growing urgency about Michael[12]. His arm was like steel[13] as he glided and stepped in perfect time to[14] the music. "Do you want to know my secret?" he whispered. "This isn't my house. It's Charley's house."

"Charley?"

Backstep.[15] Glide.[16] Turn.

"Yes, that's my real name. Edward and Janice Nash were my aunt and uncle[17]. They adopted me when I was a year old and changed my name from Charley to Michael[18]."

He was staring down at her. Darcy could not bear to look into those eyes.

Backstep. Sidestep.[19] Glide.

"What happened to your real parents?"

"My father killed my mother. They electrocuted him.[20] Whenever my uncle was mad at me[21], he said

1. Tourner, un petit saut, tourner encore.
2. haletait
3. brillaient
4. Il se mit à danser le fox-trot avec aisance.
5. Sans peine
6. la serrait contre lui
7. en l'écrasant
8. isolée
9. de lui échapper
10. relié
11. S'il savait que quelqu'un allait arriver
12. Michael semblait de plus en plus déterminé
13. de l'acier
14. parfaitement en rythme avec
15. Un pas en arrière.
16. Un pas glissé.
17. mon oncle et ma tante
18. m'ont rebaptisé Michael
19. Un pas de côté.
20. Il est passé à la chaise électrique.
21. furieux contre moi

I was getting just like him[1]. My aunt was nice to me when I was little, but then she stopped loving me. She said they'd been crazy to adopt me. She said bad blood shows[2]."

A new song. Frank Sinatra crooning[3], "Hey there, Cutes[4], put on your dancing boots and come dance with me."

Step. Step. Glide.

"I'm glad you're telling me this, Michael. It helps to talk[5], doesn't it?"

"I want you to call me Charley."

"All right." She tried not to sound tentative[6]. He mustn't see her fear[7].

"Don't you want to know what happened to my mother and father? I mean, the people who raised me[8]?"

"Yes, I do." Darcy thought of how tired her legs were[9]. She was not used to the spike heels. She felt as though the tight ankle straps[10] were cutting off her circulation[11].

Sidestep. Turn.

Sinatra urged[12], "Romance with me on a crowded floor[13] ..."

"When I was twenty-one, they were in a boating accident[14]. The boat blew up[15]."

"I'm sorry."

"I'm not. I rigged[16] the boat. I *am* just like my real father. You're getting tired, Darcy."

"No. No. I'm fine. I enjoy dancing with you." Stay calm ... stay calm.

"You can rest soon[17]. Were you surprised when you got Erin's shoes back?"

"Yes, very surprised."

"She was so pretty. She liked me. On our date I told her about my book and she talked about the program and about how you and she were answer-

1. que je devenais exactement comme lui
2. que mauvais sang ne saurait mentir
3. chantant de sa voix de crooner
4. mignonne
5. Ça fait du bien de parler
6. de ne pas marquer d'hésitation
7. sentir sa peur
8. qui m'ont élevé
9. sentait la fatigue dans ses jambes
10. C'était comme si les brides
11. lui coupaient la circulation
12. la pressait
13. sur une piste pleine de monde
14. ont eu un accident de bateau
15. a explosé
16. C'est moi qui avais trafiqué
17. pourrez bientôt vous reposer

ing personal ads. That was really funny. I'd already decided you'd be next after her.[1]"

Next after her.

"Why did you choose us?"

"And while the rhythm pings[2], what coo-coo things[3] I'll be saying," Sinatra sang.

"You both answered the special ad. All the girls I brought here did. But Erin wrote to one of my other ads too, the one I showed the FBI agent."

"You're very clever, Charley."

"Do you like the spike heels I bought for Erin? They match[4] her dress."

"I know they do."

"I was at the Playwrights' Benefit too. I recognized Erin from the picture she sent me[5] and I looked up her name[6] on the seating list[7] to make sure I was right. She was sitting four tables away[8]. It was fate that[9] I already had a date to meet her the very next night[10]."

Step. Step. Glide. Turn.

"How did you know Erin's shoe size? My size?"

"It was so easy. I bought Erin's shoes in different sizes[11]. I wanted just that pair for her. Remember last week when you had a pebble[12] in your boot and I helped you take it out[13]? I saw your size then."

"And the others?"

"Girls like to be flattered. I'd say, 'You have such pretty feet. What size are you?' Sometimes I bought shoes specially. Other times I'd take them from the ones I already had."

"The real Charles North didn't place any personal ads, did he?"

"No. I met him at that benefit too. He kept talking about himself[14] and I asked him for his business card. I never use my own name when I call people

1. J'avais déjà décidé que vous seriez la prochaine.
2. la musique fait ping
3. mots d'amour
4. sont assorties à
5. d'après la photo qu'elle m'avait envoyée
6. ai cherché son nom
7. sur le plan de table
8. à quatre tables de moi
9. C'était la loi du destin si
10. lendemain soir
11. dans plusieurs tailles
12. un caillou
13. vous ai aidée à le retirer
14. ne parlait que de lui

who answer the special ad. You made it easy[1]. You called me.

Yes, she had called him.

"You say Erin liked you when you met her the first time. Weren't you afraid she'd recognize your voice when you called and said you were Charles North?"

"I phoned from Penn Station, where there's a lot of noise[2]. I told her I was running to catch a train[3] to Philadelphia. I lowered my voice[4] and spoke faster than usual. Just like this afternoon when I talked to your secretary." The timbre of his voice changed, became high-pitched[5]. "Don't I sound like a woman now?[6]"

"Suppose I hadn't been able to go to that bar tonight? What would you have done?"

"You told me you didn't have any plans for this evening. I knew you'd do anything to find[7] the man Erin met the night she disappeared. And I was right."

"Yes, Charley, you were right."

He nuzzled her neck.

Step. Step. Glide.

"I'm so glad you both answered my special ad. You know what it is, don't you? It begins, *'Loves Music, Loves to Dance.'* "

"Because what is dancing but making love set to music playing[8]?" Sinatra continued.

"That's one of my favorite songs," Michael whispered. He twirled her[9], never relaxing his grip on her hand[10]. When he drew her back in[11], his tone became confidential, even regretful[12]. "It was Nan's fault that I started killing girls."

"Nan Sheridan?" Chris Sheridan's face filled Darcy's mind. The sadness in his eyes[13] when he talked about his sister. The authority and presence he had in the gallery. The way his staff obviously

1. m'avez facilité les choses
2. bruit
3. que je me dépêchais pour ne pas rater mon train
4. ai baissé la voix
5. monta dans les aigus
6. N'ai-je pas une voix de femme, là ?
7. que vous seriez prête à faire n'importe quoi pour trouver
8. si ce n'est faire l'amour au son de la musique
9. la fit virevolter
10. ne relâchant jamais son emprise
11. la rapprocha de lui
12. désolé, même
13. tristesse de son regard

loved him.[1] His mother. The easy relationship between them.[2] She could hear him saying, "I hope you're not a vegetarian, Darcy. Gourmet delight time."

His concern that she was answering these ads. How right he'd been.[3] I wish I'd had a chance[4] to get to know you[5], Chris. I wish I'd had a chance to tell my mother and father I loved them.

"Yes, Nan Sheridan. After I graduated from Stanford, I spent a year in Boston before I started med school[6]. I used to drive down to Brown a lot[7]. That's where I met Nan. She was a wonderful dancer. You're good, but she was wonderful."

The familiar opening bars of "Good Night, Sweetheart."

No, Darcy thought. No.

Backstep. Sidestep. Glide.

"Michael, something else I meant to ask you about my mother," she began.

He pushed her head down on his shoulder. "I told you to call me Charley. Don't talk anymore," he said firmly. "We'll just dance."

"Time will heal your sorrow[8]," floated through the room[9]. Darcy didn't recognize the singer's voice.

"Good night, sweetheart, good night." The last notes faded into the air[10].

Michael dropped his arms and smiled at Darcy. "It's time[11]," he said in a friendly voice, although his expression was blankly terrifying[12]. "I'll give you to the count of ten[13] to try to get away. Isn't that fair[14]?"

1. L'affection de ses employés.
2. La bonne entente entre eux.
3. Il avait bien eu raison !
4. J'aurais aimé avoir le temps
5. d'apprendre à mieux vous connaître
6. de commencer mes études de médecine
7. allais souvent sur le campus de Brown
8. guérira ta peine
9. disait la chanson
10. se dissipèrent
11. C'est l'heure
12. proprement terrifiante
13. jusqu'à dix
14. loyal

THEY WERE BACK on the road. "The signal is coming from the left. Wait a minute, we're going too far," the Bridgewater cop said. "There must be a side road here somewhere[1]." The wheels screeched[2] as they made a U-turn[3].

The sense of impending disaster had grown in Chris to the explosive point.[4] He opened the car window. "There, for God's sake[5], *there's* a driveway."

The squad car ground to a halt[6], backed up[7], turned sharply right, raced along the rutted ground.

Darcy slipped and slid on the polished floor. The high-heeled slippers were her enemies as she ran for[8] the door. She took a precious instant to stop and try to yank the shoes off[9], but she couldn't. The double knots[10] on the straps were too tight[11].

"One," Charley called from behind her.

She reached the door and tugged at the bolt[12]. It did not release.[13] She twisted the knob[14]. It did not turn.

"Two. Three. Four. Five. Six. I'm counting, Darcy."

The panic button. She jammed her finger against it[15].

Hahahahahahaha. ... A hollow[16], mocking laugh echoed through[17] the room. Hahahaha. ... The sound was coming from the panic button.

With a shriek[18], Darcy jumped back[19]. Now Charley was laughing too.

"Seven. Eight. Nine ..."

She turned, saw the stairway[20], began to run to it.

"Ten!"

Charley was rushing toward her[21], his hands outstretched[22], his fingers bent[23], his thumbs rigid.

"No! No!" Darcy tried to reach the staircase, skidded. Her ankle turned.[24] Sharp, stabbing pain.[25]

1. une petite route par ici
2. Les pneus crissèrent
3. demi-tour
4. Chris crut qu'il allait exploser devant l'imminence de la catastrophe.
5. l'amour du ciel
6. s'arrêta en crissant
7. recula
8. vers
9. d'enlever ses chaussures
10. nœuds
11. trop serrés
12. tira sur le verrou
13. Il ne s'ouvrit pas.
14. la poignée
15. appuya à fond dessus
16. forcé
17. emplit
18. Poussant un cri aigu
19. sursauta en arrière
20. l'escalier
21. lui fonçait dessus
22. mains en avant
23. crochus
24. Elle se tordit la cheville.
25. Une douleur suraiguë.

Moaning[1], she hobbled onto the first step[2] and felt herself pulled back[3].

She didn't know she was screaming.

1. En gémissant
2. monta la première marche en boitillant
3. sentit qu'il la tirait en arrière

"THERE'S THE MERCEDES," Vince cried. The squad car slammed to a stop[4] behind it.

He sprang out[5] of the car, Chris and the cop with him. "Stay back[6]," Vince shouted to Nona.

"Listen." Chris held up his hand. "Someone's screaming. It's Darcy." He and Vince threw themselves against the thick oak door[7]. It didn't budge.[8]

The cop pulled out his gun[9] and pumped six bullets[10] into the lock.

This time when Chris and Vince attacked the door, it opened.

4. pila
5. bondit hors
6. là
7. l'épaisse porte en chêne
8. Elle ne céda pas.
9. dégaina son revolver
10. tira six balles coup sur coup

DARCY TRIED TO kick Charley with the sharp stiletto heels. He spun her around[11], seeming not to feel the heels stabbing at[12] his legs. His hands were around her neck. She tried to claw them away[13]. Erin, Erin, is this the way it was for you? She couldn't scream anymore. She opened her mouth, frantic to gulp in air[14], and could find none[15]. Were those moans coming from her? She tried to keep fighting but couldn't raise her arms again.

Vaguely, she heard loud staccato sounds[16]. Was someone trying to help her? It's … too … late … she thought as she felt herself fall into darkness[17].

11. la retourna
12. qui s'enfonçaient dans
13. lui faire lâcher prise à coups de griffe
14. tentant désespérément de reprendre une bouffée d'air
15. mais en vain
16. de grands coups saccadés
17. et ne vit plus que du noir

Chris got through the doorway first[1]. Darcy was dangling[2] like a rag doll[3], her arms drooping at her sides[4], her legs buckled under her[5]. Long, powerful fingers were squeezing her throat. Her screams had stopped.

With a cry of rage, Chris flew across the room and tackled[6] Nash, who sagged and fell[7], pulling Darcy with him. His hands convulsed[8], then tightened their grip around her neck.

Vince threw himself next to Nash, snapped his arm[9] around Nash's neck, forcing his head back[10]. The Bridgewater cop grabbed Nash's thrashing feet[11].

Charley's hands seemed to have a life of their own. Chris could not pry his fingers loose[12] from Darcy's throat. Nash seemed to be possessed of superhuman strength and impervious to pain[13]. Desperately Chris sank his teeth[14] into the right hand of the man who was snuffing out Darcy's life[15].

With a howl of pain[16] Charley yanked back[17] his right hand and relaxed the left one.

Vince and the cop twisted his arms behind him and snapped handcuffs on his wrists[18] as Chris grabbed Darcy.

Nona had been watching from the doorway. Now she rushed into the house and dropped to her knees[19] at Darcy's feet. Darcy's eyes were not focusing[20]. There were ugly red bruises[21] on her slender throat.

Chris covered Darcy's mouth with his own, pinched her nostrils closed[22], forced breath[23] into her lungs[24].

Vince looked at Darcy's staring eyes and began to pound her chest[25].

1. fut le premier à passer la porte
2. se balançait
3. une poupée de chiffon
4. les bras ballants
5. les jambes molles
6. attaqua
7. tomba lourdement
8. eurent des secousses
9. passa le bras
10. lui tirant la tête en arrière
11. les pieds remuants
12. n'arrivait pas à desserrer ses doigts
13. être insensible à la douleur
14. plongea les dents
15. étranglait Darcy
16. Hurlant de douleur,
17. retira brusquement
18. lui passèrent les menottes
19. tomba à genoux
20. avait le regard fixe
21. d'affreuses contusions rougeâtres
22. lui pinça le nez
23. insuffla de l'air
24. poumons
25. des compressions thoraciques

The Bridgewater cop was guarding Michael Nash, who was handcuffed to the banister[1]. Nash began to recite in a singsong voice[2], "Eeney, meeney, miney, mo, Catch a dancer by the toe ..."

She's not responding[3], Nona thought frantically. She grasped Darcy's ankles[4] and for the first time realized Darcy was wearing dancing slippers. I can't stand it[5], Nona thought, I can't stand it. Almost unaware[6] of what she was doing, Nona began to struggle with the knots[7] on the ankle straps.

"One little piggy went to market. One little piggy stayed home. Sing it again, Mama. I have ten piggy toes."

We may be too late, Vince thought furiously as he searched for some response from Darcy, but if we are, you lousy bastard[8], you'd better not think that spouting nursery rhymes[9] now will help you prove insanity[10].

Chris raised his head as he gulped in air[11] and for a split second[12] stared at Darcy's face. The same look as Nan when he found her that morning. The bruised throat. The blue-white tone to her skin. *No! I won't let it happen.* Darcy, *breathe.*

Nona, weeping now[13], had finally untied[14] one of the ankle straps. She pushed it back and began to pull the high-heeled slipper from Darcy's foot.

She felt something. Was she wrong? No.

"Her foot is moving!" she cried. "She's trying to get it out of the shoe."

At the same instant, Vince saw a pulse[15] begin to beat in Darcy's throat and Chris heard a long, drawn-out sigh[16] come from her lips.

1. menotté à la rampe
2. à fredonner
3. ne réagit pas
4. lui saisit les chevilles
5. C'est insupportable
6. inconsciente
7. à s'acharner sur les nœuds
8. espèce d'enfoiré
9. débiter des comptines
10. à plaider la folie
11. pour inspirer
12. fraction de seconde
13. en larmes
14. réussi à dénouer
15. son pouls
16. un long soupir

XXIII
THURSDAY
March 14

THE NEXT MORNING, Vince phoned Susan. "Mrs. Fox, your husband may be a philanderer but he's not a criminal. We have the serial killer in custody[1] and we have absolute proof that he is solely responsible for[2] the dancing-shoe deaths starting with Nan Sheridan."

"Thank you. I guess you can understand what this means to me."

"Who was that?" Doug had stayed home from work. He felt lousy[3]. Not sick, just lousy.

Susan told him.

He stared at her. "You mean you told the FBI you thought I was a murderer! You actually thought[4] I killed Nan Sheridan and all those other women!" His face darkened in incredulous rage.

Susan stared back at him[5]. "I thought that was a possibility, and that by lying for you fifteen years ago I might also be responsible for those other deaths."

"I swore to you that I never went near Nan the morning she died."

"Obviously you didn't. Then where were you, Doug? At least level with me[6] now."

The anger faded[7] from his face. He looked away[8], then turned back with a cajoling smile. "Susan, I

1. en garde à vue
2. le seul responsable de
3. était mal fichu
4. Tu croyais sérieusement
5. le regarda droit dans les yeux
6. dis-le moi franchement
7. disparut
8. détourna le regard

told you then. I repeat it. The car broke down that morning."

"*I want the truth.* You owe it to me[1]."

Doug hesitated, then said slowly, "I was with Penny Knowles. Susan, I'm sorry. I didn't want you to know because I was afraid of losing you[2]."

"You mean Penny Knowles was about to get engaged to[3] Bob Carver and didn't want to take a chance on losing out on[4] the Carver money. She'd have let you be accused of murder[5] before she'd speak up for you[6]."

"Susan, I know I played around a lot then[7] …"

"Then?" Susan's laugh was harsh[8]. "You played around *then?* Listen to me, Doug. All these years my father has never gotten over the fact[9] that I perjured myself[10] for you. Go pack your clothes. Move into your bachelor apartment. I'm filing for divorce.[11]"

All day he begged for another chance[12]. "Susan, I promise."

"Get out."

He would not leave before Donny and Beth came home from school. "I'll see a lot of you kids, I promise." When he walked down the driveway, Trish ran after him[13] and grabbed his knees. He carried her back and handed her to Susan. "Susan, please."

"Good-bye, Doug."

They watched him drive away. Donny was crying. "Mom, last weekend. I mean, if he was like that all the time …"

Susan tried to blink back her own tears[14]. "Never say never[15], Donny. Your father has a lot of growing up to do[16]. Let's see if he can handle it[17]."

1. me dois bien ça
2. je craignais de te perdre
3. se fiancer avec
4. risquer de passer à côté de
5. Elle t'aurait laissé accuser de meurtre
6. plutôt que d'avouer la vérité
7. à l'époque
8. ricana
9. ne s'est jamais remis du fait
10. que j'aie fait un faux témoignage
11. Je vais demander le divorce.
12. la supplia de lui accorder une deuxième chance
13. lui courut après
14. ravaler ses larmes
15. On ne sait jamais
16. va devoir beaucoup mûrir
17. s'il en est capable

"ARE YOU GOING to watch your program?" Vince asked Nona when he phoned Thursday afternoon.

"Absolutely not. We prepared a special wrap[1]. I wrote it. I lived it."

"What do you feel like eating tonight?"

"A steak."

"Me too. What are you doing over the weekend?"

"It's supposed to be mild.[2] I thought I'd drive out to the Hamptons. After the last few weeks, I must go down to the sea again[3]."

"You have a house there."

"Yes. I think I'm changing my mind about buying Matt out. I love my place[4] and he really is very forgettable[5]. Want to come along for the ride?[6]"

"I'd love to."

CHRIS BROUGHT AN antique cane for Darcy to use while her sprained ankle mended[7].

"It's very grand[8]," she told him.

He wrapped his arms around her.[9] "Are you all set?[10] Where are your things?"

"Just that bag." Greta had phoned insisting that Chris bring Darcy to Darien for a long weekend.

The phone rang. "I'll skip it[11]," Darcy said. "No, wait. I tried to reach my folks[12] in Australia. Maybe the operator finally caught up with them[13]."

1. une nouvelle conclusion
2. Il doit faire doux.
3. j'ai besoin de retourner au bord de la mer
4. cette maison
5. ce n'est vraiment pas quelqu'un d'intéressant
6. Ça vous dit de venir ?
7. sa cheville foulée se remettait
8. superbe
9. Il la prit dans ses bras.
10. Tu es prête ?
11. Je ne vais pas répondre
12. joindre mes parents
13. a enfin mis la main dessus

It was both her mother and father on the line[1]. "I'm absolutely fine. I just wanted to say ..." She hesitated. "... that I really miss you guys[2]. I ... I love you. ..." Darcy laughed. "What do you mean, I must have met somebody?"

She winked[3] at Chris. "As a matter of fact[4], I have met a nice young man. His name is Chris Sheridan. You'll approve. He's in my business, only upscale[5]. He has an antiques gallery. He's good-looking, nice, and has a way of showing up[6] when you need him[7]. ... How did I meet him?"

Only Erin, she thought, could really appreciate the irony of her answer. "Believe it or not, I met him through the personal ads."

She looked up at Chris and their eyes met[8]. He smiled. I'm wrong, she thought. Chris understands too.

1. au bout du fil
2. vous me manquez beaucoup
3. fit un clin d'œil
4. Pour tout te dire
5. mais un cran au-dessus
6. est très doué pour débarquer
7. quand on a besoin de lui
8. leurs regards se croisèrent

La collection Yes you can!

Faux débutants

Ken Follett *The Modigliani Scandal*

Mary Higgins Clark *A Stranger is Watching*

Mary Higgins Clark *Loves Music, Loves to Dance*

Mary Higgins Clark *Where are the Children?*

Anthony Horowitz *The House of Silk*

Yann Martel *Life of Pi*

Nicholas Sparks *Message in a Bottle*

Intermédiaires

Harlan Coben *Play Dead*

Harlan Coben *Stay Close*

Harlan Coben *Tell No One*

Harlan Coben *The Woods*

Michael Connelly *The Black Box*

Michael Connelly *The Drop*

Ken Follett *Paper Money*

Mary Higgins Clark *A Cry in the Night*

P.D. James *A Mind to Murder*

Douglas Kennedy *The Big Picture*

John le Carré *A Most Wanted Man*

Avancés

Paul Auster *Oracle Night*

Julian Barnes *The Sense of an Ending*

Michael Cunningham *By Nightfall*

Michael Cunningham *The Hours*

Helen Fielding *Bridget Jones's Diary*

Elizabeth George *A Great Deliverance*

Stephen King *Misery*

Imprimé en Italie par La Tipografica Varese Srl
Dépôt légal : mai 2015
314165-01/11026514-mai 2015